Portal to Passion

Time Travel, Love & the Great Fire

Kathy J. Forti

ISBN: 979-8-218-73809-9
Printed in the United States of America

Cover Art & Design: Alana Ross

PART 1

Table of Contents

Chapter 1

It was a 10-minute crosstown walk on most days but today would prove to be no ordinary day, especially in torrential rain. With no available taxis-for-hire, Katherine "Kat" Branigan's long red tresses were already an unruly mass of wet dripping ringlets. Mother Nature was having her way with all those who had failed to grab an umbrella on this April Fool's Day.

Kat was no fool, just an optimist. It was bright and sunny without a cloud in the sky when she left her Brooklyn home that morning. Like most New Yorkers, she sucked it up and went with the flow. All around her harried Manhattanites, sporting the latest in brand-name sneakers, maneuvered around dog droppings and dirty puddles, only to be splattered at pedestrian crosswalks by passing drivers. Tempers were running high today and making it to work on time would be a dim prospect at best.

Kat's clothes were hopelessly soaked, while her hair was running rivulets down her freckled face. Storefront display windows reflected just how disheveled she looked, causing her to quickly glance away, but not before seeing a strange woman's face waver in the glass pane back at her. She blinked, unsure if her eyes were playing tricks on her. Was it a store employee? No, it was definitely an apparition of a lady in a vintage-looking bonnet closely scrutinizing her. Damn. Kat took a swig of her takeout coffee and quickened her step.

Rainy days were a bad omen. Her parents had died in a car accident on a rainy day on her 21st birthday. Then two years ago, while vacationing in the Bahamas, she had barely escaped a hurricane surge which destroyed her hotel. Her mind wandered to those vicious flash floods that unexpectedly struck when she was in California during what was supposed to be drought season. No, no, no. Rainy days were not her friend.

If only she had thought to check the weather this morning in her haste to get to work on time. Damage control would have to be done before the head of the department caught sight of her. Her job at The Metropolitan Museum of Art demanded she always look and be at her absolute best. A wealthy patron would be making an appearance at The Costume Institute's offices before the museum opened at 10:00 a.m.

The Met's main entrance was located on Fifth Avenue and 82nd Street which, unfortunately, did not have a convenient subway stop. Getting to work from Brooklyn was always a trek for Kat. It consisted of a half-mile walk from the Lexington Avenue subway station, then crosstown over to Fifth, come rain or shine. On most days Kat enjoyed the exercise. There were the endless window displays informing New York women what was currently fashionable along with what styles were on their way out from signs proclaiming: "Discounts" or "Big Sale." She dutifully took note of it all.

Fashion was Kat's business. Her background in textile conservation and costume studies had served her well, landing her a permanent position in The Anna Wintour Costume Center that housed The Costume Institute Department at The Met. Her uncanny photographic memory for historic detail made her an asset in her chosen field. She could name any year and its fashion trend going back to the 15th century. Rarely did she have to consult The Met's extensive Fashion Library.

Kat's brain functioned like a quantum computer craving historical information. She could also name the year of any dress design or accessory in the over 33,000 costume objects the Museum had in its vast collection. She had studied them all—extensively. The department jokingly referred to her as "The Red Brain," which helped boost her career and allow her to rise quickly in the ranks. She now held the coveted position of Assistant Installation Coordinator of The Costume Institute's Exhibition & Special Projects Department.

A majority of The Met's vast costume collection had been donated and/or was on loan from a designer's vintage archives or someone's private estate. It was not unusual for Kat to personally interact with the city's famous or wealthy patrons when taking temporary possession of their historic costume treasures. Everything had to be inspected, laid flat in large slide-out dresser drawers, and covered with very thin, acid-free tissue paper to protect old fabrics from accumulating dust, dirt, and insect infestation. Most were too fragile to be hung due to tearing. The conservation and storage rooms were all temperature controlled to preserve textiles and fragile fabrics. Preservation was of utmost importance to every staff member in the department.

It was a demanding job, but Kat loved it. Flashing her employee ID, she breezed through the metal detectors flanking the ground floor entrance and hung a hard right towards The Costume Institute and Gallery Rooms 980 and 981.

April was final preparation month for The Met. The Annual Met Gala, always held the first Monday in May, would take place in just four weeks. The "by-invitation-only" guest list, a $75,000 a ticket fundraising event which turned the Temple of Dendur gallery into a red-carpet extravaganza night, would always outrank Hollywood's Academy Awards. It was fashion's "biggest night out," with designers purchasing entire tables of ten for $350,000 a pop or more, a charitable write-off, which managed to raise the bulk of funds needed to run The Costume Institute's annual budget and pay everyone's salaries. Kat was one of the lucky ones. As a key staff member, she did not need a ticket to attend nor even be placed on the coveted "waitlist." She worked behind the scenes helping make it happen.

Right on time for this Gala event, a new exhibition would premiere heralding "The Great Fire: A Fashion Phoenix"—a time in history when Lower Manhattan, including the Financial District of Wall Street, was consumed in a fire during a wintery inferno. Over 700 structures, encompassing 13 acres, went up in flames on that deadly freezing night of December 16, 1835.

Textiles warehouses, filled with imported Chinese silks and satins, English wools and cotton, and the finest Spanish laces and floral trimmings to be bought, went up in a blaze of fire and smoke. The tragic event would change the landscape of fashion to come—tapering down the cut of exaggerated sleeves and skirts in a conservation attempt as Manhattanites struggled to survive and rebuild.

Most New Yorkers had no idea that the aftermath of this fire, occurring more than 200 years ago, would so profoundly impact the future of their city. It had become a forgotten watershed moment in history. Everything from clothing styles to finance appeared to collapse into a "drooping sentimentality." The aftermath of the fire had demanded substantial change. A new city-planning model would be adopted which would reshape the city for centuries to come as new sources of reliable water and stricter street and building codes were enacted.

Kat Branigan's ancestral family had been New Yorkers for several generations. They had come to America as immigrants, fleeing from Ireland in the early 1820s prior to the great "Irish Potato Famine." Her great-great-great-great-grandparents had the foresight to emigrate from Dublin prior to the widespread deaths resulting from potato blight and disease. She was a red-headed Irish descendent through and through and damn proud of it.

Because it was part of her heritage, Kat had taken a personal interest in this particular costume exhibition. Her own ancestors had managed to escape the devastating 1835 conflagration and go on to prosper, buying property and relocating to the Borough of Brooklyn where she was born and still resided. The Brooklyn Heights brownstone they had painstakingly built, which Kat had inherited upon her parents' death, was now a historic landmark property in the midst of picturesque streets and highly-prized real estate.

Situated on the East River with scenic views of the Brooklyn Promenade and Lower Manhattan across the river, Kat had spent all her inheritance renovating and making it her own. Had her great-great-great-great-grandparents not made such a timely investment and relocation before others discovered the charm of Brooklyn, they might have died in Manhattan along with others who lost life and property that fateful night in 1835. Kat might not even be alive today to enjoy the fruits of their early labor had destiny not intervened. While she knew history did not determine one's destiny, it came pretty damn close to it in her own family.

Kat's thoughts returned to her job as Assistant Installation Coordinator of Exhibitions & Special Projects. Her departmental boss was out on maternity leave, so she was pretty much in charge, stepping into the role of Senior Installation Manager. It was a demanding position, requiring close coordination with the other twenty staff members, the Curator and, of course, the big money people, trustees, and patrons who were too numerous to mention. She was well aware that she had a lot on the line, as well as a plenty to prove.

Toweling down her hair, she quickly changed from wet attire to more proper attire—a beige Chanel vintage two-piece suit with matching two-tone heeled slingbacks which she kept in her locker for such emergencies. She tied up her hair in a tight knot and hoped for the best. A quick dab of cherry-red lipstick almost made her look presentable before heading to her meeting.

She was intercepted on the way. One look at her boss' face told her he was irritated and not able to hide it. Adam Lowell came from old European family money and was Curator of The Institute. He liked to run a tight ship.

"Where have you been?" he demanded, without uttering even a cordial "good morning."

Kat consulted her watch. What the hell? She was right on time. The meeting had been a last-minute arrangement, but here she was.

"I thought this meeting was scheduled for 9:00 a.m.?" she pointed out.

Adam was being prickly as usual. "I texted you this morning that the patron changed it to 8:00 a.m. due to a business commitment. Didn't you check your messages?"

Damn, she had failed to consult her phone texts in her rush to be here on time. "I'm sorry, sir. I will gladly send an apology to..." She stopped, realizing she had yet to be informed of the patron's name.

Adam finished her thought. "Never mind. He's come and gone and wishes to remain anonymous. His people delivered two large, sealed crates which were placed in Conservation Room Number One. The man left legal documents stating that the crates' contents were to be designated as a museum donation."

Well, that was a very big plus, Kat thought. Adam also seemed extremely pleased. He flashed an excited smile, forgetting his initial irritation at her tardiness. "I've been informed that the artifacts have been meticulously preserved from 1835 and are to be included in the current *Great Fire* exhibition." He handed her a leather-bound binder filled with itemized pictures. "See for yourself."

Kat scanned the photos, stunned at how the garments looked like they were brand new, despite their almost 200-year-old dating. There were at least ten men's and ten or more women's clothing items, complete with matching accessories. Stunned, she looked up questioningly. "These are all originals?"

Adam nodded, walking back to his office where he showed her authentication papers. Kat was dumbfounded. "Where did this person come by such an extensive find?"

Adam sucked air through his teeth and paused, hesitant to reveal what he knew. "It's somewhat of an odd story. The costumes were preserved and placed in an airtight container by the original owner during that time period. The contents were locked in a vault with legal instructions to the law firm that is now Kendle & Kendle, LLP to keep the collection sealed until this year and date when it was to be delivered to The Metropolitan Museum of Art's Costume Institute."

Kat's mouth dropped open in disbelief. The unvoiced question on her mind was how had the original preserver known that The Met, founded in 1870, would have a Costume Institute which wouldn't open until the year 2014? And what was so special about delivery being made on April 1st? Was this some sort of April Fool's joke?

"But how…?" she began. But Adam was already on his way out the door, clearly moving on to more pressing matters. The man never stood still for long. He was a whirlwind in motion. Quite frankly, she was surprised she had gotten this much out of him. Now she truly regretted having missed the earlier meeting with the anonymous patron if nothing else then to probe deeper into the donation's origins. Was the anonymous patron an attorney from Kendle & Kendle or a representative of the original owner? If Adam knew more about this mysterious donation, he certainly was not saying.

Kat could not wait to get her hands on the contents and verify their authenticity for herself.

The department was on a tight deadline with the exhibit opening in only four weeks. Staff would be busy finalizing all aspects of the coming exhibition and now there would be added items to make way for in the limited space allotted.

Due to the nature of this exhibit's great historical significance, The Costume Institute was partnering with the New York Historical Society to maintain timeline accuracy of *The Great Fire*. The backdrop displays of the raging inferno, along with techno-lighting effects, would be spectacular in scope. Kat was certain the exhibition launch would break all museum attendance records. And for The Met Gala co-event, the fire theme would be sure to bring out an explosion of star-studded celebrities dressed in gowns blazing in fiery red and orange design, like the Phoenix Rising from the ashes. Everything would need to be perfect. If not, Kat would surely be held accountable.

Conservation Room One was locked, which was the practice upon an unattended donor delivery before staff arrived. It was considered the "waiting room"—the first stage before garments were sent to different departments. Soon the room would be swarming with staff, but Kat wanted to be the first to examine its contents. She never failed to be enthralled with such donor gifts, as if they were meant just for her. Call it crazy, but today's delivery felt—special.

Kat donned her white lab coat and cotton gloves. She stepped back from the two large rectangular-shaped cartons, taking in its pre-conservation mode. Someone had taken great care with sealing all the seams, but not too much that the costumes inside couldn't breathe. The last thing a conservator wanted to encounter was the musty smell that often accompanied mold from traces of moisture still remaining in the clothing prior to packing.

It was a toss-up of which carton to open first, since there were no content descriptions listed on the outside. The first one she opened held ten individual costume-size boxes containing men's wear. After carefully lifting each item from its individual flat box, she stopped to admire the hand-worked buttonholes and detailed stitching of each item. The craftmanship was excellent. There were double-breasted frock coats, several light-colored fly-front trousers, a few dark cravats for day wear, an elegant shawl-collar waistcoat, imported linen shirts, and even an unusual patterned-silk dressing gown. The clothes were of the finest materials and whomever its past owner was, he was undoubtedly a person of means.

Kat brought the man's silk dressing gown to her nose for signs of mustiness but instead smelled the faintest hint of men's cologne, even after all this time. It was a pleasant smell—different yet unidentifiable. It reminded her of the earth and sea.

Kat moved on to the women's costume carton with a heightened sense of excitement. Her fingers trembled as she opened the first dress box of many. It contained an exquisite emerald-green silk evening gown with full ballooned-sleeves, an off-the-shoulder neckline, and molded waist. The enormous puff sleeves were stuffed with sausage-like rolls of tissue paper to keep their padded shape which, amazingly, they had. The garment quite literally took Kat's breath away. Indisputably it would have to be featured in the exhibition. They had nothing else like it of its kind or quality.

The other boxes held more modest day wear, equally stunning in finery with only one glaring exception. A simple creamy yellow light cotton printed day dress, with a pleated bodice and voluminous puff gigot sleeves, had noticeable hem stains that would have to be addressed by their restoration department. The garment's oily-like damage was on the inside of the hem as well as the outside.

The back of the garment had a definite muddy-looking splatter pattern. How odd that this very feminine garment, with its delicate imported European lace and white sateen ribboned waist, had been included in the collection without proper cleaning. It stood out like the black sheep of the lot. It was obvious that whoever the lady was that had worn the garment, she had dragged her hems through fairly dirty streets. It happened quite often during early historical times. But why had the soiled garment been included in this costume donation in its current state?

Kat laid the garment aside for special care, while she continued her appraisal of the remainder of the collection. There were boxes filled with undergarments, long stayed-corsets, chemises, silk shoes, small reticule purse bags, even hats. A sizable find such as this had to belong to someone working in the garment industry, perhaps even a high-quality couture dressmaker. But whom? There were no identifying labels or marks sewn in the inside seams, as was sometimes the case.

She examined every item with an appreciative, yet scrutinizing eye. She went back to check every pocket, as was required, only to discover a rough-hewn pinky ring hidden away in the inner pocket lining of a man's black velvet waistcoat. It had somehow fallen through a small tear in the lining and gone undetected. Kat turned it over to inspect the "R" fashioned upon it in raised lettering. While the inside of the ring was lined in gold with indecipherable markings, the outside was forged from a dark dense metal substance. Kat frowned. Metallurgy was not her area of expertise. It looked like iron but could very well be something else.

The jewelry piece would have to be reported and archived separately due to its potential antique value. The donor might not have known about it and would definitely want it back. She placed the ring into a small cloth jewelry pouch and slipped it into the inside pocket of her lab coat after noting it in the records. Adam would definitely want to take possession of it.

Just to be certain, Kat rechecked the women's clothing items for any missed personal objects as well. The men's ring had been an easy oversight by the collection's patron. However, after diligently searching she found nothing else of note.

A knock on the door reminded her that she could not keep this incredible donor find to herself. As conservation staff filtered in, she let them take over. Every item would have to be catalogued and registered before being thoroughly inspected for stitching repair and proper shaping. The costumes' dyes would need to be analyzed and preserved for low level staged lighting to avoid fading. There was a lengthy process every costume went through before she could begin choreographing the garments for display.

Kat eased out of the room, knowing that her colleagues were experts in their field and the costumes were now in the best professional hands. Twenty plus new garments made for a sizable collection. Care would need to be taken, despite the excellent condition of the donation, especially the stain-splattered dress.

Several hours later, Portia from textile repairs informed her that the stains on the yellow dress were not responding to any preservation solutions.

"It looks like a mixture of tar, oil, some grease, and mud of the worst kind," Portia informed. "The staining is incredibly stubborn. If we use a hardier cleaning solvent on such a bright fabric, it's certain to cause color loss. The garment would be permanently ruined."

Portia paused, weighing the options. "We could re-cut it and give it a shorter hemline to hide the stains, making sure the back splatter pattern is hidden from public view. It's up to you. What do you want to do?"

Kat was disappointed. She liked the yellow dress and hated the thought of altering it. Even the dirt from the 1830s told their own unique story. "That's a shame," she sighed. "Just leave the dress in my office—at least for now. Let me see if I can find a workaround solution for it."

When Kat later returned to her office, she spied the yellow dress lying flat in an open dress box on her worktable. It stared forlornly back at her silently beckoning her: "Please don't reject me." There was something about this particular gown that felt irresistible. She was determined to find a way to use it without damaging it further.

Her cellphone buzzed in her pocket, disrupting her thoughts. Kat removed her white gloves and answered the call, knowing it would be Lexi calling about tonight's pool tournament. Lexi and she were best friends going back to their early high school days in Brooklyn. Back then Kat had only been interested in the world of costume fashion and history, having never missed any of The Met's Costume Exhibitions since the Institute's inception. During her teen years, she had set her mind on someday working in this very institution, and she had worked hard to eventually manifest and make that dream come true. It felt like destiny calling.

Lexi, on the other hand, was an athletic jock and a personal trainer at an Upper East Side fitness gym. As freshmen in high school, Lexi had nagged Kat relentlessly to join their school's billiard club with her, because "that's where all the really cool guys hang out."

Kat finally caved. What had started out as an appeasement to make her friend happy, soon turned into an obsession. To Kat's surprise, she realized that she had a natural flair for playing pool and, even more shocking, that it brought out a ruthless competitive spirit in her she had not known existed. She could play 8-ball, snooker, blackball, 9-ball, 10-ball, 7-ball, English billiards, and straight pool. You name it, she played it, whether it was on a billiards table with or without pockets. No one at The Met knew of her secret passion, and that was the way she preferred it. Gaming simply did not fit in with the decorum required of her job.

Tonight, their billiards team was competing against the reigning champs from another crosstown Manhattan pool bar. Their game was always Team 8-ball and this evening they would be playing on their home turf—a popular Lower East Side pool bar called, "Out of Pocket."

As usual Lexi was all hyped before the match. Forever the fast talker—literally as well as figuratively, she was known to talk a New York minute. "The new lineup shows we're now scheduled for 8:30. I talked them into switching us so we would be first up," Lexi rattled off with the sound of her running a treadmill marathon in the background. "I've got my car today, so I'm going to swing by The Met, say around 5:30, pick you up and we can get a quick bite to eat first. Okay?"

Kat had no problem with that. Lexi let out a low whistle. "Oh, my. It says right here in today's daily horoscope that I'm going to get lucky tonight. It's a lunar eclipse and all my stars are aligned. Well good God, it's about time!" There was the loud sound of an object hitting the floor on the other end. "Oh shit! Gotta go! See ya!"

Kat had not gotten a word in before Lexi hung up. She glanced at the wall clock. Damn. Where had the time gone? Her stomach rumbled reminding her she had worked straight through lunch and was quite ravenous. It was almost 5:00 p.m. and she still needed to finish and change. She quickly texted her friend that she would let her know when she was leaving the building. Rush hour traffic would be a bitch at this time of day. It would have been faster to take the subway.

Work often required staying late, but today she had planned ahead. The pool tournament was a big deal—something she had been looking forward to. As their team's best player, she wanted nothing better than to cream their crosstown competition and take the $1000 purse along with the free drinks awarded the winner.

Kat closed her office door and removed her lab coat, stripping down to her crimson lace bra and red string panties. One never knew whom one would meet at a tournament, and it was best to always come prepared. Sexy underwear always made her feel powerful and undefeatable. Who knew—she might even get lucky tonight and meet someone she fancied who would give her talents a run for the money. The other team had pro-like players who weren't bad on the eyes—Wall Street types, hedge fund babies, veritable wolves in the pool hall, as well as in their day jobs. Some with money and brains, but all with a talent she liked to take a crack at.

Every player had their special talisman. For Kat it was the small gold locket she always wore around her neck, now tucked safely in her bra, close to her heart. It contained miniature pictures of both her parents. They had gifted the gold necklace to her on her 16th birthday, 12 years ago. Engraved on the back were her initials "KB" and the endearing words: "With love until the end of time."

The antique-looking piece had become her forever good luck charm. Kat wore it hidden beneath her clothes to every tournament. She patted it now, three times, as was her norm. It was a silly practice, much like a baseball player's elaborate ritual before going out on the field, but it was her own. She activated her wish by silently appealing to the universe-at-large: *"May I meet my match and be granted victory over New York's most formidable opponent,"* she whispered before adding, *"Tonight and always—until the end of time."*

There, she was ready to do battle. She turned to reach for her tournament outfit, but instead, as if compelled by some unknown force, found herself gently lifting the old gown from its box and, without a moment's hesitation, carefully slipping it over her head—an act that would be taboo at The Met or anywhere else.

Kat was immediately transfixed. The gown fit her perfectly, molded to her every curve, as she somehow knew it would. It was as if someone had fashioned it with her very height and measurements in mind. The moment her body was encased in the creamy yellow fabric, she realized she felt different, lighter, almost trance-like. Time fell away, despite knowing Lexi would be outside any minute waiting to pick her up.

Remembering the hidden ring she had found in the pocket lining of the men's waistcoat she retrieved it from her lab coat and placed it on her right-hand finger as a reminder lest she forget to give it to Adam before leaving. Within milliseconds of placing the "R" initialed ring on her finger, it came alive. Kat jumped back, watching it take shape and mold to her finger size. At the same time her cellphone flew out of her hands as if magnetically repelled.

A tingling sensation shot up her arm, straight to her head, causing her to feel slightly dizzy. Or was that her imagination? Kat shrugged, trying to dismiss the strange reaction, but it persisted. She tried to take the ring off but couldn't. What the hell?

Kat felt invisible hands draw her towards the floor-to-ceiling mirrored wall which flanked one side of her small office. She stared back at her reflection, mesmerized by how fetching she looked and how the woman from 1835 must have appeared in such a garment before it got soiled. A strange magnetic pull bought her closer to the mirror, scant inches away, where she became completely entranced. The ring on her finger was now pulsing a glowing red. While a part of her thought she should be concerned at this strange happening, instead she felt a deep calmness take root, immediately followed by a wooziness that left her head spinning.

Kat closed her eyes for just a second and braced her hands against the mirror. She really should have eaten today, she thought. What she was feeling were probably the effects of low blood sugar. Suddenly the earth moved under her feet and the electrical power in the museum shut down, plunging her and everything around her into total darkness. That's when she felt herself slip into a swirling vortex that rattled her entire being.

Chapter 2

Kat's first thought was that the power had been knocked out due to bad weather, even though it felt more like an earthquake had rattled the museum. Manhattan sat on several fault lines, and it *had* happened before. It *was* possible, but rare. Any minute now, the buildings' back-up generators should kick in, but they didn't.

When Kat opened her eyes, she was stunned to feel the harsh afternoon sun on her face and, more alarming still, that she was standing outside in a noisy and densely trafficked place on the river's edge. Confusion seized her. Where was she and how had she gotten there?

A fleet of clipper ships and fast schooners lined the boat slips up and down the harbor front, telling her she must be at the South Street Seaport, a well-known historic tourist mecca which often had a few old sailing ships docked in their harbor. Chugging across the East River were steam-powered ferries and other strange looking water-craft. Kat glanced sideways and received an even bigger shock. The Brooklyn Bridge, connecting Manhattan to the Borough of Brooklyn, was nowhere to be seen.

Her pulse raced as she whipped around expecting to see the usual assortment of seafood restaurants, coffee shops, and the shopping mall where tourists flocked on a daily basis, only to experience a heart-stopping moment. The historic seaport was totally transformed, a picture postcard out of time, teeming with horse drawn carriages, open buggies, and wagon carts laden with goods. Everywhere she looked people were dressed in early 19th century period costumes—from homespun laborer garb to fashionable finery.

Kat blinked in rapid succession, hoping her eyes weren't playing tricks on her. Was this some type of large-scale historical re-enactment or was she dreaming? Glancing down she saw that she was wearing the same yellow cotton dress she had slipped into moments ago, only now it was pristine and spotless. On her head was a ghastly bonnet with white satin ribbons which barely covered the unruly mass of red ringlets cascading down her back. No this was not a dream at all, but a veritable nightmare.

Her feet unceremoniously refused to move, as if crazy-glued to the dirty cobblestone street she found herself on. She inched up her voluminous skirts, catching site of a petticoat but also taking stock that she was wearing incredibly unpractical, soft-soled yellow slippers, with absolutely no arch support whatsoever.

Kat closed her eyes and pinched herself in case she was still in the throes of some lucid dream state. But when she re-opened her eyes, nothing had changed. The clatter of horse hooves against the uneven cobblestone pavement was deafening to her ears. A throng of what appeared to be poor immigrants were seen disembarking from a nearby ship. They pushed their way onto the wooden pier and stopped to gape at the strange new landscape, much as she herself was doing right now.

The strains of an Irish folk song, both joyful and lamenting, could be heard as the foreigners moved slowly forward into their new home lugging cloth sacks filled with their meager possessions. She watched transfixed and spellbound. Yet, it all felt so real.

On the docks, an army of sweaty laborers unloaded barrels and crates of all sizes and shapes from the hold of a ship proudly displaying a naked lady's breasts on its wooden masthead. Shocking and bold, it reminded her of a masthead she had once seen at the Mystic Seaport Museum in Connecticut. Such sexist displays seen long ago, no longer existed.

All down the riverfront, slips housed all manner of sea-going vessels arriving or departing like some watery Grand Central Station. The busy main street, which ran the length of the seaport, housed maritime and shipping offices that posted sailing schedules on boards outside their doors. Everywhere she looked, historic South Street was a dirty and bustling mess of humanity in constant motion. It was daunting.

Dockworkers, many of whom looked like they had not bathed in ages, vied with the stench of rotting fish and garbage swept in by the river tide. Kat tried not to gag. Horse excrement was everywhere, stopping her from moving forward lest she step in some huge pile of shit. What she wouldn't give right now for a pair of Doc Marten boots.

The day felt hotter than hell for April. Beads of sweat ran down her neck and between her breasts from all the yards of material encasing her body in the oppressive heat. The dampness spread like an insidious rash down the inside of her legs. There would be no relief in sight without stripping down to her underwear, which she wasn't sure she was still wearing.

Her doubting mind scoffed at the idea that she had somehow traveled back in time, but her eyes told a different story. How had such a thing happened? Was it because she had donned the dress and the ring? Was there a curse attached to either article? And, if so, how would she ever get back to her time?

Such thoughts suddenly made her hand itch like the devil. A quick glance showed it was puffy and red. With a start she realized that the ring with the "R" insignia was no longer on her finger. Fuck, no! Where had she lost it? Panic swept through her. Without a moment's hesitation, she dropped down on all fours, searching the ground around her, but the ring had vanished. She had to find it; she had already written it up in her notes. Alan would certainly learn of its existence and certainly demand she produce it.

Kat swore loudly, making heads turn, causing men to stop and stare at her pitiful sight groveling on hands and knees. She must look like a lunatic and undisguised laughter around her confirmed it. With a sinking feeling, Kat realized that she was a woman alone, unprotected, and that women of this time, whatever that time happened to be, stayed inside the safety of their carriages not traipsing along a man-infested waterfront acting strangely like she was now doing.

Kat stumbled to her feet, looking around nervously, hoping that few had witnessed her lapse in judgment. But from the pitiful looks and sneers thrown her way, she knew she had made a spectacle of herself for all to see. That's when matters took a noticeable turn for the worse. It started to rain. Not just a midday spring drizzle, but the heavens opened and dropped a deluge on her and everything around her. Like rats, people scurried in all directions to escape the sudden onslaught, taking cover and shelter wherever they could. Others were not so fortunate; they had work to finish. Unloading cargo in the rain only made them move faster.

Her perky little bonnet was useless in such weather and in less than a minute she was drenched through like this morning. Kat looked around desperately for help, appealing to the first well-dressed gentlemen she came upon—a man impeccably dressed, wearing a brown beaver top hat and carrying a large open umbrella as he heralded an approaching carriage.

"Excuse me, sir. Can you tell me today's date?" she asked, stopping him.

The gentleman frowned, staring with distaste at the bedraggled person who was now pestering him, as if she had lost her mind.

"Why it's the first of August!" he answered dismissively.

"August!" she screeched, not believing her ears. The panic in her eyes made the man step back from her. Just this morning it had been the first of April. How had she lost so much time?

"Now begone, harlot. I have no business for you or your kind," he reprimanded.

Harlot? No business for her kind?! She grabbed his arm, pulling him back from the waiting carriage, anger welling up in her. "I'm no harlot you rude little prick. Just tell me what goddamn year this is?"

The man looked aghast and swatted her arm away, showing his disdain by spitting a nasty wad of tobacco scant inches from her feet. "It's 1835. Now take your filthy hands off me before I summon the authorities."

Kat let him go, still reeling from the realization that she was indeed in the year 1835 and men here seemed to be a hostile lot. Chivalry appeared to be dead as well—at least on the waterfront. All around her dockworkers shoved her out of their way in a haste to cover precious cargo or get their goods to the numerous storehouses dotting the harbor front. Carriages sped by splashing dirt and mud all over her, along with a host of other substances, which she now knew to be tar and grease. So, this was how the yellow dress had gotten soiled, but it still didn't answer *why* she was here? The ring had to be the answer. She needed it; there was no other way around it.

Had she not been so distracted attempting to find a solution, she might have been faster in getting out of the way of dockside traffic, but Kat was used to taking Ubers and subways, not dodging horses and wagons. Lugging around a wet gown, complete with layered petticoats, made her feel like she was saddled with a 20-pound weight belt threatening to drag her down. She could barely walk anywhere, being practically shoeless, and where to go was an even bigger conundrum. Not knowing what to do, she did something totally out of character for her. She sank to the ground and cried.

~~*~~

Kat's pity party caught the attention of a man who observed her behavior with keen interest from the window of the Eastern Star Line's maritime offices at the corner of Maiden Lane and South Street. This particular specimen of woman he had never seen before. Her flaming red hair was impossible to miss, like a warning beacon signaling treacherous shoals ahead. That she was clearly lost and agitated was abundantly clear. Whatever her business was that took her to the docks on this day, it was a miscalculation if she had chosen the location for the purpose of soliciting clients. Even the lowliest whores avoided the rough and tumble business of the harbor. It was no place for any woman, especially a woman alone.

Sheltered from the rain by a wooden overhang, Rem Randall stepped outside the shipping office door to watch the confrontation the red-haired woman had with Abbott Lockwood, someone he knew to have no interest whatsoever in the female sex, being cut from an entirely different cloth. It was a well-known social secret, but this sopping wet creature was oblivious to what everyone else knew. It told him that the woman was not from here and was desperate.

Rem knew everyone of standing in this town, especially those who had business within the shipping and China trade, which Lockwood did. Everything that happened in the harbor was of interest to him, even an unknown unaccompanied female trying to ply her trade. He knew many of the females from the better sporting houses, and this creature was clearly not one of them. A red-headed courtesan would be hard to forget.

Rem swore. Damn, now the wench was crying! His better instincts told him to turn around and return to more pressing matters. There were business accounts to review and no time for saving sobbing damsels in distress. That is until he saw the woman stagger to her feet and put herself right in the path of a fast-moving wagon loaded with barrels of China tea—a most precious cargo—belonging to the Eastern Star line. That suddenly made it his business.

In that moment he knew she would be struck and killed, and he could not allow such a thing to happen. His long legs ran towards the oncoming disaster, reaching her within seconds to tackle and roll with her out of harm's way. There was that split second of shock on the woman's face as he grabbed her body and they both hit the ground with a thud, his weight atop hers to protect her from the horse's flailing hooves. Seconds later, out of nowhere, he felt a solid right hook to his jaw, only to realize that the woman had hit him—and damn hard, too, like a seasoned boxer.

"Get the fuck off me!" she screamed, quickly followed by a swift knee jab to his groin. He moaned, blinded by a constellation of stars as his balls racked up with intense pain from the second direct hit. He wasted no time rolling off her, wanting to get as far away from this red menace as was possible. The ordeal rendered him speechless as he waited for the pain to subside. He was certain that everyone on the harbor front within a stone's throw had witnessed the incident. By tomorrow there would be a price to pay for his unwelcome gallantry. Gossip spread like wildfire in this town.

In the time it took him to recover his manly pride, the woman had already dragged herself up, along with skirts coated in grime. She ran from him like the devil himself was after her—fear written in her flashing green eyes. Those eyes he would never forget. Rem only hoped to God he never ran into them again.

~~*~~

Kat couldn't get the incident out of her mind as she wandered the crowded and unfamiliar streets of 1835 trying to formulate a plan—any plan. But her thoughts kept returning to the filthy perv who had his hand on her breast when he attacked her. Did he think he could cop a quick feel and get away with it? Hell, no.

The dockworker in question was tall, with hardened muscle like the bodybuilders in her time and had to have outweighed her by a fucking ton. There was no mistaking what was packaged under his breeches when he was pressed atop her with no breathing room in between. Instinctively her self-defense training kicked in, causing her to immediately react to the potential threat like she had been taught and drilled. First a punch to the jaw then a quick jab to the balls. Her unexpected response had taken the man by total surprise, which pleased her immensely. She might be a woman alone in a strange new world, but she was certainly not defenseless.

The rain had finally stopped, but the air was still damp and muggy. Kat had no idea where she was, for street names had changed over the years, and truly little looked the same in 1835. There were rolling hills, ponds, and the crooked lanes were a tangled mess where one could get easily lost. This was a time before New York was laid out in a traversable gridwork of avenues and streets, something which she was familiar with.

If she remembered correctly, city limits only reached to 14th Street and everything up to that point was tightly congested. Her father had been a tenured History Professor at Columbia University and as a child she had been expected to know her American history. She searched her memory now for how the Dutch settlers had first laid out the street gridwork of early Manhattan. Keeping this in mind, it served to guide her away from areas that were known to be dangerous—like the Five Points neighborhood and Hell's Kitchen.

Somewhere on Maiden Lane, close to Broadway, in what would later become the New York Diamond District, Kat came upon a well-kept looking brick rooming house with a sign advertising, "For Genteel Young Ladies." What was considered "genteel" during these times was anyone's guess. Taking in her present state of appearance, entry into this female bastion might be questionable. There was, of course, a small issue of payment. She was penniless, hungry, and would give anything right now for a hot shower and dry clothes. However, she knew there was no way she could wander the streets of old New York forever as it would soon be dark.

The two-story house situated at 14 Maiden Lane had whitewashed shutters open to catch the late afternoon breeze. Large shady elms surrounded the white picket-fenced property. Kat was struck at how much it looked like a scene straight off a Hallmark greeting card.

Kat tentatively opened the unlocked gate and slowly walked up the stairs to an ivy-laden trellis porch. Her tired feet hurt like the devil and were already sporting tender blisters. Hoping for the best, she knocked on the door praying to encounter a good Samaritan. Her silent prayer came in the form of a little old lady, gray-haired and rosy-cheeked, named Mrs. Begley, who took one look at her wet, bedraggled, and extremely pitiful state, and pulled her inside her rooming house.

Kat was fussed over like a wayward orphan, then prayed over like the harlot sinner she must have appeared to be once Mrs. Begley got her out of her wet clothes and spied the racy crimson string bikini underwear she wore underneath. By 1835 "genteel lady" standards it must have seemed quite shocking.

Mrs. Begley clucked over her like a woe begotten lost chick and promptly fed her a hot bowl of mutton chowder soup and cornmeal biscuits. Granted, it was not her meal of choice by any stretch of the imagination, but she heartily ate the meal not knowing where or when she might eat again. In this new world she would have to learn to eat meat and carbs.

Chapter 3

Kat awakened from a fitful dream state, only to realize that she was still living in the past. She covered her face and emitted a silent scream. When she re-opened her eyes and took in the small sleeping quarters, it confirmed once again her worst nightmare. Her situation had not changed one iota. Clad only in a white muslin shift of unknown origin, she felt the lumpy feather bed beneath her which she must have passed out on. A Marriott Hotel mattress it was not.

A "genteel" woman's boardinghouse offered extraordinarily little besides the bare necessities. A bed, dresser, mirror, and washstand graced one side of the room, with a few hooks placed on flower-papered walls to hang one's clothes. But Kat was grateful. The only frilly decor to be seen was the white lacy curtains framing an open window, which accounted for the flies currently buzzing around the room. She didn't even want to think of the mosquitos entering freely that had brought about countless cholera epidemics throughout New York's early years.

Being a good little pescatarian and not having eaten meat in a long time, her digestive tract must have gone into shock at the stronger tasting, fattier, animal offering, and had passed out soon thereafter. But beggars could not be choosers. Kat had practically choked with suppressed laughter when Mrs. Begley duly informed her that a clean private room with two meals a day (breakfast and dinner), which included housekeeping services, would cost her a whopping twenty-five cents per day or around $7.50 per month. She didn't need a calculator to know that would come to about one, vente-size, personalized Starbuck's drink. If she was going to be stuck in this time universe for a while, then she would have to find a job fast, even if it paid slave wages.

Last night she had removed one 14K gold studded diamond pierced earring and offered it as a down payment on her room deposit, which was a joke knowing what it was really worth. Mrs. Begley was kind enough to also advance her about $3.00 in pocket change for "incidentals" as she called it. How far that would get her was anyone's guess.

The other earring Kat vowed to hold onto for future emergencies. No way would she barter the necklace her parents had given her either, which… Panic struck as she scrambled out of bed looking for it. It had been tucked inside the pleated bodice of the yellow dress she had so fatefully donned back in her time. The locket and dress were nowhere to be seen.

Still semi-dressed, Kat threw open the door to her room and raced out into a long, narrow, upstairs hallway. She ran headlong into another woman exiting the room opposite hers, practically knocking her down. The woman's purse or reticule, as it was called in these times, skittered down the highly polished wooden flooring.

"Oh, I am so sorry!" Kat exclaimed, helping the woman up and scrambling to retrieve her purse. The woman was wearing a beautifully tailored day dress in robin's egg blue. Atop her head was perched a fetching straw bonnet adorned with silk ribbons that hugged her heart-shaped face. Fashion would always be the first thing Kat saw. In this time and place it was certainly no different. In fact, it was like walking through a vintage museum collection everywhere she looked.

"You must be the new girl Ida spoke about last night," the woman said with a smile and a noticeable French accent. "Your name is Katherine, correct?"

"Just Kat," she corrected.

"I'm Justine. I would love to converse, but I'm running late for work and my boss is quite the harridan."

"Where do you work?" Kat hurriedly asked, wondering what jobs might be available to someone with her skillset.

Justine shook her head. "It's not an easy job. I'm a seamstress at Madame Vesey's."

The name meant nothing to her. "Who's she?"

Justine looked completely taken aback at the simple question. "Why she's the most sought-after couture dressmaker in all of New York. All the elegant ladies of society frequent her house. Surely you've heard of her?"

Kat shook her head, wracking her brain for any mention in the historical records of such a name. There was Vesey Street in Lower Manhattan named after the Reverend William Vesey, the first rector of Trinity Church. Was Madame Vesey a distant relation?

"I'm not from here," she replied when she really wanted to say, *I'm not from this time.* Common sense told her that fact would have to remain a secret, or she might find herself locked away in an asylum. Who in their right mind would believe her anyway?

"Does this Madame Vesey have any employment openings?" Kat wondered aloud.

"Oh, heaven's no," Justine laughed. "I don't mean to be arrogant, but the Madame is very particular about her staff. We all come from couture houses in France, where we have worked for many years before she brought us to America. Madame Vesey has a reputation to uphold. I came to New York a year ago and am working my way up from a fitting seamstress. It is extremely hard work, especially with Madame's demanding clientele. They are worse here than the French aristocracy."

"Oh," Kat murmured, thinking of her own impressive resume and the elite society she dealt with regularly at The Met. None of which she could use in the here and now. "But of course. Silly me. What was I thinking?"

Justine shot Kat a departing smile. "Mrs. Begley has clothes you can wear for now. As for your hair—it is quite stunning. But then I'm sure you already know that." And with that she hurried down the stairs and off to her demanding job.

Yes. Her hair, a growing mass of unruly curls, was expanding by the second in this summer humidity. Curly hair was both a blessing and a curse, especially when it was flaming red. She doubted anyone would call her "ginger head" or "carrot top" in 1835, but she was determined to find a ribbon to bind it up and avoid unnecessary stares.

"There you are," Mrs. Begley said removing breakfast plates from the downstairs dining area when Kat finally entered the room. Everyone had already taken off for the day and Kat had slept right through it. "I saved you boiled eggs and buttered toast with cheese. If you want porridge, I can make more."

Holy shit! Usually, Kat skipped breakfast and grabbed a coffee on her way to work. If people ate this much at breakfast she would need to find a gym or Stairmaster before long.

"I'm not hungry. Coffee is fine," she said, immediately registering the disapproving frown spreading across Mrs. Begley's face.

"You must eat, young lady. I'll have none of my girls starving," she said sternly.

"Right." Kat immediately changed the subject. "By the way, do you know where my dress and locket are?"

Mrs. Begley dug down into her kitchen apron pocket, extracted the gold locket, and handed it to her. "It's a very pretty piece of jewelry. What are those strange looking likenesses inside the necklace? I've never seen anything like it."

Oh crap! The old lady had examined her locket. Of course, it would seem bizarre. The early daguerreotype photography process on tin had not been invented yet and her parents' digital camera portraits would come a long time after that.

"It's a new process, born in England," she truthfully said, failing to mention it was two years early from being officially unveiled by its inventor, Louis Daguerre. "Those are my parents."

"And where are your parents now, dear?" Mrs. Begley questioned with genuine concern.

"They died a long… I mean recently," she corrected herself, or the photo explanation she had just lied about wouldn't make sense.

Mrs. Begley, a widow, seemed to know all about death, putting her arm around Kat's shoulders to comfort her. "I am so sorry, dear. You're all alone in the world with no one to help you. How terrible."

"Yes," Kat murmured, looking down. "I need to find a job to live, and Justine told me you might have some clothes I could borrow until I can secure financial means."

"Of course I do, you poor thing. God put me on this earth to help the unfortunate women of the world and I'm sure I have just what you need."

Surprisingly, Ida Begley, possessed a small collection of dresses left behind by prior women boarders who had discarded them upon departure. All of them would have been wonderful samples for The Met's vast 19th century collection but, during this time in history, they were considered functionally plain by present day standards.

Kat picked out the best of the lot that actually fit, noticing the worn hem and seams on the light pumpkin-colored cotton frock she was forced to choose, a color she usually avoided like the plague. It would have to do until she could afford better, something she had never had to worry about before. Being penniless was quickly becoming a humbling experience for someone The Met paid quite well.

On the dining room sideboard, Kat spied a penny newspaper, sporting the masthead of The New York Herald. She scoured it, shocked to find it filled with society gossip and even more scandalous news. It disclosed information on corrupt politicians, stock market swindlers, and even had a personal section where one could locate missing persons, or lonely hearts could seek marriage and/or bed partners.

Wives routinely placed notices beseeching wayward husbands to return home, "No questions asked." There were men, advertising their net worth, while others asked for women respondents to "state your full particulars" which made her laugh. Who would have thought things were racier during these times than ever imagined?

The paper appeared to be the sole brainchild of one James Gordon Bennett, the publisher and sole reporter of what was ten times worse than the tabloid magazines during Kat's time.

Mrs. Begley leaned over her shoulder. "It's truly shocking what the Herald prints. Overnight that paper is selling out faster than all the others in the city, and it just started publishing. That Bennett man has absolutely no scruples whatsoever. And to think he was destined for the priesthood."

Kat was totally intrigued. The New York Herald had been a large-distribution paper and a phenomenally successful one for a long time. She had no idea it went back this far in history.

Mrs. Begley, despite her condemnation, appeared to be a secret fan. "He's always getting into fights with his readers. That's because his editorials are downright outrageous, and he says what no one else will print. They say the man has as many enemies as he does fans, which is a lot. My girls here absolutely love him!"

Kat found a few job listings—none which she was qualified for. Railway welder, fur skinner, pipe manufacturing work, canal workers, shipbuilding, housekeeper… 12 to 16-hour workdays, six days a week, no breaks. The factories were death traps back then. Outside of prostitution, there was no way for a woman to make fast money. But, then again, maybe there was.

A half-page public announcement on the second page of the newspaper caught her attention, making her pulses race and her eyes grow wide with excitement. In bold typeface it proudly reported that the City Hotel, located at 123 Broadway in the Financial District, had just procured the *"very highest-quality, slate-bed, American-made, four-pocketed billiards table, made by New York craftsman, Abraham Bassford."*

The City Hotel was a prestigious New York meeting place for society's gentlemen and ladies, well-known for holding lavish receptions, balls and even concerts. It also held the unique distinction of having the "longest bar" in the city, making it a favorite watering hole for the elite.

Damn lucky she was to have spotted this divinely sent little news tidbit. An idea began to percolate, sending her thoughts into overdrive. She had played on all kinds of billiards tables from the 19th century— Bassford, John Thurston, and later Brunswick tables to name just a few. Bassford had invented the gum elastic cushion which made the ball roll further. In her time, most tables were made with vulcanized rubber cushions which had yet to be invented in 1835. Playing on a Bassford table would be like running in combat boots, but she could handle it. Bank shots would have to be made with more force due to a lack of rubber bounce.

While other players of this time would still be adapting to the introduction of four pockets, what she knew would give her a clear advantage—something she might need depending on her opponent's skill. A slate table was also a positive. It would eliminate surface warping which often plagued the older carved wooden tables making play unstable.

In her mind Kat ran through the evolution of the game, preparing herself for whatever she might come up against. Early American billiards tables were either pocketless or had four pockets, unlike later English billiard tables which had six—hence the arrival of the "6-pocket *pool* game vs. a billiards game." The City Hotel's newest gaming table addition would be considered big news for serious players. Rules could be slightly different regarding number of balls in play, which was usually four, but she could adjust.

If memory served her well, a Bassford table should be larger and longer with deeper pockets, requiring greater skill. Kat was practically dancing with uncontained excitement. It was the first ray of hope she had felt since landing in the past. She itched to see how well the men and women of this time played. That's when her runaway thoughts screeched to a halt. Did women socially play the sport during this time? For centuries it was known to be a "gentlemen's activity," and women were barred from such gaming establishments. Wealthy ladies were known to play in Europe, mostly in the privacy of their own homes. Only a few dared to play in public, but in America it could be a different story altogether.

Would she even be allowed into the City Hotel's gaming room—an establishment owned by John Jacob Astor? Kat pushed the unacceptable thought aside. She would cross that bridge when she got to it. "No" was a word she rarely heeded upon first hearing it.

As far as she could see, there was only one stumbling block to playing men with money. She needed to procure a dress and not just any dress. It would have to be something stunning if she was to be taken seriously as a woman of betting means.

~~*~~

Kat decided she would pay Justine a surprise visit at Madame Vesey's later in the day prior to closing. She realized she *did* have something extremely valuable to trade—her knowledge of future fashion history. She could name any year and its fashion trend going back to the 15th century—French, American, or otherwise. However, wearing the discarded pumpkin dress, which was all she had right now, would not be an affirming choice to present herself in if she was attempting to sell such knowledge. Therefore, she would wait until the shop closed for the day to remain unobtrusive.

In the meantime, Kat took off for the offices of the infamous New York Herald. There was the remote chance she might be lucky enough to locate the whereabouts of her paternal great-great-great-great-grandparents who existed somewhere in the midst of this city. She knew their names, but not where they had initially lived prior to relocating to Brooklyn Heights.

Being a fast walker, and even an early morning jogger on good days, Kat didn't mind the trek to the newspaper's Lower Broadway area offices located in the basement of a two-story building on Wall Street. It gave her a chance to get the lay of the land in a city she knew so well in her time but was vastly different now. If only her father were here to walk this path with her; she knew he would have loved every moment.

Underneath this new adventure, there was always the persistent fear— how will I ever get back to *my* time? She no longer had the ring which might or might not hold the answer to her dilemma. Ruminating on it was a luxury she didn't have. Right now her primary goal was to consciously watch her every step. It was a dangerous jungle out there. There were no traffic lights or crossing lanes in this new world. People could be easily run over by all manner of vehicles, animals, or carts if they weren't careful.

There was congested carriage traffic and horse-drawn omnibuses running along a track up and down the wider thoroughfares. People jumped on and off public transportation as they felt like it. The looming sight of buildings becoming larger in size told Kat she was in the midst of the city's business and financial district. She searched for the correct address as she headed east on Wall Street, quickening her step.

At the end of the street, housed in a basement storefront, the newspaper's humble headquarters displayed a large banner proclaiming:

"The New York Herald, News Not Vi*ews*—James Gordon Bennett, Publisher." It had only been three months since its establishment, and it was already making its mark on the city's landscape. The place was buzzing with activity.

Inside the cluttered one-room office, the pungent smell of printer's ink permeated the air, while the rhythmic beat of a newspaper press kept syncopated time to the procession of ragged, shoeless urchins that came and went with fresh bundles of penny news sheets. Kat stepped aside to let them pass.

She had already witnessed these tough little vagabonds barking out the day's news leads on her city walk. They occupied every street corner, tempting each passing person with the lurid "hot news" of the day. They were crafty little ones that looked to be creating their own sensational headlines, duping customers while looking to sell their penny papers. One had loudly proclaimed how the world was "ending on the morrow" and that "President Andrew Jackson had narrowly escaped a second assassination attempt and how the militia would be occupying and safeguarding the Capitol by nightfall."

She had seen a bloody fight break out between two such ragamuffins after one dared to encroach upon the other's territorial domain. She was shocked to see they carried knives and weren't afraid to use them. It was a rough, tough business and these young kids were learning to fight for their turf.

Kat stepped aside in the entryway as black ink-smudged hands hoisted bundles on their small shoulders and out the door to the crowded streets where they went about their job hawking morning and afternoon news editions. This reminded Kat that she needed to hustle as well, or she would find herself also out on the streets. Some things would never change in this cut-throat city.

"And what'll it be today, ma'am?" called out a brawny man with a thick Scottish brogue. She could see he was busy setting typeface from a series of wooden racks but had yet to look up.

Kat had to shout over the din of the one-man press that thumped out each news sheet with a grating screech. The constant sound would drive anyone mad. Finally, the man looked up. He set down the letters, wiping his grimy hands in a rag as he came over.

"I would like to place an item in your 'Personals' section," she repeated loudly. "I'm trying to find someone."

The man grunted knowingly, as he wiped sweat from his brow with the back of his dirty sleeve. Certainly, he had heard that line countless times before.

"No," she clarified, knowing what he must be thinking. "I'm trying to locate family members. Can I do that here?"

"You can advertise for whatever you want," he said with a touch of sarcasm. He reached for a pen and a sheaf of papers listing the advertisements that would appear in the next edition. He shuffled to the last page. "I still have room. Now—what do you want to say and how long do you want me to run it?"

Kat had labored over the text that morning. The whole thing was a longshot by any means. Frankly, she didn't even know whether her distant relatives knew how to write, let alone read a newspaper. They were poor immigrants, Dublin transplants, more likely unskilled laborers. Irish immigrants were treated like dirty scum during this time and Kat knew it. "Potato Eaters," they were called. Was this a mistake trying to find them? Would they even answer such an ad? More importantly, what would she say to them if they *did* meet? Kat bit her lip in indecision.

"I ain't got all day, ma'am," Bennett reminded her impatiently. "Now what will it be?"

She handed over the parchment paper containing her ad copy.

The Scotsman read it over quickly. "Okay. You want it to read:

> *Young lady looking for any information that will help locate her*
> *relatives,*
> *Colleen and Duncan Branigan, and son Aiden, of County*
> *Galway, Dublin.*

It was simple and to the point. "Yes, that's right. I'd like to run it for a week if that's possible."

"Anything's possible for a price. How do you want to sign it?"

She went with the first thought that popped into her head. "Just sign it: *HOPEFUL*."

Bennett snorted. "Okay, HOPEFUL. This will be tagged to Box 140 and responses can be checked daily. I'll set the type right now and you can expect it in tomorrow's morning edition." He finally afforded her a small smile and recorded the information in his ledger. "We aim to please. Especially for 'Hopeful' young ladies."

As she paid him his few coins, it occurred to her that this man might be the publisher himself. It was evident he was lacking in social skills, which might explain why he was always getting into fights with his readers.

"Are you James Gordon Bennet?" she asked, realizing if so, she was meeting the man who would eventually become a millionaire and be written about in the annuals of New York City journalism history. His small paper would eventually become The New York Herald Tribune.

"That I am, ma'am. Jim Bennett, publisher, editor, circulation manager, advertising salesperson, typesetter, and..." he gave her a mischievous wink, "printer's devil."

"Keep up the good work," she said, before adding with a knowing smile. "Mark my words, Mr. Bennett. You and your newspaper are destined to go far in this town."

"Thank you, ma'am. I certainly hope so."

Kat had patiently waited outside on a shady park bench until the last carriage departed outside Madame Vesey's dressmaker's establishment before approaching the salon's main entrance. Justine was about to lock the door when she caught sight of Kat, her face registering surprise.

"Oh my. What are you doing here?" Justine whispered, a mite frantically, as her head bobbed this way and that to make sure no one was observing them. "Come in, quick," she beckoned, before locking the heavy door securely behind them.

"Madame Vesey's is not here at the moment," she informed, as Kat strolled into the salon, taking in the lavish decor.

The drawing room was straight out of an opulent French fashion house with dark forest green tufted velvet settees, matching sconced drapery adorning tall paned windows, and an assortment of large golden goddess statues strategically placed about.

Gas-powered crystal chandeliers cast a warm glow of light around the room's interior for the purpose of catching every ladies' reflection in nearby mirrors. Gilded floor mirrors were strategically placed to afford the client a view of themselves from all angles. Artistically overdone, Kat felt like she was in a palace drawing room at Versailles.

The Madame of the house was attempting to style her establishment on the Parisian model, even though big name Parisian haute couture was not yet born. It wouldn't be until 1837 when Hermes International came on the scene with ready-to-wear accessories and leather goods, and not until 1858 when British designer, Charles Frederick Worth, would be given the official title of *father of haute couture*. But any piece of fashion that was handmade and one-of-a-kind was considered couture.

Justine took one look at the pumpkin-colored day dress Kat was outfitted in and tried not to openly frown. Kat looked down at it and voiced the obvious. "Yes, I know. It's ghastly. There was nothing else Mrs. Begley had to offer that fit, which is why I'm here. I need your help."

Justine looked dubious, which was understandable. Kat knew a little white lie would be called for under the circumstances to get her toe in the door. The bait flowed off her tongue, as she spied a dress box and the gown inside waiting to be delivered. She studied it quickly.

"Madame Vesey needs to know that in only a few short months, such full gigot sleeves are going to be totally out of fashion, like this gown here. The French houses are already re-thinking and re-designing sleeves with less material and making bigger skirts instead. It's only a matter of time before New York women follow suit. If Madame wants to stay ahead of her competition, she needs a fashion trends consultant."

"A what?" Justine asked, having never heard of such a position.

It was only a little white lie. "All the best houses in Europe secretly employ such a person," Kat proclaimed.

"And how would you know this?" Justine asked.

"It's complicated," Kat muttered under her breath. Instead of explaining, she asked for paper and pencil and began sketching. She did three quick drawings in succession, showing what she knew would come true in the next 6-12 months. Justine quietly examined the innovative designs with intense interest.

"The sleeves will be the first to change, then the skirts, eventually getting fuller and shorter to ankle length in another year or two." This last bit of news actually shocked Justine. "Show Madame these sketches and tell her I am available for a fashion futures consult. Trust me. She won't regret it."

"She won't pay you. The woman is cheaper than a tight-arse," Justine flatly pointed out.

Kat had a better idea. "I'm willing to waive my fee and take it out in trade instead."

"And what would that trade be?" Justine inquired.

It was time she got to the point of her visit. "Well, I need new day clothes and a spectacular evening gown as well." There, she had declared her true needs. "Do you have anything ready-to-wear like Lord & Taylor is now offering?"

"Oh. Yes. Them." Justine uttered with a hint of disdain. She continued to look thoughtful. "Well, we have only one spectacular gown at the moment that might fit. It was a returned item which would be considered 'ready-to-wear' if someone wanted to buy it."

"Let me see it," Kat interrupted.

She followed Justine to a back workroom, filled with shelves of all manner of fabrics, bric-a-brac trimmings, baskets overflowing with buttons, and a rainbow assortment of colored threads. Justine pulled aside a gray curtain to another room and brought a large box over to one of the worktables. She carefully lifted the lightweight wrapping paper to reveal a soft lavender voile gown with embroidered silk lacing in a delicate alabaster white. It was stunning. The design alone was flawlessly perfected.

"This piece was commissioned by a rather difficult client of Madam's who brought it back complaining that it was 'too ordinary,' and she couldn't be seen in it," Justine explained.

Kat silently lifted the gown out of the box, knowing instinctively that there had to be another reason. This was no "ordinary" gown. The design was cut devilishly low and made for a temptress. Nothing about it could be coined 'ordinary' by a long shot.

"It's already been worn," Kat pointed out with a discerning eye. There were always tell-tale signs, even subtle, that merchandise had been used. She didn't know what the policy was in Old New York, but such a practice was considered illegal during her time and could lead to arrest. They called it "*wardrobing.*"

Justine shook her head. "I'm sure you're right. I don't know why Madame lets Miss Melanie get away with such behavior. She's already delinquent in her account, which is sizeable, and she has done this before to get a free ensemble. I don't know what we will do with it, as it can't be resold. Madame doesn't want to offend anyone from elite society, so it will probably just sit on the shelf."

Justine put the gown up against Kat's body, sizing her up. "With your flaming red hair, this dress would be better suited to you. Would you like to try it on?"

Kat wasted no time disrobing and, with Justine's help, pulled the gown over her head. The bodice was slightly snug, which she could live with, but the rest fit like a glove. The waist hugged her perfectly and whomever "Miss Melanie" was she was of the same height, which was 5'7".

Kat viewed herself from all angles in the workroom mirror, pleased with what she saw. Playing billiards in such a dress might be a tad challenging compared to the tight black pencil-leg pants she was accustomed to wearing. The city heat would be more challenging. Modern air-conditioning had clearly spoiled her. She couldn't remember when it had been invented, surely a long way off, making every room feel unbearably warm, even with open windows. How the ladies of these times managed to wear so much material was a wonder to her, but she would have to adapt. With one last look at her reflection, Kat made up her mind and spun around to face Justine.

"I'll take it!" she declared. "Can I borrow it for a night before paying for it?"

Justine suddenly looked perplexed. "Oh, dear. If Madame won't hire you as a 'fashion consultant,' then how will you pay for it?"

Kat took out the remaining small diamond stud gold earring in her ear. "Take this as a down payment for the gown, just until tomorrow night. I promise I'll find a way to fully pay for the gown, whatever Madam decides."

Justine brightened. "I guess I could wait another day or two before telling Madam that Miss Melanie returned the outfit. But you're going to have to be extremely careful with it."

She would guard it with her life. No eating or drinking anything in it. "I will," she promised. "And thank you!" Excitement bubbled up inside her. Tomorrow could not come soon enough.

~~*~~

Kat awoke to the early chattering of birds outside her open window—the kind of sounds she barely heard in present day New York City where nature was drowned out by street cleaners, garbage trucks rumbling by, and early morning construction workers jack-hammering through concrete.

Reconnecting with nature, Kat felt totally psyched, ready to start her day. She had not slept this well in ages. However, no longer having the luxury of jumping into a quick steaming hot shower whenever she desired was something sorely missed. Having to sponge-bathe with tepid water from a portable washstand was a concept that would take time adjusting to. That, and so much more.

At times it was unthinkable. The lack of flush toilets and proper indoor plumbing was at the very top of her list. It was either a chamber pot or using the outhouse in back of the rooming house for such needs. The city had yet to construct a sewer system infrastructure which could adequately address the elimination needs of an ever growing population now pushing 220,000 inhabitants. Hence, filth and lack of hygiene flourished.

Granted, she would be the first to admit that she had led a charmed life compared to what was expected of people during this time. A spoiled city girl through and through, she had never wilderness-camped a day in her life and knew nothing about roughing it. Even "glamping" might be a stretch for her required tastes.

How in the world would she ever manage to exist before finding a way to get back to her time? She had yet to come up with any kind of escape plan, which only frustrated her more. Kat was a doer and everything in life she had ever accomplished she had done through sheer will and unflagging perseverance, like her parents had taught her. Growing up in New York City had taught her to be aggressive if she wanted to realize her dreams and/or survive. The question uppermost on her mind right now was how would an aggressive woman be treated in these times?

It wasn't quite 7:00 a.m. when she heard the sound of footsteps moving past her door, accompanied by high-pitched sporadic chatter. Kat dressed quickly in another cast-off from Mrs. Begley's secret dress stash—a chocolate brown cotton with staid cut, not much better than yesterday's selection.

She descended the stairs to find the downstairs dining room was already a beehive of activity as a large breakfast buffet was laid out on the sideboard for those whose jobs demanded they start at 8:00 a.m. sharp. Last night, Kat had met a few of the women inhabiting Mrs. Begley's house. These same women straggled home every night after toiling for 12-15 hours a day for low wages, enough to make weekly room and board, but not much else. Some came home too late to have dinner, so breakfast was a big meal. These women had decent jobs, but they were the working poor. They usually retired to their room early after dinner, exhausted.

"Hello, I'm Kat Branigan," she introduced herself the next morning to a tableful of curious eyes.

"Good morning, Kat," came a chorus of responses before they returned to their food.

Kat reminded herself that she must learn to eat breakfast for who knew when her next meal might be. She filled her plate with coddled eggs, avoiding all meat, and grabbed plenty of flatbread and rhubarb jam. Carbs it would have to be.

She took a seat beside a petite, blond-haired woman named Celeste, who worked in a millinery shop and chattered away about their newest inventory of hats from Italy. Across from her, Rebecca worked in the kitchens of the recently opened Military and Civic Hotel on the Bowery and Broome Streets. Daphne was an office stenographer at the private elite Collegiate School for boys on the Upper West Side. Kat knew the K-12 school was still in existence, costing more than $63K per year.

Everyone wanted to hear all about where she was from, what brought her to New York, and what type of work she did. She gave them all the same story she had given Justine and was spared the finer details when Mrs. Begley brought in the morning edition of The New York Herald, fussing over an article on the front page, which she read aloud:

> *"Throngs of greeting citizens stood by to welcome the U.S. Constitution frigate as it sailed into New York Harbor Tuesday morning carrying none other than the Minister to France, Edward Livingston. Reports say the ship was a floating sea of trouble and the men up-in-arms…"*

Mrs. Begley stopped reading, "Well, that certainly has a ring of mutiny to it," she remarked thoughtfully.

Kat chimed in before thinking. "Not mutiny, just exaggeration meant to impress the 'right' people into seeing the need for the formation of a military naval academy. The ship's commissioned officers drew up a list of resolutions they are going to present to the Secretary of the Navy and…"

All eyes silently stared at her. Oops. Too much information. "At least that's what I heard on the docks the day I arrived," she added, backpedaling.

"Is that where you lost your belongings?" Mrs. Begley asked.

Kat shifted in her chair uncomfortably, feeling like she was now in the hot seat. She didn't need to invite more suspicion about her past, or in this case "future." "Yes," she answered simply. "It's a rather long complicated story."

Justine pushed back from the table and rose to her feet. "I'd love to hear it, but I have to go." She glanced at Kat and winked. "I'll see you later." And with that the table quickly cleared out, leaving Kat by herself. She scooped up The New York Herald hoping to see her ad placement.

There it was smack in between a remedy for curing the ailment of consumption and a woman pleading for her runaway husband to come home—no questions asked. Satisfied, she tried not to think how long it might take to receive an answer, if any. She would have to check her box daily and hope for the best.

~~*~~

It was early evening when a flustered looking Justine welcomed Kat into Madame Vesey's Salon via a back door entrance. Beautifully attired in a cobalt blue evening gown, which complimented her eyes, Justine looked ready to go out for the evening.

"Quick. Come in," her new friend whispered in a rush of words, nervously checking to make sure no one on the outside had seen her admit Kat before locking the door. Without another word she turned and motioned for Kat to follow her to the back room.

"There's not much time," Justine said, retrieving a dress box from a worktable before thrusting it into Kat's arms. "Just make sure this dress is back by tomorrow before Madame finds out."

"Thank you, I will," Kat murmured. She stalled a moment longer, quite curious about Justine's appearance. "You look quite fetching. Do you have special plans for this evening?"

Justine nodded, her eyes brightening. "Oh, yes, which is why I can't dawdle. I have a gentleman friend who is coming to pick me up fairly soon."

"That's wonderful," Kat said, stalling before Justine booted her out the door. "Where are you two going?"

"Phillipe, that's my gentlemen friend, is a barrister," Justine explained. "He's taking me to the City Hotel for the farewell celebration for the U.S. Minister to France, Edward Livingston. Mr. Livingston is his client." She practically bubbled with excitement. "I'm so nervous. It should be a quite grand affair with many of the upper gentry attending."

Kat's ears perked up the second she heard "City Hotel."

Justine continued. "It was in The New York Herald this morning if you recall. Mr. Livingston returned home from France on the U.S. Constitution two days ago. They say he will be retiring at the end of this month, which is why they are honoring him in the City Hotel's grand assembly ballroom. You might not know this, but Edward Livingston was a former mayor of New York and a State Senator, too. Everyone will be there—even the Navy's top brass."

Everyone, but her, if Kat didn't act fast. She started stripping off her bland brown day dress, a new plan taking form.

Justine's jaw dropped open, aghast. "Whatever are you doing?"

Kat would make it up as she went along. "Well, it just so happens that I had planned on going to the City Hotel this evening as well," she informed. "Not to this Livingston gala, of course, but to make a job connection that's rather important." It was another small lie, but it would have to suffice. The prospect of a job hustling pool would send Justine into a fit of the vapors.

"Can you and your gentleman friend drop me off there?" Kat asked nicely as she quickly stepped into the lavender gown, encasing herself in the voile fabric that molded to her body as if made to order. Kat twirled once, before striking a fashion pose in the mirror.

Justine speechlessly stared at Kat, before finally exclaiming incredulously: "*You* were planning to go to the City Hotel tonight— *alone*?"

"Of course," Kat uttered matter-of-factly. "I just need a ride."

She pinched her cheeks for color, scrutinizing her appearance with a critical eye before furiously attacking her hair, tying it into a tight topknot, letting soft red tendrils frame her oval face. It was the best she could do at the moment without a makeup kit and professional hair stylist.

Kat was only interested in playing pool with the opposite sex and hopefully make enough funds to pay this month's rent. The gown would be distracting enough with its low cut off the shoulder bodice for anyone to find fault with her fresh skin appearance. Showing a little skin never hurt when you knew how to make it work for you. This she knew from experience and was counting on it.

Justine continued to mumble quietly to herself in her native French tongue as she watched Kat's preparation with skeptical eyes. Two years of high school French was more than enough for her to understand that her new friend and accomplice found such independent, progressive-sounding, notions quite foolish. The suffragette movement had yet to happen, so Kat reminded herself that her way of life *would* seem quite radical. But to Justine's credit, she was quick to produce white satin evening slippers for Kat to complete her look.

~~*~~

Phillipe Auclair presented himself as the stereotypical French barrister pushing 40. Possessing an elegantly chiseled patrician nose, graying temples, and a stylish fashion sense, he outwardly appeared painstakingly proper. However, once introduced and socially engaged he expressed delight at the prospect of escorting not one but two ladies to the City Hotel and gallantly extended his arm to help them into his waiting carriage.

Sitting across from the two of them sitting side by in their evening finery, Kat could see he had eyes for Justine. But he appeared equally curious about Kat as the carriage ambled through the city's streets. "Your inflection of speech is most unusual, Miss Branigan—not Irish sounding at all," he pointed out. "Where are you originally from?"

She jestingly said: "too many places to list" instead of the truth: *Lower Brooklyn, more than 175 years from now.* However, she had learned to steer away from such inevitable inquiries. She knew she spoke like a modern-day New Yorker/Brooklynite and was trying not to sound so strange.

"Do you play billiards, Mr. Auclair? I hear that the City Hotel's gaming parlor is now world famous for its American handcrafted tables," she said, attempting to change the subject.

"That it is," he said, taking the bait. "Best in the city, with some of the best players, as well. There should be some interesting matches tonight for those who like that sort of thing."

Oh, she definitely liked that sort of thing, which was all she needed to hear. Kat cleared her throat, before tentatively asking. "We would love to see such excitement, wouldn't we Justine?" She caught Justine's inquiring look. "I mean not many women get to see how billiards is played, let alone take part in such a game, do they?"

Phillipe nodded. "True. Wielding the stick is difficult for women. It's a gentleman's game." Kat inwardly rolled her eyes.

He looked to Justine for confirmation. "Would you like to see such a thing?" he asked.

Kat threw Justine a pleading *say yes* look.

"Yes, Phillipe," she agreed. "That would be most interesting to see before attending the Livingston event. Do we have time?"

Phillipe was all smiles when it came to Justine and was ready to take on the mantle.

Kat smiled inwardly. She knew it would be exponentially better to enter such a male den on the arms of an already well-accepted gentleman. And so, it was.

~~*~~

The City Hotel was the most distinguished of New York hostelries and Kat found herself in awe as their carriage pulled up to its brilliantly illuminated entrance. By night it was known to be the scene of important balls and social functions where the city's privileged strutted and preened either in the sumptuous eating salon or the splendidly furnished ballroom where attendance was tantamount to wearing a badge of honor. Everywhere she looked there was an abundance of Old World elegance, the likes of which she rarely saw in the hotels of her time.

By day, the hotel catered to the secluded ambience of its select guests who often rented whole suites for a full year. Located at 123 Broadway, it occupied the entire block between Thames and Cedar Streets. The establishment attracted the upper crust who gathered there for social relaxation and entertainment. Tonight, would be no different.

The farewell affair tonight in honor of the retiring U.S. Minister to France, Edward Livingston, was by invitation only. The guest list included the top naval brass from the newly arrived frigate U.S. Constitution who were easily recognized in their white dress uniforms, along with the Secretary of the Navy and the Admiralty.

Phillipe Auclair's specialty was Admiralty Maritime Law and as soon as they entered the polished marble entry on his arm, he was greeted by those who knew him. When he presented his engraved invitation card at the door, no one seemed to mind that he was now accompanied by a *plus two*.

Kat's eyes darted everywhere, totally enthralled with everything she encountered. The elegant attire that surrounded her, the lavish décor, and the people who had built this great city over time.

She had no idea the City Hotel's 5-story structure would be so luxurious. Had she foolishly tried to gate crash it alone, she would not have been so lucky. Security was tight and now it was clear that Phillipe Auclair was an unexpected Godsend. Justine's incredulous look of disbelief when she had told her earlier she intended to go to the City Hotel alone, now made total sense. No respectable woman would have been seen there unaccompanied.

Guests milled about outside the crowded ballroom which was ablaze with scores of glowing gas-lit chandeliers that sent light bouncing off crystal prisms, bathing the room in a spectrum of glittering flecks that looked like a thousand dancing fireflies. Against the expansive oak-paneled walls, a conservatory of lush potted palms and verdant ferns flourished, sweeping their graceful fronds upward to reach the light that enveloped the expansive ballroom.

"This way," Phillipe said, steering them towards the back billiards parlor.

Kat had just enough time to peek into the ballroom and take a series of mental snapshots. Scattered throughout and along the thriving indoor forest of greenery were tables covered in fine European linen with a nosegay of summer flowers gracing the center of each. The dance floor was a kaleidoscope of faces, swishing petticoats, and burgeoning color. Couples kept step to a lively quadrille the orchestra had taken up—a dance Kat knew to be popular during the time.

All around there was an abundance of laughter and merriment, reminding her of The Met's Gala Ball with its myriad of celebrities. The steady clinking of champagne glasses toasting the guest of honor was non-stop as Livingston mingled among his guests. It was all so enticing and mesmerizing, but Phillipe walked them right past it, making a beeline to the entrance of another large room which proved to be a hub of the male kind—the hotel's gaming room.

The room was smoke-filled, with the strong scent of acrid cigars, which made Kat almost gag and want to flee, but she held firm. She needed money desperately and was on a mission. Her lungs would just have to take one for the team.

Several billiards tables were already in the process of play, but her knowing instincts told her to go where the most action usually gathered—in the back which brought out the better players. She coaxed Phillipe and Justine along, feigning a "just one more look" approach, weaving her way through the bystanders situated around the very last table.

There, a tall man, his back to her, leaned over the table and sank a perfect shot into the pocket, taking the game. The men cheered as a voluptuous woman, her breasts practically spilling out of a tight pink bodice, came over to the victor and brazenly planted a kiss right on his cheek.

Next to her, Justine gasped, before informing her in a panic: "Oh, dear God. We must leave now. That's Melanie Van Eaton and you're wearing her cast-off dress. If she sees it, it will be a social disaster."

Not wanting to cause her friend any distress, Kat was about to agree. That is until the man Melanie had showed such brazen affection for, turned around, and offered a challenge to anyone wanting to defeat him. This time *she* gasped. It was the same man who had tried to cop a feel of her breast at the South Street Seaport the other day. He must have thought she was a prostitute—a woman he could take liberties with. It had pissed her off then and it still pissed her off now.

Kat would remember the bastard's face anywhere. No longer wearing the worn work clothes of the docks, he was now elegantly attired in dark blue dress tails and white satin waistcoat. His silk cravat was tied in an impeccable bow displaying a brilliant diamond stud. But despite his nice clothes, she knew him to be no gentleman.

Her blood boiled just seeing him again and the next words out of her mouth shocked even her. "I'll meet that challenge. Unless, of course, you're afraid to play a lady?"

Her challenge had been loudly made, intentionally. The room instantly hushed. Smokers paused in their incessant puffing, as every eye darted towards her and openly stared at this new challenger. Kat was willing to bet no female had ever dared challenge a man in this very room before tonight from the shocked looks she was now witnessing. She dismissed their speculative appraisal waiting for the only thing that mattered—her opponent's answer to her challenge.

There was the faintest hint of a frown at the corner of his mouth before it was replaced with a sly smile. "I am afraid of no lady," he replied gallantly.

Not a pin drop could be heard in the male bastion as he accepted her challenge. Sudden movement behind her told her that curious players and spectators from other tables were now wandering over to watch the unfolding drama.

Her opponent made a graceful bow towards her. "I not only accept the lady's challenge, but I will give her a two-point lead advantage," he stated magnanimously. The crowd behind him murmured their approval.

Kat was not one to be coddled nor publicly mocked. "That won't be necessary. Perhaps I should offer you the same advantage."

Her sassy comeback made the room roar with laughter. She suspected they knew something she didn't and that could only mean that she was up against a worthy opponent, and they thought she was a female fool. Behind her Phillipe gave her arm a slight tug, wanting to either tell her something or stop her, but she paid him no mind. Justine looked pale as a ghost while Melanie Van Eaton took to scrutinizing not only Kat but her lavender, low cut dress with growing suspicion.

"Name your game," Kat said stepping forward with confidence. It was a bold move which her opponent should have been offering her, but she beat him to it.

Across the table, he smiled. "Three Ball Carom, 50 points," he replied with a knowing smirk before adding, "same standing stakes," which made bystanders gasp, something her opponent had clearly anticipated.

Kat knew 3-Ball Carom was *the* most difficult game imaginable in billiards. It required skill and precision. With only three balls: red, white, and yellow, one had to successfully strike both their opponent's ball and the red ball in one shot to score a point. It was clear that her competitor foe was out for blood. She would have to hustle to beat him if he were any good. If he had really wanted to be cutthroat, he could have called for an 18-inch balk line variation of the game where distance lines were measured as well, but she wasn't sure if such a thing was even practiced during this time.

She nodded in agreement, chose a cue stick, and followed him to a larger table without pockets. The crowd shifted with them. "White," she announced, calling her cue ball color.

She wasn't sure what the "standing stakes" were, but she would deal with the terms of that later. Right now, she was too caught up in the thrill of the game. The thought of losing was not even remotely in her equation despite her awareness that wagers were already being placed against her. The betting only served to further foster her determination.

They tossed a silver coin for the opening break shot, which he won. He wasted no time chalking up and taking his shot as if he knew exactly what he was doing, and she soon realized he did. Each of his moves were precisely judged, analyzed, and skillfully caried out. He had already racked up a five point lead before missing and turning it over to her, but not before she spotted a detail that totally unnerved her—his pinky ring finger. Her opponent was wearing the same initialed ring she had been wearing when she was propelled back into this time period.

Kat stood there confused, unmoving, and calculating what to do. Had he found the ring that day? It was an expensive piece of jewelry from the looks of it, and the strange metal gleamed as if recently polished. He paused confidently waiting for her to take her turn, as did the crowd. Yet her mind was still on the mysterious ring when she finally took her shot, tense as a rubber band ready to snap. Her hand gripped the butt of the cue stick too tightly, her hand trembling slightly and it cost her. She miscued, the worst possible thing she could have done. The crowd fidgeted, surmising that the match would be quite ordinary after all. In their eyes she had marked herself as a novice. Skillful players rarely miscued. The play returned to her opponent who seemed confidently at ease.

She studied his style as she unconsciously studied the man and the ring before her. His rakishly handsome features, now more visible to her, were a hardened line of concentration as he leaned into his shot, taking aim and executing another successful carom off the other two balls. He shot tight keeping the three balls close, making it easier to score repeatedly on one play. The score was 8-0 when he returned it to her.

Forget the ring, she told herself. Just concentrate and focus. Her hand went to her breast, where tucked beneath was the gold locket with her parents' pictures—her lucky talisman. She patted it three times and silently called on the god of billiards to guide her every move. She wanted that ring and more than anything she wanted to wipe the smile off her opponent's face. Her prayers were soon paid off.

Determination coursed through her, bringing her nerves in check. She scored her first point as it struck each of the other two balls in quick succession. Then she did it again, causing whispering to break out amongst the rank and file. When she leaned deep over the table, intentionally revealing cleavage that rivaled Melanie Van Eaton's, she glanced at her opponent who had not failed to look, before pounding her ball into his ball, then the red ball and giving herself another point. Fuck yes!!!

It managed to slightly surprise and unnerve him, but he quickly covered it. Then, just as carefully, she walked around the table, brushing up against him as she lined it up again, gauging her angle of attack and did it again. The male bystanders looked just as shocked, shit-faced would be more accurate. They must be thinking she had been sandbagging them in order to drive up the betting odds against her. The match was now tied at 8-8.

Her control had returned. She hadn't won local Manhattan billiard championships without putting in some hard practice. She was certain every man there, including her opponent, was wondering where she had acquired such skill—for a woman. There were lots of things they wouldn't ever know about her, like she could shoot a gun quite well and had run a 26.2 mile marathon in just slightly under 3.5 hours—and, of course, that she was from the future.

She didn't even know her opponent's name, nor he hers, not that it would mean anything. When she missed on her next play, her opponent's face resembled a warrior's determined to do battle. They were starting to play a psychological game. He would move purposely towards her, his height looming over her, bare inches separating them at times as he conducted his maneuver. There was the barest hint of fresh soap or perhaps the cologne he wore, which marked his scent.

Since men were such mammalian creatures, she wasn't averse to flaunting her breasts and femininity to distract him. Sometimes, he would even smile knowing exactly what she was doing. The hell if she knew whether it was effective or not. His face was quickly becoming a closed mask as they continued to go neck and neck.

By the time they reached 24-23 in his favor, they were both executing well-coordinated moves. The crowd in the room only grew in size as word spread. Kat was matching him every step of the way but only at the expense of pushing beyond herself. He was forcing the best out of her whether he knew it or not.

Kat couldn't help but admire the figure her opponent cut, though she was loathe to admit it. His jacket was well-cut over broad shoulders. His tapered and tightly fitted dark trousers, made of a fine broadcloth, looked custom-tailored to hug firmly muscled thighs. His strong hands, tanned by the sun, looked like they had seen outside manual work, yet his nails were well manicured and polished bespeaking a gentlemen. Realization hit her that these were not the clothes of an ordinary clerk or even a longshoreman, despite his roughened dockworker appearance on the day they met. The man possessed a confident manner, which hinted at education and finer breeding. He was a contradiction in terms, which only made Kat more curious to find out who the hell he really was and how he had come to be wearing *her* ring.

She quickly reminded herself that appearances could be ever so deceiving. Look how many people here tonight had been taken in by her appearance. In her current state of dress attire, beautiful as she might look, it would be so easy to mistake her as also coming from money and stature.

During her moves she was acutely aware that her opponent was also scrutinizing her. He had not yet recognized her and identified her as the same woman from the docks he had so blatantly groped before being kneed in the groin. She had been mud-splattered, bedraggled looking, and soaking wet at the time of their encounter. Her red hair might jog his memory, but she was certain she wasn't the only red-headed woman in all of Manhattan.

But just as she was having such thoughts, he stared at her as instant recognition struck. And there it was—she knew that he knew. He hit his ball with such force it practically bounced off the table, managing to make him miss and pass the baton back to her. He did his best to hide it, but his irritation betrayed him.

~~*~~

Remington Randall silently swore, as he felt his balls recoil inside him recalling the excruciating pain the woman before him had unexpectedly inflicted upon him. She was the same pitiful crying creature he had tried to save from being hit by a carriage on the docks and gotten kneed in the groin for his white knight behavior. He had thought to never see her again, and here she was openly trying to best him.

If it hadn't been for her red hair, he might not have made the connection, but her accent was slightly different, unlike others, and that had been the determining and damning factor. Tonight, she didn't look like a street prostitute, but an incredibly beautiful woman who appeared bent on beating him with a cue stick. But why? And who was she?

Had one of his gaming rivals or even a business competitor brought her in to unseat him? Rem was known to be unbeatable in billiards and only fools or blowhards dared challenge him. That a woman was attempting to trounce him, made the crowd in the room swell with curious bystanders, men and women alike. After his last miss, he reined in his irritation, replacing it instead with a knowing smile, only to see her coyly smile back. Innocent, but clever that one. Okay, let the games really begin. No holds barred his look conveyed back at her.

The score was now in her favor 38-36 when she yielded back to him. Rubbing chalk over the tip of his stick, he stood back chuckling to himself, while analyzing the ball spread. "I have the feeling the lady is out for blood," he commented before adding. "Shall we make this game more interesting?"

A titter ran through the crowd at such a proposal. Everyone waited on baited-breath to hear the terms. His opponent hitched up one finely arched eyebrow. "And what would that be?" she inquired.

"Double the stakes," he proposed as the crowd erupted in shock. Suddenly there was a frantic scrambling to place new bets. Kat realized with a start that she wasn't even sure what the initial stakes were. Her uncertain look must have conveyed as much.

"Let's make it an even 20," he clarified.

Her brain scrambled. Twenty dollars would be almost three month's rent. Not much of a wager during her time, but hell, this was 1835 and that was considered a lot of money. She glanced briefly at Justine who looked about to faint, while Phillipe made a hand signal, a "no" which she mistook for being to go for it.

"I accept," she replied. "And when I win, I want that ring on your finger as well," she pointed out.

From the crowd's chatter, they must have thought she wanted to marry the man.

"Just the ring, not you," she clarified, hearing the women in the room gasp.

Rem threw back his head and let out a loud raucous laugh. He shook his head, still not believing his ears. "Never thought I would hear that one," he remarked. "The ring is not a part of any deal. If it was, then I would be entitled to one personal request from you as well when I win."

Kat knew this kind of negotiating was getting into dangerous territory. Did he want to grope her other breast or something more? "I'll accept double stakes only," she conceded.

"And the lady is good to cover the wager?" he inquired.

She cared not one bit for his smug confident look. "You're questioning my integrity?" she responded.

"I question everything," he threw back, goading her.

"Yes. I'm good," she lied, hoping that he didn't suddenly become a crack shot after their little wager hike.

"Very well, then," he said. His steely blue eyes tried to penetrate through her reserve as he took up his cue stick. From then on out there were no words between them and the rank and file behind them grew deathly quiet as well. A palpable intensity was felt around the room.

Kat followed her opponent's every more, realizing that there was a machine behind those eyes—a machine computing all the odds, playing an imaginary 3-D chess game with her. She tried to create her own invisible wall, blocking him out, but was only mildly successful. He was beating her, and she would not have it.

The score was now 44 - 41 in his favor. As she leaned over her shot, she saw his eyes once again travel to the dipping decolletage of her bodice, which unknown to her had been providing him and everyone else quite a view every time she bent low over the gaming table. A satisfied and cunning smile toyed at the corners of his mouth when he saw that it only served to further dent her composure.

The game was now evolving into a psychological match. Opening his evening jacket, he looped one thumb into the waistband of his trousers, striking an effective pose—hips thrust out, impatiently waiting for her to continue as if he didn't have all day to waste. It was blatantly sexual. She hit the balls harder than she had planned, subconsciously hoping they would keep right on going, fly off the table, and hit him smack in the gut or better yet, his lower regions.

However, the fates were with her and instead of ruining the shot and suffering a foul, she actually managed to score another point, showing him that his little display of flagrant masculinity had failed to get her to throw a shot. He reached for his unfinished brandy and raised it to her in mock salute before downing it in one swallow.

They were now approaching their final countdown shots, tied 48 - 48. If she missed on her next play, he could easily overtake her on his turn and win the match. He knew it; she knew it.

The room took on a cloying air, filled with the choking smoke of a dozen or more anxious human chimneys. Eyes watched them from every angle. Kat felt like she was in a Roman arena and she and her opponent were dueling gladiators. Two skilled players, tied, with only two points away from game. Together they were locked in what would later be called "a most magnificent match." The final outcome was anyone's guess.

The palms of her hands began to sweat as she lined up her shot, but as fate would have it she was only able to score one more point away from game. She feared the worst. If he beat her by only one point she was screwed.

Stepping back, her opponent judged the distance and the desired angle, taking his time. He knew what was at stake. It was an extremely difficult move to carry out as the balls were all over the table. If he pulled it off, she would forever believe he had a pact with the devil himself. Both brows were knit together as he took precise aim of his target and delivered the stroke. Please miss, she silently prayed. The entire audience held their collective breath as his yellow ball rolled toward the red ball, hitting it, resulting in a spin which then missed her ball by a hair. Her heart began to beat again, silently rejoicing that fate had given her a second chance. The crowd, on the other hand, was clearly disappointed. They felt cheated of what had looked like a sure victory for their favored player.

Oddly enough, his miss didn't seem to bother her opponent. He simply shrugged it off, his eyes remaining cool, which puzzled her. The crowd, in turn, shifted their focus back to her, waiting to see what she would do. She could make the remaining point and win the game, or fumble and face the consequences. The latter was not an option.

In her mind she told herself over and over again that she could do it. It would be a victory for her to even the score between them. The embarrassment at losing to a woman might be even worth it all.

Kat knew she would take great delight in taking every penny of the $20 he would owe her. She kept that thought firmly placed in her mind as she lined up her final play. It looked like an easy shot. Without intending to, her opponent had put all three balls close together near an end corner. While such a shot appeared easy on the surface, it could be tricky especially if one ball went rogue.

Across the table her opponent's eyes met hers, almost taunting her to defeat him. Every line in his rugged face told her he didn't think she could do it yet daring her to try—daring her to win. Dammit. She suddenly realized that he was enjoying their sparring match. Would she be robbing him of a month's wages if she did? Did he care?

Kat got into position to shoot knowing exactly how she would play it. She had done such a shot before—sometimes missing, sometimes not. Her hand shook slightly as she anchored it on the table for support. This would not do at all. She stopped and reset her position, knowing that she was prolonging the suspense, but not caring. Either she would do this right or not at all. Nothing was going to rush her.

Lit cheroot cigars burned slowly as they paused midway between puffs. Everyone froze for a fraction of a second it took her to bring the point of her stick backward then let it loose to strike her ball.

In that very delicate balance of time, she hit the ball's center point, not to the right of it as she had intended. With a sinking feeling of dread, she held her breath and watched the ball slide forward. It struck the red ball before slowly rolling backward until it stopped side-by-side against her opponent's ball, tapping it a hairline of an inch before stopping. She was stunned; the crowd was stunned. She had actually won!

A sudden barrage of congratulations came at her from all sides, as she got caught up in the excitement of the moment. Someone actually picked her up and swirled her around. Hair pins jostled loose causing her red tresses to come tumbling down around her shoulders. Never had she received such an unbridled reception from winning a tournament during her time. Praises rang in her ears. She smiled magnanimously like the champion she was.

Kat craned her neck to see her opponent making his way over to her. Nowhere on his face was written the embarrassment of defeat, especially by a woman, that she had expected to see. He was clearly taking it all in stride and for some reason it aggravated her. The crowd parted, making room for him as he stepped before her and made the most elegant bow.

"Let me add my own congratulations on a most interesting match," he replied, a flawless example of charm and good sportsmanship. From the inside of his waistcoat, he withdrew a soft leather billfold of brown calfskin and produced a bank draft. He motioned for an attendant who immediately supplied him with quill pen and ink. Thanking the hotel servant, he leaned over to fill it out pausing in mid-stroke to glance back at her.

"To whom shall I make this out to?"

"Miss Katherine Branigan," she answered triumphantly.

He nodded, not likely to forget the name. She watched him sign it in a bold flourishing script before handing it over. "Miss Branigan, I'd like to say that it has indeed been a pleasure." And with that he turned and made his exit.

Kat watched his progress as he made his way through the crowd, pausing briefly every now and again as other men stopped him to exchange words or condolences, for she knew not what. With his departure, the gallery of spectators began to disperse as if on cue. The show was over, and they now sought other entertainment. Holding nothing more than a bank marker as recompense, her victory left her feeing somehow unfulfilled. She had wanted to see him shaken and embarrassed or something—not acting as if he had thoroughly enjoyed himself.

Phillipe and Justine made their way to her side looking beyond stunned. Justine was the first to speak, the words tumbling from her mouth. "You are now a woman of means. You can afford anything your heart desires… starting with this borrowed gown."

Twenty dollars was hardly what she would consider a windfall purse, which is until she looked down at the bank draft clutched in her hand. A shock wave coursed through her. She began to shake as the amount written on the note registered. Weak-kneed she thought her legs would buckle beneath her. It was the only time in her life she felt close to fainting.

The words stumbled out of her. "I think I need to sit down—now."

Phillipe quickly led her to an armchair at an empty faro card table, telling her how incredible she had been as she stared at her winnings in a state of bewilderment. The bank draft she now held in her hand had way too many zeros. Instead of $20, it said $20,000 causing numbness to set in as she realized the true stakes she had been playing for all along. Had she lost, she would have become an indentured servant or something much worse. Who the hell was this man?

Kat peered at the bold signature on the note, but the name "Remington Randall" meant nothing to her.

"You were magnificent," Phillipe kept saying. "This will be a day long remembered. I'm sure Randall is licking his wounds as we speak."

"I probably cleaned him out, didn't I?" she commented, staring at the note.

Phillipe threw back his head and laughed uproariously. "Oh, Kat you are indeed a funny one. Isn't she, Justine?" he added while her friend suppressed a knowing giggle.

When Kat continued to look bewildered and did not laugh with them, Phillipe became a shade more serious. "Please tell me you knew who you were playing against?" he asked in disbelief.

"Of course I did," she replied. "He works on the docks at the South Street Seaport."

This time it was Justine's turn to laugh. "Oh Kat. Remington Randall is no dockworker. He owns the Eastern Star Line shipping company."

As the shock of that took hold, Phillipe chimed in. "It would take more than $20,000 to clean him out. They say he is worth a thousand times more than that with his China trade."

Kat visibly paled. "Oh," was all she could manage to utter.

"Wherever did you get the idea he was a dockworker?" Phillipe asked askance.

Kat mumbled something under her breath that he couldn't possibly understand. Suddenly she felt like a bigger fool than ever and cursed softly. Thankfully, it was lost in the sounds of billiards balls colliding over green felt as the room once again resumed its regular play. There was some comfort in the fact that no one had overheard their conversation. Imagine what a story that would have made had it been widely known.

Kat could picture it now in The New York Herald's gossip column: "Woman of little means challenges millionaire in billiards match and wins big, claiming she didn't know who he really was, nor the high stakes involved."

She wanted to go home, even if home right now meant Mrs. Begley's boardinghouse. If they attended the Livingston ball, people would be pointing her out as the news quickly travelled. She would become just another oddity in a freak show.

Justine was of a different opinion. "Kat, if you walked into the ballroom right now every man and woman there would know who you are and what you accomplished. Oh, I'm sure some of the women would be appalled by a woman who dared best a powerful man, but others would absolutely adore and envy you for it. Think of the possibilities and the doors that could open! You must stay. Please."

Against her better judgment, she did. Getting a hired cab at this time would not be safe—especially with a $20,000 bank note in her purse. And taking Phillipe and Justine away from an evening out to accompany her was inconsiderate. So, Kat tried walking into the ballroom like she owned it, only to spot Melanie Van Eaton fawning all over the man she had just trounced.

~~*~~

Remington Randall missed nothing, which made him an astute businessperson and an excellent judge of character. It would take more than a woman beating him to bruise his pride. Yet his mind could not dismiss the vision of the mysterious Katherine Branigan. The woman played like a pro and had initially fooled him into believing she was a streetwalker—not to mention her unseemly self-defense skills.

He hadn't planned to hit the gaming room that evening, but his earlier talk with Secretary of State, Edward Livingston, had left him feeling unsettled and looking for an outlet for his frustration. The man had President Andrew Jackson's ear and had confirmed the growing political situation in China, which was stabilized one moment and chaotic the next. The prevailing "hands-off" political policy their government was taking would not last and before long Rem expected there would be a naval confrontation. There was only so much the Chinese would tolerate.

Expansion and consolidation of American trade influence in China was heating up and rapidly changing the economic climate. Rem knew this would impact his lucrative Far East routes as well as many other international shipping companies. His escape to the City Hotel's gaming parlor had merely been intended to clear his head from news from China, not to get embroiled in a billiards battle of the sexes.

Come morning he would have someone thoroughly investigate Katherine Branigan's background and also find out if someone he knew had put her up to such a public challenge. While he hated to lose $20K under any circumstances, he found himself open to the challenge of playing her again if only to learn if her winning had been a mere fluke or a strange twist of fate yet to be played out.

Melanie Van Eaton saw where Rem's eyes kept straying and was livid. This Branigan woman had not only stolen her thunder, but even her dress! While she could not bring herself to admit the other woman looked better in it, one thing was certain. Come tomorrow morning she would deliver a severe tongue-lashing to Madame Vesey, a spectacle already staging itself in her fertile mind. Selling her one-of-a-kind returned gown was simply unacceptable. Someone would have to pay for it!

Rem waited until Melanie was a twitter with others discussing the match to quietly extricate himself from the group and saunter over to the table Miss Branigan occupied. Wasting no time after making a name for herself, she was already surrounded by potential suitors and gold diggers. Yet, despite the attention the woman looked quite miserable, which he found surprising. As soon as he approached, the crowd parted letting him through as if they had front row seats to the next scene in this evolving drama.

"Miss Branigan," he began, gallantly extending his hand. "Would you do me the honor of joining me on the dance floor?"

Kat couldn't dance a quadrille if her life depended upon it, but she couldn't bring herself to say "no" either. She placed her hand in his, grateful to escape the solicitous crowd of men who had flocked around her wanting to introduce themselves.

Her opponent guided her to the dance floor just as the orchestra struck up a slow waltz. This she could manage as he slid his arm around her waist, and they began to move as one on the dance floor. He was a smooth dancer and probably just as smooth in other things as well, so she was thinking. An awkward silence hung between them until he was the first to break it.

"We haven't been properly introduced," he said inclining his head towards hers. "My name is Remington Randall. Those who know me call me 'Rem'..." Kat immediately flashed on the raised initial "R" on the metal ring he wore. Could the ring actually be his? And, if so, what did that mean?

"Do I have the distinction of being the first woman to beat you at billiards?" she blurted out.

Rem smiled. "Yes, I suppose that's true. But perhaps not the last."

She looked at him pointedly, not missing a beat. "Well, Rem. If you insist on being on a first name basis, you may call me 'Kat'."

"Hello Kat," he said simply before lapsing into thoughtful silence, his eyes never wavering from her face.

His gaze unnerved her. What was he thinking? "I hope you harbor no ill will after I deprived you of such a sizeable purse," she stated.

Rem heard a hint of sarcasm in her last words. Was she mocking him or was she just one of those frigid women who hated all men and liked beating them both literally and figuratively?

"On the contrary, *Kat*," he said, stressing her name. "You won fair and square."

Rem knew he was opening a pandora's box, but he went there anyway. "I have to admit that I find myself puzzled. Why did you attack me that day on the docks after I tried saving you from being run over?"

She looked indignant then aghast. "Do you enjoy groping women's breasts?"

Whoa! He had not seen that response coming. It took a moment to recover from such a blatant accusation. From her stone-cold eyes, he could see she was downright serious. This wouldn't do at all.

"I admit that I enjoy women's breasts very much," he ruefully admitted, "but I'm no groper as you call it. Never have been and never will be. So where are you going with this…"

Kat's eyes narrowed a fraction. "Then you don't recall when you tackled me to save my life, as you seem to imply, that your hand fully groped my breast?"

He wanted to say: *Hell No.* Instead, he held his tongue and tried for contriteness instead. "If I did so, it wasn't intentional on my part."

In fact, he didn't even remember having done such a thing, but he wasn't about to question her veracity. "My heartfelt apologies if I hurt or offended you in any way. However, it would be remiss of me not to point out that my quick actions *did* save your life."

Kat couldn't deny that. "Thank you," she replied, sighing. It would be childish to keep sparring with the man after he had made his apology. "Perhaps we need to start over. Please accept my gratitude for your gallantry."

People on the sidelines were staring at them, wondering what on earth they were discussing. Rem noticed. His mouth suddenly dipped closer to her ear, his body pressing closer. "Grateful enough to play me again? This time without a crowd?" he whispered.

"You don't like losing money, do you?" she shot back, trying to block out the room, the color, the gaiety, and the noise that was pressing in upon her.

He chuckled, sweeping her around the corner of the room, her skirts flaring. "Can't say I do. Do you?"

Kat had to catch her breath, the waltz was picking up, becoming faster, like the man who she recognized to be flirting with her. What about Melanie Van Eaton she wanted to ask, but instead murmured, "Touché. But you might find yourself losing even more were we to ever play again."

Rem smiled. "What makes you so confident you can beat me again?"

Kat didn't have an answer for that. Her own confidence came from playing and beating some of the best Manhattan and Brooklyn club members, men, and women alike—something she would never reveal.

There was only one thing she wanted from their encounter. Kat glanced over at the hand that firmly held hers. "Next time we play for your ring, or we don't play at all."

Chapter 4

Kat wasted no time attempting to cash out her winnings at the Second Bank of the United States, the oldest financial institution in the city, founded by Alexander Hamilton who would later be appointed Secretary of the U.S. Treasury. It also happened to be the bank name written on Remington Randall's note.

If, *God forbid*, she became stuck in this time zone, she would have to find a way to safeguard her financial winnings. Historical factors would also have to be considered. Recorded history had chronicled the ugly details of the "Banking Wars of 1836" and the "Panic of 1837" when a financial crisis hit the country, affecting the solvency of big banks and institutions.

Today and right now was what she had to worry about more than anything. The social rules of 1835 were not at all friendly to independent-minded women. To her surprise, she learned that in order to cash Randall's bank draft she had to first open a bank account, which was not an easy thing for a 19th century female to do. A woman first needed the consent and co-signature of a husband or male benefactor to bank money. The story was the same for loan borrowing. Unfortunately for her, it would be well over a hundred years before such a draconian law would be challenged and changed. Women didn't even have the right to vote.

The bankers she encountered knew who she was the second they saw the bank draft note, as they smiled amongst themselves knowingly. Scandalous news spread like wildfire in this town. Much to her consternation she encountered speculative glances and even a few disdaining sneers.

Kat demanded to see the bank manager, who promptly informed her that Mr. Randall would need to accompany her to the bank to verify the draft to collect her funds. She swore between gritted teeth. Even if she somehow managed to haul him into the bank, she couldn't just stuff her pockets with a hell of a lot of money and leave. She needed a safe place to temporarily store her nest egg and for that she sorely realized that she needed a man.

Without a Google search engine, Kat had to rely on what she had gleaned about Remington Randall from the other female boarders in the house that morning at breakfast.

"They say he's a shipping genius," she kept hearing over and over again until she was ready to vomit. She listened to the stories, finding them hard to believe.

The man was an urban legend. In the thriving business world of New York, the news of a Randall cargo making port was enough to send merchants scurrying for their hats and coats, practically tripping over each other in their haste to get to the auction houses in time to be first to bid on what went up on the selling block.

Randall's shipping line carried almost exclusively the whole China trade and he himself was known to be responsible for the changes that up until a few years ago were nonexistent for cargos from the Orient—cargos which were made up of tea, silk, ginger, firecrackers and so much more.

The legend went that after visiting the Far East a number of times, Randall was quick to surmise the Chinese were capable of untapped human resources. He observed they could be a very imitative race of people and that in the Orient one could get anything duplicated at a fraction of the cost. It was a concept he gave much thought to, prompting him to travel extensively through European ports gathering articles and goods that were outrageously expensive to import, yet in big demand. Through appointed agents he had samples sent to China to be copied at one-tenth of what it cost to make elsewhere. The profit was immense. Passage could be made out in 97 days and returned home in 90. Such cargos were never heard of before. The quantity of articles ordered was quite extensive at times, but Randall was careful to avoid overstocking the market. If prices ranged lower in New York than in Canton, it meant the merchant's profit would be cut considerably. Randall was known to keep a tight control on this practice which in turn earned him the immediate respect of every merchant in the city. In the end they all made a financial killing.

Kat listened to her sources gush about how he sent over samples of Parisian fans that the New York ladies were clamoring for and finding hard to obtain. Soon cases of such feathers, palm, silk, ivory, mother-of-pearl, and peacock fans were available to any woman who desired one, with some of the finer ones costing as little as five dollars. It soon became customary practice for European ladies to wait and purchase certain desired items in New York rather than back home where prices were ever so much higher.

It did not end there. Kat had to then hear about how Randall had taken on the drug markets as well. Every drug and/or medicinal product known in Europe was also duplicated in China along with the rarest of perfumes. Kat learned that upon attending some social function, Randall had heard a lady casually remark how intolerably high pure attar of roses was at $25 an ounce and what she wouldn't give to be able to afford this tantalizing scent. As a result, he sent a vial of the exotic perfume over to China to see what could be done. Within no time, Randall's Oriental agents had duplicated it perfectly at about six pence an ounce. About 10,000 ounces of the sweet fragrance arrived in one ship load and New York druggists and perfumers bought it up rapidly, paying between $10 and $15 an ounce.

It was no wonder ladies were known to seek out Randall for more than his handsome looks and deep bank accounts. They usually sought his ear when they found something difficult to attain. It was said that Randall often joked about the fact that nothing inspired him more than a lady's vanity and he certainly proved he knew how to give them what they wanted.

As for the sport-minded, chessmen and backgammon boards were replicated in large quantities and were readily snatched up when his ships arrived in port. Every article of horn was also imitated—with one invoice for 100,000 horn scoops to be used in the drawers of grocers and druggists to ladle out sugar, salt, or any other powdered or granulated substance. Hardly a druggist in the city didn't possess one or more of these Chinese scoops. Apothecary shelves were usually well stocked with other Eastern imports as well, such as cassia buds and chamomile flowers which were used for medicinal purposes. Then, of course, there was the lucrative opium/morphine/heroin trade.

Kat's head was spinning. The background facts on the man kept pouring in. She learned that up until 1833 only a few varieties of China silk were imported. When Oriental copies of Italian, French, and English silks arrived in port, dressmakers soon found out that the Chinese had in fact improved on the textures and patterns of their European counterparts. As a result, silk prices were reduced drastically, and Randall was quickly besieged with merchant requests to import even more of the rich fabric.

Enough already, Kat was thinking. Okay, so she would give him kudos for being a good businessperson since importing goods from the East did involve a bit of a gamble. The shipper had to be shrewd and exercise foresight, for on these Canton runs the duty was high and the freight charges were enormous. Importing an item that might sell poorly could be financially disastrous. However, Randall seemed to be extremely lucky in his China trade and the Eastern Star Line flourished. It continued to remain unshakeable while his competitors scrambled to keep up.

Somehow he had managed to prosper domestically as well, being that not all of his packet ships concentrated on the lucrative Far East trade. He had regular routes between New York and the foreign ports of Belfast, Cartagena, Greenock, Havana, Harve, Hull, Liverpool, Veracruz and, of course, London and Paris. From the latter two European cities, in addition to textile goods, he also provided a variety of gourmet delights for the palates of American food connoisseurs. The most famous of sauces, condiments, reserves, sweetmeats, syrups, and other non-perishables were procured and shipped out regularly. The man proved to have a discerning culinary taste.

His domestic runs included Charleston, Savannah, Mobile and New Orleans which made up the Cotton Route. The South was still the golden key, for without the cotton to trade in the foreign ports, Northern shippers would be left with little bargaining power. When Southern crops suffered and harvest production dropped, shippers were known to experience considerable financial losses, but Randall's resources remained stable due to his fast China trade. His wealth continued to steadily increase as more ships were bought, and more goods shipped. In some circles his name became almost synonymous with the exotics of the Far East itself.

Kat stubbornly admitted his accomplishments *did* appear impressive. It sounded like everything he touched turned to gold. He probably had every unmarried girl and her mama desperately trying to bring him to the altar. It would be a fitting justice if Melanie Van Eaton did indeed sink her sharpened claws into him, married him and his money, and they made each other supremely miserable. His indecent good looks convinced her that he was the type of man who discarded women along the wayside, leaving a path of broken hearts behind him as he tired of each conquest.

Kat now knew more than she wanted to know about Remington Randall from all the unsolicited reports she was getting. In her time, New York City was filled with such characters who used their money, social stature, and good looks to attain anything they wanted. Now that she knew Randall's background, she would be wise to proceed with caution. She needed him, but not in any way other than business. A little horse trading would be called for.

Kat set off to track down the infamous shipper. He was not to be found at his South Street Seaport maritime offices, nor his formal accounting offices for the Eastern Star Line housed on Broad Street. Through some finagling she managed to learn he was presently at his residence on "The Old Row," a place where many of the city's wealthy and elite maintained homes.

Randall resided across the street from Washington Square Park, a well-known public and social meeting place. When she approached the area she had to geographically re-orient herself. This area of New York was noticeably different from the Greenwich Village of her day. Decades later a circular fountain would be located in the plaza area nearer to the yet-to-be-built Washington Square Arch as the park went through a metamorphosis in community development design. She took a moment to appreciate the original beauty of the area that held many modern-day memories for her.

On the northeast block of the Square, the University of the City of New York, later to be called New York University in 1896, was getting ready to open its first constructed building whose campus would change the area's landscape forever.

In the 21st century the remaining rowhouses on the North Square were all considered to be historical landmarks. They would keep their grand façades, yet their interiors would be converted into apartments worth a small fortune. What Kat was now observing were the first original row houses in all their architectural glory. They were indeed architectural beauties as was the original Washington Square.

Kat's father had once told her that there were over 20,000 bodies buried under Washington Square before the city purchased it in 1825. Being it was once a Potter's Field for the poor, mentally ill, and cholera and yellow fever victims, it was known to be the gruesome site of a "Hangman's Elm" where early in the 1700's executions were held. This might explain why it was known as the most haunted neighborhood in all of New York, with paranormal activity registering off the charts.

A stately elm shaded the façade of No. 8, Randall's three-story red brick Greek Revival townhouse. With white marble trim, Ionic and Doric columns, and marble balustrades, it was as impressive as the other newly constructed structures on the private tree-lined street. Black wrought iron railing of the bourbon style ornamented the steps and blended with the dark shuttered windows that hung open against the pale sun-bleached brick. On the door was a small bronze knocker shaped in the form of a sailing ship.

Kat rapped lightly, hearing approaching steps, followed by the glimpse of a man through the white-leaded glass windows that ran along each side of the door. The mores and culture of these times forced her to walk a thin line. Being an extremely independent woman, she had to rein in her true nature. She knew damn well it would be considered extremely forward going to a single man's house unchaperoned to solicit his help. However, being a modern-day girl who preferred taking the initiative to getting what she wanted, she threw caution to the wind.

The door to the mansion was answered by a manservant named Higgins, who made her wait in a highly-polished marbled foyer while he summoned his employer. French doors adjoining the foyer were closed off to her view and curiosity. But the foyer itself was bold and impressive. Large oil paintings of sailing ships graced the walls, a gallery of nautical assets owned by the Eastern Star Line. Kat didn't know how old Randall was, but he seemed quite young to have amassed such an early fortune. Did he come from old money? Was he a trust fund baby like so many she dealt with in her time?

The servant returned without Randall and instructed her to follow him. She wasn't prepared for scaling three flights of stairs in such heavy skirts but damn the man for making her. Bypassing the upper bedrooms, the servant led the way towards the roof. Kat stepped out on a rooftop terraced deck with black iron railings spanning the length of all sides. There, perched atop a riser was Randall, without a jacket, his shirt partially exposing the dark thatch of hair on his muscled chest, surveying the harbor with a spyglass to his eye.

"I can't say I'm surprised to see you," he commented, with a sidewise glance her way. "I surmised that you would be calling sooner rather than later."

Oh, did he? She walked over to him, getting straight to the point. "Don't get too excited. I only came as a last resort, against my better judgment and, I might add, under extreme frustration and duress." Kat sighed and spit it out. "It appears I need your help."

Randall lowered his spyglass and looked her in the eyes. "The bank note, I presume. A bank messenger informed me that you tried to redeem it. What I can't understand is why you tried to open a bank account— alone. Have you no other men in your life to ask for help?"

Grrrr, she wanted to scream. She wasn't used to being in a man's world with female limitations. It was exasperating and unseemly. "Can you help me, or do you expect me to beg?"

That actually made him laugh. The jerk was probably picturing her on her knees right now. But instead of lording it over her, he gestured to her good-naturedly.

"Come here," he beckoned. "There's something I want to show you."

Kat stepped up on the perch next to him as he handed her the spyglass. "Tell me what you see," he said, as she adjusted the lens to her vision.

"Two ships coming through the Narrows," she reported, scanning the harbor front and beyond. She could just make out their country's flags. "One is American; the other is British."

"Good eye. Which one has the full cargo?" he prompted.

Kat peered closer. So, he was bent on testing her. "The ship displaying the British flag is riding low in the water. I'm guessing that's the full one. It's iron-hulled—probably carrying iron ore or steel. The American ship is older and made of wood. My guess is it's carrying something lighter, perhaps mercantile, and/or dry goods."

There was dead silence behind her. Kat had been watching ships come and go from her Brooklyn Heights home since she was a small child but never ships such as these. She turned to see how correct she was and saw the surprised look on his face. Oh My God. Remington Randall was actually stunned, possibly even impressed by her nautical knowledge!

"That's correct," he said, without elaborating.

"Did you think I was all skill and no brains?" she joked as she handed him back the spyglass.

"Not at all. I find you to be a most unusual woman." He continued to stare at her quizzically. "You speak differently than most others and your manners are ... Where are you from?"

It was a question she had been repeatedly asked since arriving in this time. Was it her hint of a Brooklyn accent? "It's complicated," she said avoiding the question altogether and promptly changing the subject. "So will you help me with the bank issue?"

Rem was not so easily sidestepped. "That is exactly what I was referring to. You have a strange use of words. What does 'it's complicated' mean? Please explain yourself."

Good God, would she have to give him a lesson in 21st century colloquialisms? She knew he wasn't about to let the subject drop. This was a man with a need to know all things great and small, a factor which had earned him a reputation for having an astute business sense. Kat suspected he was like a dog with a bone who wouldn't let go.

Rem *was* thinking along those very lines. Just this morning, the private investigator he retained had given him a full report on the mysterious Katherine Branigan. She came from no-where and no one knew her. She hadn't arrived on any transport ship or train, had no husband or living relative of record, and had no criminal history of note. She was a blank slate—a woman without a past which intrigued him all the more. All he knew, other than she was a crack shot at billiards, was that she was staying at a low-level boarding house on Maiden Lane, having arrived less than a week ago. In fact, she had arrived at the hostel the same day he had seen her on the docks. Yet no manifest ledger or seafaring Captain could recall a red-headed passenger booking passage on their ship or one of her description disembarking in New York.

Rem could tell she had taken particular care with her appearance for this meeting, even wearing a hint of the perfume "Night Blooming Jasmine" if he wasn't mistaken. He knew them all. It was not an expensive brand by any means. He watched her purse her lips while informing him she was skillful in more than just billiards.

"It won't work," he drawled, measuring her reaction.

She frowned, not understanding. "Excuse me. What won't work?"

"My head is not so easily turned by beauty—yours or any other woman's," he stated flatly.

Kat was stunned by his words. A few choice curses sprang to her lips ready to be hurled in his direction, but she reined them back in, not wanting to alienate him further. Unfortunately, she needed him, and he knew it.

His assessment and advice to her continued. "The perfume was a nice touch, but you'll have to try a different approach if you intend to win me over," he continued, collapsing the spyglass, as he stepped down from his watchtower perch.

She caught the hint of amusement in his eyes. The arrogant bastard was enjoying this! Did he treat all women this way? If so, that would explain the rumors of him going through female companions as fast as his ships came and went. However, Kat Brannigan was not going to play this particular game with him.

"I believe you have misread my intent, sir," she replied curtly.

"Then tell me the truth," he prompted, weighing her words. "Then, and only then, will I decide if I wish to help you or not."

If he wanted the truth then she would give it to him. He wouldn't believe her anyway. "I'm from the future," she replied matter-of-factly. "Something you know nothing about, which puts you at a disadvantage."

His hearty laugh was immediate—confirming what she already suspected to be true. He didn't believe her and thought her mad. "Well, you asked for the truth. And I told you it's complicated."

From the determined look on her face, Rem saw she was dead serious. Was the woman insane? Perhaps his source had failed to check the sanitoriums or mental hospitals for records of her as well.

Kat could see she was at an impasse. She needed her money—or rather his relinquished money to survive—to pay for the dress, to pay rent, and to live in this unfriendly women's time. She would have to make a deal fast, even if she had to beg.

"Listen," she began. "If you can beat me at billiards I promise to tell you the whole story and anything you want to know. I guarantee you won't be disappointed." How far she would have to go was uncertain, but she would cross that bridge once she got to it.

Kat extended her hand. "Is it a deal?"

~~*~~

When Kat walked into the Second Bank of the United States with Remington Randall at her side, bank managers snapped to attention, dropped what they were doing and practically came running. That was enough to tell her Randall must have a hell of a lot of money in their financial institution.

She watched personnel which she had encountered earlier suddenly change their demeanor and tone. They fawned over the man beside her, smiling solicitously, finally turning their undivided attention to her as he issued curt instructions to his bankers, which to her ears sounded more like barking orders. She had to admit he was impressive when it came to getting things done.

"Gentlemen, this is Miss Katherine Branigan," he said his hand resting at her back, as if *she* were *his* woman. "I expect her to be treated as if you are personally dealing with me. The lady wants to open a bank account. Get it done."

"Very good sir," they replied nodding and bobbing their heads in acquiesce. "Will you be personally co-signing for Miss Branigan?"

"Yes," he stated, without further elaboration.

Kat balked. She wasn't thrilled to hand over joint access of her money to any man, especially one she didn't really know. Granted, he had plenty of money of his own, but there was always the possibility he could use it as a bargaining weapon against her. She tugged on Randall's coat sleeve and raised herself on tiptoes to whisper in his ear.

"Just a minute, gentlemen. The lady has a concern," Rem responded, holding up his hand and gently taking her aside. The bankers, already preparing account papers, looked away, but Kat knew they were straining to hear the nature of her "concern."

Kat made it clear up front. "Mr. Randall," she began.

"Rem," he quickly corrected. "Call me Rem."

"Okay then, Rem," she complied before forging forward. "There will be no strings. I want it in writing and attached as an addendum to the account. We are agreeing to your being a co-signor to open the account, but nothing more. Under no circumstances will you have authority to block, withdraw, or hold up my funds in any shape, manner, or form. I specifically want your guarantee, as well as the bank's, that I do not need your consent should I wish to withdraw my funds in the future. Is that agreed?"

"Agreed," he said with a rueful smile. "Tell me—do you distrust all men or just me?"

Kat wasn't sure whom to trust. She didn't know all the rules of this time, but history had informed her of some of the stranger ones. Powerful men had the right to lock women away and institutionalize them in mental wards if they didn't comply to their demands. Look at what had happened to poor Sophia Johnson Vanderbilt when her husband Cornelius Vanderbilt, the Commodore, had done that very such thing. He had locked her away for her refusing to play the social scene, finally forcing her to do his bidding, when all she really wanted was to stay home and care for their twelve children.

If she became trapped in this time and couldn't find a way back, she would have to secure an attorney, but right now she would have to forge a contract with Rem making it clear she was not a woman to be hoodwinked by any man.

While her demands surprised him, he didn't argue the point and additional papers were drawn up laying out her stipulations and were quickly signed off on. They left the bank with Kat Branigan being a woman of means with coin and bank drafts in her pocket. It was an exhilarating feeling of freedom.

"Shall we celebrate?" Rem asked as they exited the bank and stepped back out onto the Broadway Boulevard where his personal carriage and driver awaited them.

Kat declined. She had other plans, but so did he. "Might I remind you that you promised me a re-match for my help here today," he began. "I intend to hold you to that promise. I'll send my driver to pick you up at 9:00 a.m. Saturday morning. Please be ready and waiting."

The General in him had spoken. Rem threw her a devilish smile before getting back into his carriage. "I believe it will be a most interesting day."

Interesting, indeed! She rolled her eyes and watched him depart before taking off at a brisk walk. Her step felt lighter now that she had accomplished the feat of procuring herself a bank account. Now if only she could also procure herself a decent pair of sneakers to move around the city more easily.

The basement offices of The New York Herald were nearby on Wall Street. Today the print shop was quiet having already dispatched their morning and afternoon news editions. Jim Bennett was hunched over his desk with pen in hand, furiously scratching out tomorrow's editorial column. He waved as she headed for her box number. Disappointment crept in when she found the box empty of any response to her ad attempting to locate her ancestors. That's when it hit her. She had the financial means to a much faster approach; she could simply hire someone to find them for her.

Bennett, his face smudged with black ink, stepped up to the counter and called out, "Are you the same Katherine Branigan that made news last night at the City Hotel?"

Good lord! Had their billiards match made The New York Herald's gossip column? To confirm her worst suspicion, Bennett handed over a copy of his morning edition where he laid it out for the world to see:

Gentlemen, hold onto your purses! News has it that there is a female billiards shark in town who swished her pretty little skirts into the gaming room at the City Hotel last evening, where she took the high stakes betting world by storm. This billiards vixen quickly overshadowed Edward Livingston's Grand Gala event held in the Grand Ballroom next door, as curious bystanders caught the whiff of slaughter and made their way over to witness a slice of history in the making. Eastern Star Lines' Remington Randall, known to be unbeatable at the tables, was the first to take the fall. Speculation is that he is hanging his head in shame this very morning at being beaten by a woman. The lady they call "Kat," is one sly and clever feline behind a cue stick, not to mention incredibly richer...

Kat couldn't read any more. Never in her life had she been called a "shark" or a "vixen" and she could attest to the fact that Rem was not hanging his head in shame when *she* saw him. The damn fool wanted to give it another go. The man was made of Teflon. It would take a hell of a lot to accomplish a state of shame in him.

"So, are you *the* 'Kat'?" he repeated.

"Yes," she murmured, turning to go.

"Wait," he said. "Care to give an exclusive with your side of the story?"

Kat thought about it for less than a second. "Yes. I got lucky, nothing more. Mr. Randall was the epitome of a gentlemen possessing a high degree of good sportsmanship. I suspect he let me win for the entertainment factor alone—and to give you something scandalous to write about." She turned and left, not missing the raised eyebrow of surprise Bennett displayed at her parting words.

There was obvious truth and lies mixed in with her statement, but she couldn't dig the knife in any deeper for the man. Rem wasn't the type to throw a game for anyone—that much she was certain of. He was a formidable opponent, good at whatever he did, and deserved to be respected for that. Those bankers didn't treat him like he had been pussy-whipped at all. They didn't dare. The name *Remington Randall* represented a captain of industry.

Somewhere between yesterday and today she realized with a start that she had softened a bit and was now defending the man. Why? Because, if she was honest with herself, he had come to her rescue not once but three times. He had thrown himself in her path to avoid her being run over; he had provided the financial resources she desperately needed to exist in this world; and he had good-naturedly helped her open an account with those nasty little banker cartel men.

For that last good deed alone, she should engage in wild thank you sex with him. This unexpected and salacious last thought made her laugh. An almost inaudible sigh escaped her as visions of Rem's tall naked body pressed against her, doing all manner of nasty things, filtered through her 21st century mind. *Stop that*, she scolded herself!

In the past Kat had gotten it on with a few of her other gaming opponents whether they beat her or not. Like politics, billiards also made for strange bedfellows. Would Rem be shocked to know she had harbored such fleeting thoughts about him?

She sighed, reluctantly stuffing down the vivid and erotic thoughts that wanted to take on a life of their own. Kat did not poach other women's men, nor mess with the married kind. Melanie Van Eaton had been all over Rem like a bad rash and there was a high degree of probability she was his current bedmate. Powerful men with money and prominence who looked like Rem and were still single to boot, meant he never lacked for sexual partners. Some things never changed, despite the times. Melanie would be hell bent to protect her turf, which reminded her that she had better get to Madame Vesey's and pay for Melanie's dress quickly before Justine found herself in deep water.

~~*~~

As fate would have it, Melanie Van Eaton beat her to Madame Vesey's salon. When she stepped inside the shop, Rem's paramour was entrenched in full tyrant mode. Accusations were flying as Melanie threatened to ruin Madame Vesey if Justine was not immediately terminated. With her job at The Met, Kat had been dealing with the petty elite and privileged her whole life. It was time to step up and do damage control to save her friend.

Kat walked over to them like she was attending a coronation. "Madame Vesey, I'm here to pay a bonus for your creation, which became famous last night."

Melanie whipped her head around, eyes blazing, pointing her finger at Kat. "That woman stole my gown!"

Madame Vesey was clearly confused. She was blank-faced as she turned her attention to Kat. "Who are you?"

"I'm Katherine Branigan, the woman who made your gown so famous last night that even The New York Herald wrote about my 'pretty little skirts' in today's morning post. I shall have to tell Jim Bennett, the publisher, to give you and your salon full attribution in tomorrow's paper."

Across the room, she heard Justine audibly gasp as Kat faced-off with Melanie. "You never paid for the gown, did you? I put a down payment on it, so your accusations are without merit. And let me remind you that possession is nine-tenths of the law."

Melanie clearly didn't know what the hell she was talking about. When citing the law, people's eyes usually glaze over, which was exactly as Kat intended.

"Mark my words. You'll pay for this," Melanie indignantly shot back.

"I just told you I already did," Kat responded. "Which part didn't you understand?"

Melanie was aghast. Clearly she was not used to being confronted in such a manner by anyone. That's when she pulled out what she thought was her most potent ammunition in her arsenal. "I'll see to it that Remington Randall ruins you for this. You'll regret treating me in such a disrespectful manner. Just you wait…"

Kat was growing tired of the woman; it was time to end this little cat fight. "Perhaps it's you who should be worried, Ms. Van Eaton," she responded. "It is evident that you wore Madame's creation, then returned it without payment. That's blatant *wardrobing* and fraud. I know the law in this area. It is not only illegal, but Madame could have you arrested for it right now—on the spot."

Madame Vesey's eyes grew big. She babbled something incoherent as she stepped away, backing off. Her bony hands frantically waved in front of her as if warding off some type of evil spirit. She was too scared to deal with such a threat to her clientele.

Kat knew she had laid it on thick, but it accomplished her goal. Melanie huffed out, slamming the salon door behind her as she made her exit. What Kat wouldn't give to be a fly on the wall when Melanie came storming to Rem to try and make good her threat.

After Melanie's departure, it took Kat a while to calm things down and make sure Justine still had a job. Madame was paid handsomely for the gown that had contributed to her success and Kat bought several others— some ready-to-wear, and others that were couture made-to-order. It was the first bank note she wrote on her new account, and it didn't even make a dent in her total winnings. Kat was through with Ms. Begley's hand-me-down cast-offs. If Kat was going to make her way in this new world, she could need a wardrobe of designer wear.

Chapter 5

Kat knew she would eventually have to consider finding a place of her own. While she certainly enjoyed the company of some of the undeniably interesting mix of female characters staying at Mrs. Begley's rooming house, such a decision to move out would be akin to resigning herself to the unfathomable fate that she might be forever trapped in this primitive time period. It was a possibility she couldn't dismiss.

By breakfast the next morning, everyone in the house knew about Kat's opening a bank account the day before, something unthinkable for an unmarried woman. There was a chorus of congratulations expressed all around the table, coupled with awe, a tinge of envy, and even a few shocked stares. That she had taken up a gentlemen's sport and managed to beat a powerful and rich man, was almost unthinkable. That she now possessed a bank account, securing her financial freedom, practically made her a rock star.

Justine took center stage as she once again gave them a dramatic play-by-play of Kat's consummate billiards skills. That was soon followed with an exaggerated telling of Kat's confrontation with Melanie Van Eaton at Madame Vesey's salon. Justine repeated their word-for-word exchange, mimicking Kat's slight Brooklyn accent as she did.

Kat found all the new-found attention quite curious. It made her uncomfortable, as it placed her life under greater scrutiny. She downplayed her gaming skills, claiming instead to be just lucky and Randall had had an "off" night.

"Is he as handsome, as they claim he is?" Celeste gushed. "They say he is a notorious rake and that women throw themselves at him."

"I hadn't noticed," Kat lied, not wanting to go down that road. "I suppose some would consider him good-looking," she conceded, as they all stared at her in disbelief.

Whether Rem was a consummate "rake" as some seemed to imply, was not her business. She was no virgin herself, and Kat was pretty certain she was surrounded by women who had never been intimate with the opposite sex. Rather than judge and be judged, she opted to keep her mouth shut and not have them think her a harlot as well.

Rebecca, who taught school and barely got by on her meager salary, turned to Kat. "I for one want to know what you plan on doing with all your money?"

It was a good question, which everyone else seemed curious about as well. Daphne, who had dreams of marriage and a house of her own, immediately chimed in. "Oh, Kat—if it were me I would buy land somewhere in a quiet little place with a view of the river. A place where I could have my own garden and raise rabbits and chickens, and lots of children."

While the others smiled ruefully at Daphne's picturesque dream, it gave Kat an idea. Real estate would always be key in Manhattan—a city that was growing and would continue to expand northward with each passing year. Daphne's dreams of living happily ever after on a little tract of her own was a good suggestion. Kat had been giving that very idea some thought on her way to opening her bank account.

So much had transpired since coming into her newfound fortune, that her head was still spinning. Come evening, her fellow female boarders wanted to know all the details of her day as a woman of financial means. She decided to keep the personal details about having gone to Randall's house, alone and unchaperoned, the day before and then opening a joint bank account with him after setting the terms. It bordered on indecent and would set tongues to wagging.

Divine providence saved her from further scrutiny. Mrs. Begley had an old friend over that evening who not only brightened up the dinner table with colorful tales but proved to be an endless source of even more interesting news concerning Randall.

Travis McBee, known as "Captain Buzzy," was a short, husky man of middle years. His round jovial face sprouted bushy mutton chop whiskers, while his portly belly spoke of a fondness for rich food. The playful glimmer in his eye, coupled with his charm and salty humor, won them over. The man was like a giant teddy bear, worn around the edges, but extremely lovable.

From the moment he sat down, the captain lavished praise on Mrs. Begley, her meal, and her gracious hospitality. It was evident that the crusty old seafarer had more than a passing fancy for her landlady and from Mrs. Begley's blushing response, it looked to be a mutual attraction.

"How did you get such a nickname?" Daphne asked, obviously missing the fact that his last name was "McBee."

Buzzy winked unabashedly at the ladies. "Well, I have been known to have quite a temper—like 'an angry nest of hornets' so they say. But that's only if a crewman disobeys my orders. At sea there is only one authority—the captain's, or else you invite mutiny."

Buzzy was the ship commander of a tall commercial trade ship known as the *Canton Witch* which had trade routes between Manchester, England and Canton, China. As coincidence would have it, the *Canton Witch* was owned by none other than the Eastern Star Line's, Remington Randall.

"Oh my," Celeste gasped. "That's the same man Kat beat at billiards the other night!"

Buzzy turned his attention to Kat. "Ahhh, so you're the one." His look was quietly speculative. "That bit of stunning news was the first thing I heard when I made port," he informed. "You caused quite a stir, young lady. It's had everyone talking. Rem is a hard one to beat at any game. But I hear tell he took it like a good sport. Not much ruffles his feathers."

After several months at sea, the *Canton Witch* making port the following morning was why Rem was on his rooftop perch awaiting its passage through the Narrows. The *Canton Witch* had to be the ship she had spotted and remarked on.

"Then you know him well?" Kat questioned.

"Since he was a lad," Buzzy replied. "He was a smart one and even quite devilish at times."

Kat could certainly believe that. "Do tell," she encouraged, trying not to appear too interested in the man. There was a chorus of agreement heard around the table and so the captain, between bites of vegetable beef stew and sips of the imported wine he had brought Mrs. Begley as a gift, began his tale knowing he had the undivided attention of every female there.

"Well, there's a bit of history to be told before we get to what I'm guessing you ladies really want to know about the current owner of the Eastern Star Line." There was an eager nodding of heads, wondering what secrets Captain Buzzy might reveal. Kat sat back confident the other women would do the questioning for her.

"The *Canton Witch* goes back to the days when she was first called the *Sea Erne*," Buzzy began. "She came straight out of a London shipyard with wood shavings still on her planks and not a scratch on her bow. Ezra Stark, the man who owned her, and never a harder man to work for I might add, put his mark on her right off he did. She was the best ship in his fleet.

"I was first officer on another of Stark's ships at the time and it was decided I was to be given the commission for the Sea Erne's maiden voyage. She was a real beauty in her day—one of the first transatlantic packet ships and faster than most anything on the seas back then. Many a man would have given anything to command her. I counted myself lucky to get the first go at her. But a lot has happened since then. The old girl is getting on in years…"

Buzzy looked off waxing nostalgically. "These days everyone wants bigger and faster ships, but I suspect Rem held on to her this long for sentimental reasons. But I'm getting ahead of myself …"

The captain drained his wine glass, only to refill it as he recalled the earlier years. "The Sea Erne was my first big commission, and no sooner did I get the good news then I learn old Mr. Stark would be making that first voyage with me—watching my every move. He had a way of not missing the most insignificant little detail and could make a man jumpier than hell in no time. We sometimes wondered if he stayed up half the night thinking of things to find fault with. It was rare to see him smile or laugh. He was a serious and cantankerous old scrooge.

"We're not a week out of port when the old man learns that we got ourselves a young stowaway hiding in the cargo hold. No one knew how he got there, only that Stark would have our hides for such a thing. The lad couldn't have been more than 10 years old at the time. Ezra had him hauled up on deck, then lined up every man topside demanding to know who was responsible for hiding and aiding the lad.

"He threatened to flog every last one of us personally unless someone confessed. You see, the boy was found with food and the old man knew the lad hadn't obtained it without help. A stowaway was as good as a thief, and it wasn't unheard of for the culprit to be thrown overboard and left to drown…"

There was a collective gasp heard all around. "Oh, no. That's terrible!" Daphne lamented. "Did they actually do such a thing?"

The captain continued. "Everyone was shaking in their boots waiting for the punishment to begin, me included. Then the strangest thing happened. The lad went over and whispered something in the old man's ear, and I swear if it didn't make Stark flinch. It was even more mystifying when Ezra shook his head, whispered something back to the boy, then let out one hell of a belly laugh that seemed to shake the very timbers of the ship. No one dared move, wondering what incredible thing might happen next. And that's when the old man turned around and stared us straight in the face and yelled: 'What the devil are you *swabbies* standing around gawking at? Get back to work, now, you miserable tar!'

"For a reason none of us could fathom, the whole affair was dismissed without another word. The men were laying down bets trying to figure out what had just happened, especially when the very next day Stark decides the lad should be made a cabin boy."

"Was that boy Remington Randall?" Justine asked, cutting to the chase.

The captain smiled knowingly but didn't say.

Celeste leaned forward in her seat, unable to contain herself. "What did he say to Mr. Stark? Oh please, you must tell us! I cannot wait another second."

Kat was curious to know as well, but the captain was enjoying his little tale and was not one to be rushed.

"There's more," Buzzy said, heading off their questions. "Not more than a week goes by and old Ezra and the young stowaway are the epitome of best mates. In my entire life, I have never seen such an abrupt change. There simply was no explaining it. But let me tell you that every crew member was grateful to that lad. And yes—the lad was none other than Remington Randall. Many a time I wondered what he whispered in the old man's ear, but to my knowledge he has never told a soul."

Kat couldn't believe her ears. "Oh my God. Are you telling us you don't know after all this time?!" Could the good captain be gaslighting them? It was like telling a joke and omitting the punch line.

"Tis true," Captain Buzzy admitted, lighting up his weathered pipe and drawing it out until the aroma filled the room. Then and only then did he return his attention back to his audience. "I've asked him many a time, but he claims if I make it to my seventy-fifth year, he'll have the words engraved in gold and given to me as a birthday present."

Buzzy laughed ruefully. "This old, weathered body still has a way to go. But it's a possibility I may never know."

Daphne still wasn't satisfied. "That's an amazing story. But what's he like now?"

Buzzy continued. "As they say, the boy is no longer a boy, but a man. Ezra really likened to him like no other human being on earth. And having no family of his own, Stark finally adopted Rem and took him under his wing."

Kat rolled her eyes. "It sounds like a fantastic fairytale."

The captain shrugged. "Ezra was no fool. The boy was smart, and Ezra saw it—everyone did. He was a quick learner and a fast problem solver. Ezra sent him to the very best schools and started him out doing small jobs in his shipping office. He made the kid work his way up and Rem was a diligent worker."

Kat still wasn't buying it. "And no doubt he eventually took the old man for a bundle. Correct?"

Buzzy found her presumption amusing. "Quite the contrary, Miss Branigan. You see, the lad not only had an astonishing head for figures but a shrewd business sense as well. He was instrumental in establishing trade routes with China, and not just for tea and silk. His contractual negotiations helped make many men very wealthy, including Stark himself."

Kat was frantically recalling history. The truth came crashing into her consciousness. Her father had told her what had really made America wealthy. "On drug money," she uttered aloud, before stopping herself.

Buzzy nodded. "That's right. The very pain medicines that fill our apothecaries are due to Rem's foresight. Supply and demand are powerful incentives."

Kat became deathly quiet. This sudden knowledge was worse than she could have imagined. Remington Randall might be serious eye candy, but you can't always spot a leopard by its colors. Eventually, they show through. She couldn't believe she had even entertained thoughts of having wild sex with the man. With his name on her bank accounts, she was now, theoretically speaking, in league with a drug dealer of the worst acceptable kind that operated under the guise of helping humanity.

The infamous Opium Wars, which must now be brewing behind the scenes, would in time lead to senseless deaths and billions being addicted for decades to come by the likes of fentanyl and other opioids that had started with Rem's China trade routes. Knowing the future was agonizing.

The captain continued his tale, oblivious to Kat's astonishing realization. "Yes, Rem steered Ezra into changing some old ways that were costing him quite a bit of money, while at the same time making new trade deals that would amass the old man an even bigger fortune. I'd say that Ezra knew exactly what he was doing from the start. He could spot potential when he saw it. Some even say that he got dealt a royal flush the day the lad picked his ship to stowaway on. Eventually he let his prodigy run the business and it flourished. Old man Ezra upped and died from a weak heart six years ago after contracting cholera, leaving everything to his protege. The Eastern Star Line is now one of the biggest shipping companies on this coast, with trade routes all over the world," he added proudly.

And with that, Buzzy sighed along with a number of others at the table. It sounded like a celebrated Horatio Alger rags-to-riches story—a romantic tale of man triumphing from humble beginnings to become a Goliath in his field. No wonder it made the men at the bank jump to attention. It made Kat want to vomit.

Tomorrow morning Rem would be sending a carriage to pick her up. As promised, Kat would fulfill the replay game agreement they had made in exchange for procuring her bank account. After that she would hopefully be done with the man. Knowing the historical truth about what he had helped set in motion, made him nothing more than a drug cartel monster.

The rest of the evening became a blur, even bidding goodbye to Captain McBee. Kat lost sleep picking her brain for details surrounding the Great Opium Wars of 1839. There was not one war, but two wars spanning from 1839 and even as late as 1860. All told, it would result in thousands of lives being destroyed and/or lost. More than 175 years later, they were still paying the price for such crimes against humanity. China would always hate the West for addicting its countrymen, turning them into opium-induced mind slaves. Was it any wonder that they would return the deed, wreaking revenge on our countrymen by flooding the West with synthetic fentanyl well over a century later—turning our men, women, and children, into zombie addicts as well.

Chapter 6

After a restless night, relentlessly tossing and turning and cursing the fact that sleep eluded her, Kat woke to a sultry and stifling heat wave that permeated and hung low over the city. Temperatures were pushing 90 degrees before 9:00 a.m. The day promised to be a scorcher, with no sign of rain in sight.

Kat vowed she would never take air conditioning for granted ever again, along with the wonders of modern plumbing. When one has never experienced such luxuries, one never knows what they are missing. These days she was missing everything.

It occurred to her that she might be missing in her time as well and her friends and colleagues would have no clue of what had become of her. Would she become just another one of thousands of missing persons that vanished into thin air? Would they look for her and if she didn't return soon, would they give up on her—along with her job, her Brooklyn brownstone, and everything else she owned? The thought was too depressing to contemplate. If she couldn't find a way back to her time, she would be forced to forge a whole new life for herself here. And while $20,000 was a hell of a lot of money in this time, it wouldn't last forever.

Kat meticulously sponge-bathed and donned a lightweight peach-colored day dress, one of the many ready-to-wear ensembles she had purchased the day before at Madame Vesey's, along with a proper ribboned bonnet, soft kid leather slippers, and a cutesy little white parasol to top it all off. The last touch was not at all to her style, but for women during these times it was their only defense against the harsh rays of the sun. The truth of the matter was that she didn't relish getting any more freckles. Today she would present herself as a fashionable and proper young lady. She opted to pull back her hair and braid it so that it fell off her shoulders, knowing full well that if she didn't the humidity would expand it to unseemly proportions in record time. She would have to keep her cool in more ways than one when dealing with Randall.

As a precautionary measure, she told Justine who she would be meeting with that morning. Justine's eyes grew wide. Her face conveyed her worry. "Do you think it's safe to go alone? I mean, shouldn't you have someone go with you to make it *proper*?"

"Proper" was fast becoming a boring concept that had managed to invade her world. Kat was not about to reveal to Justine or anyone else that she had already been with Rem alone in the privacy of his Washington Square house, where he would take her today. There was no way he would want to repeat another defeat anywhere in public like the City Hotel. There had to be a billiards table tucked away somewhere in that big old house of his.

While nothing untoward had occurred during their last encounter, outside of her forging a Faustian agreement to play him again, Kat felt confident she could hold her own no matter what happened. This time she was playing for so much more. His ring had to be the key to returning to her world. How long could it take to do a replay game, get the ring, and skedaddle out of there? An hour or two?

Her transport arrived promptly at 9:00 a.m. Kat glanced out the front window and was surprised to see Rem had not sent a hansom carriage to come get her as she had assumed would be the case. Instead, he occupied the driver's seat of a double-rigged Amish-looking, horse-drawn, black buggy. One that was small and cozy.

Kat watched him jump down from the buggy's seat dressed in casual attire, only a cut above the rough homespun shirt and trousers she had first encountered him wearing on the South Street docks. Atop his head he sported a classic Irish flat cap, giving him a country gentlemen's look. Kat panicked, knowing she was clearly overdressed, but realizing it was too late to change.

From the front window she observed him throw the reins to a small barefoot street urchin sitting on the curb resting his feet on the cool blades of grass to avoid the blistering heat of the pavement. The boy clutched the leather straps tightly and was rewarded with the toss of a few coins.

Rem proceeded to the boardinghouse's front gate causing Kat to fly into action. She scurried out the front door to avoid other female boarders from being alerted to his presence and any resulting scrutiny. It occurred to her that somehow Rem had managed to learn where she was staying. What else had he tried to find out as well?

His eyes took in her appearance, but before he could comment, she made light of it. "I guess I failed to get the proper dress memo?"

"You look quite pretty," he remarked, extending his hand to help her into the conveyance. He gave her a rueful, yet sly look once she was seated. "Should I be concerned that this is a ploy to dazzle and distract me in order to win once again?"

"Such amateur tactics are unnecessary," she stated, as he seated himself quite comfortably beside her, his thigh touching hers. She looked down pointedly and inched a fraction away. "Hmm. Am I to assume I need to be on guard as well?"

Rem laughed. "If there's anything you need to know about me it's that I play fair and square. For the life of me I can't understand why you are dead set on possessing my ring."

He held it up for her to see. "It's just a ring. But if you want it that bad, you're going to have one hell of a fight obtaining it. Are you seriously up for that?'

"I've never been afraid to take on any man," she replied, before adding: "Personally or professionally."

"So, you're not going to divulge your reasons?" he countered, maneuvering the horses around a tight bend and into the flow of morning traffic.

"That all depends," she murmured, preferring not to say any more.

"On what?" he inquired, pressing further.

When she didn't immediately answer, he added: "Just what kind of game are you playing?"

Surely, if he knew how really valuable the ring was to her, he'd only make it impossible for her to win it. It was better to change the subject and play nice.

"Where I come from we have a game called 'Truth or Dare.' Would you care to play?"

Rem hesitated. "Another game, huh? Are you good at this one, too?"

Kat had to admit she was starting to enjoy their banter. "I'm an overachiever. I'm good at most everything. Where I come from I've always been on the winning team."

"And just where is it that you *do* come from?" he asked.

Kat looked away to avoid his intense scrutiny. "Your private investigator didn't find that out, did he? How disappointed you must have been when all he learned was where I currently reside?"

It surprised him that she knew he had looked into her background. "On the contrary. Your address was listed on the bank account records."

Kat had forgotten about that. "So, you didn't have me investigated?"

"Truth? Of course I did. I like to know everything about a person I have financial dealings with. And you, my dear, are no exception." He hesitated, then looked her straight in the eye. "I found it odd indeed that no one has heard of you or that no one has ever played billiards with you before the other evening. You showed up on the docks, but you weren't listed on any ship manifest in the last year, and no records in City Hall exist on your birth or parentage. I don't even know if Katherine Branigan is your real name. You seem to have dropped down from out of nowhere and into my world. What else would you have me believe?"

Traffic moved slowly, plodding its way down the avenue as even the horses balked at having to work in such sweltering temperatures. Rem mirrored their frustration. "If you're from the future as you claim, tell me something that will happen this year that no one else would know about."

Kat took the bait. "There will be a devastating fire on December 16th that will wipe out most all of the Wall Street area. Warehouses will go up in flames, property will be destroyed, the New York Stock & Exchange Board will cease operating, insurance companies will go bust and millions will be lost. And that's just for starters. The city will have to rebuild. History will call it: 'The Great New York Fire of 1835'."

It took a moment for him to take it all in. "And you know this because…?" he prompted.

"Because I come from the 21st century and my father, who has since passed, was once a tenured History Professor at Columbia University, which is now known as Columbia College. My father loved New York history and drilled such historical facts into my head since I was a child. Go ahead—ask me anything."

Instead, he commented. "That's quite a fanciful tale. It doesn't take a fortune teller, or someone from the future as you claim, to know that there will continue to be fires in this city. More than half the structures are wooden and the water for firefighting is often scarce. In June, a fire broke out at a stable near St. Patrick's Cathedral on Mulberry Street. It spread so fast it destroyed 20 houses and left close to 200 people homeless."

Kat didn't know that. "Mark my words. This one will be much bigger." She hesitated, knowing it was none of her business. "Who's your fire insurance carrier?"

"Are you an insurance expert as well?" he inquired, dismissively.

"I'm serious, Rem. I'm doing you a favor here so don't look a gift horse in the mouth. Who do you have insurance with?"

She could tell he was reluctant to say. "Franklin Fire," he finally replied.

Kat shook her head. "Change it. All 26 insurance companies will go bankrupt from this fire, except for Hartford Fire Insurance which will pay off all of their claims."

Rem looked visibly shaken. What kind of tragedy would bankrupt so many companies? How did this woman know the exact number of fire insurers? When he should have been peppering her with more questions, he chose to remain silent. The truth was he was afraid to ask what else the future held. He preferred to believe she was making it up instead, but despite trying hard to convince himself of this, he felt jumpier than hell.

Kat chastised herself for saying too much. Damn! What must he be thinking right now? She stole a sidelong glance only to see he was lost in deep thought. Then suddenly he made a sharp right turn and swung the carriage off the main thoroughfare and in an entirely new direction.

"Where are we going?" she inquired, seeing he was still rattled by her revelations.

"To escape this blasted heat," he replied.

"I'm not crazy," she stated, just for the record.

He nodded. "I never said you were."

As they silently wove their way through streets that were now cluttered with vendors whose meats and vegetables looked dried out and shriveled from the heat, she noticed the parks were filled with people staking out their ground under some shady elm as if it might be the last cool haven to be found anywhere in the city. What she wouldn't give to strip off the layers of petticoats she had thoughtlessly encompassed herself in, which now grew heavy in the muggy air.

She took to fanning herself, debating whether this day had been a mistake and would only end in disaster. In truth, she had no idea where they were going to escape the heat, except that they were quickly approaching the East River. The pungent smell of fish hung in the air assaulting her nostrils. As they rounded a corner, coming upon the Fulton Fish Market, Rem eased up on the reins and brought the horses to a slow gait.

The set of matching bays seemed to know where he was taking them from the soft nickering, indicating they were not at all thrilled with the route their owner had chosen. Kat understood why soon enough. A line of carriages, being driven onto a flatbed, steam-powered ferry, was transporting freight and passengers back and forth across the fast-flowing waters of the East River.

Before she could question Rem further, he jumped down off the seat, took hold of the horses' harness and guided the animals over the pier's wooden planks. Two ferry hands, wearing ragged breeches and graying bandannas tied across their brow to catch dripping sweat, sprung to his aid as one of the horses reared back its head in protest.

"It's better if you get down," Rem suggested, coming towards her.

Reaching up to encircle her waist, he effortlessly lifted her down from the vehicle in one swift movement. As the deck hands took control of their conveyance and horses, Rem helped her aboard the ferry and over to its iron railing.

Kat couldn't help but think that someday the Brooklyn Bridge as well as others would be built with massive freeways and tunnels taking one over and under this very river—making it a quick and easy crossing to the Long Island side.

Water transportation was not always kind to her stomach. She breathed in the salty air having been known to have had bouts of seasickness on rough waters. Today was not one of them for which she was grateful. There was something to be said for actually feeling the power of the river all around you. The ferry's steam-powered engines rumbled beneath them, which continued to spook the horses. Kat edged away from them. Truth be known—horses scared her. Riding them was one of the few things she would never be good at, nor cared to be. Thankfully, it was not something required of her in her modern day life.

While this little excursion was enjoyable, she still had no idea what Rem's plans were. He must have read her thoughts. "The ferry will be stopping a little farther down along the shore where we can catch a road leading directly to the ocean. It will be a far cry cooler there than in the city."

Kat loved to be out in nature, but she suspected Long Island would be like being out in the hinterland. She couldn't help herself from commenting: "Someday in the future this will be densely populated with summer vacation and beach rentals, expensive homes, and gated estates. It will be a playground for the wealthy."

Rem filed that tidbit of information away. Her prediction of the future didn't surprise him, like the news of the big fire she spoke about. This whole premise about her being from the future he found unsettling and theoretically impossible. Yet, Kat seemed not only convinced of it, but knew specific details which he had to admit, he found interesting. He prided himself on being a man who listened and weighed options before taking appropriate action. He hadn't gotten this far in life by being close-minded.

"Right now, it's still pretty rural land. Mostly farms, a few private residences and summer resorts. I come out here whenever I can," he told her, putting aside the future for the time being.

"You have a home here?" she asked, already suspecting the answer.

He grinned. "Yes, and it has a fine billiards table."

The ferry made land. No sooner did they disembark, then the horses were off at a fast gait happy to be back again on solid ground. At least they knew where they were going if she didn't.

Away from the city heat, Kat sighed in contented relief as the cooler ocean breeze gently caressed her face. No matter what century one was in, the city had a tenseness to it. They had left it behind to just enjoy the day.

Rem stole a sidelong glance at her, his eyes suddenly mischievous. "Tell me how you play this game of *Truth or Dare*?"

~~*~~

Rem's first "truth" question was an easy one. "Where did you learn to play billiards so well? Who taught you?"

"Mr. Shapiro taught me when I joined the billiards club at Brooklyn High School," she informed. "I was 13 years old, too brainy for my own good, and my best friend Lexi thought the sport would broaden my horizons and open me up to greater possibilities. She was convinced that the billiards club was where all the really cool hunks hung out, which was where she wanted to be."

Her answer perplexed him. "Define what *cool hunks* are."

Kat hesitated, then softly giggled, as she self-consciously searched for adequate words. They had an urban language difference spanning over a century. How to explain a term objectifying men?

"This is something embarrassing?" he asked curious, yet dead serious.

"Oh, no," she assured him. "A *cool hunk* is a handsome virile male which most women find highly-desirable for several reasons. They tend to be alpha males with a good strong body—like yourself."

Rem found her explanation interesting. "So, you think *I'm* a hunk?"

"Oh, please. STOP it!" She said laughing, not willing to admit to any such thing. "Seriously, do you not own a mirror? Melanie Van Eaton practically falls on her knees at your feet when you're around. My eyes do not deceive me. The woman is all over you. Like you haven't noticed?"

Kat paused, realizing from his curious look that she might have put her foot in her mouth and gone too far. She was being unnecessarily bold and blunt. Too much truth could prove potentially deadly. She quickly backpedaled.

"Oh my God. Rem, I am so sorry. If she's your girlfriend, I shouldn't have said that."

"No offense taken," he said, smoothly.

When he didn't elaborate with either a *nay* or a *yea*, she asked again. "Well, *is* she your girlfriend?"

There was that curious look on his face once again and she realized the term was not a familiar one. "Girlfriend means someone who is a close or beloved female companion," she explained.

Rem nodded, understanding. "I will count this as another 'Truth' question," he clarified before answering. "No. She's not my *girlfriend* as you term it."

Melanie might not be his official girlfriend, but she should have asked whether they were occasional lovers, bedmates—not that she expected him to tell her, but what the hell. Afterall, it *was* "Truth or Dare" and one could ask anything. Before this day was over she would find out anyway.

An involuntary sigh escaped her lips, which Rem took note of with a sly little smile. Did this have something to do with why Melanie had stormed into his office late yesterday afternoon to give him an earful about the "wicked" likes of Katherine Branigan.

After a distance, Rem pulled up the buggy along a deserted stretch of white sandy beach and tied the reins to the hitching horn. To Kat's surprise he reached behind them and pulled out a wicker basket from under the leather seat.

The man continued to astound her. "You planned for a picnic?" she asked incredulously.

"Is it okay if we stop here and have an early repast by the sea? We're not far from my home where we can play our match. I promise to have you back before nightfall."

Well, okay. He had laid out the day accordingly and was trying to make it as pleasant as possible before they both went their separate ways.

When he took off his shoes and socks, she did as well, only to be surprised when he looked away as if exposing her bare feet was the same as displaying one's private parts. They made their way down to the water's edge, where she lifted her skirts to feel the water and sand rush between her toes. Alongside her, Rem filled his lungs with ocean air, his dark hair ruffled by the wind.

They found a comfortable spot on the soft sand for their little picnic. Rem pulled out a blanket from the basket and invited her to sit down as he brought forth an assortment of fruit, cheese, and bread—accompanied by two stemmed glasses and a bottle of vintage French wine.

It felt like a *date*, but she wasn't even sure such a term was used in these days. Perhaps everyone brought such provisions when they went for a buggy ride in the country just in case they got stranded. Best not to read anything more into it than it was. She had to admit today he seemed like a genuinely nice drug lord. Her better instincts told her that she should refrain from bringing up the subject of opium or they were bound to get into an intense argument. Kat nibbled on the bread and cheese and waved off the wine. She was determined to keep a clear head since she would soon play him for important stakes.

The lull from the buggy ride, coupled with the sun overhead, made her want to lay down, close her eyes and just feel the ocean breeze wash over the heat of her body, but she didn't. She found herself staring at the inviting blue waters wishing she could strip down naked and get into the water and rid herself of all these useless layers of clothing once and for all.

Yesterday Kat had commissioned Madame Vesey to make her several sets of woman's trousers and shirts. Such a proposal had managed to shock the salon owner, but Kat didn't care. She craved the comfort of jeans and a tank top, or the next best thing to it—men's clothing. Of course, they would gossip about her if she dressed like a man, but this dress wearing thing was quickly wearing thin on her. From day one she had refused to don the long tight corsets of this time which were like being encased in a straitjacket. No wonder women of the 19th century often had consumption.

"You look wistful," Rem commented, observing the longing on her face. "Are you missing your home?"

His assessment was astute. There was a longing in her in more ways than he could understand. She continued staring out to sea, observing the waves crash against the shore. "Yes," she finally admitted. "I was just thinking how much I wanted to dive into the water and feel totally free."

He nodded, taking her words seriously. "Then since it's my turn to play the game, I *dare* you to do it."

Kat was never one to turn down a challenge and an easy one at that. She would take his dare. She stood up and started peeling off the first outer layer before she remembered who she was with and that such things were not done in such a manner. Rem would not be used to a woman intimately stripping for him outside the privacy of a bedroom.

She turned her head and gave him a pointed look. "Close your eyes," she ordered.

Like a gentlemen he did as she instructed.

"And don't you peek either," she added for good measure.

A low chuckle was heard behind her. It's not like he wouldn't be seeing anything he hadn't seen before, but it was unlikely he would know that skinny-dipping was not such a shocking thing to do in her time.

The peach dress and all its many layers were discarded in a rumpled heap on the blankets next to him. Thank God, she hadn't needed to discard a corset as well. Running naked and free, the soft white grains of sand squishing between her toes, she raced for the ocean and uninhibitedly dived in. The saltwater felt glorious against her heated skin as she sluiced through the waves, not having a care in the world. It felt like she was leaving this other world behind—a world that felt too constricting for someone who had been raised to be a free spirit.

Kat happened to glance behind her only to find, much to her consternation, that not only were Rem's eyes wide open, but he, too, was stripping down and… She heard her own audible gasp as her eyes grew big with what was now packaged in front of her in plain sight. Rem was as naked as a jay bird, his tall frame racing for the water's edge, his manhood on full display without shrinkage.

Yikes! Remington Randall *was* a "hunk"! His had the kind of body most men get by spending endless hours in a 24-hour fitness gym, lifting weights, and flexing their muscles. Rem's physique and musculature were not gym-made. His looked natural, the kind acquired the old-fashioned way—by arduous work and not afraid to get dirty doing manual labor. Geez. Did he unload his own ships?

Kat dove under and swam out farther, afraid that should he catch up with her, it would present an entirely new problem. Her "let's get naked" actions had been nothing short of an open invitation to trouble.

~~*~~

Rem *had* peeked big time and was not ashamed to admit it. He was a man who liked what he saw, and Kat Branigan was stunningly beautiful with or without clothes. Not much surprised him when it came to women, but he hadn't expected her to take him up on his little dare without outright protest. So, when she readily took the bait and began to semi-modestly strip right in front of him, he was more than shocked. It turned him instantly hard.

If Kat was from the future as she claimed, he wondered if all women were like her. Hell, now he was even more curious to find out what other disinhibitions she also possessed. In some ways she was very much like a male competitor encased in female form. Joining her in the water was a foregone decision, if only to learn what else she might be open to and to save her should she flounder in the tidal currents that frequently sprang up in these waters.

A strong swimmer he had always been, but while he knew that most women couldn't swim at all, he wasn't surprised to see that Kat did it with ease and confidence. If the woman swam anything like she played billiards, then he might not so easily overtake her in the water. "Overachiever" was another term he had never heard of but could easily figure out, unlike the term "hunk." It told him she didn't like to lose and was by nature highly competitive. Unfortunately, so was he. Rem picked up his pace, shortening the distance between them with each powerful stroke.

He saw Kat glance back and witnessed the exact moment when realization hit her that he was in hot pursuit and was quickly gaining on her. That only served to accelerate her pace. They were well beyond the breaking waves when a warning signal went off in his head. Up ahead he spotted a patch of sea where the color had changed to a deeper, darker blue, telling him she was approaching an area past the sandbar where rip currents could easily sweep one away. Rem knew these waters better than anyone; she didn't. If he didn't act fast, they would both be in serious trouble.

Rem called out a warning. Kat heard it as she struggled to swim against the current, trying to not let it take her down. That's when he swam like their lives depended upon it, reaching her and pulling her away from a swirling heap of seaweed and other debris the churning water had coughed up, before forcing them both into a floating position.

"Relax, don't fight the current. Stay parallel to the shore," he shouted. Rem could see the look of rising panic in Kat's eyes even as she complied. Rip currents could make one feel like something was pulling you down under and further away from shore. Panic only led to drowning. Rem held on to her, steering them at an angle away from the current until they made it safely back to shallow waters.

"I suppose that was pretty stupid of me," Kat assessed as they dragged themselves out of the water, neither caring about propriety or modesty. She avoided his eyes and that body of his. "Thanks for coming to my rescue. That makes it twice now. I suppose I owe you for this."

Rem refrained from commenting, his back now to her as he jogged towards their clothes. Kat's eyes did a thorough sweep over the sight of his long wet torso moving over the sand. She swallowed hard, feeling her nipples harden. No, no, no, she chastised herself. Don't even think about going there!

Rem snatched up the picnic blanket and wrapped it tightly around her. "I will exercise more restraint should I ever dare you to do something of that nature in the future. Low tides in this area can get nasty and riptides can occur unexpectedly. It could have happened to anyone."

He shook the water from his hair, running a quick hand over its brown lengths to slick it out of the way. Without a towel of his own, Kat tried not to stare at the water dripping down his chest, straight to his lower parts, which he seemed oblivious to.

She closed her eyes feeling overly self-conscious, which was unusual for her. A chill was setting in, despite the sun beating down on them. Her lips involuntarily chattered prompting Rem to wrap himself around her and the blanket, warming them both. It was a strange sensation having him pressed intimately against her even with a wool layer of separation between them. They remained silent, soaking in the warmth.

"Get dressed," Rem suddenly said, pulling away. "We should go."

"Okay," she murmured, breaking the spell.

Rem held up the blanket as a curtain for her to dress behind. Not like he hadn't already seen everything there was to see, she was thinking. While it took her longer to put everything back on, it took him no time to scramble back into his own clothes. They got back into the waiting buggy and glanced at each other, waiting to see what the other would say first. It was such an awkward moment that Kat began laughing. Then, Rem did as well.

She stated the obvious. "Well now that we've both seen each other without clothes, and there's no surprises there, shall we get on with the business of the day?"

They had encountered only one other vehicle since steering the horses off the main road. It was a farmer and his young son hauling a half-empty wagon of fresh hay. Upon seeing them, the man spat out a wad of chewing tobacco into the grass, took off his cap, and yelled out a hearty greeting. Kat was surprised to hear Rem return the greeting, addressing the farmer by name.

"Does he work for you?" Kat asked.

"No, but he delivers fresh hay for my horses. His farm is about two miles back, off that last bend in the road. This is primarily agricultural land. Out here a man does not feel compelled to build on top of his neighbor, but rather carve out his own niche, in his own corner, away from the clamor of other men."

Rem sounded almost poetic. He talked about his neighbors, how they all helped each other, but most of all he expressed his reverence for the rich land and the plentiful bounty it provided for so many. Kat debated whether to tell him that someday this very land would be filled with hordes of weekenders, gridlock jammed highways, all of which would displace the farmers and the agricultural land he cherished—all in the name of progress.

Just over the next hilly rise, Rem eased back on the reins, leading the horses off the dusty lane and onto a grassy knoll where clusters of lady ferns and purple coneflowers flourished along a scenic panorama of the ocean below.

For as far as her eyes could see, the vast shoreline stretched on endlessly like a wiggling snake through curved coves and inlets. It took her breath away. She had never seen such island views in her time without a parade of motorboats, catamarans, yachts, and other sailing craft trafficking the busy waterways.

Rem pointed out a ship further out, as he reached for a small spyglass strapped to the side of his seat. "That's the *Deliverance*. It's a packet schooner that makes weekly runs to North and South Carolina for southern cotton and to carry mail." He passed the spyglass to her for a better look. It was a three-masted beauty, moving fast through the water.

"Is it one of your ships?" she asked looking through the lens.

He nodded. "One of twenty-six."

"You're lucky to have all that you have," she remarked, handing him back the spyglass.

Rem hmphed. "I had to make my luck."

Kat remembered what she had learned from Captain McBee about Rem as a young lad.

"Truth question," she began. "What did you tell Ezra Stark to stop him from throwing you overboard when you were found as a stowaway?"

Rem broke out in raucous laughter, shaking his head. His eyes twinkled with a knowing look. "So, you've been talking about me with that old scoundrel Buzzy."

"Heavens, no," she shot back, mortified should he think that she had been checking him out. "He has a thing for my landlady and when he came to dinner last night we all got quite an earful of salty tales. And, of course, your name came up…"

Kat eyed him. "So, Mr. Randall. What's your rags-to-riches story?"

"It's not that interesting," he replied.

Kat rolled her eyes, not buying it. "Let me be the judge of that."

Rem steered the horses into a long private drive. "My parents are both dead," he began. "My father by the sharp edge of a blade thrust into his back for the meager wages he earned laboring on the London docks, and my mother…" He paused. She caught a hint of raw sadness lingering behind his eyes.

"My mother died by the hands of injustice for stealing a half-dead, scrawny chicken with barely enough meat on its bones to feed a small child. I was four at the time."

"I'm so sorry," she murmured, quite shocked.

He continued, barely nodding at her condolences. "They dragged us both before a magistrate and sentenced her to life imprisonment for her crime. I can still remember how the judge belched when he declared the sentence, grease still lingering at the corners of his mouth from some midday repast. He dismissed her off to some festering prison cell at Newgate without even so much as a second glance. She died within the year, but I never knew it until years later, for I was immediately made a ward of the state and whisked off to an orphan asylum."

Kat unconsciously put her hand on his. "That's awful."

He noted her hand on his and that she had yet to remove it. "The place was a snake pit," he continued. "Where anyone wanting cheap labor was quickly accommodated. I couldn't have been of much use to the wardens being so young, but I was sent, nevertheless. For 14 hours every day they had us working either in the coal mines or textile mills, lifting, or carrying until our backs were ready to break, or we collapsed from sheer fatigue. We were paid a shilling a week for our labors, but we never saw it. Each day seemed worse than the last. The food was not fit for a pig's slop, and it doesn't take long with conditions like that before the will to live is quickly sucked out of you. We were beaten when we didn't comply and at night, they used the boys to …"

He stopped, realizing he had said too much. "I don't need to tell you all the details. It's best forgotten. When I saw other lads my age or older dropping like flies from either abuse or inhumane conditions, you wonder if each day will be your last. It brought out a strong survival instinct in me. I spent several years there, but it seemed like a lifetime. It's not important how I managed to escape, but I did. And I did whatever was necessary to avoid being caught and sent back. There are so many places in London a young boy can hide and never be seen again. You quickly find them all when you have to.

"But salvation came in the form of a lady. This lady's buggy had slid in the wet mud of the road where it got stuck in a rut and wouldn't budge. It was late in the evening. She was driving alone on a street not safe for man nor beast, which was unwise. She was in a panic, and I suspected she was fleeing something or someone, which was why she had no driver. I happened to witness her dilemma from my makeshift bed in a hallway of a deserted building. What little help I could I offered her and managed to free the wheel by maneuvering a board under it.

"In return, I was given a warm place in her stables to sleep that night and a job the next morning as her stableboy. It was a fresh start in life for me. A little more than a year later I was on a ship bound for the States where I met the man who would be instrumental in giving me a chance to make something of myself. That was more than twenty years ago. The rest is history."

Kat waited for him to elaborate, but he didn't as he steered the horses onto a back road running parallel to the ocean cliffs. The land was verdant with green rolling hills and white paddock fencing. Here it felt so much cooler than the heat of the city.

Kat elbowed him wanting to hear more of his tale. "That's it? You're not going to tell me how you came to be aboard that ship, or what immortal words you whispered in Ezra Stark's ear to save you from being tossed overboard?"

"No," he said, ending the subject. He pulled up on the reins and announced, "We're here."

"Here," for all purposes, meant his place. It was a far cry from the Long Island beach houses of her time. The three-story whitewashed house, set center stage at the far end of a long stone driveway, was surrounded by grazing land, a small lake, and in the distance dense forestry. This sizable estate was much too grand to be just a weekend country home.

"This is yours?" she questioned taking in the tall, white-shuttered windows looking out over the distant blue ocean. The house had several strategically placed balconies to capture the view. Stone steps, chiseled out of solid bedrock, led to the front entrance's massive double doors. And yet in the grandeur there was a touch of homey quaintness. A large wraparound shaded porch with rocking chairs made it seem downright hospitable. There were outbuildings towards the rear, which she suspected were the barns and livery stables.

Rem glanced up at the sky where dark clouds were fast forming. "We don't have a lot of time. Come." He jumped down, just as a servant and stableboy came running, having spotted them rounding the bend. He tossed the boy the reins and helped her down.

The manservant appeared surprised at his employer's arrival. Clearly he had not been expected or informed of Rem's pending visit or that he would be bringing a guest. "Sir, the staff were given the day off, as we had not expected you until later in the week."

"It's alright. We're not staying long," Rem informed, before pointing out. "A light squall is brewing. It may blow over quickly, but the lady and I are here on quick business, and it shouldn't take long. No need to call the staff back."

Kat almost gasped aloud. Rem's declaration sounded like they were only there for a quick romp in the hay. Business, indeed! If the man was thinking such thoughts, he gave no indication.

The servant looked relieved. "Very well, sir."

"We will be occupying the billiards room. No need to prepare any other rooms."

Kat stifled a small laugh. Surely the man would not think they were going to do it right on the billiards table—a hit and run before departing. Rem threw her a questioning look which she avoided. The last thing she needed was for him to read her thoughts.

"Is there anything else you will be needing, sir?" his servant inquired cautiously.

Kat was feeling itchy from the salt water still lingering on her hair and skin. "Is there any way to draw me a bath? I feel quite…" She searched for words, then settled with "do we have time?"

They both looked at her curiously, like she had just asked for a round-trip ticket to the moon. Oops. Tub bathing was considered a luxury even for the rich. It would take hours to heat and haul up enough hot water to fill a tub. A pitcher of cold water, some soap, and a washstand basin would have to suffice. Since hair dryers didn't exist either, her hair would just have to air-dry. She sighed. The drawbacks of this era were a hundred times worse than modern-day camping.

~~*~~

Kat plunged her head in the basin's cold water and furiously soaped up her hair, scalp, and body. From an upstairs bedroom window, she spied the freshwater pond out back and figured this was the source from which the house drew its water. Probably spring fed, it would have been a hell of a lot faster and more convenient to have just dived into it instead and soaped up.

There was no way around it. She was loathe to put back on her sandy petticoats and sweaty undergarments. The guest room she had been directed to use to wash up held no feminine garb. It looked like a male's lair, but not the master's bedroom. Forced to forage in the room's large armoire for any castoffs or suitable attire, Kat found a man's silk dressing gown, which she quickly rejected. Such a thing would be too large and much too challenging to play in.

There was a pair of soft fawn-colored men's breeches hanging on a side hook that were the kind intended to be worn with tall riding boots. It immediately took her fancy. She wiggled into the legs seeing that it had been made for a tall person. Were they Rem's? The breeches came down to her ankles which worked simply fine for her needs, like short trousers or capris. However, the waist was too big and without something to hold it tightly in place, it would undoubtedly slip down.

Kat glanced around the room and spied a pair of braided curtain ties, which she quickly knotted together to fashion into a makeshift belt. With that problem solved, she donned a white silk shirt, rolled up the sleeves several times to fit her arms' length, and marveled at how she felt like a brand new person. For the first time since dropping down into 1835, she felt fashionably free.

Kat scrutinized herself in a tall mirror and took stock. She presented a strange appearance for this time, but it would have to do. Despite towel drying her hair, it was hopelessly unmanageable. She finger-combed her slightly damp red tresses attempting to look presentable, which only made it worse. It was the nature of curly hair, despite its heavy length. If only she had a scrunchie or some hair pins to tie it back, but there were no more curtain ties to be had.

She opted to remain barefoot. Back home she never wore shoes in her own house. New York was a filthy place to be tramping in such street dirt and country roads were no different. It was no secret that Kat loved playing pool barefoot. It served to ground her.

She sighed, taking one last glance, knowing she shouldn't linger much longer. Dark clouds were gathering outside. She stopped and turned, knowing she was forgetting something. Her lucky locket. She searched her reticule bag where she thought she had placed it but came up empty. With a sinking feeling she realized that in the rush to tell Justine where she was going, she had forgotten to take it with her. Double Damn! Her family talisman had never failed her. It was something she brought to every game. How could she have left it behind on today of all days?

Kat sighed, looked in the mirror and gave herself a major pep talk. "You've got this girl. Just pretend it's with you. You know you can win this. Now go do it!"

All fired up, Kat practically pranced down the carpeted stairs, found the billiards room on instinct alone, and quietly entered. She was ready to do battle for the ring that would take her home.

Rem was pouring himself a glass of brandy from a sideboard array of liquors when she entered the dark mahogany wood-paneled room unnoticed. His back to her, his eyes were drawn to the sky outside an open window which held his focus.

Kat's eyes were immediately drawn to the imported, exquisitely carved, European billiards table on display in the center of the room. It was a nine-foot tournament length table and a real beauty. Large and without pockets, its green felt surface resembled his manicured lawns surrounding the house. She was certain the table must have cost a small fortune. Next to it, its owner struck a handsome figure, resembling a country squire in a dark pair of fitted breeches, polished Hessian boots, and silk shirt much like what she was now wearing.

Kat cleared her throat, making the lord of the manor turn. The shocked look on his face when he took in her attire was priceless. It was a picture-perfect moment seeing the man rendered speechless. Good, she thought with a feeling of triumph. Hopefully, her indecent attire would serve to throw him off his game. Without her lucky locket, she would have to do whatever it took to beat him once again.

~~*~~

Rem was thinking along the same lines. For the second time that day this unusual woman had managed to surprise—no, shock him. Unnerving on numerous fronts, he was certain this had been her intentional plan from the start. It had not escaped him that she was presently encased in an old pair of *his* breeches. He watched her twirl around, displaying her attire for his full view.

"Quite fetching, isn't it?" she asked barely containing a smile. "Are you ready for a man- to-man game of it?"

Rem downed his brandy, searching for the right words. Instead, he walked over to the double doors of the room and firmly closed them. While his help was discreet, he frankly did not know if tongues could be kept from wagging about something of this sort occurring. A woman in man's clothes was downright unseemly. Thank God, most of the local staff were currently away.

Frankly, he didn't care what she wore. But if she was determined to throw him off kilter, he could also play that game. "You look better without clothes. Perhaps you should reconsider," he suggested pointedly.

"Are you asking or daring me to take them off?"

A strong gust of wind blew in from the window, fluttering the draped curtains, followed by a loud far off crack of thunder which made Kat jump. Rain was coming. You could smell it in the air.

Rem secured the window latch and voiced what she already knew. "We may not be able to get back tonight. If it's raining, the ferry won't be running."

Kat visibly shrugged. It wasn't as if she had some teenage curfew and/or hadn't crashed before at someone's place if it became difficult to get home. There were more than enough bedrooms in this big old house. Did he think she would be mad or somehow mortified to stay the night? He seemed generally concerned, which was actually endearing.

"I'm sorry, Kat," he said as another clap of thunder struck closer to ground. The storm was approaching fast and there would be no outrunning it. At least it would bring a much needed respite from the heat.

"It's okay," she murmured, looking to the upside. At least now they could take their time without having to try to beat the storm back. Any suggestion of her taking her clothes off was quickly forgotten. "Let's play," she said taking up a cue stick from a wall rack.

They would have to stick to carom billiards. If Rem had owned a billiards table with pockets, something she would certainly encourage him to procure, they could stay up all night and she could teach him a thing or two from her time. Instead, they opted to play "cushion" billiards, which was just as challenging as their first game but with different rules. Here one had to carom the cue ball off both object balls while contacting the rail cushion.

They agreed to a warm-up game, no stakes involved, to get her used to his table. Without a crowd betting and scrutinizing their every move, they both felt more at ease. Whether Rem was in the comfort of his own environment or the crowded gaming room of the City Hotel, he was still in every way a formidable opponent. Kat hated to admit it, but he had a better grasp of geometry and physics than she did, calculating the angle of incidence, and using the laws of reflection and refraction to predict where the ball would bounce off the rail.

Remington Randall had a sharp mind. His bank and backspin shots were undeniably awesome, and she grudgingly told him as much. "Do you practice every day?" she asked.

"Sometimes," he admitted. "It clears my head on nights I can't sleep."

Kat wished she could say as much. Right now, she was strung higher than a kite being in the same room as him knowing what the stakes were. She patted her chest three times where her lucky locket should have been. In her mind, she pictured it with her. *Don't fail me*, she thought.

Outside the tropical storm surged, bringing heavy rain which pelted the windowpanes like hail. Rain always made her uneasy. It was not a good omen with which to start such a critical game.

"Are you ready for our match?" Rem finally asked, having given her plenty of practice time.

Kat nodded. "Yes. Let the games begin."

~~*~~

Rem hawkishly watched her every move. He knew he would beat her, even if she had yet to figure that out. She was a skillful player, but he could see the weather was making her jumpy. Why, he wasn't sure, but there was one thing in life he had learned the hard way and that was if you wanted something too badly, it strangled off the breath of success. It also played havoc on your ability to focus. Some of his best business deals had come about when he had remained neutral, detached, and not emotionally invested in the outcome.

Right now, his focus was crystal clear, despite the fact that the lady in front of him, currently leaning low over the billiards table to make a bank shot, did not have a stitch of undergarments on. He had perfect eyesight. From across the table, he could clearly see her bare nipples, sans corset or chemise, pressed up against the oversized silk shirt she wore—a shirt that was his.

Rem mused that this strange woman continued to confound and intrigue him. She was a determined creature. Any other woman would use her bare breasts to lure him into bed to get what she wanted, not play a game of cutthroat billiards. He hadn't decided what he would ask for when she lost—something she had dismissed as not even remotely possible. Should he demand his initial $20,000 back and even the score? No. It wasn't like he needed the money. She had no idea of his true wealth. Perhaps no one did. What did she have that *he* most wanted?

Rem smiled inwardly. Kat Branigan had no idea that besides skill he possessed an unusual penchant for luck. Which was why he was not about to easily hand over his potent talisman to one Kat Branigan. She had unknowingly underestimated him.

The ring that she was so dead set on obtaining had been made for him by a sea witch herself—Lady Portia Darcy, the very benefactor that had set him upon the life he now led. "Keep it close to your heart, always," she had instructed with a hint of warning. "It can bestow power beyond the human realm to those who have a pure heart."

As a mere lad, Lady Darcy often spoke about things he did not understand, but she saw something in him as Ezra had as well. Some had claimed that Lady Darcy was an enchantress who could see into the future. Beautiful and compassionate, even Ezra had fallen under her spell. Up until the day he died, the old man still held a fond place in his heart for her despite her having departed years before him. *Hell, no! There was no way Kat Branigan was getting his lucky ring! She could flaunt her hard little nipples in his face, and he would still remain unmoved.*

Kat glanced over at Rem wondering what was making him grin like a silly fool. It unnerved her. What was he plotting? He was points ahead of her, and he didn't even seem to be trying that hard—damn him! Now she wondered if he had sandbagged her at the City Hotel. You just could not trust an opium-shipping drug lord one iota!

The driving rain and gale force winds which didn't want to abate were playing a number on her head. That and the fear of losing. *What was wrong with her?* Usually, she could remain cool when it came to playing tournaments, but Rem's eyes kept boring into her, like he was performing psychic surgery on her thoughts. She kept wanting to slap him, knowing damn well that anger or irritation was a disastrous head game to engage in.

Stop it, she silently scolded herself. Her blood sugar was too low, and she just needed sustenance. She stood back from the table, taking a minute to breathe and regroup. "Have you got any food?" she asked, smiling prettily.

Rem saw right through her non-subtlety. Of course, he knew she was stalling. He had a five-point lead on her. "What would you like?" he asked.

Certainly not a leg of mutton, but something to assuage the butterflies in the pit of her stomach. "Do you have any of those little soda crackers?"

Rem frowned, not familiar with the term. "You mean corn crackers?"

Kat brightened. She had no idea when Nabisco invented saltines, but some form of crackers was now available. "Yes. That will work or maybe some biscuits. Have you got any of those, too? I'm starving."

She was testing his patience. Rem sighed and nodded. He poked his head out the room's double doors and called for his manservant, who came running. Within minutes there was a knock on the door and a plate of both crackers and tea biscuits magically materialized. Even before Rem closed the door to his servant, Kat snatched a few and began nibbling away.

"Your turn," she said, leaning against the table as she devoured the bland-tasting crackers.

Despite knowing she was committing a gross mortal sin, Kat did the unthinkable. Everyone knew you didn't eat or drink anywhere near the surface of a billiards table. Billiards was the indoor extension of lawn croquet. The green felt was one's lawn, and she had just strewn crumbs on Rem's private indoor lawn. He looked at it pointedly and frowned. He paused his play, came over and picked off the crumbs with a loud clicking of his tongue.

"That's a 2-point penalty," he announced. "House rules."

"What?!" she replied, openly aghast. "That's not fair!"

Rem would have none of her protests. "If you weren't dressed like a lad, and indeed were one, it would merit a prompt and proper switching for such an egregious infraction."

Kat stood back. Those were big disciplinary words from the master of the house. "You mean a spanking? You want to spank me?" she tried asking with a straight face. "Ooh, Rem. That's kinky!"

He obviously understood the slang meaning of *kinky*. His face turned a slight shade redder, surprising her. Rem always seemed so cool and smooth. *Had she just finally managed to ruffle his feathers?* She placed both hands on her hips defiantly and took it a step further. "Go ahead. Spank me. I double dare you."

Rem gritted his teeth and exhaled. He would have liked nothing better than to have turned her over his knee and done more than that, but he prided himself on being a gentleman. One did not strike a lady—not even one dressed as a lad.

He slowly chalked his cue stick, giving himself a moment to regain his composure. Damn, she was getting under his skin, which was exactly her intention. "Maybe I will, but not now," he replied. "Let's finish this game first and get it behind us." And with that he was all business again.

Kat lost by three fucking points despite having given it her all. Rem played like the devil himself was on his side, successfully making shots that looked impossible to pull off. Her defeat came with a big serving of humble pie for believing so wholeheartedly she could beat him, take possession of his ring, and go home to her time once and for all. That she felt disheartened was putting it mildly. Unless she could come up with a viable Plan B, it looked like she was staying here in this time until further notice. C'est la vie!

Kat extended her hand for the usual congratulatory handshake that came at the end of a match between two formidable opponents. "You played an incredible game," she said trying to be a good sport about losing, while trying not to think about the repercussions. Short of stealing, she would have to find another way to obtain his ring.

Rem shook her extended hand, pulling her closer as he did until they were scant inches apart. His firm grip on her felt absolute. She smiled nervously, bent on taking a new tack. "Shall we make it two out of three matches for the evening's final winner?"

"No, Kat." There was a tone of finality in his answer. "Let's be honest with each other. You now owe *ME*. It's time to pay up."

Kat froze in place, recognizing that his words were serious. She caught her breath, trying to think fast. Did Rem want his money back? She was afraid to ask but had to. Swallowing hard and keeping the trepidation out of her voice, she voiced the question uppermost on her mind. "And in what form are you requesting payment, Mr. Randall? Money?"

He was thoughtfully considering, taking his time in answering, his eyes never wavering from hers yet recognizing her hint of fear.

"Not money. Just a kiss to the victor," he stated simply. "Certainly, that's not asking too much. Is it?"

No, it was not too much to ask. Inwardly she sighed with relief knowing he was letting her off lightly. A kiss it would have to be. Kat unconsciously wetted her lips. She leaned in closer to give him a quick peck.

It was all Rem needed to act. Drawing her into his arms, his lips tentatively touched hers, testing the waters. Then he was kissing her, and she found herself kissing him back, all the while feeling tiny electrical currents shoot through her as she did. In a nanosecond her sensual senses were awakened to high alert status. Like two circuits connecting to a power station, the kiss intensified, taking on a life of its own. She might never know who initiated that exact moment when things shifted, but it was evident that a kiss was not just a kiss to the likes of a man such as Remington Randall, but a prelude to much more.

Rem's mouth and lips became more insistent, finding no resistance to his advances. His tongue probed the entrance to her mouth seeking a deeper connection and was rewarded when she readily welcomed him in. Their breath intermingled, fueling the flames. Kat found herself being swept away with the passion of the moment as they began their dance of intimacy.

There was no denying she knew exactly where this was all going and decided not to fight it but openly embrace it and get it out of her system. Perhaps it was the intensity of the storm outside seeking a human outlet, or the memory forever etched in her brain of Rem's virile wet body on full display leaving little to her imagination. If she was being truly honest, it might just be that she was feeling hornier than hell right now and there would be no stopping what was inevitable. Her defeat at his hands made for a strange connection between the two of them—something she had yet to fully understand.

Being the brazen 21st century woman she was, she let her needs be known. Lightly running her hand down the front of his breeches, she heard his breath catch as she gently cupped his bulging manhood through his clothing, realizing he was already hard.

Rem felt his body straining. They were practically having sex with their mouths and once she touched him, he knew she wanted more. But he was not about to rush things, for his sake or hers. This was his prize winnings, and he would fully enjoy it and her to the full degree imaginable.

His hand moved to cup the contours of her breast through the silk fabric of her/his shirt. It was the same breast he had been kneed in the groin for having accidentally touched on the docks that first day. This time there was no retribution, no rebukes, nor hesitancy, as she allowed him to finger her engorged nipple through the silky material. Her breath quickened, spurring him on.

Rem felt his manhood fairly bursting to be freed. He reluctantly released his tongue from the full wetness of her mouth to look deep into her eyes. "Yes?"

Kat knew what he was asking permission for. She nodded. Unbuttoning the top two buttons of her shirt, she let it slip down off her shoulders, dropping to her waist. As intended, it exposed her naked breasts to his full view. His eyes took them in like he was treasuring a priceless Rembrandt painting. They were full, lush, and more than a mouthful for any man. He wanted to taste them. He wanted to run his lips over the softness of her skin and so much more. Under his intense admiration, he saw her nipples stand at full attention.

Rem wanted more than just an eyeful of Kat's beautiful breasts. He lifted her off her feet and planted her on the cushion rail of the billiards table to have unfettered access. Both hands reached out and reverently cupped each luscious breast as he felt the weight and creamy smooth texture of her pale skin now in his care. He caressed her erect nipples, finding them incredibly responsive to his touch, eliciting a small soft moan to escape her lips. Her eyes encouraged him to go further, and he did without further prompting. No longer confined by the blockage of fabric, Rem drew a nipple into his mouth and lavished it with his tongue.

"Yes. Harder," he heard her almost pleading whisper. He sucked it in skimming his teeth lightly over the teat's turgid pebbled surface, feeling her immediately respond with a gasp—letting him know what she liked. He gave her more of it, giving equal time to each breast until she frantically reached for the silly-looking cord that held up her breaches. Rem was one step ahead of her and pulled them down to find soft downy red hair covering her womanhood. He yanked the pants off and spread her legs slightly to get a better view of what he had already glimpsed on the beach. There was nothing he wanted more than to bury his face in her personal female scent and come inside her.

As if reading his thoughts, Kat leaned both arms back on the billiards table to support herself and slowly opened her legs further. Then she did something Rem found so seductive it simply unglued him. She brought two emboldened fingers down to separate her vaginal folds, pulling the hood back just enough to give him not only an unobstructed view, but total access to do whatever he desired. Damn if he wouldn't!

Rem was acutely aware that as his gaze swept over her sensual body and back down to the jewel she was offering him, Kat knew exactly what she was doing to him. She had bewitched him. Taken possession of his sanity. In that moment he doubted once with this unusual woman would be enough.

Kat observed the deep blue pupils of Rem's eyes dilate with instant arousal. His cool businesslike reserve dissolved and was replaced with unbridled male desire. The transformation made her juices flow, making her wet—for him.

Unlike the crumb incident, there was no talk of house rules or potential penalties for engaging in foreplay on his billiards table. Rem was clearly not thinking of any such silly things—only that he wanted *her*.

Kat watched him quickly divest of his own clothing, freeing his manhood which, from any vantage point, looked daunting. She had not misjudged what she saw on the beach. This man was poised to deliver and deliver he would.

Positioned between her open legs, Rem pulled her closer to the edge of the billiards table, exactly where he wanted her. If she was going to bewitch him, he would do the same until she was desperate to have him.

He would have her no other way. Rem knew his way around the female body, but Kat's was more than fiery and luscious. She was so incredibly sexy he might lose his mind.

Kat knew he was intentionally teasing her as he brushed his manhood against her engorged clitoris, causing her body to tremble from the electrical currents of desire that instantly zipped through her. The sexual tension building was palpable. Inside she felt like a rubber band ready to snap.

Beyond entranced, she watched him wet his fingers with her vaginal juices and fondle her hardened nub, massaging its sensual circuity masterfully like a virtuoso playing a Stradivarius instrument. Kat practically came right then and there. Rem was painstakingly drawing out their foreplay, trying to bring her to the brink, then retreating. The man was a devil.

The conflagration building inside her was slowly consuming her. Kat felt on fire. She craved for Rem to enter her and experience the totality of him. Her impatience would be her undoing. Unable to wait another second, she reached for him, pulling him back down to her hungry mouth as she suggestively moved her pelvis against his hardened penis. He got the message and plunged into her, filling her with his length, his ball sack rubbing against her bare bottom. It felt absolutely glorious. No holds barred, they thrust and rocked vigorously against each other, only to pick up the intense pace as her moans grew louder with the sensation of rising sexual energy. As Rem brought her to the brink of climactic release, she tumbled over the edge, soaring with the pleasure that flooded through every cell of her body.

Like a gentlemen, Rem waited seconds for her release before quickly following with an exerted grunt that shook his entire body as he stiffened and came inside her. Good God! Remington Randall definitely knew how to properly fuck a woman, whatever century she came from. That was definitely a 10+ on her chart. Her heart was still erratically beating, forcing her to take deep breaths to calm down what he had just awakened. *How in the world had this man escaped the marriage bed in his time?*

That there was now mutual sex sweat and probably some bodily juices on his prized billiards table seemed not to matter one bit to the master of the house. Kat had to admit that sex with Rem on a billiards table had been the sexiest most erotic thing she had ever experienced. And unbelievably, Kat had never had sex on a billiards or pool table. This was definitely a first for her.

Rem, however, was far from finished. He reached one strong arm under her, pressing her naked body against him as he wrapped her legs securely around his waist to pull them both off the table. His lips met hers and he kissed her again. This time it felt slightly different, softer—or was it more conquering? Kat dismissed the thought, reminding herself that they were merely scratching each other's sexual itch and fulfilling the stakes of their bet.

Rem carried her over to a side sofa where he settled her comfortably on his lap, legs straddling and facing him. It felt incredibly intimate. There was light sweat on his chest that brought out the familiar scent of ocean and earth, the natural cologne of the times which felt vaguely reminiscent.

"Thank you," he murmured, running his hands lightly down her back to firmly cup her buttocks. The blue of his eyes deepened, his nostrils flared as he quietly spoke. "I find you to be a surprising woman in so many ways."

Kat already knew that, but then so was he. She ran her fingers through his hair playfully. "So, tell me Mr. Randall. Is my debt now paid in full?"

He was taken aback for a moment, as if momentarily offended, but then chuckled deep in his throat. "Not by a long shot, Miss Branigan. I think you will find that I am a man of many desires."

Yes, this she could believe. Underneath her bare bottom, she felt him stir and grow hard again. She reached down and lightly stroked him until he was panting heavily with new desire.

A complete wantonness stole over her. Without words Kat raised herself to her knees and impaled herself on him, reeling in the power of switching dominant roles. She rode him, fully in control, until he came once again inside her.

For both of them it began a night that would never end, as together they discovered all manner of sexual positions and pleasures in the master's large upstairs bed. As the storm continued to plummet

Manhattan and Long Island with hard rain, they remained oblivious to the outer world as they explored the inner world of their sensuality.

Chapter 7

Kat awoke in the early hours, just prior to dawn, feeling a warm body entwined with hers under the goose down coverlet. Everything about the night before came rushing back in vivid detail, causing her to actually blush as she recalled the carnal memories they had created. It had been a marathon night on all fronts. From the sound of his breathing, a warm whisper now caressing the back of her neck, the man who had given her a night to remember was still in the throes of deep sleep.

Kat took note of the fact that Rem's leg was draped possessively over her hip as he hugged her against him. It felt so natural. By nature she was a restless sleeper of the worst kind, but last night Rem had somehow managed to tame that inclination in her. When sleep had finally overtaken her, she had slept like a baby.

This morning, she felt reborn and raring to go. A knowing smile spread across her lips as she felt something poke against her thigh. Rem was feeling the same, for he was already sporting a morning boner. The man was insatiable.

Kat stifled a laugh. Yes, there was a God after all! But the street definitely ran both ways. Sometime between yesterday and today she had morphed into a 19th century nymphomaniac of the worst kind. Remington Randall was like a sexually addictive drug she couldn't get enough of. Thoughts of sticking around this century a little longer, if only to get a lifetime's worth of great sex, invaded her waking consciousness.

Snap out of it, she chastised herself. One couldn't allow such prurient thoughts to highjack one's better judgment and she had almost gone down that slippery slope without thinking. Unfortunately, great sex could do that—muddle one's brain until it was downright mushy and just plain stupid.

Right now, there were more important bridges to cross, and she knew it—like getting Rem's ring. Kat glanced down at the hand currently cupping her breast and the pinky ring which the man so zealously refused to relinquish. It beckoned to her, almost mocking her to come get it. She ran a finger over the raised "R" wondering at its power, if indeed it had the power to take her back to her time. She wasn't certain of anything. But both the man and the ring now consumed her waking thoughts.

Rem watched the little seductress under hooded eyes. She was trying to work out something in that busy little head of hers. Like an experienced poker player, he had identified some of her more obvious *tell* signs. She would purse both lips together when confronted with a particularly troublesome problem.

Right now, she was intently staring at his ring—her lips pursed in such a manner, debating what to do. He hadn't moved a muscle since waking, knowing he was being studied and preferring to see what she might do next. Last night she had done things with him that only experienced courtesans knew how to do, but being a good judge of character, he knew she was not one of their kind. A virgin she was not, but perhaps things were indeed different during her time if she was really from the future.

The heady scent of their intimacy permeated the bed sheets, and he breathed it in. He would know her scent anywhere with its hint of jasmine and rose. There wasn't an inch of her body she hadn't let him explore, which was why he was presently hard again. Sometime, during the early morning hours they had finally both fallen into an exhausted yet sated sleep.

Rem was acutely aware of his morning erection, surprised there was anything left in him after last night, but his member had a mind of its own. He pushed the thought away of just slipping into her from behind and focused instead on what path they would take from here on forward. One didn't walk away from such a night as they had experienced together. Everything about her intrigued him, demanding more.

He was dying to know what was going on right now in that little head of hers and whispered close to her ear. "What is this obsession you have with my ring?"

Kat startled, as if caught red-handed, and quickly deflected to an innocent tone. "I was just thinking how unusual it was. May I try it on?"

Rem knew better. The woman was up to something. "The ring was made to be worn only by me," he replied. "So, I'm going to have to say NO."

Kat snorted. "Well, you're no fun—this morning." She sat up, her hair tousled from the night before. The bed sheets dropped down around her, fanning out and once again displaying her naked beauty. Her disarming angelic face and body fooled him not one bit. He now knew a lot more about her than he had 24 hours earlier. Kat was quite clever when it came to getting her needs met.

Rem playfully tackled her, his body pressing down upon hers. They were now face to face. "I'm calling for a Truth question," he declared.

Not to be denied, Kat shot back. "I am, too! But as master of the house, you go first."

Rem chuckled. "Bollocks. Ladies first."

Kat felt captured in his arms. "Oh, for heaven's sake, Rem. Stop being childish! Tell me what *you* know about the ring and then I'll tell you what *I* know." She looked downright petulant, extending her own pinky towards him to shake on it. "Pinky promise."

Rem would give the little minx the benefit of the doubt, but only up to a point. Boundaries still needed to be established. "Very well," he conceded. "But I'm holding you to your promise."

She nodded, but not before swallowing hard. It was another one of her little *tells*. It told him it was highly probable Kat wouldn't be entirely truthful about what she would reveal. Not a problem. Rem felt quite confident that he could get the facts out of her in other ways if he had to. That alone gave him pause to smile.

And so, his tale began. He told her all about Lady Portia Darcy, his London benefactor, and how she had gifted him the ring before placing him on Ezra Stark's ship the *Sea Erne* prior to it setting sail for the States. He even revealed her departing instruction to him regarding the ring:

"Keep it close to your heart, always. It can bestow power beyond the human realm to those who have a pure heart."

Kat listened, totally fascinated regarding the ring's unfolding history. She waited patiently before grilling him with questions: "Where did Lady Darcy get the ring? What's it made of? What did she mean by 'it bestows great powers'?"

Rem rolled her over on the bed so that they were once again facing each other. Last night Kat had called such information exchange "pillow talk." Pillow talk with the likes of this woman was something he found extremely enlightening. Last night there had been less pillow talk between them and more copulation than he had thought possible. It was hard to dismiss the images flooding back into his mind. And his morning erection certainly wasn't helping either.

Kat nibbled on his ear, bringing him back to the present. "Are you going to tell me or not?"

The woman had a way of making him come around just by touching him. "The ring is made from meteorite iron with a gold inset," he replied. "It's said to be quite rare."

The meteorite part got Kat's attention. She already knew it was inlayed with gold, with strange markings, but revealing such knowledge would only serve to make him wary. There was no way for to her to have known this about his ring if he never took it off.

"And this Lady Darcy told you this? That it came from outer space?" she prompted.

Rem nodded. "Yes. She called it 'sky iron' and that it fell from the heavens on the night of a lunar eclipse. It streaked across the sky like a fireball, splitting off, and a part of it landed right in front of her. She told me it was too hot to touch until two days later."

Rem paused, debating how much to reveal. His hesitancy prompted Kat to entwine her fingers around the nape of his neck, playing with the strands of his hair. Unconsciously his hands moved down to her firm little ass and squeezed. Damn if she didn't wiggle it enticingly in his hands. The woman was torturing him.

"Tell me more," she whispered. "This is soooo exciting."

"Exciting" wasn't exactly the word he would use to describe their interactions. More like combustible—like two flames in the night perpetually fueling each other.

Rem sighed and threw caution to the wind. "Lady Darcy claimed she could draw elemental energies from this rock. I don't know how, but she did. That's why many called her a *seer,* while others called her an *enchantress.* They thought she possessed magical powers to see into the future. Noblemen and women came to her and paid her well for her predictions. This is how she met Ezra Stark who, surprisingly, believed in such things. The old man would never admit to it, but those two had a strange connection. I think he was actually in love with her or, at the very least, had a softness in his heart for the lady."

Kats eyes grew big at the mention of mysterious otherworldly circumstances surrounding the unusual ring. What had Lady Darcy known about its powers? Had she been a time traveler, too?

"Did she tell you about the future—your future and what she saw?" Kat asked.

Rem closed his eyes a not wanting to go there. There were things Lady Darcy had told him as a young lad he hadn't fully understood. Fantastic things. While he hadn't thought much about it in the passing years, it got him remembering the sealed letter she had penned to Ezra before stowing him away on the old man's ship. Rem had never read it. It might still be buried away in Ezra's personal papers.

Instead, of answering outright, Rem hedged: "Lady Darcy talked about lots of things that never made sense. Yet, she said she told me that she had a dream to fashion a signet ring for me out of the original rock, and she did. It's my lucky talisman. I've never taken it off."

Kat's head was spinning, her thoughts going in all directions. Never taken it off? Well, he must have eventually done so to have it show up during her time. Would it have been taken off upon his death? Death, especially his, was not something she wanted to contemplate right now. Kat pushed the thought to the back of her mind and focused instead on the present. So, the ring was his good luck charm, his talisman. This she understood. She was sure that she had lost their match last night because she didn't have her favorite gold locket with her. A meteorite talisman might be ten times stronger than *her* good-luck piece. Yet the universe had managed to compensate her loss in other more delightful ways. A night of unlimited sensual pleasure would certainly count as one of them—and that had been handed to her in spades.

Unfortunately, Kat didn't have access to an internet search engine to learn if meteorite iron possessed any mystical properties. There were too many missing pieces in this confounded puzzle with nowhere to turn for real answers. *Or was there?* Perhaps there was someone knowledgeable during this time who might know about such things. But whom?

Rem noted Kat was pursing her lips again—this time with a faraway look in her dancing green eyes. He pulled her closer, capturing her in his arms to bring her back to the present. "It's your turn," he reminded her. "You promised."

Kat sighed. She had more questions about Lady Darcy and why Rem was a stowaway on Ezra's ship if Lady Darcy was such good friends with the shipper. It didn't add up. But Rem was pressing her to fulfill her part of the truth question. She sighed once again, wondering where to begin. In her mind she kept hearing the song lyrics, "It's so crazy right now." What she was about to tell him was beyond crazy. He might not believe her, which was more likely than not.

Before beginning her strange tale, a soft knock at the master bedroom door was heard. A maid had brought up an early morning breakfast tray. Rem scrambled off the bed and called out to leave the tray outside the door. Quickly, he went over to his wardrobe armoire where he donned a silk dressing gown before going to retrieve their waiting meal. Behind him, Kat's surprised gasp caught him off-guard. Rem turned his head to see shock and confusion on her face.

Kat's reaction had been almost immediate. The silk garment Rem now wore was one of the men's items from the costume collection given to The Met by the legal firm of Kendle & Kendle in her time. The memory came crashing back of how she had smelled this very clothing item for signs of mildew, only to encounter the faint long ago hint of ocean and sea instead. She now knew it to be his scent—the scent of Remington Randall—the man who had managed to sexually send her to the stars.

~~*~~

Rem was certain there was something about his ring which Kat Branigan was hiding from him. She had promised to tell him what she knew and dammit if he wouldn't hold her to it, but something had caused her to clam up and inwardly retreat. The playful laughter that had been openly displayed just minutes earlier was quickly replaced with an all pervading silence.

Something had shifted in the time he had left their bed until the time he had walked to the bedroom door to head off his servant from coming in upon their little love nest. While he was mystified as to the cause of Kat's sudden change, his instincts told him not to press the matter. From experience, he had learned that women like to mull things over until they're good and ready to let you know what's really on their mind—or what in God's name they thought *you* had done wrong that needed righting. Under such circumstances he decided to wait her out until she was prepared to talk.

After last night's storm, there was land cleanup to see to and a pressing problem in the riding stables where one of his prize thoroughbred mares was requiring immediate attention. As a working horse farm and breeding stable for Long Island racetrack horses, there was an endless host of work that took up his and the farm staff's time.

Horses had been in Rem's blood since his early stableboy days working for Lady Darcy in London. Ships had been Ezra's dream; horses had been his. Shipping had been a means to fund his true love of the equestrian world. Rem looked forward to showing Kat the farm he was so proud of.

That morning, he had sent out a groom and stableboy on horseback to check the roads back to the city. The road directly to the ferry was still a muddy mess, the deep ruts not easily traversable without getting stuck. It was evident from the road condition report that Kat and he would, in all likelihood, be confined here until tomorrow. While he reveled in the thought of another day of her sharing his bed, he wasn't sure how Kat would take to being delayed from returning. He had left her in a strange mood.

Rem had instructed a maid servant to see to Kat's needs with that hot bath she craved, while he disappeared to take care of estate matters. Physical labor was something Rem found enjoyable and satisfying. It provided a welcome break from the financial world of maritime shipping that occupied most of his days. While he had managers, stewards, and accountants to see to the day-to-day running of his shipping line, he still liked to take a hands-on approach to all aspects of his thriving business. Ezra had taught him as much and the man had been a good teacher.

Which brought his thoughts back to Ezra's private papers currently stored away in his private vault in his Washington Square house. He had yet to go through all the man's personal files after his death—the loss being too acute at the time. Ezra had been a prolific writer. There were journals and stacks of correspondence with friends, business partners, and even Lady Portia Darcy. Perhaps there was something in the lot of it which he had overlooked and needed to know about. Up until now, he had practically forgotten about the cache the old man had left behind. Rem made a mental note to look into it upon his return.

~~*~~

Kat sank down into the large copper tub, submerging herself in the hot water hoping to cleanse both mind and body from all she had experienced within the last 24 hours. The sight of Rem's dressing gown being the same one delivered to The Met had thrown her for a loop. Could things get any stranger?

What she needed was a large whiteboard, the kind they used in mystery-solving movies to write down all the gathered facts and evidence in order to solve the case. There were similarities on the day she had been transported from her time to his time. First off—it was raining. But that could be mere coincidence. However, the ring, the unstained yellow dress from the donated collection she had arrived in his time wearing, and now Rem's dressing gown pointed to something more than mere coincidence.

Hearing Rem tell of the meteorite rock falling to Earth on a lunar eclipse, served to jog her memory further. Hadn't her friend Lexi said that there was a lunar eclipse on the same night they were to meet for their tournament? Did it somehow have significance?

Kat was stumped as to why she had arrived in 1835 on August 1, instead of April 1st in her time. It made absolutely no sense. Had there been a lunar eclipse on August 1,1835 as well? Who could she ask? Well, duh. She would ask Rem, of course.

After an hour languishing in the steamy bath water until it was now tepid, Kat finished her toilette smelling like the lavender soap she had generously used. She felt renewed and determined. A maid servant had laid out a fresh pair of breeches and shirt, a lad's size smaller, along with boots. That must have taken a bit of moxie for Rem to have instructed his servants to find something she would find more desirable in boy's wear. The dress she had arrived in was nowhere to be seen. Hopefully, it was being laundered.

Kat devoured the large tray of food that had been left for her. Eggs, haddock, tea, and even a stack of cornmeal pancakes with maple syrup— her favorite. They were just like the flapjacks her mom used to make on Sunday mornings as an end-of-week treat. After last night she was running on empty. Never-ending sex with a Greek God required plenty of nourishment. Her cheeks turned crimson just thinking about it, sending quivers zinging to nether regions. Enough, already! Kat needed to find Rem and get some answers.

~~*~~

Rem was saddling up a white Arabian stallion when Kat entered the stables. After riding out the storm in their stalls, most of his thoroughbred horses had been let out to pasture that morning. Rem held back two of his prize Arabians, hoping Kat might join him for a morning ride to show her his land and the surrounding countryside.

"There you are," she called out, stopping just inside the stable door where she glued herself to the spot. She watched with wide eyes as Rem took the reins of two saddled horses and walked them towards her. Kat backed up against the tack room door, making like the pancakes she had just eaten that morning.

"I thought I would show you my ranch," Rem said, all smiles. "Come, let's ride together."

Kat's instant reaction to his offer made Rem stop dead in his tracks. She looked downright terrified, something he had yet to witness.

"You do know how to ride a horse, don't you?" he asked. "I figured since you do everything else so competitively well, you would want the chance to outrace me given the chance."

The chestnut mare snorted, causing the stallion to toss his head from side to side at the challenge. *HELL NO*, Kat thought! Not in a million years. She would ride Rem Randall from here to eternity and back, but not his damned horse.

Kat licked her lips nervously. "I think it's better if you ride alone," she replied. "Horses don't generally fancy me."

Rem stared at her as if she had just announced the sky was falling. "C'mon Kat. That's utter nonsense. These two here are the finest bred and trained Arabians. They're highly intelligent, sound, and will respond to whatever command you give them."

These were racehorses, not old gray mares. She hated being scared, but it was sending shivers of fear throughout her body. "I said, NO!" she shouted at him. "No means No!"

Rem raised both eyebrows, stunned at her overreaction. He frowned but remained thoughtful. "Don't tell me the brave and bold Kat Branigan is scared of a horse?"

She tried to utter a convincing *Fuck No,* but no words came out of her gaping mouth. Instead, a flood of memories spilled forth, paralyzing her from moving. It was hard for Kat to admit to anyone that yes, horses, of any kind, even an old gray mare, terrified her. This new life she found herself thrust into kept challenging her comfort zone. She had managed it and hid it well up until today but now felt totally vulnerable.

She was certain that Rem's Zeus-size horses could smell her heightened fear a mile away. They would either charge or run her over the second they got the chance. She would die right here in 1835, and no one would ever be the wiser of what had become of her. It was an irrational thought, and she knew it; but there is nothing rational about fear. Strong emotions raged to the surface. Tears welled up in her eyes.

Rem was stunned. A crying female was unnerving to any man, but over the years he had had plenty of experience with such incidents. He did the only thing he could do under the circumstances, which wasn't much. He tied the horses' reins firmly to a stall post, then went over to Kat and wrapped his arms around her letting her cry against his work shirt.

The floodgates, which must have been dammed up for some time, finally broke free. Within seconds Kat was simultaneously sobbing and trying to apologize for her emotional meltdown. He just held her closer, his hand patting her back trying to comfort her.

He vividly remembered the very first day he spotted her on the docks. A pitiful-looking creature she was, with drenched hair and bonnet, her clothes mud-splattered from passing carriages and an expression which appeared completely lost. But he was surprised to learn the hard way that she was a little fighter from the physical trouncing she had given him. Then and now were the only times he had seen her let down her strong-woman persona and show her vulnerable side. Rem suddenly felt an overwhelming need to rescue her—once again.

"It's okay, Kat," he assured, his lips pressed against her hair. "You don't have to ride today or ever if you don't want to."

She sniffled against his shirt. He waited before finally asking: "Do you want to tell me what happened?"

Her voice trembled remembering. "I can't erase an old memory that still haunts me. I know it's silly, but I just can't. I was once thrown from a horse and almost paralyzed a few years ago," she admitted, her words spilling out, unable to hold them back.

"I was in Egypt at the time, and I really wanted to tour an ancient temple deep in the desert, far from any paved road. The only way to get there was either by camel or horse—and there were no camels available. I'm not an experienced rider. I never *have* been. I told my guide this, but he didn't understand. They gave me a spirited Arabian mare to ride as they had nothing else available. I should have said 'no' right off, but I didn't. I figured if I took it slow, everything would be okay. After all, the distance was only over desert sand. But Arabians are born and bred to run, not walk in the sands, which I soon learned.

"Halfway to the temple this riderless white Arabian stallion came charging across the desert sands headed straight for my horse and my guide's horse. It totally spooked my mare, which caused her to rear up and throw me off. My horse then continued to rear up mauling the head of the charging stallion with her hooves. It left ugly bloody gashes on his forehead. Hooves were coming down everywhere and I had to roll and crawl away as fast as I could, or I would have been stomped on. I was terrified. The horses scattered in all directions and fled, leaving myself and two others stranded in the desert without help. I was in real pain. I broke a leg in the fall and landed up having to do physical therapy for several months. Seeing your two Arabians brought it all back."

Kat wiped her nose with her hand. Rem produced a handkerchief from his pocket and handed it to her. "I haven't been back on a horse since then. It scares the bejesus out of me," she confessed.

"I'm really sorry that happened to you," he said, rubbing her back.

Rem knew horse behavior and understood what had happened. He would wager the mare had been in heat and the stallion was ready for some action, but the mare was not willing to comply, which was sometimes the case. From years of experience breeding horses, Rem knew the mare always set the tone and, much like their human counterparts, a stallion's courting style and temperament were a significant factor. Mares were known to kick oafish suitors. Breeding was a tricky business no matter what the species. Kat shouldn't have been given a horse in heat in the first place. But that's not what she needed to hear right now. The damage and accompanying fear had already taken its toll.

One of his groomsmen picked that moment to return to the stables to wash down a horse he had been working with in one of the ranch's round pens. Clearly embarrassed, Kat backed away from him, looking for an escape route. Rem quickly instructed the man to unsaddle the two reined horses and let them graze. He turned them both around and made for the other end of the stable's breezeway. Riding would have to wait. Right now, he needed to distract Kat from her vivid memories. He grabbed her hand and whisked them away from the stable. Together they walked across a rolling green field, until they arrived at a shady poplar tree where they plopped down against its sturdy trunk.

"Are you okay?" he finally asked.

"Yes. No." She sighed wearily. "I don't know what got into me."

Kat knew exactly what had gotten into her—Rem Randall and 1835. She turned to him and bluntly asked: "August 1—the day I first met you on the docks, was there a full moon lunar eclipse on that day?"

The out-of-the-blue question took him by total surprise, like everything else the woman did. They had gone from dealing with her fear of horses to lunar eclipses. "No. Had there been such a lunar event, my ship captains would have to had to adjust for higher tides and stronger currents and I would have known."

"Oh," she said clearly disappointed, thinking aloud. "Hmm. Then what's the significance of that day? I left my time on April 1 and landed up here on August 1. A four month time span must mean something."

Rem chuckled, hearing her thoughts. "Maybe it was because it was my birthday. You were my birthday present. The kind I least expected."

Her head whipped around, excited by this new bit of information. Rem's birthday was August 1?! The man was a Leo, a fire sign, like herself. Born on July 31, she had missed her birthday by one day when she traveled to his time. But then again, she hadn't been born yet, so it didn't matter. This one degree separation in birthdates could mean something, but she was dammed if she knew what it was. Lexi would know such things. Lexi was an astrological junkie. Her friend had known about the lunar eclipse that day when she had been clueless as to what was happening in the heavens. As far as Kat was concerned, it was just another day in her busy New York life.

Kat lay back in the grass, staring up at the blue sky. "I am so fucked!" she proclaimed to the universe at large.

Rem found her statement amusing, thinking she was referring to their sexual escapade of the night before. But he hadn't forgotten that it was long past for her to come clean about other matters. There would be no escaping her time of truth. He laid down next to her, propping his head up with one arm to more closely study her. Her eyes were closed, trying to shut the world out, but he would have none of it.

"Kat, look at me," he instructed.

She opened her eyes and turned slightly to see that Rem was serious and resolute.

"You claim you're from the future," he began. "But not much of what you've expressed thus far makes any sense. I've been patient, but now I'm holding you to your promise for helping you open a bank account. You need to tell me what brought you here."

"You'll think I'm mad or crazy," she proclaimed on a loud exhale.

Rem didn't bat an eye. "I already think you're crazy–wonderfully crazy," he stated with droll amusement before getting serious once again. "The roads are still too muddy to travel, so it looks like we have another day here. I'm not going to let you leave until I hear the truth."

It came as no surprise to hear they would be delayed another day. It was as if the universe was deliberately conspiring to keep them captive. "You're really going to hold me hostage if I don't tell you?" she asked, testing him.

"If I have to, Kat. Would that be so bad?"

No, it wouldn't be, she thought with a secret smile.

"Alright," she sighed, surrendering to what was to come.

If he wanted all the details she would give them to him until his head was spinning from overload. Kat cleared her throat and started from the beginning of that fateful April 1st day in 21st century New York which started with a torrential rainstorm. She set the stage for her tale, telling him that she lived alone in a highly desirable Brooklyn Heights brownstone that had been in her family for decades, of which she now owned.

She told him that every day she went to work using an extensive underground subway system on rails which was fast and efficient. From Brooklyn she took the Lexington Avenue subway line to 86th Street, then did a westbound walk to Fifth Avenue, and then southbound to 82nd where she worked at The Metropolitan Museum of Art, a large structure where priceless treasures were displayed. She explained that horse-drawn carriages no longer existed except for tourist rides in Central Park. A few times she paused to explain the various transportation modes available during her time—gas-guzzling buses, electric cars and bicycles, scooters, and motorcycles. He seemed perplexed to learn that tall ships were rarely used for fast travel and those that were used were mammoth cruise ships the size of extra-large floating hotels. She omitted the existence of airplanes, space shuttles, and supersonic transports or they would have been there all day and would never have gotten to the true story of how she arrived in his time.

Kat was painstakingly patient in answering all his questions as she painted a vivid picture of her modern world. He mulled it over while making mental notes. Rem asked her to describe The Met, what it contained, and what her job consisted of. He seemed quite fascinated, even impressed, by the scientific methods she and her staff employed in their costume preservation methods.

"And you went to school for such things?" he inquired.

"Yes," she replied. "I have a master's degree in Textile Conservation with an expertise in historical 19th century costumes. It was the silk dressing gown you put on this morning that I recognized…"

Rem inclined his head. "What do you mean?"

"It came in a large patron donation on the morning of April 1st. Twenty men's outfits and twenty women's garments, all from 1835 and in impeccable condition. Your dressing gown was one of the items in the collection. I would recognize its unique style and pattern anywhere."

Rem's next question was astute. "Who was the donor of this collection?"

"I was told that it was arranged by the law firm of Kendle & Kendle," she replied. "I never learned the patron's name. I was late that morning getting to work due to the rain and never got to meet their representative or the patron."

Rem remained stoically silent. He stared off, his thoughts a million miles away.

"You know this firm?" she questioned.

Rem shook his head, changing the subject. "Tell me everything that happened after you opened this costume donation."

This was the hardest part for her. The part about donning the stained yellow dress, the beckoning mirror, the earthquake that shook The Met and subsequent power loss and, of course, finding and putting on the strange-looking ring—which now appeared to be Rem's ring unless there were others just like it out there.

"It all happened so fast. One minute, I was in my office examining the ring and dress. The next minute I found myself on South Street Seaport docks wearing a pristinely clean yellow dress with no ring on my finger. I thought it had fallen off somewhere on the harbor front."

Rem mentally scrambled to put the pieces together. No wonder she had been groveling on her hands and knees when he first spotted her. She had been searching for the lost ring. The whole story sounded utterly fantastic. Did he believe her? While some elements rang true, others he would need to look further into. Until then, he would play his cards close to the chest. And for reasons he was not yet ready to divulge, he would keep Kat Branigan close as well. What he was about to do was totally out of character for a man of his standing, but the world be damned, for it made not one iota of difference to him. He was captain of his own ship and would steer it in whichever damned direction he pleased. Kat might not be a relationship bed of roses, but in that moment his mind was clearly made up.

"And you're eager to return to your time?" he asked. "Even if you could leave right this very moment?"

Kat frowned, wondering what Rem had up his sleeve. Was he reconsidering? Would he hand over his ring and send her on her merry way? She had been enjoying their 24-hour sex-a-thon a little too much. Perhaps one more romp in the hay with him would be enough to sate her desire for the man. Tomorrow would be a much better day to travel forward in time.

Kat's next words didn't sound nearly as convincing as intended. "Well, yes, of course I want to go back. I can't stay here forever. I have responsibilities, just like you do. I need to return to my time and my life there. It's important."

"Why?" he asked simply.

Kat was at a loss for words. "Well, because it is..." Kat stopped in mid-thought. Rem's face had softened considerably. He leaned in, looking to kiss her, but instead softly caressed her cheek. It unnerved her. She needed to stay strong. She would not and could not fall for this man!

"Stay," he whispered, running his thumb over her lower lip. "If you really must leave, I'll find a way to help you if I can." He exhaled knowing his next words would be the hardest part. "I would like you to stay with me until that time. I can provide for whatever you need. Let me do this for you, Kat."

Rem's offer shocked her. While he looked to be sincere, something felt off. Right now, she was merely a shiny new toy for him. Unique for the moment. But in all honesty she knew this was a man who could easily procure willing sexual partners anywhere. He didn't need to sacrifice his bachelorhood for her.

Kat sat up straight, protectively hugging her knees to her chest. Her mind was caught in a maelstrom. Was Rem actually serious? Was this a marriage or more likely a mistress proposal or something else entirely? The thought of being a kept mistress in the year 1835 didn't bother her one bit, despite knowing that society would probably scorn and ridicule her as a woman of loose morals. Did she care what they thought? Hell, no. Once she left this time she would never see any of them again. They would be footnotes in history.

Kat temporarily pushed the thought aside of Rem merely being a footnote in her personal history, which she might not even remember when she got back. What was uppermost on her mind right now was a far more disturbing thought that she couldn't give voice to. At least not yet.

Rem sat up, intently waiting for her answer.

Kat swallowed hard and looked him straight in the eye. "Absolutely, not," she declared with a note of finality. "Never in a million years would I do anything so utterly foolish."

PART 2

Chapter 8

Nothing is ever written in stone, not even the best avowed intentions. One week later Kat Branigan had to eat her words when she became the new mistress of No. 8 Washington Square North. Some of life's errors of judgment result in dire change. This happened to be one of those times, for living with Rem Randall was indeed life changing on numerous fronts. Like she really needed any more change in her life to make it any more confusing.

Kat had made the ultimate mistake of agreeing to play another blasted billiards match with Rem Randall. The stakes were for his ring, which is all she really wanted in the first place, and he damn well knew it, so he had her over a barrel on that front. Their game had been another close match, but as fate would have it she lost again, resulting in her living with him in his Old Row house. For this wager, she forfeited her freedom.

Trying to regain the upper hand, she insisted on separate bedrooms, as he had plenty of them. She desperately needed to establish some sort of boundary for fear that she would be easily swallowed up by his powerful presence. Rem had that effect on people. When he talked, people listened.

Kat considered herself an independent woman who needed no man to take care of her. Rem merely chuckled knowingly at her protests. She wasn't fooling him one bit. He merely shrugged and laconically told her: "As you wish" which was the 19th century version of saying, "whatever."

They took meals together, discussing everything from her time period which fascinated him to no end. Pillow talk was often replaced with table talk. It was like Rem was taking an immersive crash course in the future of the world. He took in everything, analyzed it, and questioned her on every facet involved. His mind was as sharp as a knife, his memory for detail even keener.

They ferociously played billiards against each other every night betting on anything that took their fancy. Kat's separate bedrooms rule disappeared after the very first day. Foolish her. Rem was quickly becoming her lifeline to navigating his world. Despite their differences, they continued to fuck like rabbits in heat. The servants were discreet, but she saw their exchanged knowing looks. They believed that the red-headed woman was not only strange in many ways but had somehow bewitched their employer.

Rem discovered that he preferred staying home at nights. With Kat he didn't crave outside sport or entertainment. Life with Kat, although trying at times, was never boring. He knew all too well that she might disappear back to her world at any time—possibly forever. He was determined to make the best of whatever time they had left, realizing that he would miss her once she was gone.

Kat was so bold and fearless at times (except for horses), that he worried about her. She preferred to wear men's attire, and he knew there was talk going around, which he tried to ignore. It didn't seem to faze her, but he couldn't say the same for others. There was the matter of her safety if she continued to want to traipse out alone in the city when he wasn't with her. He contracted to have one of his security people accompany her despite her arguments to the contrary. On this front he would not compromise or back down.

If everything seemed idyllic between them it wasn't always. Some of their ideologies differed due to the nature of the time. One issue in particular stood out like a sore thumb—the issue of his company and the British East India Company exporting opium from Turkey and "pushing it on the Chinese people," as Kat termed it, in order to establish a trade monopoly on China's silk and tea products. The subject always sparked serious debate.

Kat lorded her knowledge of the course of history over his limited here and now view.

Rem dutifully listened to her rants, but it was evident that he thought the profits were so large and his investors so vast that he held firm to his business practices.

Kat felt like she was a small David going up against a big Goliath. Could one actually change the future—even if just a little? Perhaps if she was stuck in this time, she might at least attempt to diffuse the impact of the nature of these drugs on an unsuspecting society who were clueless as to its future negative effects.

"You don't understand," Rem tried to laconically point out.

She glared at him through narrow eyes. "Stop being a condescending prick," she shot back. "I understand and know a hell of a lot more than you think."

Rem hmphed. He secretly enjoyed watching Kat get all riled up, her eyes shooting daggers at him while her pretty little mouth spouted salty words. There was real passion in her whatever the subject matter. But she was missing the greater benefits of what the drug provided. He tried to enlighten her.

"The medicinal properties of opium provide miraculous relief to so many pain suffers," he uttered, lighting up a cheroot cigar, which he knew bothered her. The woman was against smoking as well. Thank God she wasn't also against copulation, he thought ruefully.

"Ugh! That's disgusting, Rem," she commented, wrinkling up her nose at the acrid tobacco smell.

Rem calmly puffed away, brushing aside her disdain. "All apothecary tonics now contain a form of opium. You can't tell me that's not a good thing. This is not something words can stop the progress of. Even the physicians call opium, 'God's own medicine'."

Kat was no fool. She knew all about the usefulness of opiate narcotics. Introduced in Europe as "laudanum" or in black pill form as the "stones of immortality" it quickly went from medicinal to recreational use in no time. Opium was made into morphine; morphine was then manufactured into heroin to combat the effects of opium addiction, which ironically only caused addiction to soar. Eventually a derivative of morphine would be synthesized into the lethal drug called *fentanyl*. Kat had known too many people in New York who had succumbed to this dangerous street drug.

She exhaled, feeling like she was spinning her wheels and dealing with El Chapo the drug lord. "You're just being greedy, self-centered, and narcissistic. Where is your integrity and morality?"

That made Rem pause in mid-puff. Those were words he had never been accused of by any woman, especially a lover. The woman was brazen for challenging his business sense and his *integrity*. He would have much preferred taking her to bed then sparring it out over drugs and his China trade.

Kat recognized she had managed to make a slight chink in his armor and continued. "Someday China will get their revenge for our introducing opium to their people and enslaving them to the drug. They will wait it out until they can make a synthetic version of the drug called *fentanyl*, and then they will flood our streets with this destructive drug to get back at us. It will enslave our citizens and turn millions into drug addicts, just like opium shippers and traders are doing to their people during your time. Babies and children will become addicted too. It will take out generations of those between 18-45 years of age. It is not 'God's own medicine,' as you call it, but a curse. There's not much time. War will be coming very soon."

Now the talk of war caught Rem's attention. It could financially devastate him and countless others. Some of the things Kat had pointed out were true so far, but he rather enjoyed watching her debate abilities and those flashing green eyes of hers. He knew there was a British dependence on opium for medicine and that recreational use was at an all-time high. They were importing approximately 22,000 pounds or more per year of the poppy seed drug. The demand kept rising. However, war would quickly put a damper on such trade routes and profits. Rem was a businessman first and foremost. War was good for some, but not for him.

They had just finished dinner and were enjoying a fine cognac together in the drawing room before retiring for the night, when this heated conversation had arisen. Rem leaned slightly forward in his high-back chair, suddenly all ears.

"You say that the U.S. will be at war? With whom?"

Kat shook her head. "In 1839 the Chinese will order all foreign traders to surrender their opium. The British will send their warships, sparking the 1st Opium War of 1839."

"The first?" Rem questioned.

She nodded. "Yes. The British will defeat the Chinese and China will be forced to cede Hong Kong to them. But a second Opium War will restart in 1856."

While 1839 was not far off, 1856 was far enough in the future. However, in his business you had to read the signs. "Why the second war?" he asked.

"Britain and France will both get involved against China who will attempt to stop the spread of this drug on their shores. China will be defeated once again. The victors will force them to legalize opium and to increase production as a condition of war."

"So, it all turns out well," Rem surmised.

Kat snorted. "Of course not! Opium and heroin trafficking explodes. Illegal smuggling thrives. The U.S. tries to impose a tax on opium, followed by Congress banning it, but it's like a broken dam you can't fix. Addiction becomes a worldwide epidemic. Our intelligence agencies begin trading in opium with warlords to destabilize governments, cause wars, and wreak havoc on the world. And China is smiling through it all. They become the leader in opium production, marketing heroin for all the world's drug cartels, and amassing a fortune to build up their country while it destroys other countries and millions of lives. And they did it all by not having to fire a single shot. This is what you are setting in motion."

Rem frowned. He sat back pondering her words. Could such a thing really happen, like this Great Fire she claimed would happen at the end of the year, wiping out lower Manhattan? Was there anything good she could foretell?

~~*~~

A week later Rem was gone, having set sail for business in Canton, China. Kat refused to go with him. Her fear of horses was one thing, but she couldn't bring herself to admit she also had a serious seasickness affliction. Long distance travel by boat was an exercise in stomach torture, something she avoided like the plague.

The Old Row house felt empty without him. She busied herself with a long "To-Do List" she was determined to tackle now that she was a woman alone on a mission. Sometimes in the early morning she would walk across the street to Washington Square Park to stroll and do some serious thinking. She longed to run a few laps around the park, but wherever she went in men's attire, she saw the covered gasps and withering looks. The women were especially scornful, or perhaps envious, she wasn't quite sure.

The men usually looked on in interest, sometimes even staring as they watched her retreating derriere in form-fitting breeches move past them. It was obvious what *they* were thinking. Which is why Rem had assigned Frank Calvin to her protection, whether she chose to dress like a lady or not. A former constable, Calvin was eager to please his employer and was paid well to look after her. At times, his dogging behavior irritated her to no end, but they soon came to a working agreement.

When Kat wanted his protection in male-dominated domains, Calvin walked by her side, otherwise he walked several paces behind her. She knew he carried a pistol under his jacket and a knife in his right boot. In her opinion it was overkill, but Rem had insisted. Kat was learning that there were some things you did not argue about with Rem Randall once his mind was set, and this was one of them.

In the early morning she often occupied a certain bench in Washington Square Park. It was a good spot for deep thought. She could look across the street at the Old Row houses, admiring their beauty, knowing some would no longer be around during her time, while others would be added. It was a place of reflective calm and solitude.

Calvin almost drew his pistol the day a stranger decided to sit down next to her. The well-dressed gentleman, barely in his 20's, stared ahead at the Greek Revival architecture of the homes on the Old Row and attempted to venture a neighborly conversation.

"This is one of my favorite spots," he remarked. "I've seen you before. Do you live nearby?"

Having grown up a street-savvy New Yorker, such personal information gathering by a total stranger was usually a red flag inside or outside a bar. But before she could reply, he quickly added. "I'm going to build a grand house on this street someday."

She couldn't help but agree. "You should. It will be promising investment property—worth a million someday."

His head turned curiously towards her. "Is that so?"

"Yes. Mark my words," she stated. "I happen to know such things."

"And how is that?"

Kat shrugged. "I can see into the future."

The man seemed to seriously consider her air of certainty. "My name is John Jay," he informed her extending his hand with a smile. "And what is yours?"

Behind her, lounging against a nearby tree, Calvin was ready to spring into action. Kat waved him off. Instincts told her that the guy on the bench, probably a college student, looked to be quite harmless.

"Nice to meet you Mr. Jay," she said shaking his hand. "I'm Kat Branigan and I'm new to the Old Row."

Jay? A light bulb went off in her head. She pivoted to face him head on. "Are you any relation to *that* Jay family? You know—Chief Justice Jay and the second New York Governor?"

"That was my grandfather," he said matter-of-factly. "He died a few years ago."

Holy shit. Kat could barely contain the excitement bubbling up inside her ready to explode. This was a serendipitous and fortuitous meeting. John Jay II, while only a young man at the time, would indeed build a home on the Old Row in the future just as he was envisioning. That and so much more. This was the opportunity of a lifetime to connect directly with a future leader.

"Do you go to Columbia College?" she asked, already knowing the answer.

He nodded. "Yes, ma'am. I'm studying law. I graduate next year."

"Do you have plans after that?' she inquired.

He shrugged. "I'll set up a law practice like my father and grandfather before me."

Kat knew he was on the right track. Should she give him a suggestion to point him in the right direction? She didn't need to bother, for he was already thinking along those lines.

"You said you can see into the future," he tentatively began, hesitating before continuing. "Are you able to see anything in my future?"

He looked abashed by his bold question. Kat could see he was practically holding his breath with curiosity.

"That is, if you can," he added hopefully.

Kat took a while, closing her eyes to look more psychically authentic. "Well, I'm seeing that you should focus your legal practice on civil rights. Particularly anti-slavery."

He nodded. "It angers me that Jackson's postmaster general prohibits anti-slavery literature from being delivered to the South."

Kat had forgotten about that. President Andrew Jackson had been a staunch slave owner, having made many enemies for his views, which was one of many reasons an assassination attempt had been made against him that very year.

"Well, this is a human rights area where you can excel and make a name for yourself," Kat pointed out. "In fact, your efforts will take you to the highest courts in the land to argue such cases. Eventually you will be instrumental in organizing a new political party—the Republican Party—the party of anti-slavery. This will bring you into international ministerial circles and even higher offices, bringing you wealth and opportunities beyond what your grandfather and father accomplished."

Okay. She could see from his face that she might have gone a tad too far and blown him away. His mouth dropped open. He was staring at her almost bug-eyed. Someday in the mid 1950's a John Jay College for Criminal Justice would come into being, named after his famous grandfather, so his name would be long remembered in New York history. But she didn't need to add this additional fact.

She waited, drawing out the moment. There was more. Something really quite important as far as she was concerned personally, but there was the chance that revealing too much might somehow mess with the future. She decided to throw caution to the wind and just go for it.

"I see that you have an important mission in this lifetime that won't kick in until the second half of your life sometime around the age of 50."

John Jay leaned in closer as Kat's voice became a whisper. "During the summer of 1866 you will be called to France to speak at an event celebrating the 90th birthday of the United States. You will accept it and talk about New York being one of the greatest cities in the world, but how it lacks the one important thing all other big cities in Europe have..."

Kat noted he was nodding his head, waiting for her to tell him the punchline. "...and you will suggest to these men of major influence and wealth to build a national museum of art for this city. A museum rivalling all others. This is your legacy John—to build The Metropolitan Museum of Art."

There. She had laid out to her founder boss what his historical job would be. It would hopefully cement the foundation of her job future. The land The Met would be built on was currently rocky and swampy with nothing beyond farms and small settlements. The only accessible route up there and to parts further north was Kingsbridge Road which ran the length of Manhattan.

Kat had made Calvin drive the carriage northward to take a look at the future home of her employer. She secretly harbored the idea that if she returned to the exact spot, a portal in time and space would miraculously open and she could return to her time. However, such a notion proved futile. It was nothing more than hopium on her part.

The exact spot where the Museum would be built was hard to pinpoint. The area had yet to be made into an urban park and the concept for Central Park hadn't even been envisioned. But John Jay didn't know anything of this and what she had divulged would be more than enough to get the ball rolling on his end.

"And I will be able to accomplish such a project?" Jay prompted.

"Yes, and you will be remembered throughout history, even centuries to follow, for having done so," she added for good measure.

The next day John Jay returned with several friends and so began the Kat Branigan secret "Future Forecasting Group." A week later he suggested they move the group to Fraunces Tavern, an old multi-story yellow-brick building on the corner of Pearl and Broad Street where, in the 1700's, it became the favorite watering hole for the Sons of Liberty and the revolutionary Founding Fathers. It looked nothing like the renovated landmark museum building it was in her time. Kat longed for a camera to document all she was witnessing. It was times such as these that she wished her history-loving father was here with her to see it all for himself. Whatever would he think of her strange otherworldly plight?

With Kat's new group leader status, it was no surprise when she turned psychic celebrity overnight. Suddenly she was surrounded by gentlemen of all ages wanting her future advice and slipping her coins or tips when she did. She could have become instantly rich, but for her it filled the boredom felt from Rem being gone and having his big old house to tool around in alone with only a few servants. She had to have something to do to fill her days besides sightseeing and, having a keen photographic memory, it would be wasteful not putting her knowledge to beneficial use. Her male admirers seemed to agree. There was only one rule she stuck to in case it messed up her return to the future. No mention of The Great Fire of 1835 would ever pass her lips. Telling Rem might have already changed history.

Her entourage fondly dubbed her "Madam K" (despite her preference for pants). With the new moniker came an elaborate back story created on the fly. She was a military widow of several years, which gave her social stature—hence the "Madam" address. More importantly it gave her license to be unaccompanied by a chaperone in the presence of men. Due to her true age of 28 and the times she was currently residing in, she was considered not only a spinster, but an old maid. The grieving widow story gave her an excuse as to why she had not remarried. It was okay for widows to discreetly have affairs or sexual liaisons, just not chaste single women—which she was not. Instead of being labeled an unmarried harlot, she opted for the label of horny widow with second-sight abilities instead.

The attention and respect she received was flattering to say the least. Some of the older men proposed marriage to her outright to help her forget her grief. Thank God for Calvin. He attended to her, often standing behind her like a loyal magician's assistant. It was obvious that he was fascinated with all she revealed yet never failed to warn her that she was playing a dangerous game and that Mr. Randall would not be pleased to learn of her new career endeavor. Well, Mr. Randall was nowhere in sight—off enjoying Canton, Peking Duck, and who knew what else.

Kat was carving out her own little niche in a man's world and enjoying herself. The women of this time, mostly a suppressed, male-dominated lot, didn't quite know what to make of her bold fearless style and manner. But behind closed doors, Kat bet they had plenty to say and not all of it nice.

Not everyone in their future forecasting group would go down in the annals of history like John Jay, so Kat kept her predictions primarily focused on the rapid growth of New York, the coming wars, the future of banking, evolving fashion trends and, of course, valuable real estate development. That was more than enough to keep her followers enthralled and ecstatic.

Invites to private dinner parties and social events started pouring in, quickly marking her as the notorious red-headed "Belle of New York"—the one that had beat Remington Randall at billiards and had taken him for a bundle. Kat preferred to not become a part of early American history by making a name for herself. She turned down all the offers, preferring to remain the mystery woman in the background.

For centuries, celebrated women throughout history had openly dressed in men's trousers, some disguising themselves as males, while others openly displayed their feminine gender. Kat had nothing to prove by opting for men's pants. In her time, she lived in black pencil leg pants and tight jeans. No, her primary reason was that men's clothes were ever so much more comfortable. Once again, she realized why so many women had consumption during these early times. Laced corsets and hard whalebone stays left one unable to fully breathe or eat. Having a small, compressed waist was not worth the pressure endured on one's internal organs or the deformity perpetrated on one's ribs.

Kat took no money for her knowledge but exchanged it in the form of valuable favors and tips instead. It troubled her that her advertisement in The New York Herald trying to locate her great-great-great-great-grandparents had not borne any fruit. A group member offered his firm's private detective. She took it and in two days' time he located Colleen and Duncan Branigan of County Galway, Dublin, now living in the overcrowded, dangerous slums of the Five Points neighborhood. She was still debating on what approach to take—a plan which would positively impact her own future.

~~*~~

That night, Kat fought chronic restlessness. Ideas kept bouncing around in her head about what was safe and what wasn't regarding contact with her ancestors. She had yet to approach them or set up a meeting date, afraid they might refuse. The prospect of seeing them in the flesh filled her with unknown anxiety. She certainly couldn't tell them she was a relative from the future. They would think she was batshit crazy.

Kat tossed and turned in Rem's big old bed, where despite clean sheets his scent still lingered. There were some nights she could almost feel him spooned up against her and wondered if he was thinking of her as well. As mistress of his house, his bed was now hers. It was where she preferred to sleep. His belongings, his clothes, and even his personal toiletries provided an odd sense of comfort. In many ways he was her lifeline, whether there or not.

Finding the prospect of sleep futile, Kat donned one of Rem's silk dressing gowns and barefooted down to his library study hoping to find an enjoyable book to read. Quite frankly, she had no idea where his literary interests lie but was surprised to see that many of the leather-bound books on his shelves were old classics: *Oliver Twist, The Hunchback of Notre Dame, The Last of the Mohicans.* There was a good assortment of biographical adventure stories, as well as conquering heroes and the likes which appeared worn from several reads, telling her these were his favorites. On another shelf she found a sprinkling of poetry, philosophy, and maritime books and charts.

Kat pulled out a copy of *Confessions of an English Opium Eater* and realized Rem knew damn well the repercussions from the drug. People were already writing about it. She plopped herself down in his big brown leather tufted desk chair, feeling like the master of the house in a room that emanated Rem's energy. She tightened the dressing gown tie around her waist and settled back for a long read.

She suspected if he were here right now he would shoo her out of his private domain. The man could be territorial when protecting what was his. Curiosity struck causing her to momentarily set the book aside. Was there anything in this room which could tell her more about Remington Randall, that she didn't already know? She suddenly found herself waging an internal struggle between right and wrong.

Kat knew only too well what Rem kept hidden inside his pants, but what he kept inside his desk drawers was a mystery. Did he have any terrible secrets? It was wrong to invade his personal space, but somehow she managed to convince herself she might want to write down some of her thoughts and his desk would provide the necessary writing materials to do so. Would it be so bad if she opened a few desk drawers and poked around?

His desktop was neat and orderly with only a bronze inkwell and quill pen holder. She smiled, picturing him wielding his quill like the stroke of a knife. His bold, flourishing signature on the bank note he had written her was so like the man himself.

Kat slid open a top right-hand drawer only to find stationery adorned with the insignia of the Eastern Star Line. Beside it was a wax stick and his personal seal, with two raised "R" initials stamped upon it signifying its owner, Remington Randall.

Another drawer contained blank sheets of parchment paper and a household account book for this month which she found rather interesting. The maintenance expenses for this house were not cheap, even for the time. There were servants' salaries, food and cleaning bills, house repairs, the stabling of his horses and carriages in the Square's back alley mews and much more. The list was quite extensive and detailed. Rem was definitely a numbers man.

One particularly expensive entry immediately caught her eye. Rem had recently purchased a new customized billiards table. This one had six pockets, was made of durable slate, and had a tournament size length of twelve feet. Her heart actually skipped a beat when she saw the enormous price tag.

Rem had actually taken it to heart when she promised to someday teach him how to play snooker. He had a good mind for details and had remembered her description to the tee of the type of table required. The date of the order had been made just prior to his leaving. Was it to be a surprise for her upon his return?

A warm glow spread throughout her being. What a charmer Rem Randall could be. Under his smooth, take-charge exterior, he was a real softie. She would keep the knowledge of his surprise a secret and when it came, act deliriously happy, which was what she was feeling at the moment.

She moved on to the bottom drawer only to find it was locked. Kat tugged on it in case it was stuck on the track, but it refused to budge. It was definitely locked. Sitting back in her chair, she stared at it debating what to do. Spurred to action she riffled through other drawers looking to see if there was a key. She found a ring of housekeys, but no key which fit the lock.

She had heard that some old desks had hidden spring mechanisms to hide valuables in, like a key, but her search produced nothing of the sort. Kat felt under each drawer, behind it, and still came up empty. This would have been the right time to give up and let it go, but she couldn't.

Picking a lock was not her forte, but she retrieved a metal hair pin from her hair, opened it wide to a right angle and wiggled it into the lock's mechanism. It took about 15 minutes to lift the tumblers using a second hair pin to jimmy them into the proper alignment—a trick she had once seen on a "how to" YouTube video but had never actually tried. She was more surprised than not to find that it actually worked.

Kat opened the drawer slowly in case there was some type of trip wire. It was a crazy notion but not out of the realm of possibility. She had been wise to exercise caution. Sitting atop a metal box was a bronze-barreled pistol which looked to be loaded. She gingerly moved it aside and pulled out the metal box underneath. It, too, was locked.

"You have got to be kidding me!" she uttered exasperated.

After coming this far, she was not about to give up so easily and repeated her painstaking lock-picking procedure. In the end her curiosity would do her in, but she would think about that later and threw caution to the wind. When the lock clicked open, she was disappointed to find it contained papers and nothing else.

As she studied each envelope, some sealed, some open, enormous guilt surged through her. Kat almost stuffed it all back in the box, immediately regretting such a blatant breach of Rem's personal matters. That is until she spotted the familiar name "Kendle" on one of the envelopes. To be exact—Braden Kendle, Attorney-at-Law, 35 Chambers Street, New York, New York.

Kat gasped in confusion. When she had revealed to Rem how the costume collection had been delivered during her time by a Kendle & Kendle LLP, he had said nothing. Her recollection was crystal clear. Rem had hidden from her the fact that he was not only familiar with the Kendle name but was in correspondence with them. Why?

With trembling hands, Kat opened the folded white parchment paper, whose dated envelope showed it had been delivered via courier prior to Rem's recent departure. What was written in a neat, elegant script was brief, but cryptic at best:

> *Dear Sir:*
> *We are in receipt of your explicit instructions on the delicate matter we recently discussed. We appreciate your continued generous patronage and will personally see to it that your wishes are discreetly carried out in a judicious and timely manner.*
> *Very Respectfully,*
> *Braden Kendle, Esquire*

What the hell? Kat stared out into space, buried in deep thought. Exactly what was this "delicate matter" to which Kendle was referring? "Continued" told her that theirs was an ongoing relationship. What were the odds that this was just an ongoing legal matter and had absolutely nothing to do with the costume delivery in her time?

Kat looked for other letters from Braden Kendle, but the metal box contained only one. Why would Rem lock it away? Did he fear she would snoop and find it? She examined the other papers in the box and turned pale when she saw one addressed from a Lady Portia Darcy to Ezra Stark, dated February 27, 1812:

My Beloved Ezra,

You must be livid right now at the very thought of a stowaway on your ship. The boy was my doing and I did so born out of an act of love. Forgive me for that. I am entrusting you with the care of this young, but intelligent 10-year-old lad you see before you. His name is Remington Randall, and I have come to know and love him as if he were ours.

I have seen into his future and know he is marked for remarkable things in your world, which is where he now belongs under your tutelage. You have always wanted a son, an heir, and now the heavens are smiling down upon you and making this possible. I am grateful to be able to make him my birthday present to you on your voyage home.

My heart is heavy with the news now on the horizon. I must warn you that in four months' time your country will declare war against Britain. I'm sure you are well aware of Britain's violation of U.S. maritime rights. This war will wreak unspeakable carnage, so be prepared. It will last for several years and take many lives. Blockades will be placed preventing trade between our countries as well as our visits, which deeply saddens me.

My dearest one—it comes with a heavy heart to know we may never see each other again in this lifetime, so it is imperative that I impart information to you which is crucial to the boy's future. I have enclosed a separate letter to be entrusted to Rem in his 33rd year of life. It is sealed and for his eyes only which, I trust, will explain everything. Do not worry, my love. You will be a fine father and dearly loved by your new son as I love you. Your legacy will live on through him.

I will always regret that I did not accept your marriage proposal made so many years ago, but I knew we were destined for different paths, despite our love and deep affection. I rest confident knowing I am providing you with this wonderful parting gift before you. Treasure him as he is pure of heart.

Your Devoted Love, Lady Portia Darcy

Kat sighed as she wiped a stray tear from her eye. It was a love letter and final goodbye. This had to be the letter which had saved the young stowaway from being tossed overboard—not that she believed anyone would actually do such a barbaric thing.

Rem had to have read this letter, but when? Recently? She shuffled through the papers looking for the personal letter Lady Darcy had penned to Rem to be opened in his… She paused, quickly doing the math. Born on August 1, 1802, *this* was his 33rd year!

The letter was not in the packet. She searched other drawers just in case but came up empty-handed. Where could it be?

Chapter 9

Rem was not on his way to Canton as Kat had been informed but bound instead for the English Channel. Last minute developments had forced him to change plans. The China negotiations would have to wait. The trip to Britain would require his immediate presence without proxy intermediaries becoming involved.

Time being of the utmost importance, Rem took his newest steam-powered acquisition, the *Lady Darcy,* on what would be her maiden transatlantic voyage. A faster ship, she would cut sailing time down from 30 days to 15. Being away from Kat too long made him more anxious than he cared to admit. If only she had agreed to come with him, he could keep an eye on her himself. The woman was painstakingly obstinate.

Rem had read and re-read Lady Darcy's letter to him so many times it was now committed to memory. What she had divulged defied logic on so many levels. Being a man of science, this pushed his boundaries of believability and acceptance. But as of late, there were just too many strange things surrounding the appearance of Kat which forced him to examine his beliefs more closely.

Scant days before setting sail, the 23-year-old unopened letter had been personally placed in his hands by the attorney Braden Kendle. Ezra had been wise to entrust the sealed letter into the attorney's care upon falling ill six years ago. By doing so, his benefactor had ensured that whatever happened to him, Rem would receive it when he turned thirty-three.

Kendle had been one of many of Ezra's personal attorneys, something Rem hadn't known. The Eastern Star Line's maritime business matters were handled by two other New York legal firms. So, while the name Kendle sounded vaguely familiar to him when Kat first mentioned it, it hadn't seemed significant at the time. Now it was uppermost in his mind.

What was contained in the sealed letter was astounding, bordering on incredible. While he knew Lady Darcy was a gifted seer, her words and tales from the past now made more sense to him. Like a loving mother, she had made sure that he led an unburdened life under the strong mentorship of Ezra Stark. This had allowed him to hone his inherent strengths and evolve as a man until destiny kicked in. Lady Darcy had spelled out everything she knew and seen concerning his future in this lengthy letter. The problem was what was he to do with her life-changing information?

Overnight a frenzied exchange of legal correspondence took place— right up until the time he sailed. Kendle was now his personal attorney and the knowledge of that would be kept strictly confidential. As more information became known, which was the reason for this sudden trip, the man would manage all of Rem's "delicate matters."

Rem hadn't breathed a word to Kat about what he now knew, especially with his leaving so shortly after taking her into his home. But he knew the time would come. In so many ways the past week had been idyllic for him, despite their differences. If she were to learn what he had deliberately failed to tell her, she would be seething with righteous indignation. The woman was a hellcat both in and out of bed. Her passions ran deep. So did her ideals. His only hope was that she managed to stay out of trouble during his absence.

To assure that, as well as to see to her personal safety, he was counting on his man Frank Calvin to protect her from such influences. The mere mention of him providing a security detail for her was something she vehemently protested, arguing that she valued her "freedom and independence" and that he was being a "male chauvinist," "a sexist," and that she could take care of herself.

"I have defense skills you know nothing about," she informed him with a sly smile.

Rem just bet she did. He wouldn't argue that point, but he still flatly refused to back down. Kat's unwavering insistence on wearing men's attire marked her as a woman of interest — a visible target. He knew damn well that other men were imagining what was under those tight breeches, that firm little ass of hers, like he had when he first encountered her sporting his figure-revealing clothes.

It was ironic that for a woman who claimed to be obsessed with historical women's fashion, she was not keen on wearing it. She lamented the tyranny of wearing laced corsets (which he could not blame her for). Kat had taken needle and thread and fashioned herself with little whisps of see-thru lace pieces she called "panties and bra."

Rem had to secretly admit he preferred her version of "lacy underwear" to straight-jacketed corsets. The red pair she claimed to have been wearing when she arrived in his time, made his heart stop short when she modeled it one night. God, how it made foreplay and sex so much easier when you were not fighting the confines of layers of women's undergarments. Just the thought of it made his pulse race with desire.

Life at sea was oftentimes lonely, which is why so many married sea captains took their wives with them. Sitting alone in his cabin with time on his hands after the dinner meal, Rem was acutely aware of being separated from the most intriguing woman he had ever met. He missed their playful banter, the way she wielded a cue stick determined to best him, and the nightly pillow talk where she told him about outrageous inventions she claimed her future possessed.

She spoke of such things wistfully, telling him that there were so many things she missed. Like "hot showers, indoor flushable toilets, cellphones and something called a Mocha Frappuccino." Some of the inventions intrigued him and had valuable merit. He had actually looked into how difficult it would be to design and make her a flushable toilet and found, to his surprise, that someone had already come up with the idea and patented it in 1775. It had yet to become widespread due to the extensive underground plumbing required, but it got him thinking. When he returned he would find a way to rig such a device for her if only to make her happy and abandon any thoughts of returning to her time where such amenities existed.

There were times when Kat's brilliant smile took his breath away. Her green eyes sparkled when she was genuinely excited and there was a slight dimpling of her chin. Pleasing her became his newfound goal. It was the first time in his life he was focused on making someone else happy rather than just himself—like the pocketed billiards table he had special ordered to surprise her, knowing she would be deliriously pleased when it arrived. Was this love or just lust, he wondered?

Rem pushed the thought aside. Such emotions muddled his thinking. It was just too early to know. If she left him to return home to her time, they might never know. No sense putting the cart before the horse. Then again there was the matter of Lady Darcy's letter and that something was waiting for him in London that would help him understand what was to come.

Rem wrapped the cabin's rope hammock around his body, which allowed him to roll with the ocean waves surrounding them. He preferred it to the fixed bunk of the Captain's or Officer cabins which he had fallen out of too many times to count during rough seas. Motion lulled him into a meditative reverie. Kat had told him that big ships during her time had something called "stabilizers" causing them not to roll. It made sense to him, but she was sorely lacking on the mechanics of how it worked.

He closed his eyes and tried to sleep. But his dreams led him back to his own bed in New York, where he found himself spooning up against the woman patiently awaiting his return.

~~*~~

Kat didn't know what to tackle first—arranging to meet her great-great-great-great-grandparents, trying to find out what Braden Kendle knew about Lady Darcy's letter, or attending her future forecasting group at Fraunces Tavern at the prescribed time. She opted for two out of three. Before long she would need to hire a social secretary for her now busy and robust life.

Calvin brought the carriage around from the back alley mews and pointed it in the direction of Pearl and Broad Streets. The lunch crowd made it busier today than usual, but the far corner table in the back of the tavern was reserved for her group. Here she held court.

Today there were ten participants—men from all professions, young and old alike. She got their names, hoping to snag a historical big fish. She practically leapt from her chair when a very dapper-looking man in his 40's, sporting dark black curly hair and a patrician nose, stopped by the table and the others addressed him respectfully as "Mayor."

Philip Hone, former Mayor of New York for only one term from 1826 - 1827 was indeed a big fish in a big pond. Often referred to as "the Famous Beau of Old Manhattan," he knew everyone from senators to presidents to great literary figures. A wealthy auctioneer and merchant by trade, there was one thing that set his legacy apart during her time—his diaries.

Clearly he was surprised to find a lone woman in a tavern surrounded by a flock of men he knew. Those same men promptly informed him of "Madam K's" astounding abilities predicting the future.

"Go ahead," one man chimed in. "Ask her a question."

Kat couldn't tell if Hone thought the idea was ridiculous, but he good-naturedly played along.

"Tell me something about my future," he prompted, holding back the hint of a grin.

It was like feeding candy to a baby. Kat closed her eyes getting into character, letting them wait on bated breath for what she might reveal about such a noted figure.

Kat opened her eyes. "Mr. Hone. I'm being shown that you will be remembered, not for being mayor, but for your detailed diaries about Old New York—its society events, its immigrant problems, your disdain for its constant construction, your disapproval of President Andrew Jackson and…"

She paused in mid-sentence seeing Hone pale at her words, then continued. "… in the future your numerous diaries will be kept at a place called the New York Historical Society where millions of people will know about you and these years from what you have written. You will be an invaluable historian, and your name long remembered. So keep writing—about everything."

The table quieted, everyone looking to Hone for his reaction. His face remained stoic, not revealing his thoughts but his body had stiffened. Kat's words had affected him all right.

"Thank you Miss…" he stumbled, not knowing her name.

"It's Katherine Branigan," she finished.

"Thank you, Miss Branigan. Your gift of insight has been most enlightening, especially since no one knows of my diaries. I will strive to do what you have advised. Good day to you all."

With that Hone turned tail and went to join his friends at another table, where he must have revealed what she had just forecasted. Curious glances were thrown her way.

"I have something to ask," a man named William Baker voiced, pulling out that morning's August 25th newspaper edition of The New York Sun. The headline proclaimed: *Great Astronomical Discoveries Lately Made* by a Sir John Herschel.

"Is it true?" Baker asked.

Kat hadn't read it. "What does it say?"

Baker went on to elaborate. "It says they used an immense telescope aimed at the moon and discovered 'bison, single-horned goats, miniature zebras, tailless beavers and bat-winged humanoids' living on the surface." He displayed the drawing of the bat-winged human creature, called the "bat man."

Kat practically fell off her chair laughing. "It's a hoax," she stated outright. "The Great Moon Hoax is meant to sell papers." They looked at her, still not sure. "It's hogwash, gentlemen," she added. "The truth will eventually be revealed in a few weeks after many more articles come out proclaiming such nonsense. The Sun's newspaper circulation will have dramatically increased by then, which was the true purpose."

They looked at her skeptically. "Do you know what IS on the moon?" one brave man dared to ask.

Kat was not about to give a long lecture on NASA. "Look—man will not have the technology to get to the moon until 1968 or even after. That's a long way off. You have to get through the Van Allen radiation belt, and this is no small feat. In 1969 the National Aeronautics and Space Administration, which they will call 'NASA' will allegedly land a manned spaceship on the moon, leave an American flag behind, claim to go back a few more times, then stop going altogether. This will cost countless billions of taxpayer dollars."

They looked at her dumbfounded, but someone was brave enough to ask what was still uppermost on their mind: "Will they stop going back because they fear the bat men?"

The strange creatures mentioned in the hoax article had taken root in their imagination. Kat opted not to tell them about the comic book character "Batman." It would only confuse the matter more.

"They will report back that the moon is uninhabited with no such creatures," Kat informed. "Of course, you can't trust the government to tell you the truth—about anything. Remember that gentlemen. That is why they will call NASA, the "Never A Straight Answer Agency." In the future there will be claims of ancient pyramid structures on the moon and evidence of a more advanced alien race from another time, but no bat men. This is all I can see right now. The real truth will not be known for some time."

That was more than they needed to hear or comprehend. They sat back in their chairs, speechless and openly gob-smacked. It was time to adjourn for the day. Kat felt Calvin lightly tap her on the shoulder, ready to escort her out. She was certain the unearthly discussion would continue long after her departure. Was she stirring up a hornet's nest with too much information?

~~*~~

Braden Kendle had a small family practice located on Chambers Street along with other older and more established law firms that currently inhabited the bustling Courthouse area. There was no masthead sign emblazoned on the building's exterior advertising its legal services, only a small unobtrusive placard next to the door knocker which Kat almost missed.

She instructed Calvin to remain outside and that she would let him know if or when she needed him. He balked, but gave in. When Kat walked inside, she produced the same desired effect that followed her entrance everywhere else she went. A bespectacled older gentleman at the front desk glanced up from his account ledger, slightly taken aback by the sight of a woman dressed in men's apparel.

The confused man rose to his feet in line with social etiquette while she got right to the point. "I wish to speak with Mr. Braden Kendle regarding an important personal matter. Is he in?"

"Which one, Sir—I mean Ma'am?" the gentleman inquired respectfully. "Are you wishing to speak with Kendle Senior or Kendle Junior?"

So, there *was* more than one Kendle. Well, of course there would be if eventually this practice grew and became the likes of Kendle & Kendle, LLP.

Kat had no idea which one was Rem's attorney, so she lied. "I'm here on behalf of Remington Randall."

The old man removed his spectacles, put down his quill, and closed the account ledger he had been diligently working on. "That would be Kendle Senior," he informed. "And your name, please?"

"Miss Katherine Branigan."

Kendle's desk warden nodded and went to summon his boss. She knew her name would mean nothing to him, but she was not prepared for his rejection either.

"Mr. Kendle says he is not at liberty to talk with you," he announced upon his return.

She was completely taken aback. "Well why not?" she shot back. "He hasn't even met me. How can he not be at liberty to see me?!"

A voice behind the clerk, having heard the front office exchange, came out of his office to make himself known. "Perhaps I can be of service instead," he cordially suggested. "My name is also Braden Kendle."

The man now before her was the junior son who looked to be straight out of law school. He had yet to earn his name being added to the firm's masthead. She extended her hand, and he shook it like she was another man. Good. He was not intimidated at all by her male attire.

"Mr. Kendle," she acknowledged, nodding her head. "I'm Katherine Branigan and I wish to retain your legal services. I am a close associate of Remington Randall."

Junior raised one hairy eyebrow having heard Rem's name. He quickly ushered her into his small, spartanly decorated office. A wooden-framed law degree from Columbia College hung on the wall behind his desk, verifying that he had been a lawyer for only the last year. He beckoned her to take a seat across from his desk and took a seat once she did.

"My father cannot see you due to confidential reasons neither of us are at liberty to discuss. But I can help you. What are you in legal need of?"

Where to begin? The old man wouldn't acknowledge that Rem was his client, but he didn't need to. His outright refusal to see her because of a potential conflict of interest confirmed as much. He had recognized her name and the only way he would have known it was if Rem had mentioned it. Confidentiality be damned! She had seen their letter. Not knowing what they had discussed or agreed to, was driving her crazy. Was she Rem's "delicate matter?"

"I would like to arrange a land trust," she began, taking a different tack. "Is this something you can help me with?"

"Certainly," he replied. "Do you have a particular parcel of land in mind?"

"Yes, I do. It's in Brooklyn."

~~*~~

It took some doing, but Kat had managed to drag Calvin out to the Fulton Street ferry slip earlier in the week. Since the time of 1819, the steam-powered ferry had been making daily runs across the East River and connecting it to its corresponding Fulton Street stop in Brooklyn. Kat was a Brooklyn girl through and through. She knew the borough like the back of her hand but wasn't prepared for how vastly different it looked from what she was familiar with.

The Village of Brooklyn was America's first Manhattan suburb. Although it was still undeveloped in 1835, Kat knew that it would quickly change. Once the Brooklyn Bridge, originally called the "East River Bridge," opened in 1883, it would carry thousands across the river to populate the fast-growing borough.

What was now called "Brooklyn Village" would later be known as "Brooklyn Heights." This was to be Kat's future family "hood." The brownstone rowhouses that would soon line the streets would eventually become landmarks, all the more prized for their stunning park and river views of the Manhattan skyline. Kat had lived her entire life in Brooklyn Heights and loved it.

But since things looked so different, she was taking mental snapshots of everything she saw. The area was showing recent signs of a building boom after adding the ferry service. The streets were laid out in a grid pattern, sidewalks were paved, and water pumps had been installed. Seen as a "country retreat" from Manhattan, Brooklyn proudly touted itself as having New York's "healthiest air." The population was already around 23,000, comprised mostly of hard-working Irish and German immigrants. It was a perfect place for her family to lay down roots.

There were real estate companies in 1835, but not many. Most were developers who had the foresight to realize the city would grow and prosper. It could and would make them rich in the process if they played their cards right. These powerhouse men were mostly in New York, not Brooklyn, but were willing to branch out. A gentlemen in her future forecasting group gave her the name of real estate developer, Thomas E. Davis, who agreed to meet both her and Calvin that afternoon on the other side of the river.

"This is the lot I want," she announced standing in front of the vacant, undeveloped piece of land where her family's home would stand in the future. "Is it available for purchase?"

It was, and she bought it on the spot for $7,400 — a veritable steal. The prices would go up all over New York and surrounding boroughs after The Great Fire in December of that year. Which was why she was telling members of her future forecasting group to "buy, buy, buy," in certain untouched areas, then hold onto the property, making no improvements until prices escalated and they could flip it to make a profit — which they would. Buying the Brooklyn Heights property was taking her own advice, as she knew its true worth.

Unlike the gross amount of paperwork required in her time to complete a land or house sale, it was easy to accomplish her goal in 1835. It was hard to resist her own "buy, buy, buy" mantra. Kat purchased an adjoining lot as well, hoping it wouldn't change her future too much.

Her billiards winning money was exchanged with the land development owner, one of the forefathers of Brooklyn, a man by the name of Hezekiah Beers Pierrepont, who named her future home street after himself. The Clerk of Court reassigned the claim deed, and both properties were now hers. Her mission was accomplished. Which led her to securing her new attorney Braden Kendle, Jr., and the second part of her plan, which would be the trickiest—meeting her great-great-great-great-grandparents.

Chapter 10

Between the ranks of England's solicitors and the U.S. lawyers who had suddenly come into his life, Rem felt he had been thrown into a never-ending treasure hunt. Cut from the same cloth as Ezra, Lady Darcy had entrusted what was valuable to her, as well as personal correspondence upon her death, to the likes of Jeremiah E. Whitehall, a solicitor who had risen to the high rank of barrister before retiring five years earlier.

Unfortunately, Whitehall was deceased having died of a weakened heart two years earlier. As a high-profile trial litigator, barristers were known to have their lifespans shortened by at least ten years and Whitehall was just another casualty of his chosen profession.

This complicated matters considerably. Rem was stuck in London tracking down leads to any or all of Whitehall's associates who might know what became of his legal records. One such associate, Peter Hansen, suggested contacting Whitehall's family. As it turned out, Whitehall's only surviving relative, a spinster daughter, was located in Yorkshire. Hansen arranged a meeting, so he went to see her.

While Hansen had warned him she was a peculiar one, he understood now why the man had not accompanied him. Delphina Whitehall was a cat lady and a morbidly overzealous collector of memorabilia and outright junk. Everywhere Rem looked there were stacks of old newspapers, books, piles of unopened correspondence, clothes boxes, and discarded food. Rem almost backed out, but he gritted his teeth and ventured into her parlor where every available sitting space contained a cat, animal hair or... good God! Was that a rat scurrying around the sofa? Apparently so.

A large cat, perched atop a box, hissed and leapt for it. Delphina Whitehall, quite the cheerful sort who seemed content with her life, was oblivious to the chaos and filth all around her that would have driven any sane man quite mad.

"Now you behave, Morpheus and leave Henry alone," she admonished, before turning to Rem to explain. "He's such a naughty little renegade."

Exactly. Apparently no one had informed Delphina Whitehall that cats were supposed to hunt mice and their larger rodent cousins. The woman was batty. Not knowing where to sit, with cats everywhere, Rem leaned up against a large box, that he soon noticed was exuding a peculiar smell. He cautiously moved away, hoping it did not contain rotting rodents from Morpheus' more successful hunts, or something worse. Maggots came to mind. At a loss for where to plant himself down, as proper etiquette demanded in the presence of a lady, he tossed convention aside and chose to stand.

In contrast to the disarray around her, Whitehall's daughter was dressed impeccably, her gray hair pulled back in a neat little bun atop her head, but inside she was a mass of nerves. From her perpetual hand-wringing he wondered if the prospect of a guest had sent her into a tizzy to look presentable and hide the insanity around her.

"Would you like some tea?" she graciously offered.

Not in a million years, he thought. "No thank you. I'm here on an important but pressing matter and wonder if you might be of some help."

The thought of someone asking for her help seemed to please her immensely. "Mr. Hansen told me you are interested in my father's correspondence with a Lady Portia Darcy. Is this correct?"

"Yes, Ma'am. That's right," he replied.

Delphina grew wistful. "Such a lovely lady," she opined.

"Yes, she was," he agreed. "Then you knew her?"

Delphina smiled widely. "Oh, my, yes. We had some fascinating conversations before she passed. She possessed a third eye, you know."

"A third eye?" he questioned.

Delphina pursed her lips and pointed to the middle of her forehead. "She saw all things, but…" she sighed. "I should have listened to her."

Rem was intrigued. "And why is that?"

Her words sprang forth, without censorship. "She told me I had a deep hole inside me which would never be filled until I ..."

Delphina stopped, looking slightly aghast at her impulsive outburst. She recognized that she had said more than she had intended. Clearly she did not want to go down that particular life memory path again and scrambled for an excuse.

"I was only 18 at the time, so what did I know anyway?" she mumbled more to herself.

Immediately, she changed the subject. "The greater lot of my father's records are still stored in the upstairs attic, untouched. I could not bring myself to go through them. Too many memories, you know. He was not the easiest of fathers, but he *was* an incredible barrister."

Something then served to jog her memory, making her brighten. "In fact, it was Lady Darcy who once told me that should anything happen to her or my father I was to keep all his records safe. I believe she said that someday a man would come for them. And here you are. Imagine that!"

Rem smiled grimly. Imagine that, indeed. "May I take a look?" he asked motioning towards the upstairs attic.

"Why, yes, of course. Unfortunately, it is a bit of a mess up there," she apologized. "I hope you don't mind."

He did, but what could he do? He stoically made his way to the attic, wondering how bad it could be.

~~*~~

It was indeed a mess, as the lady had said. The attic was airless with a thick layer of dust covering every surface making it unbreathable. Rem put a handkerchief over his nose and mouth and jimmied open windows in order not to pass out.

Boxes and cartons were stacked everywhere and not a one of them was labeled as to its contents. With a sinking feeling, he groaned inwardly. This would be a time-consuming and massive task akin to looking for a needle in a haystack. But Rem knew what he was searching for was here somewhere—Kendle had implied as much.

If it were up to him he would have hired men to move the boxes out of there and go through them in a more habitable space. That was not an option for Delphina Whitehall, even after offering to pay her generously for the lot of her father's records. Apparently, there was no price to compensate for sentimentality.

Rem removed his jacket and cravat, then rolled up his sleeves. He surveyed the tightly packed attic wondering where to begin. Jeremiah E. Whitehall's life and career were stored up here in this forgotten attic space like a mausoleum honoring the dead.

As Lady Darcy had died some time ago, he started to methodically go through the older looking boxes. Most legal documents did not have to be retained and stored beyond six years unless the nature of the information marked it to be kept indefinitely—like an instructional letter of intent within an estate plan. In all likelihood Lady Darcy would have taken that legal route knowing that someday he would come looking for it. At least he hoped as much.

Several hours later Rem had yet to find any files or correspondence regarding Lady Darcy. His head was pounding from lack of proper ventilation, and he needed to get out of there. He wasn't sure if it was just the dust, or the combination of cat hair as well, but he was sneezing incessantly. His eyes itched and watered, making him miserable. The place was not only a fire trap but a death trap as well. He fought off disappointment and vowed to return the next day, and the day after if necessary — however long it took to find the answers he sought.

On the other side of the pond, Kat was equally frustrated, being consumed by doubt. What she was doing was similar to committing "insider trading" by using knowledge of "non-public information" for profit and gain. The term hadn't even been coined yet, but what she was doing was a felony in her time. Insider trading was a criminal offense leading to federal prison time. To placate her guilt, she tried to think of herself as a "whistleblower" instead.

Calvin had advised her that it would not be wise for her to tell members of her future forecasting group to refrain from investing in ideas or inventions she saw going nowhere. The health inventions were the worst. One such absurdity was "cholera pants" to keep the abdomen and stomach warm and protect it from bowel complaints, which was believed to lead to cholera—something everyone feared. The craziest idea was a "breast douche" consisting of a cupping device with a tubal hose attached to a woman's nipple to keep such mammary parts clean. That one had her chuckling at its outright insanity. She half-jokingly told them that they should think more to a woman's "lower" parts for hygiene intervention.

Of course, she knew what groundbreaking inventions were coming down the pike with some still in their infancy stage. She wholeheartedly supported anything Samuel Morse proposed, knowing the telegraph and his unique Morse Code would be revolutionary in the next two years— that and such things as typewriters and even sewing machines.

The official United States Patent Office, which would require strict examination of each patent before being granted, would not even come into existence until the Patent Act of 1836. Many of these absurd ideas she was now hearing about were flooding into the Superintendent of Patents office within the Department of State in Washington, without any scientific scrutiny. All one needed was to pay the $35 fee, making it an inventor's zoo out there.

Kat felt compelled to educate her financial members on the dangerous potential for being hoodwinked into "Ponzi" business schemes before swindler Charles Ponzi even committed such acts. When all was said and done, she was giving these men a Wharton School of Business crash course in finance management, only without the graduate diploma.

At another such meeting she moved on to how the federal government would remove deposits from the federal bank, crippling it, and leading to the financial Panic of 1837, so they better be prepared. Kat wasn't sure if there had been prior bank panics they had experienced, but this one would be disastrous, made worse by bad real estate loans for western lands and northeastern forests.

She warned them that the collapse of cotton would come first, then widespread flour riots, all of which would result in an agricultural depression lasting years. Nonexistent banking regulatory practices would lead to financial institutions shutting down after running out of precious gold and silver. A chronic currency crisis would cause bank runs and bank failures that same year. Kat alluded to such "possible" scenarios without going into greater detail, fearing her words alone might bring on a bank run.

Men of this time were concerned about only one thing—their financial future. While they listened with dread and fascination, some remained skeptical. 1835 was a year of economic boom. They did not want to believe that within a year's time it might all change for the worse. Yet, they repeated such incredible and dire predictions everywhere despite being sworn to secrecy. It was when she started warning against the China opium trade that she realized she had gone too far. It was the equivalent of attempting to slaughter a sacred cow. Anyone who had money to invest had their hand in it to some degree, whether big or small. Everyone knew which men were raking in huge profits. These men were the "untouchables" whose money gained them unimpeachable and unspeakable power.

It was error in judgment on her part, but Kat actually named a few, like John Jacob Astor, while conveniently omitting Rem's name from the culprit list. She chastised them for making their wealth off widespread opium and heroin addiction which was enslaving and killing thousands of people but making them immensely rich. The little group became deadly silent, exchanging quick glances amongst each other. This was not a subject one openly discussed in public.

However, Kat felt like she was on a roll, telling them that she foresaw how those involved in opium trade were incurring tremendous "negative karma." She warned them that if they didn't stop, they would eventually face an equal fate at a later date and time, if not sooner. Misfortune would surely follow them and their accomplices, bringing a curse upon their families.

Her followers looked outright stricken by her damning prediction. Others were not buying it or refused to hear. Everyone knew someone who was making a fortune off the opium trade. The power and money that came from it was irresistible and beyond belief.

Kat knew it was hard to combat greed regardless of what century one lived in. But, if nothing else, she hoped to plant a warning seed. That day she took on the unlikely role of pulpit preacher, reminding them of their moral duty to humanity. She knew too many during her lifetime who had succumbed to recreational drugs and had died because of it.

Men killing men for profit was simply unconscionable in her mind. Someone had to educate these foolish males and knock some sense into them. It might as well be her if no one else was willing to step up to the plate.

Kat knew damn well that New York City had been built on opium trade money. It was one of those damning little secrets no one wanted to talk about or own up to. The opium traders and China shippers had to do something with all their money besides amassing real estate. They learned to launder their immense drug profits by creating philanthropic foundations that made charitable donations to institutions that would emblazon their name across building mastheads giving them lasting name recognition and notoriety for decades, even centuries, to come.

"If they don't stop their evil opium dealing ways, then they must give back through philanthropy," she instructed, trying to present a solution. "They need to donate such profits to build great schools, teaching hospitals, libraries, cultural museums, and charitable foundations that will help all men."

The concept of coerced charity to redeem oneself did not go down well amongst her band of followers. At least not with everyone. Her warning words travelled quickly to deep and dark places—to men who did not take kindly to her unsolicited advice. That day, unbeknown to her, the final meeting of the future forecasting group would take place and abruptly end her short-run career as "Madam K." The very next day she would pay the price for having such loose lips.

The undercarriage of Kat's phaeton, a smaller open carriage, was deliberately compromised. By whom or when was never certain. The front axle was partially sheared through to intentionally cause a serious, even lethal, accident. All it took was one good bump on the road to accomplish such a disaster—which happened to come the very next day.

Kat and Calvin were on their way to a meeting with Kendle Junior when their carriage hit a deep rut in the road, cracking the axle wide apart, causing it to lurch precariously before tipping over and colliding with another carriage going in the opposite direction.

It happened so fast, and so unexpectedly, that there was little time for Calvin to save her. Kat's head crashed against the sideboard with a rattling thud. Seconds later, her body was thrown from the carriage like a lifeless ragdoll. She lost consciousness as she hit hard ground.

When she came to she was acutely aware of Calvin carrying her to a grassy area, where he gently laid her down and took stock. Fear suffused his cut-up, bloody face, as he checked her pulse.

Kat was still alive but felt unbearably sticky. Her hand came away from her face smeared with blood oozing from a cut on her head. It was way too much blood for a nick, and she feared it would require stitches. Every bone in her body ached with the tiniest exertion, but Kat was fairly certain she hadn't broken anything.

Calvin did not look to be so lucky. His left arm was dangling at an odd angle. A large crowd had assembled due to the two-carriage accident. Kat had no idea what damages the other carriage had suffered as a result of their tipping over. It all happened so fast; her head was reeling. Calvin and she were immediately rushed to a nearby medical facility near City Hall Park, which just happened to be Bellevue Hospital.

Medical facilities during these times scared Kat more than the prospect of suffering a head injury or a broken bone. Kat inwardly shuddered at the sight of the makeshift emergency room. They might decide to bore a hole in her head to relieve the pressure they believed was the cause of pain, or give her drugs like morphine, or worse yet—use bloodletting leeches. Kat was an alternative medicine adherent and naturalist at heart. Acupuncture was more to her liking if or when pain was involved.

But she was also realistic. She knew she needed immediate medical attention. Her face was continuing to swell with each passing minute, and she was getting woozier from the loss of blood and the hospital smells assaulting her senses. Lethargy was setting in, muddling her brain. If she didn't quickly take charge, she might let something verbally slip about who she really was. It would surely land her in a locked psych ward, a snake pit of the worst kind. Bellevue Hospital in the 19th century was a notorious mental asylum and a world apart from what it would become in her time.

While her head hurt like the devil itself, she was thankful to be alive. She still remembered who she was, what year it was, and where she had come from—all sad, but true facts. She demanded they bandage her up and that Calvin arrange to take her home.

Calvin's anguished look spoke volumes. He had feared for her life at the expense of his own, but now his job security was at stake. With a broken arm, he would no longer be fit to protect her. Not even he could have foreseen the sabotage done to their vehicle. It was a miracle she had not been run over and broke every bone in her body after being flung from their carriage. Calvin had acted quickly to rescue her from passing road traffic despite his broken arm. The man had saved her life!

If and when Rem found out what she had been doing, he would be beyond furious. She would have to make certain he never found out, even if it required bribing all his employees. News would certainly travel and stopping it would be impossible. If that occurred, she would have hell to pay when he returned.

It would be better for her to lay low for a while, which was not difficult. Kat could barely drag herself out of bed each morning, let alone venture out into the world-at-large. She was tired and just wanted to sleep. If she had suffered a concussion as well, there was only one way for her brain to heal; she needed plenty of rest.

For as long as possible, she put off looking at her face in the mirror. She didn't need a crystal ball or a mirror to tell her it was bruised and inflamed. She could feel its puffiness creeping around her eyes, causing her to squint at times.

By day three she couldn't be in denial any longer. She had to know how dreadful things really were. One look at her reflection, brought her to immediate tears. She looked like Rocky Balboa after a brutal boxing match. Her eyes were black and blue and would require some serious concealer, if only she had some. Her forehead and cheeks were puffy and tender, and there was still a hard knot on her head which was too sensitive to touch. Note to God: *I will not do this ever again.*

Rem's household staff averted their eyes when addressing her, silently confirming that she looked just as hideous to others as she did to herself. There was a hint of pity on their faces as well, which made it all the worse. Great! She was now a poor pitied creature as well! Yet she could find no fault with them. They dealt with her needs as if she were mistress of the house and for that she was profoundly grateful.

At times, Rem's absence weighed heavily on her mind. Now more than ever, she felt alone in a strange world in which she did not belong. She was self-imprisoned in his home not knowing what to do with an endless amount of unfilled time on her hands.

Finally, a message addressed to her was delivered via one of Rem's fastest packet ships. Her heart leapt with excitement upon receiving it. But when she broke open the wax seal, it only contained a few scribbled lines telling her that he had inadvertently been delayed on business and needed a few more weeks to complete legalities before returning home. He added that his thoughts were with her and not to worry. That was it. She was crestfallen.

A part of her had hoped for some type of flowery love letter from Rem during such a prolonged absence. It was a disappointment. He might be good at most everything else, but a prolific writer he was not.

Kat could have written a book on all that had occurred since his departure. In fact, she decided that it wasn't such a bad idea. She could begin writing her own diary, ala Philip Hone style. The man had filled 28 volumes over time, which would be hard to beat, but it would at least give her something to do to stave off cabin fever and boredom.

And so, it began. Each day Kat spent hours behind closed doors in Rem's study, painstakingly journalling. She awkwardly mastered using a steel point dip pen until her fingers were ink stained and cramped. At first she lamented not having the convenience of a laptop computer or even a typewriter to make her writing easier but soon forgot all that. Writing became her therapy against loneliness and isolation. She no longer felt bored. To her surprise, she realized she had a lot to say.

Before long she was requesting more writing paper and ink as she poured out her thoughts and observations. She wrote in detail about her family, her life back home, her job, and the infamous day and events that led to her arrival in this time. She theorized on how she had arrived here based on her limited understanding of theoretical physics. Some ideas she knew to be outlandish, but since she had no way to verify the science behind her strange and unearthly experience, she pressed on. Back in her time, she would have consulted the internet to gather and assess other peoples' opinions on the subject. But not having the benefit of the internet to provide such answers, it forced her to think for herself.

Kat wrote about all she had seen and done, both good and bad during her time in 1835, which was plenty. She wrote about the future forecasting club, the subsequent carriage accident, and her acute loneliness during her recovery. There were times when it became too painful to contemplate her plight, and she would sit back and cry—relieved no one could witness her grief. She imagined Lexi telling her to just, "Snap out of it, Chica," in her sometimes overly direct way of giving advice. She missed her friend, especially in moments like these when she became nostalgic for her past.

Her journal revelations were intended for her eyes only—the writings becoming her personal truth set to paper to hopefully gain insight into the strange trajectory of her new life. It became a cathartic experience. Not once did she question why she felt such a great need inside her to chronicle all that had taken place; it just was.

There was one glaring omission in her journalled tale. Kat could not bring herself to write about her "situationship" with Remington Randall—mainly because she didn't really know where it was going. Her father had once told her during a time when she was deciding which career path to take, that even if one doesn't see the road, it still remains there, waiting to be found. Would she find the right road and move forward instead of being stuck as she felt right now? What if one finds a road they cannot move forward on? She knew her father would have told her: "Then it's not a real road. Don't go down roads that go nowhere." These days she was waxing philosophically. Put a pen and paper in her hands and it was turning her into another Henry David Thoreau.

After each writing session, Kat would hide away her growing manuscript inside a stack of Chinese nesting boxes in Rem's study, well aware of the irony of doing so. A "China box" structure in literature was when the writer placed stories within stories, like a nesting box. She doubted any of the staff would disturb her secret hideaway but would dust around it.

Justine and the girls from Mrs. Begley's rooming house came by each week to cheer her up and bring little sweets along with news and gossip from the outside world. When they first saw her face there was a collective gasp, followed by words of utmost sympathy. She could have worn a veil to cover her healing wounds, but she didn't. Instead, she tried to make light of it, mumbling something about being Mary Shelley's 1818 Bride of Frankenstein character, which no one in her little group had read. So, she spent the afternoon enthralling them with the story of Frankenstein.

With each new day, she felt like her life was passing her by. She couldn't write herself out of this real life plot she had become captive in no matter how much mind-escape writing she did.

It felt like months since she had last seen Rem as summer turned into the cool briskness of fall. The color of the leaves slowly changed in hue as she did. Her face was healing, the swelling had disappeared, and the black and blue patches were getting fainter with each passing day. Observing the change gave her new hope, telling her it was time to move forward on her road and get back to life in the outside world. She couldn't put it off any longer; it was time to meet her long-lost Irish relatives.

Chapter 11

After what seemed an eternity, Rem found what he was searching for in Delphina Whitehall's disgustingly dirty attic. It had been worth the torture of poking through endless trial notes, daily schedules, evidentiary materials, legal pleadings, and documentary exhibits. Some boxes were a maddening hodge-podge of legal memorabilia. Items were often misfiled or out of sequential order, defying any coherent dating system. Years were comingled forcing him to go through every item for fear of overlooking something vital to his past and future. Somewhere amidst this mess was the one thing that might finally shed light on the strange connection he had to Kat Branigan.

Lady Darcy had said as much in the letter she had dispatched to Ezra. Thank God Ezra had turned it over to Braden Kendle for safekeeping until his 33rd year or he might never have known of its existence.

Rem felt like he was playing a clever game of cat and mouse. The woman who had paved the way to his future had loved playing games. Surveying the attic disarray it was evident that she was making him work for whatever the prize would be. Deep down he knew he had little choice. He could not walk away from ever knowing—not when it came to Kat.

Lady Darcy had known something incredible about his future that she had decided to keep hidden until he was ready—or until the "fates were aligned" as she had so often said. The kicker for him had been spelled out in the letter Kendle had given him.

The letter told a strange tale which most would question, but Lady Darcy was long gone and could no longer provide the answers. He had to go on what little she had divulged. Rem had committed her words to memory before setting sail, despite carrying the letter on his person for safekeeping. The penned words ran through his mind now like a mantra…

My Beloved Rem:

Where to begin, my dearest one? When you receive this letter you will be a grown man in your 33rd year of life and I will be a star shining brightly in the nighttime sky watching over you. I can picture you so clearly that it is almost uncanny. Tall, handsome, confident, accomplished in whatever business venture you choose and, I am quite sure, with a propensity to be mulishly stubborn. As a child that trait served you well in surviving the hellish streets of London and miraculously it did not tarnish you.

I could see from the very first moment we met that you had a pure heart, and that you missed your mother fiercely. In our brief time together, I tried to impart such motherly love to you, but I could see that you were destined for greater things beyond the shores of Britain and what I could give you.

Entrusting you into the mentoring hands of Ezra was not an easy decision. It meant sending you away from me in order to make your own way in the world in order to discover your true destiny. While I knew Ezra would provide you with the opportunities you needed to excel in life, yours would be a lonely journey, without a guiding mother's hand.

I want you to know that I agonized over the decision as to whether I was doing the right thing entrusting you into the sole care of Ezra Stark. I would have gladly preferred raising you as my own. However, fate intervened. Several days before I put you on Ezra's ship, I had an incredibly vivid dream where I saw your unfolding fate and the path you would take. This alone convinced me that I had made the right decision. Dreams can be powerful harbingers, and this dream was no different. Remember this.

I saw that a messenger would be sent to you in your 33rd year. A messenger not from the present or past, but from a strange distant future where large birdlike objects flew in the skies overhead and metal cans on wheels roamed noisy congested streets. It was a place where ladies did not look like ladies but were definitely female.

At first I was very scared to view this odd-looking world, but then I saw a green-eyed woman, with flaming hair, carrying a cup with a green and white mermaid on it, and she smiled at me. She saw me in the reflection of a large window glass. I recognized her, although I do not know her, which makes no sense. This woman was running to get out of the rain, like a cat avoiding water, and she told me she was going to see you soon to wish you a happy 33rd birthday. I did not understand how that was possible, but I remembered laughing when she said her name was "Kat" with a "K."

I knew in that moment that she was from the moon and the stars, and that your destinies were somehow intertwined, despite the two of you coming from vastly different worlds. A moment of total clarity showed me that in time you would come to the realization of what to do because you alone held the key.

I am certain you will meet this mysterious "Kat" woman if you have not already. If you come to love her, then sadly you must let her go. Should you choose to bridge worlds to accomplish this, I will leave something of significance with my solicitor in London, Jeremiah E. Whitehall. God Bless and God Speed...

Lady Darcy's last missive to him prompted Rem to drop everything and make the unscheduled trip to London to find the "significant" answer she had written about. He had refrained from divulging the correspondence to Kat, taking it with him so he could rest assured she would not accidentally find it. If it turned out to be nothing and he had gone on a wild goose chase, she would be sorely disappointed. At least he could spare her from such anguish.

Kat believed the signet ring on his little finger was her one-way return ticket home. While she desperately wanted him to give it to her, he did not. This was not the solution to her problem. This was something he knew with deep certainty, despite being unable to explain how. He just knew.

Lady Darcy had warned him to never take the lucky talisman off. There had to be a damn good reason for her telling him to do so and perhaps it had something to do with the dream she had. Which led him straight back to the here and now task before him. This was a personal quest he could not have assigned to anyone else. He had to be sure the search was thorough, which from experience required he do it himself. No stone would be left unturned in the process.

Rem kept searching, having gone through over half of the boxes in the days he had been cooped up in Delphina's attic space. He was tired, ravenously hungry, coughing up dirt, and having to poke his head out a window every half hour to breathe fresh air into his aching lungs. While the thought of having Kat there to help him might have made things move faster, having her around would also be too distracting. Rem needed this time to concentrate and think.

By the end of the next day, he felt he was on the precipice of making progress. He finally located Lady Portia Darcy's client file box. Unfortunately, fate quickly ripped away any ray of hope when he discovered the file had nothing inside of "significance" despite his having meticulously labored over every scrap of correspondence between her and her solicitor.

Rem was close to giving up when he literally stumbled upon it in Whitehall's personal records. He tripped over a box causing him to fall upon it and split open its seams. It was a fortuitous finding. It contained numerous letters Whitehall had written to friends, family, and colleagues over his long life. The man saved everything—like his daughter.

One letter in particular jumped out of the box as it spilt open. Marked boldly in capital letters, the envelope read: "THE STARK BOY." Rem's pulse raced erratically as he snatched it to him. The envelope was wax sealed, but he tore it open, immediately recognizing Lady Darcy's neatly penned script and her opening words:

My Dearest Rem,

I trust you will know what to do with this when the time is right, and the way has been made open. Use it wisely with no regrets…

There was more, but he was distracted by a small, black velvet pouch inside the envelope. He pulled open the drawstring close and extracted a ring. It was the exact duplicate of the meteorite ring Lady Darcy had once given him, complete with a signet "R" initial.

A chill ran through him, making him shudder. He knew exactly what it meant, but to use it would mean never seeing Kat again. An internal battle waged war inside him. If he kept this ring hidden from her and she found out, she would surely come to hate him.

Rem read the remainder of Lady Darcy's letter, sat back, and for the first time in as long as he could remember, unfettered tears ran down his dirt-smudged cheeks.

~~*~~

As Kat continued to heal, her surroundings started to feel like she was incarcerated in a high class prison. It was evident that she couldn't stay holed up forever in Rem's Old Row house, fabulous as it was, without the prospect of going insane.

Kat was instructed by her attending physician to stay in bed and rest, but such a prescription was impossible to heed. Her body craved activity to regain strength. She had hoped to while away her recuperative time practicing her pool game, but quickly discovered her limbs were still sore from the accident and raising her arms to sink a shot hurt like she was stretched out on a rack.

If she stood too long, she experienced dizziness and fatigue. Kat knew she would have to find other things to do to occupy her time which were less stressful. She avoided looking at her naked self in the full-length mirror. The black and blue patches on her body would take time to fade. It was just as well that Rem wasn't here to see the ugly mess she had become.

The bandage on her head was eventually removed, leaving only a small bump to remind her that someone had attempted to permanently silence her. Calvin had been right to warn her. If only she had been smart enough to listen and heed his advice.

After the accident, news spread quickly that Madam K had adjourned the future forecasting group meetings at Fraunces Tavern until further notice. Some participants tried to lure her back in, proposing a private meeting in someone's home, but Kat was no fool. Next time, if there was one, she might not be so lucky to come out alive. Whistleblowers who revealed too much often landed up dead or "suicided" which, in her book, was the same thing.

A one-armed Calvin, his arm in a makeshift sling, made a suspicious accident report to the proper authorities who promised to investigate the incident on behalf of an absent Remington Randall. Kat very much doubted this would happen. If one had money to line their pockets, they might attempt to solve a crime. An actual police department force had yet to exist. Paid constables, city marshals, and night watch men would fill that need until 1845. And so, the "official" investigation went nowhere.

Despite obvious signs of deliberate sabotage, the culprit who sawed halfway through the carriage's axle had yet to be identified or apprehended. Kat was certain someone had hired the responsible person to commit such a deed, but whom and for what price? How many men of wealth and influence had she threatened by revealing information they held secret? The bankers? The opium drug traders? Jealous wives or lovers who thought she held too much sway over the minds of their men? It could have been anyone.

The thought of going out again in public made Kat jumpy. There was still the matter of her meeting her great-great-great-great-grandparents. But she had put it off, not wanting to scare them with her hideous appearance. But as weeks passed, bruises faded, and she felt her strength return, there was no longer an excuse to fall back on. She summoned Braden Kendle Junior to call on her.

While she awaited his response, Kat managed to entertain herself at night reading from the vast assortment of literature Rem had available in his library. His home on the Old Row reflected his likes and dislikes. It was filled with expensive and valuable collectibles from his numerous travels around the world. Like a curator of antiquities, he possessed museum quality taste—from rare porcelain figurines and statues of the imperial Qing and Tang dynasties to the silk Persian tapestries which hung on the walls or the area rugs covering highly polished wood floors.

You could tell a lot about a person from how they decorated their home and what they chose to display. Rem was a collector of history and had obviously led an interesting life thus far travelling the world. In the brief time they had been together, he had shared with her a number of his adventures, while she shared information on her world.

Yes, she did miss him, especially as the early Fall nights turned cooler and she no longer had his body beside her to warm her bed. She wanted to learn more about him but had no one to ask. Cabin fever and partial boredom prompted her to explore every nook and cranny of his home, especially after the incredible find she had stumbled upon in his study desk drawer. But if there were more secrets to unearth, she did not come across any.

Kat wandered into the kitchen one morning to find the cooking room was equipped with a large cast iron wood stove with several grates, a brick oven kiln built into the wall, and a healthy herb garden growing out back in a small yard area.

To the surprise of the kitchen staff, Kat offered to show them how to make a New York bagel, the kind her grandmother used to make. She had a nostalgic craving for comfort food from back home. The staff indulged her whim, following her precise instructions to boil the yeasted dough in barley malt water first before baking it in a kiln oven to give it its thick outer crust and softer chewy inside.

While Jewish immigrants would bring the pretzel-like bread from Poland later in the 1800's, Kat's unique bakery creation was a big hit in Rem's household. They soon began whipping out hot fresh bagels for her every morning. Unfortunately, she didn't know how to make cream cheese, so she settled on using a creamy butter topping spread instead. It was heavenly and gave her a chance to ask questions about the Old Row House and who the neighbors were that graced this historic street.

The next day a knock on Rem's study door interrupted her daily journalling session. She was informed that Kendle Junior had come calling. Kat scrambled to hide her diary papers before Higgins, a senior manservant who also functioned as a butler, saw the gentleman in.

Kat sat behind Rem's mahogany rosewood desk like she owned it. It was a man's desk, large in size with carved lion's paw feet and a tooled leather top. She sat up straighter when Higgins opened the door to usher her attorney into the room.

"I was happy to hear of your swift recovery," Kendle stated good-naturedly before taking a seat across from her. He opened a leather portfolio and extracted a sheaf of documents.

"The land trust on your property has been drawn up and awaits your signature," he informed.

Kat nodded. "And as the grantor of the trust, my Brooklyn property will be transferred to the beneficiaries I have requested," she confirmed.

"That's correct, but only if they accept the terms of the trust," Kendle pointed out. "As a trustee of many such land trusts, I must say that the terms you spelled out were most unusual."

Kat would have to agree. She had tried to cover all the possibilities that the passage of time might present. "And you have located the correct Colleen and Duncan Branigan of County Galway, Dublin?"

He nodded.

"And they have agreed to meet?" she continued.

He nodded once again, before adding. "Well, yes. That is—upon certain conditions. They are distrusting of attorneys…"

Kat snorted. Yep, these were her ancestral folk, alright.

Kendle elaborated. "They asked that if we have official business to conduct, we will have to come to them to make it happen or not at all."

Kat shrugged. Not a problem for her.

Kendle Junior had a difference of opinion. "They live in Five Points, Miss Branigan," he informed with deep frown lines creasing his brow. "It's not a safe place for man nor beast either day or night. Even the constables go into the area in pairs of two—and reluctantly, I might add."

It was not Hell's Kitchen, but it was just as bad from what she knew. "Calvin will come with us," she declared. She trusted him to protect her, and the man would need the work.

Kendle sighed looking none too happy with her decision. "Well then Calvin had better be carrying a firearm," he advised.

~~*~~

The notorious Five Points neighborhood was ten times worse than its description. The first of Manhattan's slum areas, populated densely with Irish, Italian, and German immigrants, the district was home to thieves, pickpockets, prostitutes, and all manner of perverts and thugs openly carrying bludgeons and knives. Organized gangs roamed the streets day and night, making it a sinkhole of iniquity where gambling and prostitution flourished.

Five cross thoroughfares converged to give the area its infamous name. Only two of the street names still survived during her time: Mulberry and Water Streets. Her ancestors lived on Mulberry Bend, a narrow, back alley street near an old brewery, which could only be described as the worst imaginable street in all of New York.

Squalor was everywhere in the cramped tenements. Sanitation was practically non-existent. From inside the protection of their carriage, Kat took in the gutters piled high with putrid-smelling garbage, while feral pigs rooted through leftover scraps on rat-infested streets. Calvin took along another man, a driver, for additional safety. Both sat up front, while Kendle Junior and her sat in the safety of the enclosed carriage. Kendle looked upon the district with unseeing eyes, blocking it out, anxious to get about this business for which he had been employed.

They had chosen an early Sunday morning to meet with her relatives, a time when much of the area's riff-raff and hoodlums would still be abed from a late night of theft and debauchery. A lone wooden wagon rolled slowly through the dirt paved lanes spraying some unknown substance from a hose that was meant to prevent cholera and typhus disease. It smelled like toxic chemicals. Kat had never seen or imagined anything this bad. The place was hell-hole that took real survival skills.

The carriage stopped in front of a dilapidated building, housed next to a brothel sporting a flying penis sign. Kat was aghast. There was a man passed out on the front stoop, alive or dead, she could not tell. He had a bloodied head and was missing his pants.

Next door Colleen and Duncan Branigan, along with their 11-year-old son Aiden, lived with countless other Irish immigrants in a densely packed wooden tenement structure that looked foundationally unsound. Cramped together in a one room cellar dive that barely provided enough room for two people, let alone a family of three, they were lucky to have a small iron-barred window to provide a few rays of captured daylight.

Kat entered cautiously and was immediately struck by how spartanly furnished the room was, much like a prison cell. Yet these living quarters were neat and clean. A brightly colored kitchen tablecloth was the only festive addition to their humble little abode. In expectation of their guests, several mismatched and chipped teacups had been set out on a flowered oilcloth.

While Calvin and his man waited outside to protect the carriage from being stripped down and the horses stolen, Kat and Kendle were being keenly scrutinized by Collen and Duncan Branigan. She couldn't blame them for being suspicious, as all they knew was that an unnamed benefactor had left them something, which even to her ears sounded hard to believe.

Kat was introduced as Kendle's legal assistant, Katherine O'Malley. Being of Irish descent, like them, they welcomed her into their home for a "cup of tea." They looked too poor to offer any refreshments other than that. She was well aware that Duncan worked on the docks when work was available. Colleen took in washing and sewing. Young Aiden was nowhere to be seen, which concerned his parents.

"Who is this benefactor you speak of?" Duncan asked, getting straight to the point. "And why would they be leaving us anything?"

Kendle and Kat were prepared for such questions. "The benefactor wishes to remain anonymous," Kendle replied. "They are prepared to help you and have arranged to deed you land in Brooklyn Heights on which to build a family home. The trust they have left you is quite sizeable."

This stunning revelation caused them to exchange skeptical looks. Colleen Branigan, scoffed. "What? Sizeable you say? How much are we talking about?"

Duncan was of a different mind, sitting up straighter—a proud man. "We are not charity cases, Mr. Kendle. We are hard-working, simple people. While we may not have much, we are not destitute. Why in God's name would someone choose us? And what would they be wanting from us in return?"

Kat could see her relatives had come to this country not expecting a handout but to build their dream through honest work. These people had a quiet pride about them, whether poor or not. Charity was something they wouldn't easily accept from anyone. They were Branigans and not pushovers. If something sounded too good to be true to them, it usually was. She knew all this and decided to step in and assuage their fears.

"Mrs. Branigan, the donor's relatives came from County Galway in Dublin like yourself. Unfortunately, they are all gone, and the donor has no family member of their own to will this land to, and ..." Kat paused. "They may not have long to live here. They want to offer a fresh start to a family with a son with similar ancestry. I think you will find the terms of this land trust to be fair with no untoward strings attached."

The Branigans listened, looking to Kendle to confirm Kat's assurances. He nodded. "Yes, this is correct. We would suggest that you see the land prior to signing any trust agreements, then make up your mind. We can easily arrange for this. The only terms of the trust are that you are not to sell the land but keep it on the paternal side of the family in perpetuity. It is to be handed down to the first born son in every generation until a designated year in the future when the land trust will be released, and your ancestors will be free to do with it as they please. Until then, any and all estate taxes will be paid on the property from the trust fund, with enough money allocated for you to build a home."

The Branigans blinked several times in unison, as the extent of their good fortune set in. Kat had arranged for the land trust to be released in the year of her parents' death, thereby legally reverting to her—a woman.

"The land is beautiful with stunning river views of Manhattan," Kat added. "Someday, the land and the area will be worth a fortune. You are quite lucky. You must accept this generous offer. The donor will be so pleased to know it is going to a good family to start a new life."

Colleen Branigan made the sign of the cross, still shaking her head in disbelief. She turned to her husband. "I would like to see this land. It is the answer to our prayers. Aiden will finally be safe and away from this place."

What Kat learned was shocking. Young Aiden was being pressured to join one of the more notorious Irish slum gangs known as "the Dead Rabbits." Young children of the Five Points were taught early in age to be adept pickpockets who would shake down and terrorize merchants all over Manhattan. They hung out in saloons on 39th Street between 10th and 11th Avenues, where they made their headquarters. These young hoodlums would eventually turn from mayhem to murder; it was the way of the streets in a neighborhood where blood flowed like sewer waste.

Kat's generous intercession was coming at a critical time in her family's history. Young Aiden's potential involvement with nefarious gangs could change the course of everything, with lasting ripple effects no one could predict. The sooner they got the family out of the Five Points neighborhood, the better it would be for countless generations to come.

"Consider this your lucky day," Kat told them. "As my Irish grandmother used to say: 'May your blessings outnumber the shamrocks that grow and may trouble avoid you wherever you go'."

Colleen and Duncan simultaneously made the sign of the cross, and a deal was struck.

Chapter 12

Within days, Kendle Junior arranged to have her relatives moved to a small two bedroom farmhouse property in Brooklyn Heights close to their new land. Far away from hoodlum influence, Kat made sure Aiden was enrolled in a school where he could get proper education and stay out of trouble. If it hadn't been for her billiards winnings from Rem, none of this would have been possible. Fate did indeed work in mysterious ways.

Kat had never known much about the early history of her Irish Branigan clan, except that they had been hard-working people who had built their first house on purchased land in Brooklyn Heights. Where they had received such funds, no one seemed to know.

Kat knew her ancestors would beat the residential construction boom which skyrocketed after the Brooklyn Bridge opened in 1883. The land would eventually be worth millions in what would be marked as a New York City old historic district, marking it as a national landmark. Never in her wildest dreams would Kat have thought she would be instrumental in her early ancestors obtaining such a real estate treasure.

The history of the area alone made it invaluable. During the Revolutionary War, General George Washington had set up headquarters for his troops here to have easy access across the East River to fight the British invasion. The invention of the steamboat, and Fulton's Ferry service in 1814, made this little slice of heaven across the river more easily accessible. It soon grew in leaps and bounds.

Kat loved Brooklyn and its history. Her father used to enthrall her with amazing stories about the Canarsee Indians and the early Dutch farmers who settled the area. Seeing it almost 200 years before her time was an unbelievable treat.

When she, Kendle Junior, and Calvin transported the Branigan clan across the East River on the Fulton Ferry to see their new land, it made for a memory never forgotten. Colleen Branigan cried tears of joy. Aiden dashed off to catch rabbits, while Duncan quietly surveyed the property sporting a wide grin. With most of her remaining earnings, Kat decided to hire her relatives a local craftsman and builder to make their little dream house a reality. She even provided the builder with a detailed sketch of the layout and design of the brownstone to be built, which Colleen and Duncan absolutely loved.

They came to refer to her as "Mistress O'Malley," which was how she preferred it for the sake of any recorded family history. Kat was extremely careful not to reveal the future in their presence but did give them some gentle financial suggestions. Whether they followed through on her advice or not, she left up to them.

Her relatives were good people, and she enjoyed getting to know them, if only briefly. A small educational fund was set up for Aiden. It was a weird feeling knowing that this mere lad would produce the offspring that would eventually lead to her being born. For that reason alone, she nurtured his thoughts and ambitions, giving him a slight nudge in the right direction of his dreams, which was to "help sick animals."

"You mean a veterinarian—a doctor for animals," she clarified.

Aiden brightened and nodded. "Yes. That is what I want to do. Do you think I can?"

Kat felt like his personal fairy godmother. Her money would allow him to fulfill his dreams. She returned to Manhattan, feeling like she had accomplished a major mission. There wasn't much left in her winnings fund, but at least her paternal family's future would be secure. It was now time to let them evolve on their new path without her influence. Kat recognized she came from solid, strong stock. In her heart and mind, she knew they would thrive and flourish on their own.

~~*~~

All Hallows' Eve, known as Halloween during her time, came and went and Rem had still not returned home. August through October were the peak months for Atlantic hurricanes and the harsh tropical storms known for sinking ships. Kat justified Rem's delay by assuming he was waiting it out until November when the seas would be calmer, making the transatlantic crossing more bearable.

Of late, Kat filled her days canvassing the fashions at the modern department stores gracing Lower Manhattan: Stewart's, Lord & Taylor, and Arnold Constable & Company. It felt like retail therapy, but she coined it "costume research" instead as she sketched what she saw—from odd transient trends to the more classic styles influenced by European and American designers. It was like poking through The Met's extensive 33,000+ historical costume storage units. So many fashion nuances had been lost over time. Some had fizzled out right away leaving no evidence of their existence. The opportunity to document such transient trends in the department stores of this time was the chance of a lifetime for someone in her field.

Kat had never told Justine of her true origins as a historical preserver of fashion in a modern day world that had yet to happen. Her friend wouldn't believe her claim of being from the future anyway. She wasn't sure Rem bought her story entirely either. But he was a damn good listener when it came to talk of the inventions to come.

Justine thought Kat had good instincts for fashion. Because of this, she wasn't averse to listening to a few European trends which Kat predicted would soon hit American shores in the coming months and years. If nothing else, she left Justine with plenty of sketches to fill a portfolio of future fashions. Someday she might even open her own shop with such prior knowledge.

Big sleeves would taper off in size later in the 1830s, going to big skirts instead. Evening gowns would be cut low off the shoulder with short, full, and heavily pleated sleeves. Ankle length skirts would soon follow which would be low in the waist. Such styles would be adorned with belts and buckles, or even a sash for daytime wear. Hair pieces and huge hats would flourish with all manner of decoration. Justine picked her brain for every detail.

Kat felt like she still had one foot in the future, the other in the past. There were few whom she could truthfully confide to that would understand her plight. That was true until one day she stepped into an herbal apothecary on East Fourth Street next to the Seabury Tredwell House, an historic Federal style landmark building during her time, which would later be turned into a museum known as the "Old Merchant's House." Kat hadn't realized it had been built shortly prior to 1835. It was said to be haunted, but it looked too new to be that now.

Kat had been looking for a lavender tincture to put in her bath waters when she came upon the herbal apothecary next to it. There she met a most unusual woman.

Corinda Brown was ancient by 1835 standards. Jamaican by birth, her face had become lined and wrinkled with age, but youth and vigor still danced in her dark lively eyes. She took one look at Kat and whispered: "Do not delay. You will go home soon."

Kat paused, knowing Calvin was just outside in the carriage waiting to take her home after this last errand. She smiled at the woman and asked about the tincture.

"Listen carefully, my lady. You will go home soon," Corinda repeated more urgently. "To your real home, where you belong—in your time."

Now those words got Kat's attention. "What do you mean 'in your time'?" she murmured, glancing over her shoulder to see if they could be overheard in the small shop.

Corinda rolled her big old eyes. "Now don't go playing the fool, Missy. You know what I mean. You came from the moon and stars, travelling through time. It is written all around you. Your eyes possess a knowing of what has yet to be. But you are merely a woman, playing at a man's game—even dressing as such. You come from a time where such things are acceptable."

Kat was floored. She drew nearer, her heart racing. "What else can you tell me?"

Corinda went to the front door and locked it, putting up a "Closed" sign in the window. She swiftly returned rubbing her hands together and extended one outward palm face up towards Kat. "How much is knowing such things worth to you?"

At any other time, Kat would have dismissed such fortune-telling nonsense and told the person to piss off, but not today. There was truth in the woman's words. Her eyes reflected an element of wisdom, despite her attempt to shake Kat down for the prospect of gleaning such information. For heaven's sake—the woman somehow knew she was from the future. This was something she could not walk away from.

Kat pulled a few silver coins out of her drawstring purse and dropped them in Corinda's waiting palm. "Tell me more."

Corinda took her by the hand to the back of the shop, where she instructed Kat to take a seat at a small table. The woman lit a white candle and pulled out a well-worn tarot deck and proceeded to lay out a spread of cards with strange exotic symbols.

"I see a man," she began, thoughtfully reviewing the lineup. "A very rich and handsome man," she quickly clarified, clucking her tongue. "Someone you have been waiting for who you hope will place a ring upon your finger."

Right. Kat sat back waiting. Did all fortune-tellers tell their clients the same thing? Like you will marry a rich, handsome man and live happily ever after together?

"Forget the man," Kat replied, abruptly heading the woman off. She pointed to the card spread. "I need to know how to return to my time. Tell me what you see?"

Corinda shook her head and sighed deeply. "I cannot forget this man, and neither should you. He is the key that unlocks the door and the ring you seek. Without him you can go nowhere. You will need to be patient and release all negative thoughts. It is preventing me from seeing more."

Kat placed two more silver coins on the table. Corinda quickly whisked them away to her pocket. She continued to study the tarot cards, lightly tapping them as she did.

"Give me your hands," she finally instructed.

Kat readily complied. Corinda held them in hers for a few moments before placing them face up in front of her. She leaned in to scrutinize Kat's palm lines. Corinda smiled, then frowned, then smiled again, before shaking her head.

"What?" Kat demanded unable to contain the suspense. "Tell me what you see!"

"It is not what you think," Corinda informed. "To whom much is given, much will be expected."

What the hell did that mean? Did the woman want more money from her to speak comprehensible English? Corinda continued with the reading.

"Your fate is linked to the rings of the moon and to this man," Corinda declared. "From your palms I see that your heartline crosses over your destiny line and then briefly touches your lifeline, right here."

Corinda pointed it out and sucked air in through her teeth. "This configuration brings about sudden and abrupt life challenges. Sometimes good; sometimes not so good. However, you possess a mystical cross right here which says you will be tested by the flames of time to determine your fate. Happiness will come to you if your heart remains open. Love is a factor to your success. Wait until the winter moon is obscured in the sky and snow blankets the earth. When fire and ice commingle to cleanse the land to start anew, and a new union is forged. If the timing is right, and your heart is pure, the way will be made open to you."

Corinda sat back and quietly observed Kat. "The cards do not lie. They show that your heart is closed off. This prevents you from moving forward and will continue to put obstacles and tests in your path until you awaken and open your eyes to the truth. Do you understand what I am telling you? You will need to change to get what you most desire."

Kat bit her lower lip unable to respond. A shiver had run through her upon hearing Corinda's words, confirming that it had struck a resonant chord. Truth usually did this. It gave her much to think about. Was she really so closed off as the woman had implied?

The next day she received news from Rem on a mail packet coming from Europe, not China. He was finally coming home and would be arriving the last week in November. Closed off or not, she felt her heart flutter with such promising news.

~~*~~

Rem had read between the lines of Kat's last posted letter. She sounded lonely and bored. He learned his latter assumption was far from accurate when he received Higgins' report laying out all that had transpired in his absence. Kat might have found a way to silence Frank Calvin from reporting the truth, but Higgins had not succumbed to Kat's wily tactics. What he learned made him drop everything and book immediate passage back to New York.

The news that Kat's life had been threatened and that she had been seriously hurt, shocked him to his very core. According to Higgins it had taken a toll on her:

"Sir, she hides herself away in your study for long hours every day and will not come out. Her fingers are ink-stained so I can only conclude that she is writing some long missive. Her face is healing from the carriage accident, but there is word on the street that she brought this misfortune upon herself from making enemies through her words. She started something called a 'future forecasting group' and the men have flocked around her, some even proposing marriage. I truly fear for her continued safety, as should you..."

He cursed incessantly as he paced his quarters knowing full well that he had left her alone in a city teaming with ruthless snakes of industry. He should have been there to protect her. Everything in Higgin's letter made him angry.

Kat's outspokenness had proven dangerous, which did not surprise him one bit. Left unchecked, it could have been lethal. Yet despite her more obvious drawbacks, he still admired everything about this bold, brave, and beautiful woman. Hearing news that she had not touched the billiards table since the accident confirmed for him just how serious her physical injuries had been.

That very same day, another letter reached him. This one from his attorney, Braden Kendle, informing him that Kat had employed his son in a legal trust matter. She had purchased land, then given it away soon thereafter to some poor immigrants she had never met before who lived in the Five Points neighborhood.

Rem's head was reeling with the barrage of incoming news. What he was hearing was insane. He knew enough about Kat to know she did not do anything without good reason, but for the life of him, he could not make sense of her action. Kat had been a remarkably busy woman in his prolonged absence. God only knew what else she had done that he had yet to hear about. With both a good degree of dread and excitement, he could not wait to return home and learn the truth. No ship could sail fast enough for him.

Chapter 13

The day Kat had long waited for had finally arrived. Rem's ship the *Deliverance* was expected to make home port by midday. Kat discarded her daily menswear and in preparation for his momentous return had bought a new dress—a luxurious and stunningly cut emerald-green crepe de Chine. Its silky smooth low cut bodice intentionally showed off her more visible assets. Cleavage was the only thing women of this time were able to flaunt, and she was certainly up to the task of doing that.

Armed with Rem's long-lens spyglass, she perched herself on his rooftop viewing platform, fighting the chilly fall wind that whipped around her as she scanned the ship-filled harbor waters. She squinted against the sun, searching for a vessel coming through the Narrows flying the Eastern Star Line's identifying flags.

After what seemed like hours of waiting, she finally spotted the tall, fast schooner displaying his colorful moniker. It sliced through the choppy waters at top speed, eager to make port. Her pulse quickened with excitement. Undeniably, Rem would be standing at the rails this very minute monitoring their harbor approach. She could almost picture him, spyglass in hand, looking for the prepared slip where dockworkers would be standing by for the ship's arrival. What would he be thinking? Would he be as excited to see her again as she was to see him?

After Corinda's sage advice, Kat found herself doing some deep soul-searching. Was her heart truly blocked from attaining true love and happiness? After concerted reflection, she realized that whether she had planned to or not, she had somehow developed deep feelings for

Remington Randall that had nothing to do with the best sex of her life. Her last two entries in her journal writings had confessed as much. Here she felt safe to reveal such honest feelings, knowing no one else would be privy to her most intimate thoughts.

The crux of their relationship was whether it was doomed to be an intense brief one if she returned to her time, or a long, abiding one if she stayed. Corinda Brown had informed her that she would be going home soon, so that had to mean theirs was destined to be a brief affair.

The psychic's prediction was permanently etched in her mind, consuming her waking thoughts. On the next obscured winter moon, meaning a lunar eclipse, she had a chance to step through a portal doorway back to the future. That event would take place on December 5, 1835, 11 days before The Great Fire. There was not much time left. This homecoming would be a bittersweet reunion.

Kat half fantasized that at this very moment Rem was smiling with thoughts of her as well. Her heart fairly leapt out of her chest at the excitement of seeing him again. She raced down from the roof to relay the news to a servant, who then informed the back alley mews stableboy to bring around the closed carriage and prepare for departure. Never one to sit still for long, Kat had opted to go fetch him herself.

Kat stripped out of her long pants and donned her pretty new dress, sans corset, and the much detested undergarments women subjected themselves to. She took exceptional care with her appearance, freeing her red curly tresses so they fanned her heart-shaped face and cascaded wildly down her back. She added a hint of blush to her cheeks and reddened her lips to stand out against her pale creamy skin. It was overkill, but she wanted to look her best—for him. She was thankful that any physical evidence of her accident had long faded, and that Rem would be none the wiser of what had befallen her due to her rash actions.

~~*~~

Rem was battling both fatigue and uncertainty as he stood by watching the Deliverance's cargo hold being unloaded by his dockworkers. Several months was way too long to be away from someone such as Kat. Would she have grown tired waiting for his return? He recalled Higgins saying she had fielded gentlemen callers and invitations from those who wanted to use her for her financial foresight. How she had managed this, Higgins had not reported. He realized with a start he knew truly little outside of such brief reports and the very worst news might still await him.

As was always the case after being away for an extended period, there was a host of pressing business to see to. No sooner had he stepped off the ship then he was dealing with shipping agent and customs problems which could not wait. Documents needed his signature, and delayed shipments had to be dealt with.

Rem held up his hand, staving them off. "Gentlemen, give me a minute and I'll be in to take care of all this," he informed his managing agent. "They're opening the bottom hold for something that needs unloading before anything else."

Instructions went out and the artfully crafted billiards table he had specially ordered as a gift for Kat was first off the ship. Rem stood watch as a team of strong men managed to hoist it from the depths of the cargo hold, precariously maneuver it over the wooden gangplank and load the large crate onto a flatbed wagon sturdy enough to accommodate the weight of the pool table's slate frame. Inside the crate, the manufacturer had wrapped this exquisite beauty in many layers of heavy-duty sackcloth to prevent physical damage to its carved legs and frame. The company's shipping agent had guaranteed him it would arrive in pristine condition, and so it had.

A finer billiards table was not to be found in all of Britain or quite possibly in all the States. It was large and unwieldly to transport, but it had survived the transatlantic journey without damage. He hoped Kat would love it. She had promised to teach him snooker on a six-pocketed table and he would hold her to it. His mind painted a vivid picture of spreading her out on the table's green felt surface, like their first time, and making love to her in every conceivable way imaginable.

There was beaded sweat on his brow despite the late November temperatures. The wintry morning wind swept through the busy seaport sending a chill through him he could not shake. He had not slept well and was bone-tired and slightly feverish. But he pushed it aside as the excitement of being back in his home port overcame him.

Inside the Eastern Star Line's Maiden Lane shipping offices, he was greeted warmly by office staff and the agents who had anticipated his arrival. The *Deliverance* would be quickly unloaded and within 24 hours new cargo reloaded in its hold before sending it back out to sea. Ships never stayed in port for long—at least not his. Time was money, often providing bonuses for the captains who made fast return crossings.

At this very moment Rem just wanted to lay his head in Kat's lap and let sleep claim him. On both ends of the long room two blazing fireplaces made it a cozy refuge from the weather. He went over to one hoping the heat would dispel whatever was presently ailing him.

There was work to be done before returning to the Old Row. No sooner had he started signing off on shipping agreements then there was a commotion at the front door as if a whirlwind had stormed in. From the back of the office, he heard a familiar voice that was music to his ears. He turned his head searching out its source.

"I'm here to see Mr. Randall. Where is he?" she repeated aloud to anyone who would listen in the busy male-dominated bastion.

Wherever Kat went, she caused heads to turn and stare. Like now. This woman was not the type to stand in the shadows. Bold and beautiful, she was a cure for sore eyes. The little vixen had not been able to wait; she had come to him.

Rem stole upon her from behind, gently placing his hand on her shoulder. She spun around, eyes blazing, but instead of launching a right hook at him for touching her, she flung herself at him, hugging him to her without an ounce of social propriety. Never a finer welcome had he experienced in his lifetime. Eyebrows were raised; others openly stared before looking away as he hugged her back. Her feet lifted off the ground as he took her into his welcoming arms. He wore a silly smile, as he leaned his head back to search her face.

"Why are you smiling like that?" she demanded to know.

He could not help it. She had come to him, which told him all he needed to know. "Am I now? I was just thinking how very pretty you look all dressed up like a lady, for me."

Kat started to balk, but he held her firm. "Dare I ask, Kat? Does this mean you missed me?"

"I was bored. I had nobody to play with," she protested.

Rem frowned through narrow eyes. "That's not what I heard."

Kat blanched. What *had* he heard? And who had snitched? "Let's get out of here," she murmured prettily. "We have so much to talk about."

That, he ruefully surmised, would be the understatement of the year.

Their talk would have to wait. As their carriage arrived on the Old Row, several delivery men could be seen maneuvering the new billiards table up the entry steps and into the red stone house. Higgins was supervising, instructing them where to put it, and anguishing over it barely making it sideways through the front double doorway.

"Whatever are they delivering?" she asked, feigning ignorance.

"It's a surprise—something for you," he said winking.

"For me?" she replied, continuing to play dumb. "It's certainly BIG. Whatever can it be?"

Kat had prepared herself to feign surprise upon delivery of the new pool table. She just hadn't expected him to arrive with it. Rem must never know that she had poked through his study drawers after picking the lock. But thoughts of her surprise gift were pushed aside when she saw a sudden tremor run through him. Rem didn't look well at all. She felt his face and forehead, only to have him grab her hand away from his brow to kiss the back of it.

"Rem, you're burning up," she declared, alarmed at the clamminess of his hand. "For heavens, sake. You're sick!"

"It's nothing," he sighed. "It can wait."

No, it couldn't wait. As far as she was concerned, she would march him straight up to bed the second they got inside. But even that wasn't soon enough. As he stepped down from the carriage to take her hand, he slumped forward, nearly taking her down with him. Higgins came running to the rescue.

"Mr. Randall is not well. Please help me get him upstairs," she shouted as others swooped in around him.

It was not the homecoming Kat had envisioned, but Rem was finally home and that was all she really cared about. Their long-awaited intimate reunion would just have to wait.

~~*~~

Remington Randall made for the worst patient imaginable. He was not used to being sick and somehow thought his drive and strength made him impervious to such human failings. The doctor diagnosed influenza—in other words "the flu bug" as she knew it and told him to stay in bed and rest for as long as possible.

Influenza was thought to be a contagious killer during such backward medical times, so it sent the entire household into total panic mode. The doctor declared a household quarantine for five days so as not to spread the deadly disease to other parts of the city. Influenza epidemics, believed to have originated in China, had rapidly swept through the city in 1830 and continuing through 1833. The viral disease pathogen had killed thousands of city residents—mostly the weak and elderly, causing widespread fear at the first signs of a cough or fever.

Kat was of a different mindset. She immediately took on the role of nursemaid and medical expert. Rem's chest was deeply congested, and his lungs needed clearing. God only knew what he had been doing to cause such a debilitated state. Upon questioning, he kept referring to hunting through dusty airless attics, which made entirely no sense to her. In his feverish state, she wrote it off as the ravings of delirium.

Grannie Branigan had been the queen bee of natural, homemade remedies, so Kat knew what to do. The flu demanded the patient be constantly hydrated to flush the toxins from their body—not an easy task with Rem. He did not like being coddled one bit.

In the kitchens, she whipped up her Grannie's special concoction of elderberry tea, lemon, and honey, with a sprinkling of ginger—a syrupy brew that killed throat bacteria and would make him sweat out the toxins.

The mixture would serve to boost his immune system and heal the upper respiratory distress he was experiencing.

Kat practically had to tie Rem down to make him comply. Chicken soup with garlic, penicillin for the soul, was administered to everyone in the household, along with Grannie's flu remedy as a preventative measure. Kat instructed everyone to wash their hands frequently throughout the day, while disinfecting and wiping down surfaces to avoid the spread of bacteria and harmful germs. She was well aware that this was not a hygiene practice known at the time until Louis Pasteur would come on the scene in the 1860's. While they may have thought her fanatical, they heeded her advice and no one else got ill. Overnight she had morphed into Nurse Florence Nightingale.

By the next morning, Rem was still sweating profusely from the fever raging within him. How she wished she had a cold-water plunge pool. Instead, she repeatedly sponged down his body with cool water to soothe him, while force-feeding him her remedies. Rem mumbled something about her becoming a domineering tyrant. However, no one else questioned her intimate nursing skills. They were extremely relieved that she had taken on the task, protecting them from contracting the dreaded "killer" disease.

Kat never left his side, sleeping on a makeshift mattress cot beside his bed, administering to him like only a wife could. She was determined that he would not die on her watch if she could prevent it. They had yet to talk about so many things.

For one, they had yet to enjoy the new billiards table placed inside Rem's gaming room alongside the older billiards table. That first night, on her way to the kitchen to refill the water basin from the sink pump, she had paused at the billiards room door to admire it. It was one of the earliest six-pocketed tables to ever be made. Her pulse quickened, wanting to play to relieve the stress of the last 24 hours.

There were balls on the table—22 to be exact, and the correct colors, just like she had once described. Rem's memory was a steel trap for detail. Nothing escaped him. Snooker wouldn't even be invented for another 40 years. The man had gone through a lot of trouble to bring her this special gift, getting sick in the process. Was this not a declaration of love?

Kat returned to their bedroom and softly kissed him on his forehead, on his closed eyelids, and briefly on his lips. Rem stirred, his lips were moving, whether in a dream state or awake, he was trying to say something.

She leaned in closer and heard his almost incoherent whisper: "My love."

Startled by his words, she sat up on the edge of the bed, wide-eyed. Did he know what he was saying? Would he even remember it? And with that she watched him fall back into a deep sleep.

By the fourth day of her ministrations, Rem started to look infinitely better. The fever had broken, and his color was returning. She bathed and shaved him carefully, using a straight-edged razor and strap, but only after he raised a hand in surprise when she held the blade to his throat.

"You've done this before?" he questioned, not at all confident.

"You don't trust me? Afraid I'll slit your throat?"

He raised one eyebrow a notch, weighing his options.

"Relax. I know what I'm doing," she assured him.

Rem let her finish without protest, but he was still tense watching her wield a razor. When she moved on to bathe him, his body finally relaxed. This time he was consciously aware of her hands on his body in a different sort of way. While he silently observed her ministrations, there was a hint of amusement forming around the corners of his lips.

Her hands slowly moved the damp cloth down his bare chest, causing him to stir. Kat glanced up to see he had a sexy crooked smile on his lips. "You're enjoying this. Seeing me attend to you, aren't you?"

Rem hmphed. "Undeniably, but perhaps a little lower if you will," he instructed. "Being thorough is extremely important to your patient's overall health."

She knew damn well what he was referring do. The man was incorrigible. Like she didn't know that he was sporting a morning boner under the blanket and was wanting her to do something about it. Yes, his health was definitely returning.

"No, Rem," she said putting away the washcloth. "We need to talk first."

"Okay. Then let's talk," he replied, taking her hand in his. "Tell me what's bothering you."

Where to begin? "I feel like you're keeping secrets from me. Secrets which I need to know," she said, before carefully choosing her next words. "Lady Darcy knew your future, didn't she? Did she know about me as well?"

Rem's heart pounded as if he had been caught red-handed. He had yet to sort out the entire mess in his mind and arrive at a solution. There was the old saying: "A wise man once said nothing." He followed such sage advice and remained silent.

Kat shook her head. "Your silence tells me she did. Does Braden Kendle also know what I don't know?"

This question unnerved him. Braden would never discuss his personal business with anyone. Explicit confidentiality instructions had been given prior to moving forward with their agreement. How had Kat come to know about their interaction? Then it occurred to him.

"I heard you retained legal counsel with Kendle's son to purchase land. Does this mean you plan on staying?" He waited, hoping she would tell him this was true, but she sidestepped the issue.

"I had to do it, Rem. I set up a land trust for my direct Irish relatives who were living in the worst slum imaginable—right next to a filthy brothel!"

"You used all your money?" he asked.

Kat looked down and away. Giving her money away was tantamount to signaling she would not be needing such financial resources if she planned on leaving. "I had to do something to save them. Criminal gangs were recruiting little Aiden!" she lamented. "What would you do if these were the very people who were responsible for giving you life in the future?"

Rem had no pat answer to that, other than he would do the same thing. But he had plenty of money to spare. This was all she had that he knew of. "Did you make money from your little forecasting group?" he inquired.

Kat sucked in her breath. So, he *had* learned about that folly as well. Was this man plugged into some kind of 19th century psychic hotline? "Were you spying on me?"

Rem laughed for the first time since returning—a hearty laugh that made her acutely uncomfortable. "Hell, no. I didn't have to. Your antics spread like wildfire. Madam K. indeed! And don't think I didn't hear about your carriage mishap all the way in London. Why do you think I dropped everything to hightail it back here to make sure you were okay?"

"You weren't in China?" she questioned.

"No. Did you not hear what I just said? I was scared that something had happened to you. I raced home, with only half a ship's cargo, sick as a dog from being cooped up forever in a dusty dungeon of a place, only to arrive home to find you looking fit as a fiddle in some temptress dress. Did you not think I would care about you?"

Kat smiled light-heartedly. "Does this count as a confession of love?"

Rem sighed in exasperation. He shoved aside the bedcovers, naked as a jaybird, and got out of bed and paraded over to the armoire to retrieve his clothes. Kat's eyes followed him. He was only slightly thinner from being sick, but he was still an impressive sight.

"You need to rest," she suggested. "It's only been four days."

He dismissed such a thought. "If you haven't noticed—I heal quickly," he pointed out, grabbing a pair of gray worsted wool trousers. "I've been in bed long enough and I'm feeling quite ravenous. I want to take you out. Right now. So, dress warm and please put on a damned dress."

~~*~~

In 1835 New York, public eateries were usually located inside hotels for the convenience of their guests. Restaurants, at least the kind Kat was used to frequenting, were rare—especially ones that offered fine dining. Places like Fraunces Tavern were the more familiar places to frequent for a hearty meal, social discourse, and ale. So, it came as a surprise when Rem instructed his driver to take them to 23 William Street in the heart of the Financial District.

Kat hadn't said a word when Rem had instructed her earlier to put on a dress—not even a peep of protest. She was just so happy that he had quickly recovered, and she would no longer feel so alone in this strange world of his. Of course she had missed him desperately. And whether he would admit it or not, he *had* missed her. You don't call someone "My Love," even in the throes of feverish delirium, without there being some kernel of truth in the declaration.

This was Kat's first public outing since the accident and subsequent termination of her future forecasting group. She was excited to be going anywhere with Rem and made sure to look her best in a powder blue flounced dress with a pearled belt that cinched her tiny waist. Its Belgium lace, epitomized femininity. All she needed was a shepherd's crook and she could easily pass for Little Bo Peep.

The carriage wove its way through the noontime Broadway traffic, then down the winding curves of William Street until it pulled up outside a quaint French café called *Delmonico's*. This little European culinary oasis was tucked out of sight but appeared to be a popular choice — at least for the luncheon crowd. Outside the eatery, the street was lined with parked conveyances and hired drivers patiently waiting for their owners and/or occupants dining inside.

Rem was personally greeted by name at the door by the establishment's owner, who quickly escorted them to a private reserved table in the back. Inside the café, fine-linen covered tables were filled with other dining patrons enjoying a gourmet repast. Some craned their heads to see who Remington Randall had on his arm. There were a few faces she actually recognized from her future forecasting group, though she couldn't recall their names. So many gentlemen had popped in and out to listen to her financial advice during her short-lived career as Madam K.

Good heavens. Was that Melanie Van Eaton over in the corner dining with a woman and an older gentleman who looked vaguely familiar? No sooner did Melanie lay eyes on her than an undisguised scowl, quickly becoming a curled sneer, was spotted on her pretty little face. This wasn't such a good "restaurant date place" after all. But if Rem saw Melanie, he paid her no mind. Bless the man. Today he only had eyes for *Moi*.

The little French café's atmosphere was quite cozy and inviting with a luxurious ambiance. Clear glass-blown vases with an assortment of colored roses graced each table, giving off an aromatic scent. The owner was quite solicitous as he showed them to a table with a view of a private garden courtyard.

"Mr. Randall, we are honored to have you back at our humble establishment. We hope you and your guest will enjoy your meal," the man said, as he handed them printed menus with French script on one side and English on the other, offering such things as Lobster Newburg, Roasted Venison, Beluga Caviar and Kingfish à la Richelieu.

"Thank you Giovanni for providing us a table." Rem inclined his head towards Kat, resting his hand on her arm. "I want you to meet my guest, Miss Branigan…" he began, but Giovanni was all smiles.

"Ahh yes. I have already met the famous Madam K," he informed, brightening at the memory. "And let me say that my brother Pietro and I are honored that you have chosen to dine at Delmonico's."

Kat silently groaned. Rem shifted uneasily in his chair as Giovanni continued addressing Kat. "You may not remember but we met briefly at Fraunces Tavern a while ago. I was so sorry to hear of your unfortunate accident. I trust you are doing well after such a terrible ordeal?"

Kat nodded and thanked him for his concern as she scrambled to identify when he had popped into one of her group meetings. The Delmonico brothers, but of course! The famous eatery that went back to 1827 and would go on to become famous well into the 21st century—known worldwide for its exceptional cuisine. This café would be their original location—the one which existed before The Great Fire would consume it.

Giovanni was now gushing at her presence. "My brother, Pietro and I took your sage advice and purchased a hotel on Broad Street, which we will move to in a few weeks. My nephew will be joining us," he informed her proudly.

"That's excellent news," she said, clasping her hands together in joy. "Expansion will bring you prosperity, Giovanni. It's good you don't delay. In your case, time is of the essence. I guarantee you won't regret moving locations, despite this place being incredibly charming."

Giovanni bobbed his head in agreement. "Yes. Yes. We have outgrown this little café which was once a pastry shop. Business is so good that we have begun construction on a new location at the corner of Beaver and Williams Street. It will accommodate more seatings, and I plan on expanding our culinary menu as well."

Kat saw his excitement and fostered it further. "Make your dishes unique and name them in honor of people or events so they will always be remembered," she added. "Mark my words—many future presidents will dine at your restaurant, making Delmonico's quite famous."

Giovanni beamed at hearing such good news. The man would take her advice, as years later the dessert, Baked Alaska, would come to be created and named by a Delmonico pastry chef in honor of the purchase of Alaska from Russia. There would also be the famous "Delmonico steak" and the iconic "Eggs Benedict" to set a culinary trend.

Since their arrival, Giovanni's attention was on Kat—something Rem was not used to. He sat back, watching the interesting exchange with listless curiosity. As it continued, his mouth tightened with the stirrings of irritation. He picked up the printed menu and proceeded to intently study the French side.

"I'm thinking about the Cote de Boeuf," he announced, changing the subject. "How about you, Kat?"

Giovanni took the subtle hint. "Forgive me. I should leave you to your dining privacy." He bowed graciously, signaling the waiter to attend to their order. "Thank you again, Madam K — I mean Madam Branigan. You are most welcome at Delmonico's anytime. And you as well, Mr. Randall."

Rem snorted softly. Kat studied the English side of her menu, avoiding Rem's scrutiny as his fingers tapped impatiently on the table. She decided to cut him some slack being he was just getting over the flu and a far cry from his usual cool, unruffled self.

"The grieving Madam K widow story was quite creative," he drawled, placing his menu to the side. "I will assume that this is also a fabrication."

Kat shrugged. "Would you rather they believe I am a single woman, a harlot with no shame, living in your house?"

"Are you afraid of what they think?" he asked.

Kat scoffed. "Hell no. I was more afraid of the potential fallout for you."

"That was considerate," he replied, before adding. "Did you tell Giovanni and the rest of your admirers about the catastrophic fire you forecast will occur next month?"

"No. Of course not," she replied tersely. "Did you think I would take out a full page announcement in The New York Herald and panic all of Manhattan and Wall Street? Let's enjoy our last meal here. This place will be gone in less than a month, but at least Delmonico's the restaurant will survive due to my timely advice. Giovanni is such a nice man; I would hate to see him financially ruined. He will be one of the lucky ones to survive the fires of time."

She stared pointedly at his tapping hand. "Can you please stop that? Why are you so annoyed?"

Rem's fingers stopped. That's when she noticed his lucky signet ring was missing from his little finger. "Your ring!" she exclaimed. "Rem, what's become of your ring?"

Rem didn't answer at first. When he did, his tone was gravely serious. "Am I nothing more than a ring to you—a piece of jewelry you can use to take you home? What about us, Kat? Do you think *we* will survive the test of time?"

His bluntness took her aback. "I don't know," she admitted truthfully. "Especially when you hide things from me. I had no idea you were in London and not Canton. Can you tell me what you were doing there that took so long?"

Kat laid down her menu, causing the waiter to quickly approach, waiting to take their meal order. "I'll have the Crab Florentine," she informed, no longer hungry. The mood had quickly turned, causing a knot to form in the pit of her stomach.

"Very good, Madam. And the gentlemen will have the Ribeye Steak. Correct?"

Rem nodded. They both silently watched the waiter retreat before speaking.

"The ring is in a safe place," he finally answered.

Kat scoffed. "You mean a safe place from me?!"

Too late he realized his faux pas. "That's not what I meant."

With a ragged sigh he tried to smooth over his poor choice of words. "Kat let us please not argue—today of all days. I cannot tell you how happy I am to finally be home and have you here beside me dining together like a real couple. I didn't get a chance to tell you this morning, but I am deeply grateful for all your care in the last few days. And if I was not the best of patients, I apologize. I'm not used to being bedridden or attended to by such a beautiful nursemaid. Thank you for all you have done."

"You're welcome," she murmured.

He paused, covering her hand with his. "You look very pretty today. I know you hate wearing dresses so thank you for appeasing me. I want nothing more right now than to have you all to myself, to feast upon you without talk of all the appreciative men you helped give advice to while I was away. Had I been here I would have warned you against such dangerous actions, but it is clear you do not need a man to rein you in, but someone who will cherish you for the unique woman that you are."

Was this *her* Remington Randall expressing such words? They were downright feminist-sounding. Her resolve immediately softened at the earlier notion of him chastising her foolish venture.

Kat put her other hand over his, lightly stroking it. "Then no more gaslighting?"

He didn't understand. "Gaslighting?"

"Just the truth. No more secrets," she clarified.

He leaned in closer as if he wanted to kiss her. "No more secrets," he vowed.

She searched his eyes waiting to see whether he would be truthful or not. So much was riding on it as far as their relationship was concerned. "What was your business with Braden Kendle?" she asked.

"As you like to say: 'It's complicated'."

Kat waited. That phrase never boded well. Was he hiding bad news?

Rem continued. "Just recently I came across instructions in Ezra's personal papers that in the event of his death before I turned 33, I was to seek out Braden Kendle who he had entrusted with an important letter from Lady Darcy written to me many years ago."

This much she had learned from snooping in his study drawer—a small detail he didn't need to know right now. Was he in possession of Lady Darcy's letter to him which she had not located anywhere in his study? What had the lady told him? More importantly, would he tell her?

"And what does this have to do with going to London?" she asked instead.

He took a deep breath, telling her that this was the "complicated" part. "I went to London to locate a package Lady Darcy had placed in the safe-keeping of her former solicitor."

Kat strained forward. It sounded like an elaborate treasure hunt. How many letters or packages were there? "And did you retrieve this package from him?"

"No," he admitted, seeing her immediate disappointment.

"Her solicitor was deceased, so I had to go through his estate papers to locate it, which is in all likelihood how I got sick. The place it was stored in was a rat trap—filthy and dusty and…"

"But did you find it?" she prompted, barely holding her breath waiting for his answer.

"Yes, I found it."

She audibly sighed in relief. Why she wasn't sure, but she knew it was somehow important to them both. "And?"

"Slow down. I'm getting ahead of myself here. The letter Kendle held for Lady Darcy is quite astonishing in and of itself. It contains prophetic instructions written to my future self—intended to be opened and read in my 33rd year of life."

Kat stared back in astonishment. "You mean, right now?! Whatever did it say?"

Rem dropped the bomb of all bombs. "It was all about you, Kat. The letter was to prepare me for meeting you."

Chapter 14

Rem took the letter from his inner jacket pocket and handed it to her. It was the letter Ezra had given Kendle from Lady Darcy addressed to Rem. This is what Kat had been searching for after reading Lady Darcy's love letter to Ezra. Rem had taken it with him.

As she read it, she gasped. Shocked, she glanced up to register Rem's expression as to its authenticity. "Oh, it's real," he said confirming its validity.

"This is incredible. I don't know what to say," she uttered.

Their food came and she could barely eat what was served as the words in the letter sunk in. Lady Portia Darcy had seen her, Kat Branigan, in a prophetic dream. She had even seen glimpses of New York City in the future. The part about Rem and her destinies being inter-linked scared her. Did it mean she would forever be trapped here in the past? But the woman spoke about a "bridge" between worlds. What did she mean?

Kat bit her lip, more confused than ever. "You said you found the package she spoke of in London?"

"Yes. But it wasn't really a package, just information on the ring."

This is where she detected Rem was hedging. But why? "Let me see it," she demanded wanting to verify it for herself.

Rem cut into his prime rib, devouring it like a starving man eating his last meal. "The time is not right yet," he stated simply. He glanced at her uneaten plate of food. "Kat, you haven't eaten anything. Are you going to finish that?"

She pushed her plate towards him, watching him empty it as well. "And just when is this 'right time' you speak of?" she challenged.

"Soon," he replied, echoing the words of Corinda Brown. "Very soon."

Two elegantly dressed gentlemen diners purposely passed their table, recognized her, and stopped to inquire if she would be resuming her little forecasting group anytime soon. Their interest could not have come at a worse time. Rem knew both the men and when they questioned her about her further thoughts on the coming banking crisis she had predicted, she could see instantaneous shock on his face.

Backpedaling, she mumbled some idiotic noncommittal word salad about "time will tell what time will tell," which only served to perplex them. Kat smiled and bid them a good day. Rem remained unusually silent until they were out of earshot.

The first words out of his mouth sounded like a death knell. "Kat, you do realize those men are bankers, don't you?!"

Obviously, she did not. "Don't worry, Rem. It's alright. I'm not going to give out any more advice. I promise."

His face remained stricken with doubt, causing her to immediately switch gears, bringing them back to the real issue at hand—Lady Darcy's note. The words were etched in her mind, allowing her to repeat them.

"What does it mean: *'If you come to love her, then sadly you must let her go. Should you choose to bridge worlds to accomplish this, I will leave something of significance with my solicitor in London,'*" she questioned, re-reading the words aloud.

Rem was being intentionally sketchy about the details of the last part of the letter. Kat highly doubted it was *just* more information on the ring as he claimed. It had to be something of "significance" to Rem, but what?

Rem turned down the dessert tray when it came around, despite the apple custard tarts looking scrumptiously tempting. Instead, he kept insisting "no secrets" meant Kat had to also come clean about everything she wasn't telling him as well, which was considerable. The bankers had proved as much.

They were both playing a game of avoidance. She knew he was attempting to steer her away from further questions concerning the true contents of "the package" he had found, but Kat was having none of it.

"Okay. No secrets." She took a deep breath. "While you were gone I met an extraordinary seer—one much like Lady Darcy," she informed. "Corinda knew I was not from here and told me I would be returning home very soon. In fact, she claimed my departure date was on the next lunar eclipse, which happens to be December 5th."

From the stricken look on Rem's face, one would have thought she had just informed him she had only a few days left to live. It pierced her heart to see him shaken to his very core.

"Kat, that's only seven days away." One could cut through the silence that ensued as that fact sunk in.

Rem exhaled. "What else did this woman tell you?"

They were at an impasse when it came to an information exchange. However, fate rudely intervened, turning Delmonico's little café into Grand Central Station at rush hour. Melanie Van Eaton happened to pick that very moment to saunter over to their table like an incoming train derailment.

As was Melanie's norm, she only had eyes for Rem. She rested her white gloved hand on his broad shoulder and smiled coyly at him. Rem stood up, being the gentleman he was in the presence of a lady. Kat highly doubted the "lady" part, but even she had to admit Melanie presented a pretty picture standing there all feminine and coquettish-like.

While Kat had never asked Rem for the details of his past relationship with the woman, she didn't want to give the impression that she harbored any resentment or jealousy towards the annoying socialite. But it was clear to her that Melanie had come over to their table with an agenda in mind.

"I was so delighted to hear of your recent return," Melanie cooed, deliberately turning her back to Kat sitting beside him. "You're looking as well as ever, Rem. We must do dinner together very soon. Perhaps this week at my place, like old times."

Rem shifted uneasily. Kat's face was a blank mask which he knew spelled trouble. The sooner he nipped this in the bud, the better. "Melanie. I would like you to meet Katherine Branigan. She and I are…"

Melanie made a dismissing wave of her hand, cutting him off before he could utter another word. "Oh, yes. I've heard about her from the men all over this town. So *many* men," she stressed, letting the damning words sink in. "I hear she's quite good at what she gives them."

It was a direct insult. Rem frowned, reaching for his drink, to hold back a hot rebuke—still attempting to be the gentleman. Kat was not so nice. She had only one word for the woman—*bitch.*

She rose to her feet. "You know I'm really envious of all the people who have *never* met you," Kat shot back with a sweet innocent smile. "And for your information, Rem is not interested in the used goods hidden under your skirts. Isn't that right, Rem?"

Rem sputtered then choked on the dark ale he had just taken a swig of. A coughing jag seized him, preventing him from speaking. Shock seized Melanie. Her mouth dropped open and only word salad was tossed out. Kat had hit a direct bullseye. *Take that you bitch,* she thought with a sly smile. No one plays word warfare with a fighting Irish Branigan and gets away with a free pass. She didn't give one iota what anyone in the place thought of her raunchy retort. But then, maybe Rem did.

Kat patted Rem's back with a familiarity that could not be mistaken for anything but what it was—a lover's touch. "Oh, Honey," she cooed, caressing his back. "Let's go home where I can make you feel all better again."

In her time period, a bar crowd might have clapped at such a blatant cat fight display, but even the wait staff was quiet. Then in unison they turned and resumed their duties as did the other diners as if nothing untoward had just happened.

Rem celebrated inwardly. His little she-devil was barring jealous fangs which meant she cared. It made him feel better than he was willing to admit. A warm glow spread throughout him—lighting a fever of an entirely different sort. Hide it as she might, Kat still wanted him.

Rem took Kat's hand in his. There was a devilish twinkle in his eye, which she knowingly identified. "My thoughts, exactly," he replied.

All of Delmonico's diners witnessed the social spectacle along with the rage now plastered across Melanie's contorted face. She stood there unable to move, seething at being openly and publicly mocked. If looks could kill, Kat would already be six feet under eating dirt.

~~*~~

On the way back to the Old Row, alone again in the confines of their private carriage, Rem promptly pulled down the window shade. He finally turned to a very stoically quiet Kat, who looked guilty enough, fearing she had gone too far. She headed him off before he could chastise her egregious behavior.

"Rem, I'm so sorry. I should never have said what I did…"

Not able to resist a second longer, Rem took her in his arms and kissed her deeply, claiming her as she had claimed him as hers back in the café. She looked relieved but at the same time attempted to protest that he was still too weak to being doing such things.

"Stop talking," he said, putting a finger over her lips. "I've waited too long for this. Stop pretending. You know you want this."

That shut her up, for she did want *this*. She wholeheartedly threw herself into a smoldering response determined to make his toes curl and not be outdone. But the man was too damn competitive and way too skilled! It was *her* toes that were curling instead.

Kat finally came up for air, only to let out a long slow exhale. Her heart was still racing. "That was some kiss. Have you been practicing somewhere?"

"Only in my dreams," he replied, quite serious. "My darling Kat— let's not waste whatever time we have left together. If you're to leave soon, then let's make every moment count."

His hand reached up under her gown, only to be both shocked and delighted to find she was not wearing any undergarments—only a wisp of lacy white material she referred to as "panties," a women's "bare necessity" from her world. He pulled them off and stuffed them in his jacket pocket.

"The driver," she reminded him, bringing him to his senses.

Rem yelled out to his driver up top to keep driving around the park until he instructed him otherwise. No sooner had he done this than he raised her lacy skirts to take in the exposed beauty of Kat Branigan. This was the remedy she should have offered to him above all others. New energy surged through him. Her creamy thighs and wet vaginal lips, spread invitingly open to him, would forever be etched in his mind until the day he died. He would do his best to create a million memories to last a lifetime between now and December 5th. Rem dipped his head in and tentatively licked her, causing her smooth white thighs to quiver in anticipation.

"Yes," she whispered, eager to have him as she reclined on the velvety seat.

He dived in deeper to lap her up. Her soft moans of pleasure were songs to his heart. Of course he loved this woman and could not imagine life without her despite knowing he would eventually have to let her go. But telling her this would only make their parting more painful and difficult. The last playing card in their hand was something they were keeping close to their chest. Fate would end this game sooner than he wanted, so he would do exactly what he desired to do, and the world be damned.

~~*~~

All thoughts of the mysterious "package" slipped from her mind in the next several hours. Rem acted like a dying man on a mission to live life to the fullest. Sexy as all hell, by the time they arrived home and raced for their bedroom, they were already tearing off each other's clothes. A very naked Rem propped his arms up on the bed behind him and waited for her to remove the last of her silk stockings. But waiting was only half the game of foreplay.

Kat prolonged the moment by slowly peeling down her hosiery, exposing creamy white thighs to his view. The seductive little striptease made his eyes widen with untapped desire as she touched herself. His response was immediate, causing his cock to stand at full attention. She smiled inwardly, knowing her effect on him. How she loved watching sexual hunger rise up inside him, knowing she would be the sole beneficiary of all his testosterone-laden lust. The waiting and teasing game she was playing was well worth it.

"Stop torturing me," he groaned. "Come here right now!"

Kat sauntered over to the side of the bed, where she paused to slowly take in every inch of her lover's body. But Rem was having no more of her delays. Taking matters into hand, he clasped his hard cock and taunted her to come get it. How could she resist the irresistible?

Surprising him, she dived onto the bed, tackling him, and pushing him flat up against the pillows. Kat straddled him, her bare breasts dangling in his face, as she worked to restrain his hands. An erotic bondage scenario flashed through her fertile mind. Would her alpha male relinquish control to her?

Rem was just where she wanted him, but on all fronts he proved to be faster than her. In one swift move, he turned the tables and was now atop her where he wasted no time entering her to finally claim what was his.

~~*~~

Due to their indiscreet public behavior at Delmonico's, they overnight became the scandalous talk of the town. Her grieving widow status went the way of the wind. Unlike in her time, where public displays of affection were the norm, in 1835 it was considered unseemly to openly kiss one's husband or lover in public. But Rem did not seem to mind when she did. She would throw her arms around his neck right in Washington Square Park where they often strolled and plant a big old wet kiss right on his lips knowing it would cause a public stir—maybe even get back to that bitch Melanie Van Eaton. There were embarrassed smiles, disapproving frowns, and even looks of downright envy. It was not like they were having sex on the street, but from the reactions one would have thought as much.

In fact, Kat came to believe Rem craved such affection as an unspoken sign of her loving devotion. While the "L" word was never mentioned, she suspected they both knew it would complicate matters should they dare to go there. Afterall, she was a woman not long for his century.

At times, his transparent feelings showed through. Kat got Rem into the habit of tossing a coin in the Park's fountain whenever they walked by. He would throw it over his left shoulder and make an elaborate show at making a wish like it was the custom at the Trevi Fountain in Rome. He termed it a "courting wish" that he would not reveal despite her playful attempts to get him to come clean. In admonishment he would plant a chaste kiss on her cheek and say: "Never you mind."

As wintery fall weather swept in, the Moon grew fuller in the nighttime sky, reminding them time was quickly passing, and December 5th was almost upon them. Rem put his business affairs on hold, micro-managing it through his employees, in order to spend every waking moment together. He took her everywhere—announcing to his world that they were a twosome.

They attended music concerts at Castle Garden at Battery Park, an entertainment hall lit by gaslight chandeliers which emitted a feeble light not much better than the outdoor streetlamps. The Rialto theatre district on Broadway had yet to take off and was mostly clustered around Grand Steet, where they caught a Shakespeare production of King Lear. Kat labeled it her first "Off-Off Broadway" play.

They both loved to walk and stroll the streets, checking out the new construction going up in a city that would never stop growing. There was the newly constructed, five-story, 309 room, Astor House Hotel on Broadway and Vesey Streets, which covered a massive four-square block area and was slated to open the following year. Rem informed her that it would be a luxury hotel with bathing and toilet facilities on each floor, to which she told him such amenities were standard features in her time, complete with mani-pedi spas, hot tubs, masseuses, gym facilities, and sometimes even an indoor/outdoor swimming pool. While such news shocked him, especially the 24/7 on-demand massage services by both female and male masseurs, she was shocked to learn that women would not be allowed to enter the Astor House without being accompanied by a man in order to discourage prostitution from nearby brothels off City Hall Park.

"In my time women can go anywhere," she informed him proudly. "They can have babies without husbands, own and operate big companies, propose marriage, and even run for president."

Kat loved to shock the hell out of Rem. It made for lively conversation and debates about the rights of men versus women. During their off nights at home, Kat taught Rem snooker which he quickly excelled at. They would make snooker wagers based on an exchange of sexual favors, the more outrageous the favor the higher the stakes. Kat was sure this was the incentive that made Rem quickly learn to master the game. At times, the intensity of their lovemaking made even Kat blush. They both knew it would have to make up for a lifetime apart.

At night, they would lay awake in each other's arms and share things they would never have told another human being. Not even her friend, Lexi, knew such intimate or personal things about her. That night before the lunar eclipse was one such night.

"Tell me. What do you fear most?" Rem asked as he hugged her to him under the weight of heavy woolen covers.

It was a good question, a deep one, that she expected from a therapist, not a lover. "I don't know," she began, thinking. "I guess it would be bad, unhealthy relationships, where I should have known better but didn't. I've never been good with relationships. I don't know if I ever could be. Maybe I'm just inadequate in that department."

Rem put his forehead to hers. "I beg to differ. I certainly have no complaints. I find you to be the most incredible, smart, courageous, and loving woman I have ever known. And did I mention stunningly beautiful as well—both in and out of bed?"

Kat poked him playfully. He was just feeling the momentary afterglow of a great orgasm. "Thank you. But when I leave, you will hate or even curse me," she stated.

A sigh escaped his lips. "Why do you say such things?"

Because they usually do, she silently thought. "Rem, if you must know—men have told me I am too high maintenance—a handful so to speak. I'm too strong-willed and intimidating. Or worse yet, maybe I'm just not worth the effort they have to put in to make it work. I am forever being disappointed in relationships. This is why I leave men before they can leave me."

Oops! That last part was not meant to be spoken aloud. It contained far too much truth, even for her. Too late to take it back, she remained silent.

Rem thoughtfully weighed her confession. "So, you fear rejection and disappointment. That somehow no man will find you worthy enough to fight for you, to move heaven and earth for you—to really love you as you deserve to be loved?"

Kat buried her head in his neck. His statement had hit home. Emotion came flooding to the surface, but she did not want to spoil the moment with a display of tears. It was best if he didn't see that he had hit the nail on the head. She sighed and flipped the conversation, something she was good at doing.

"And what is it you fear most?"

Rem didn't hesitate. "I lost my mother. I lost Lady Darcy, and I lost Ezra Stark. I have no close family—something I've always desired. So, I guess you could say I fear losing those I love the most and being abandoned to a lonely life."

Guilt seized her heart. She would be just one more woman abandoning him like the others. Never had she experienced such a soul-baring discussion with a man. When one doesn't have much time left, expressed truth can often be profound.

How ironic this whole experience had been. For once in her life a man actually got her and soon she would be leaving him forever. They had played right into each other's deepest fears.

Sadness welled up in her chest and the dam that held back her disappointment broke open. Unchecked tears flowed down her cheeks which quickly became sobs of heartbreak and despair. Instead of attempting to talk her out of her emotions, or try fixing it as most men did, Rem held her tenderly, letting his bare chest absorb the flood of sorrow she spilled upon him. He lovingly kissed her on the lips, a kiss that felt different in a way she could not explain. Exhausted, she fell asleep in the comfort of his arms.

The sun had long ago risen in the morning sky when she wiped sleep from her eyes, ready for the new day. With a start, she realized she was alone, and Rem was nowhere in sight. Her dreams that night had been unsettling. Kat had dreamt of being trapped in a mega hotel with hundreds of rooms and countless floors. Frantically she searched for Rem throughout the hotel only to realize he had checked out of the hotel without telling her and leaving no forwarding address. It felt like an ominous warning.

And now, this morning upon waking, it had come true. He was gone. Had she driven him away after such an emotionally raw and revealing night or was it just separation anxiety on her part? She sat up in bed, clutching the coverlet to her breast, breathing in the lingering scent of him still upon her.

Even the room felt starkly different without him in it. Kat glanced over at the nightstand where she kept her locket and froze. There on the nightstand, next to her lucky locket, Rem had left his signet ring. The one he had said to have put away for safekeeping. Kat openly stared at it, knowing what it meant. He had left it for her to go home to her time. For him, it had been the ultimate sacrifice—an unspoken act of love.

"If you come to love her, then sadly you must let her go."

The realization hit her hard. Rem had decided to let her go. With trembling hands, she slipped the meteorite ring on her locket chain and patted it, feeling its strange energy. When the time was right and the Sun cast Earth's shadow onto the Moon, then and only then would she place the ring on her finger as Corinda Brown had instructed. The Earth would be physically between the Sun and the Moon; all three bodies aligned in a perfect powerful event like it had been the day she was transported from her world to his.

The first snow of winter swept in that day, like a romantic South Korean teledrama. In Korean culture it was believed that if two lovers witnessed the first snow of the season together, true love would blossom between them and be long-lasting. A wish made on this day would eventually come true and all lies would be forgiven. There was something about having to buy alcohol for the other party to actually seal the deal, but this was 1835 New York, not present day Korea.

Rem was not there to seal the deal. By nightfall, he still had not returned, and she realized that he had ghosted her. She couldn't blame him. No one liked saying their final goodbyes. It was time to prepare the way. A total lunar eclipse can last up to two hours and Corinda had told her not to eat or drink during that time. She had rambled on about it causing indigestion, which made no sense to her at all. It was just another silly superstition like Korean lovers witnessing the first snowfall together.

Kat had carefully preserved and saved the yellow stained dress she had been wearing that fateful August day when she found herself transported to 1835 South Street Seaport. She donned the bonnet and dress, hoping to re-create the exact details of the event.

When she was appropriately attired, she placed herself in a chair in front of the bedroom's standing floor mirror and put Rem's signet ring on her finger and waited. The Moon outside the bedroom window brightly illuminated the room. Then as if on cue, it dimmed, turning a yellowy blood red, before darkening entirely. For a brief moment, in the surrounding darkness, she felt like Dorothy in the Wizard of Oz, repeating the manta: "There's no place like home."

Three hours later she was still sitting in the chair, her head falling forward in resignation, sound asleep. She was out cold and didn't even stir when two strong arms lifted her up and put her to bed. On an unconscious level she already knew there would be no going home that night nor ever. She was forever stuck in 1835.

~~*~~

Rem had prepared to come home to an empty house. Without Kat it would no longer be a home, so he avoided returning until well past the midnight hour, attempting to find numbness at the City Hotel where he and Kat had first formally met. His bar intake of the finest bourbon, considerable even for him, was still not enough to dull the pain over the realization of him never seeing her again. After last night, he was still too raw to face her and spent the day embracing work hoping to forget the hands of time ticking down.

For a man used to being in charge and taking direct action, he felt powerless which only made him angry. Kat might be right—he *would* come to curse her in time for leaving him or even hate himself for not stopping her. She was a 21st century woman not used to being gender-restricted, and she wanted to go home. In his time, she was a fish out of water. No amount of expressed love or attention on his part seemed to sway her determination to return to her other life.

When he came home to the shock of seeing her sound asleep and not transported back to her time, he had selfishly rejoiced. Had she changed her mind or had giving her the ring simply not made any difference? There was also the possibility she would never stop trying, which he would find hard to live with.

Not knowing what to expect once she woke and realized she was still stuck with him in his time, he opted to sleep in the other room and leave her be. This decision was harder to do than he would have thought. He just wanted to crawl into bed beside her and cherish his sudden good fortune.

Kat had never asked him why a man of his wealth and stature had not taken a wife—the same question every woman and their matchmaker mama in this town had been trying to learn for years. While he had seen to his own physical needs being taken care of when it so moved him, he had avoided marriage for one simple reason. He had been waiting for an extraordinary woman to come along and had not yet found her until the day Kat catapulted into his world. She fulfilled his needs on so many fronts that he could not imagine having any other woman after her.

Rem had enjoyed every minute spent with her, even their heated debates about the opium trade. Kat may have thought he wasn't listening to her counter-arguments, but he had done some uncomfortable soul-searching on the issue. After probing deeper, he now understood her personal crusader stance on the subject of drugs. He learned both her parents had been killed in a vehicular accident by "some man hopped up on fentanyl, driving on a suspended license." This man had also died. Kat had called him a "trafficker" and a "drug dealer." Such terms were new to him, like many of her odd colloquialisms. He had certainly learned a lot in a short time from this most unusual woman claiming to be from the future.

Rem knew that while we aren't privy to the future or what the end results might be, we need to at least be cognizant of potential repercussions our actions might set in motion for generations to come. He had always thought of himself as a man of moral integrity. Once he fully understood his lucrative China trade would result in the death of thousands, even millions all over the world in the years to follow, it made him pause to reconsider his position.

Kat had dutifully reminded him of the karmic fallout if he failed to heed her warning. "Karma can be a bitch," she had pointed out.

Rem had yet to figure out a workaround. Merchants, both domestic and foreign, counted on his ships to import and export such lucrative goods. There were trade contracts which he could not just walk away from. The whole issue weighed heavily on his mind—just like Kat.

~~*~~

Kat pulled the covers over her head, letting a sense of hopelessness claim her. She knew exactly where she was and that she was still dressed in her yellow and white gown from last night. Having slept right through it, she could only surmise that Rem had finally come home, found her, and put her to bed and had opted not to join her. There was no mistaking the obvious; Rem's signet ring was still on her finger, and she was still trapped in Old New York.

Corinda Brown had scammed her. It was far safer to direct her anger and disappointment toward the Jamaican psychic feeding her hopium crap about the lunar eclipse being her ticket home, than to take the blame for her own gullibility. Rem must think her a total idiot, wherever he was.

If her fate was to permanently live in this timeline, then she would just have to make the best of it. Grannie Branigan was a firm believer that life can change depending on who one met. She used to tell Kat: "If you follow a fly you will probably land up in a bathroom. If you follow a bumble bee, you will find yourself in a flower garden. Choose wisely, my dear." Kat opted for the flower garden. But was it too late?

~~*~~

Rem left early that morning after spending the worst restless night he could recall. He could not focus, and he could not sleep. Sleeping alone no longer suited him. The bed felt cold and empty without Kat, despite the fire roaring in the guest room's hearth to keep the December chill at bay. Outside the wind howled as a desolate winter blast swept through the city, blanketing the streets with a heavy wet snow that made navigation difficult.

But business continued regardless of the conditions mother nature sprang on it. Others were up and about just as early as he. His bank had messengered him to attend an emergency meeting that morning—a rare event which did not bode well, especially in such inclement weather. Rem's carriage lumbered through snow-packed streets, yet he was still able to arrive at the designated time outside the Second Bank of New York, an impressive Greek Revival columned structure the founding fathers had built. Outside, a team of men were diligently shoveling snow off the building's grand stairway, making big piles off to the side as they prepared for another day of financial business.

It was an hour before the bank opened to the general public. The instructions he had received had been short but explicit. His bankers requested that he promptly arrive at the prescribed hour, as it concerned grave "confidential" business. There had been no explanation of what that "business" entailed.

Upon entering the marble entry hall, Rem was discreetly escorted to a closed-door boardroom, where a meeting was already in progress. The discussion was quickly curtailed the minute he stepped into the room. One quick glance round the room told him the Bank's most prominent board members were all in attendance—all 12 of them. Many of these men also held private seats on the New York Stock & Exchange Board only a stone's throw away.

Rem's presence was acknowledged with an assortment of nods and grim looks. A few of the members avoided direct eye contact, alerting him to the probability that today's unscheduled meeting had something to do with him.

Rem knew his companies were all financially sound and in good standing with the Second Bank of the United States, an institution well known for being the U.S. financial hub to the nation's wealthiest power brokers, inside and outside New York. So, it had to be something else entirely.

Nicholas Biddle, the Bank's third President since its 1816 inception, was a controversial political figure. The man was currently in the crosshairs of President Andrew Jackson, who contended Biddle's banking practices were unconstitutional and a dangerous "many-headed monster" to the Republic. Jackson, who despised national banks, and central banking in particular, had made it a re-election issue. The man ran on a platform that promoted the distrust of any bank that was not backed by gold or silver deposits. Rem tended to agree, which was why he kept his own stash of silver and gold bullion in a private secure vault outside the banking system.

But Rem and Biddle had never had any disputes—mainly because Rem's vast shipping fortune, parked in the Second Bank and others like it, was accruing the banking institution a fortune in yearly usury fees, making him *persona grata*. Bank managers usually snapped to his attention to do his bidding, like the time he had brought Kat in to open a bank account.

"Gentlemen," he acknowledged warily taking his usual seat at the director's table. "My apologies if I am late to the table. I was not aware this meeting would start before my arrival."

There. He was putting them on notice that he knew something was brewing concerning him. "What business brings us here today at such an early hour?" he added.

All eyes swung over to Nicholas Biddle, who cleared his throat nervously as he took control of the meeting. "Yes. Well, discretion was necessary." He paused before spelling it out. "Randall, it appears we have a problem. A big problem."

"I surmised as much if we're all here," Rem replied. "What exactly is the nature of this problem?"

Biddle donned his spectacles, now perched on his florid nose, and perused a report sitting in front of him. "The problem is Madam Katherine Branigan," Biddle stated.

A sinking feeling began to grow in the pit of Rem's stomach. "Can you be more specific, Nicholas? I cannot read minds."

The gathering of men shifted uncomfortably in their seats, well aware that the information, once expressed, could turn a friend and business ally into a foe. They could already sense they were treading in murky waters from Rem's tense reaction to the mere mention of the woman's name.

Biddle cut to the chase, not mincing words. "It's come to our attention that this Branigan woman, which it is said you harbor in your own home and are personally involved with, is not a predictor of the future at all but a Jacksonian spy."

Rem actually threw back his head and laughed at such a preposterous accusation, but no one else in the room was laughing with him. "Gentlemen, you can't be serious?" he questioned. The grim looks all around confirmed they were.

"That is utter nonsense! What in God's name has she done?" he asked a touch too loudly, for he suspected he already knew. He attempted to scale back his rising anger. They were talking about the woman he loved, which was none of their goddamn business.

John Jacob Astor was the first to chime in: "She is condemning anyone making a profit in the China opium trade for starters. Calling us immoral, greedy robber barons and killers of humanity. My wife and family have heard these defamatory accusations and are deeply humiliated and upset at such affronts to our character. Such spurious allegations are totally unacceptable. This woman is ruining my health."

Astor's health was already "ruined." Gout and heart disease had plagued him for years, weakening him to the point that it was said he had a wet nurse breast feed him for nutrients. Rem had heard about his "ill heath" too many times to take it seriously.

Astor continued his rant: "Madam K's so-called 'future forecasts' are destructive to decent industrious people. Did you know that she is predicting soon-to-come opium wars and thousands of deaths as a result? This woman is dangerous and needs to be stopped now. For God's sake

Randall, she called all bankers *'self-licking ice cream cones'* whatever that means!"

Rem's protective armor went up. Kat's outspokenness and dire predictions had indeed made wealthy enemies in high places while he was away. Until this very moment, he had not realized the full gravity of the matter. It was a given that these men would want her gone and in any manner accomplishable. They saw her as a grave threat and that he was standing in the way of eliminating it.

"Gentlemen, hear me out," he began. "Granted, the woman has strong opinions on the subject—all of which I have heatedly debated with her on several occasions. But when has a woman ever stopped you from plying your trade in any manner you saw fit? Are you telling me you are afraid of one woman's words?"

Rem did not expect anyone to openly admit to such an unseemly notion, but Cornelius "the Commodore" Vanderbilt, offered up another nail in Kat's coffin. "She talks openly of banking wars occurring. Specifically singling out this very bank. This could start a run on the bank and God help us all if that happens. It would be the same as shouting fire aboard a ship."

Rem quietly sighed. It was a good thing Kat also had not mentioned her Great Fire prediction which, if true, was only 10 days away. Such a fire could ruin many of them. "Miss Branigan has deposits of her own in this very bank. I am sure she did not mean what was said or perhaps was misunderstood."

Biddle quickly set the record straight. "She withdrew a huge amount while you were gone, which only fed the circulating rumors."

Okay, so the man had a point. However, it was none of these men's business that Kat had purchased Brooklyn property for her relatives with her bank holdings, and he was certainly not going to inform them of the generous transaction. They had it in for her and were looking to him to rein her in. Such a notion was futile. It would be like trying to lasso a tornado.

"Miss Branigan has no further plans to continue her little forecasting group. Of that you have her promise," he offered to put them at ease.

Thaddeus Chitwell sitting across from him openly scoffed. He had been one of the bankers to come over to their table at Delmonico's. Was he behind this inquisition? A chill ran through him as he glanced around the table, recognizing their collective hostility. The fear of losing money made sane men commit insane acts to maintain the status quo. Who amongst them had been responsible for trying to silence Kat with the carriage accident?

"And precisely what are you suggesting I do about the situation?" he asked, getting to the point. "I can attest to the fact that Miss Branigan is no spy, despite whatever damning evidence you have concocted to the contrary. The woman means no harm. Have you stopped to even consider she might be right?"

There was a chorus of derisive laughter heard around the table. Anthony Van Eaton, Melanie's railroad magnate father, was the loudest of the lot. "Rem, she has bewitched you to be talking such nonsense. I have seen with my own eyes how you look at her. You need to get rid of her or she will bring you down along with her."

Those were damning words that took him aback. The threat was now blatant and unanimous from the nods of agreement around the table.

"Arrange for that little charlatan to leave New York and stop causing trouble," he heard from the far end of the table. Abbott Lockwood's face was almost a sneer as he uttered the words. A rival China trade shipper, Kat had run into him on her very first day at the South Street Seaport. Rem recalled her telling how Lockwood had called her a "harlot" and "to be gone" from his sight. Lockwood's opinion had not changed but grown stronger. It was no secret he was a consummate woman-hater. The man could play dirty when it benefited him.

Rem found himself silently questioning who hated or feared Kat enough at this table to try to kill her. Little did they know that Kat would have liked nothing better than to be gone from their world—or that he had already tried to aid her yesterday in making that very wish come true without success. If these men only knew the truth, they would set her afire for being a witch.

They issued their final damning missive: "Take care of it, Randall, or we will." Katherine Branigan had more reasons to return to her time than she knew. She was now an officially marked woman.

Chapter 15

The bankers were forcing him to make an impossible choice. Rem simply would not let them dictate how he ran his life. His business ventures had allowed them to grow and prosper and build the very reputation of their banking institutions. They had used his money to become rich or richer—the whole damn lot of them. If he had to take extreme measures to protect Kat from them, then he would.

He needed more time to think. Their recent meal at Delmonico's took center stage. The events that had played out at the eatery were a harbinger of what was and had been brewing under the surface; events that were now coming to a fast boil. The unease he had experienced at the restaurant now confirmed it. There had been red flag warnings throughout the entire meal.

The first ominous sign was seeing Melanie Van Eaton dining with her father, something she rarely did except in the event of a crisis or impending family business. There were quite a few other familiar faces in the café that day which he had silently taken note of without mentioning it to Kat. The lot of them had looked surprised to see him. He knew they were covertly watching him as if a spy had just entered their private domain. Or was it really Kat they had been watching all along?

Rem swore. Who in God's name had drummed up that ridiculous Jacksonian spy accusation against her?! While he *had* been sick, he still had not lost his better instincts for knowing foul plan was afoot and now he knew what it was. They wanted her gone from New York and quite possibly the face of the earth.

Rem's only desire that day had been for the two of them to enjoy a simple outing and a satisfying meal after such a long separation. Even that had become impossible. The dining establishment was a popular place for the wealthy. Many of these men he had conducted business dealings with over the years, and he knew their families. The elite power brokers of New York all ran in the same social circles. This was an international trade hub where names and money meant everything, as well as who *you* knew and what you knew. In the brief time they had come to know of Kat, they had found her to be an outsider unworthy to give advice or make a name for herself. This was how the system worked. Everything had its order and place, and he would bet anything it was the same in her time as well.

Relationships, whether personal and/or business, fell under the same elite rules. Rem had been to enough elegant balls and galas to know the landscape and pitfalls—even the courting and betrothal scene. With the wealthy, it was all about merging and preserving their dynasties. Kat had referred to it in her time as "the meat market" and no truer a word could describe it. She had also informed him he would be considered "prime meat" in her time. Rem had to then field questions about how he had managed to fight off matchmaker matrons trying to get a "meat hook" into him.

"You're a big fish, Rem," she declared. "Why aren't you already married?"

Because I never loved any of them, he wanted to say. Kat was referring to Melanie, even though she refused to utter the woman's name. In fact, he had never cared much for Melanie's father, Anthony Van Eaton, and today's meeting cemented that opinion. The man was a barracuda—fast and aggressive just like his daughter. Such scoundrels of the deep could be toxic if ingested in large quantities. Which made him steer clear of the man after his brief liaison with his eldest daughter—that is until he was forced to deal with him today.

Van Eaton always had high aspirations for his first born child, which made for a spoiled grown woman used to getting her way. Melanie's father continually attempted to bring the two of them together in hopes of marrying her to his fortune. However, Rem had not gone along with such matrimonial plans. He would pick his own wife when he was good and ready. He did not need help in that department from meddlesome scheming parents.

Melanie Van Eaton had been nothing more than a brief diversion for him, a shiny new toy that one eventually tires of prior to Kat coming into his life. When Kat had asked him on their Long Island buggy ride whether he and Melanie were a couple, he had told her the truth. The finer details had been omitted. Such as that he had indeed bedded Melanie but was certain he had not been the first.

Melanie was nothing like Kat, who was vibrant and passionate and actually enjoyed everything he did with her in bed—daring him to do more. She possessed the soul of a woodland nymph. God help him—he could not get enough of her. Melanie, on the other hand, had lain there like a cold fish, relying on her beauty alone to sate him. He saw through her ruse. The woman had hoped to become impregnated to trap him into marriage. Bedding her had been a huge mistake on his part. Not only did he regret that particular transgression, but he had never gone back for seconds.

Rem did not doubt for a minute that a scorned Melanie had fueled the issue regarding the need to remove Kat from his life and Anthony Van Eaton had complied. But a murderer, she was not. Someone else had played that evil hand—a hand he now was forced to deal with.

Rem had no idea what to expect when he saw Kat again, which was par for the course. The woman could be maddeningly unpredictable.

Kat had no idea whether Rem would still want *her* in his life. She had been ready to run, abandon him, and take the first timeline portal back to her time. He might never forgive her for that. She was a terrible hit-and-run lover, but fear had overtaken her. Rem hadn't made an appearance since this morning, which spoke volumes. It only added to her doubts.

She was a grown-ass woman who had really fucked up a good thing. Not even a round of power yoga could dispel her anxiety coupled with feelings of being lost and adrift. While she had foolishly thought they were in a situationship, Rem had believed they were in a relationship. Could they ever bridge their two worlds?

Aimlessly she wandered around the house in a thick robe—her version of pajamas in an age where baggy sweatpants had yet to exist. The staff no longer looked surprised at her unseemly choice of loungewear outside the master's bedroom. She poked her head in the kitchen to see what the cook, Mrs. Potter, was preparing and felt comforted for all of the five minutes it took her to eat a hot bagel topped with chopped onion bits which had just come out of the oven.

Listless and bored, she wandered into Rem's study and fished out her hidden diary and began journaling where she left off hoping to work some disparity out of her system. But as she put her thoughts to paper, realization hit her hard. She recognized that she was a habitual pattern offender when it came to men. The truth was staring her right in the face. She could no longer deny the fact that she had turned her back on plenty of interested men in order to be free to do her own thing. She sat back in her chair contemplating why this was the case, only to put away her writings without a clear answer. Truth was often too painful to dissect.

Where in the hell was Rem right now? Kat sat on the window seat watching and waiting for him to return. The snowy weather outside had forced her inside to deal with growing cabin fever without a good Netflix movie and popcorn to curl up with.

She waxed nostalgic for a few wishful moments. In her time, she would be outside on such a day, inhaling wintery frigid air into her lungs, warmly wrapped in an all-weather ski parka, spandex leggings, woolen hat, and gloves, and most importantly—top-of-the-line winter running sneakers to jog through the snowy mess. Nothing would have kept her inside in such a winter wonderland.

The streets would have snowplows going 24/7 throughout the boroughs, and curbs would be piled high with black icy slush next to snow-blocked cars with parking tickets stuck under frozen windshield wipers.

The Old Row was empty except for a few diehard men, mostly street cleaners, shoveling walks. If it was up to Kat she would be outside this very minute making snow angels in Washington Square Park. However, women of this time did not fare well on snow days with such long skirts, so they were confined inside.

Kat would need to find boots for such days and made a mental note to purchase the best men's boots Brooks Brothers had to offer. From her "costume research" outings she had discovered the store was now offering winter accessories along with a ready-to-wear men's line.

What was wrong with her? Her thoughts were all over the place this morning. Purchasing boots should be the last thing on her mind under the circumstances. With one eye glued to the window watching for Rem's return, Kat watched the sparse street traffic come and go, causing the road to become even more snow-packed and slippery. It was starting to get treacherous out there. Would he be okay?

A man, bundled up in fur pelts, rode up on a horse and stopped outside their Old Row house. She knew instantly it wasn't Rem. The stranger dismounted, carrying a shoulder-strapped leather satchel slung across his chest. Kat watched as he proceeded to secure his steed to a hitching post before striding up their snow-covered front steps and stamping his feet to rid himself of the heavy white powder. A loud knock on the front door followed, answered by Higgins.

"Would you like some tea, Ma'am?" Higgins asked, entering the room to place a letter on Rem's study desk. Kat eyed it curiously.

"Yes, thank you. That would be nice," she said. "Have you heard word yet from Mr. Randall?"

"No, Ma'am. He had early business with his bankers this morning," Higgins informed. "I do not know when he will return."

Higgins brought her a tray of hot tea and biscuits to while away her wintery imprisonment. She had yet to change into clothes more day-time presentable but didn't care one wit if she looked like something the cat dragged in. She was fighting off an incoming bout of depression and there was no Chocolate Cookie Crumble Häagen-Daz ice cream anywhere to make it more bearable. *It will only make you fat and more sugar depressed* she scolded herself!

The letter on Rem's desk was a temporary distraction. Was it another cryptic message from his attorney, Braden Kendle, Senior? She picked up the envelope and examined the sender's seal. It was from Philip Hone, ex-mayor of New York, and was personally addressed to Rem. Despite being sealed, it had the look and feel of a social invitation.

Kat smiled. Justine had once mentioned that not being invited to a Hone party was tantamount to being branded an outcast. A slightly late invite was known to cause some matrons to be convulsed in an attack of the vapors. Kat imagined Rem got invited to many social events, but they usually came to him via his personal assistant at his maritime office. This one had the look of a holiday party, making her immediately brighten.

Christmas was fast approaching and the festive holiday season in Old New York would soon be in high swing. Kat loved Christmas. It had always been her favorite family holiday—when she still had a family. With her mother, father, and Grannie Branigan all gone, she usually hung out with Lexi and her big Italian family. Every Christmas Eve they would celebrate the Feast of the Seven Fishes with every kind of seafood dish imaginable. Pasta would be flowing with homemade cannoli, tiramisu, and lemony powdered sugar-dusted pizzelles.

The thought of experiencing Christmas in Old New York style with Rem picked up her flagging spirits. All thoughts of drowning herself in ice cream instantly faded. She had a mission to carry out.

Did Rem even have holiday decorations? Kat downed her hot tea and ran to find Higgins.

Rem could not bring himself to go home, at least not yet. There was a need in him to come bearing gifts to soften what he was certain was Kat having a tough time dealing with the fact that her plans to return to her own time had failed. If he could, he would at least try to bring a slice of it to her to lessen her homesickness.

She had told him stories about ice skating at a big building called "Rockefeller Center," where scantily-clad dancing women performed on a stage and "the biggest lit Christmas tree in all of America" was erected each year in the outside plaza to usher in the holidays. Crazier sounding yet was the fact that people actually brought real fir trees into their own home and put glowing lights on them. Kat had told him about how

Christmas trees were lit in the late 19th century using candles clipped to branches. This last bit of news was alarming and quite unbelievable to even imagine. Rem seriously wondered at the sanity of such a fire hazard.

The tradition of erecting Christmas trees in one's home had yet to be done in his time. Festive garlands and holiday wreaths dressed doors and windows, but trees belonged outside not inside. He paused to reflect on the notion and that gave him an idea.

Rem instructed his driver to take him past Central Park and to the rural forest area north of Harlem. With an axe the driver kept under his seat for added protection, Rem used it to chop down a hardy white spruce evergreen of medium height. Together the two men strapped it atop the carriage and headed south. It was indeed a strange sight to behold as he brought it home.

Nightfall was stealing upon them as they made their way to the Old Row. Both he and his driver were tired and cold, despite having stopped earlier at a tavern to give the horses a rest while they warmed their bones and filled their stomachs with hot food and ale before proceeding. But at least the snow had stopped falling and the air was clean and crisp.

~~*~~

Kat had done her best with the limited resources available to her, which wasn't much in a bachelor's house where the master rarely entertained. She had to think creatively. After emptying all of Rem's desk drawers of paper, she proceeded to cut out all manner of stars, angels, trees, candy canes, snowflakes, and snowmen shapes, before stringing red ribbons through the paper for hanging. It was her first attempt at creating handmade ornaments since being in elementary school and she threw herself wholeheartedly into the decorative task.

Paper chains with assorted holiday shapes were soon strung across the living room's fireplace mantel and front windows. Higgins managed to find red fabric for her to cut up into strips for bows and ribbons and she went to work. The man must have thought she lost her mind but didn't say a word when he saw what she was trying to do. Tomorrow she would search the park for evergreen boughs and branches she could weave into garlands and wreaths. Excitement coursed through her knowing she was creating a holiday home.

It was just what she needed to lift her flagging spirits and get her into the Christmas mood. Without the benefit of colorful electrical lighting, she lit glowing candles and placed them in every corner of the room. The only thing missing was a tree.

Kat stepped back to view and admire her handiwork when a loud commotion at the front door caused house staff to drop everything and come running. She hurried to the entry in time to witness the incredulous look on Higgin's face as Rem and another man carried a Christmas tree inside, it's fir branches dusted with recent snow. Her hand flew to her gaping mouth in surprise. Rem had brought home the very thing she had longed to add to her Christmas setting to make it real. How in God's name had he known?

He heard a gasp behind him and looked over his shoulder to find Kat standing off to the side, her reddened cheeks wet with tears as she silently stared at him and then back at his Christmas offering.

"What's wrong? You don't like this tree?" he asked bewildered. "Too big? Too small? I can take it back and get another. Just tell me what you want."

Kat shook her head, finally finding her voice. "No. No. It's perfect—absolutely perfect."

He let out a deep sigh of relief. It had been an ordeal in this weather, and he was bone tired. Yet, he would do it all again if only to make her happy.

It was now his turn to be surprised when she marched right up to him, wrapped her arms around his neck, and solemnly declared in front of the entire house staff: "I love you, Remington Randall, you wonderful man!" And all it had taken was a Christmas tree for her to realize it.

Chapter 16

Kat's heartfelt declaration turned their situationship into a real relationship in that memorable moment. Rem tossed his snowy topcoat and fur hat into Higgin's waiting hands, picked her up, swung her around, and kissed her right back. Together they laughed as one, causing her heart to melt, just like the snow forming wet puddles on the marble floor from their Christmas tree.

For Kat there would be no more denying the obvious. She had been too pigheaded and scared from the start to admit it to him or herself. She loved Remington Randall. Destiny had delivered her into the realm of Old New York to find this unusual man and she would be forever grateful. There was no going back. Her mind warmed to the idea and accepted it. Right here, with him, is where she belonged. This simple realization brought forth a flood of positive emotion that she reveled in.

All of her adult life Kat had secretly craved finding a man's man yet had never met such a person in all of Manhattan who could measure up to her fantasy ideal. Instead of a ring, Rem's declaration of love had been a simple Christmas tree. It didn't escape her that it was the first of its kind on the Old Row and perhaps all of the city. Rem had found this perfect tree, stomping through thick snow to cut it down, then bringing it home to her in the worst weather imaginable. That was going the extra mile, no matter how you viewed it.

Without knowing it, Rem had managed to give her the one gift that was surefire to lift her spirits. The tree was deeply meaningful and reminiscent of the tradition of her time—a time of the year that had always been her favorite.

Despite being tired and weary from weathering a long day, Rem spent the next several hours putting up the tree, nailing together a makeshift stand before helping her place her paper ornaments on the fragrant spruce. Kat sang Christmas carols as she waltzed around the living room, making him realize something else he did not know about her. She had a beautiful voice. Such musical lyrics he had never heard before. He found himself mirthfully chuckling when she topped off her little performance by pantomiming and singing a tune she informed him was Eartha Kitt's rendition of *Santa Baby*.

Rem's heart soared at seeing Kat so incredibly happy, but he wondered if it would last. Their relationship so far had been troubled with difficulties. Yet, for the very first time she had actually said that she *loved* him. He would have gladly cut down the entire forest if he had known one little tree would open her heart to him.

But he could not yet bring himself to declare the same true feelings for her just yet. When he did, it would be meaningful and not just because she had said it first. They made love that night with a different kind of passion—an enduring one. Rem knew that this was the woman he had been waiting for and would make his wife. Together they would become a family, hopefully have children, and create their own little Randall dynasty. Whatever it took, he vowed he would protect her with his life. His proposal of marriage would be his Christmas present to her.

Rem slipped inside her and they slept that way, wrapped around each other connected and tenderly entwined. For the first time in a long while he slept deeply, entertaining dreams of their future. Christmas could not come soon enough. So many arrangements needed to be made to make it one she would never forget.

~~*~~

December 16th finally arrived with gale force winds, snow flurries, and freezing temperatures. History would record it as being "the coldest night to hit in 36 years." Kat knew exactly what this tragic day held. That night the Great Fire of 1835 would sweep through all of lower Manhattan, causing total devastation and changing Old New York forever.

Every aspect of the conflagration was permanently etched in her mind, having helped assemble The Met's costume exhibition of the event for the May Gala Ball. Thankfully, Rem's Old Row house would be spared, being too far north of the fires.

Kat would have liked nothing better than to stay home and burrow down for the wintry night ahead. She had insisted Rem move any warehouse goods located within the 17 block radius of the fire to safer ground as a precautionary measure. It was a huge task, but he humored her and did as she instructed.

Being practical, Rem was more inclined towards preventative action. "If you know where the fire will start, wouldn't it be wiser to just station lookouts at the location to ensure it doesn't happen?"

Kat knew exactly how, when, and where the fire would start according to recorded history. Whether those reports were true or not was anyone's guess. History was known to get muddled and re-written in the time before fact-checkers.

But the known details were that sometime around 9:00 p.m. a burst gas pipe, ignited by a coal stove at the dry goods shop of Comstock & Andrews located at 25 Merchant Street, would spark an uncontainable blaze. Adjacent to the dry goods store would be buildings storing whale oil and turpentine, which would fuel the inferno. Roofs would ignite as gas pipes exploded, and coal hearth fires burned buildings of wood. Could such an event actually be stopped, she wondered? And if she tried to stop it, would her future be forever changed? There was just no way of knowing.

Rem would have to be careful. "If you warn people, they will suspect you of setting the fires, especially after moving your own stored goods to a safer ground this very week," she pointed out. "Suspicion will be cast upon you. They will wonder how you knew such a thing would happen?"

Rem was not to be deterred. "I'll suggest to Mayor Lawrence that additional Watchmen be placed on duty tonight due to rumors of thieves targeting the warehouses."

As fate would have it, they would not be spending the night safely tucked in as Kat would have preferred. The day Rem had brought home the Christmas tree was the same day an invitation had arrived addressed to him from Philip and Catherine Hone. The Hones would be hosting a Christmas Gala that night at their Broadway residence for the who's who of New York. It would be a lavish affair as all their galas were. Not attending would be a snub of the highest order and would ensure never being asked to another of their sought-out events in the future.

The Hone event was to raise money for a worthy cause—the New York Orphan Asylum Society of which Catherine Hone was a founding member. The Society had just purchased land to build a new orphanage in Bloomingdale Village, which Kat knew to be around 73rd Street and the Riverside Drive area. They had outgrown their current orphanage on Asylum Street, which would later be renamed West 4th Street in Greenwich Village. So many streets would change names over the ensuing years that Kat was forever scrambling to pinpoint where she was.

There was comfort in knowing that the Hone's Broadway residence was north of the known fire area. Despite what the night would eventually manifest, there was a level of excitement about attending a party where luminaries of the time would be in attendance. This would be the first high society ball she and Rem would attend together. Could they actually hope to dance the night away while Lower Manhattan burned?

The dress she designed and commissioned Justine to make was finished in record time after bringing on extra staff. It was beyond anything the women of the time would have ever seen and was more in the realm of the type of gown one would experience on the red carpet at The Met's Annual Gala. But a night to remember demanded a gown that would be remembered as well.

Kat's ensemble resembled a Phoenix Rising—reminiscent of the mythological bird that rose from its own ashes to be reborn. It symbolized her hope for her own future here in Rem's world. Her daringly strapless bodice, hand-beaded and done in a crimson silk, snugly fit her feminine curves. The lower part of her gown was outfitted in fiery shades of red, orange, and dyed gold ostrich feathers, with tiny flecks of black to resemble ashes. With a flared, flowing overskirt of tulle it moved like she was a bird in flight. It was a stunning and daring fashion statement for the times.

When her lady's maid helped her slip on the head-turning gown, Kat was satisfied with its dramatic effect. But what would Rem think? When he entered her dressing room in black formal attire, he stared at her in stunned silence. His eyes told her that she had accomplished what she had set out to do. It took his breath away.

"You look absolutely stunning tonight," he groaned. "And oh, so tempting."

Kat laughed with abandon. *Good answer*, she thought. Dressing for a man who appreciated how you looked, both dressed and undressed, was a heady experience for her. She wanted him to be proud of her despite all the trouble she knew she had caused him with her impetuous acts.

Rem came up behind her, sharing the vision of the two of them in the mirror. Out of a jacket pocket he extracted a black velvet jewelry box and snapped it open. He then proceeded to place an exquisite white gold diamond and cultured pearl choker around her neck. She gasped at its brilliance. It had to have cost a small fortune. Rem ran his hand down her neck and leaned in to kiss it.

Kat noticed he had gone back to wearing his signet pinky ring after she had taken it off and left it on his dresser stand. They no longer discussed the matter. They were a couple now and society would have to get used to seeing them together. The Hone's gala marked a turning point in their social relationship.

"What do you think?" he said nuzzling her neck with devilishly clear intent.

"I think we don't have time for a quickie," she said knowing where his thoughts had strayed. "But if you're referring to this incredible piece of jewelry, then I think it's extravagantly wonderful, exquisitely beautiful, and deserves an equally generous *thank you*."

She turned and kissed him deeply. "I think I may just keep you."

~~*~~

A 12-piece orchestra was tuning up for a night of festive dance when they arrived. Together they presented a stunningly attractive couple as they entered arm-in-arm into the gaslit chandeliered ballroom. When they were announced, a sea of curious eyes looked their way lingering with speculation.

Kat stood proud and tall, a statuesque beauty next to one of the most desirable and handsomest men in the room. As they made their way down the reception line gauntlet, every woman was scrutinizing her unique gown, wondering who had designed it while every man looked on for a variety of other reasons. Kat was a vision in crimson, from her flaming hair to her feathered gown, as she was officially introduced to New York's High Society. Tomorrow the buzz surrounding her, would be replaced by talk of the devastating fire. This evening she vowed she would enjoy the moment and the extravagant gaiety with her number one man, if only for a little while.

As hosts of tonight's party, Catherine Hone proved to be an elegant matron with impeccable manners, as was her famous husband. If she had heard the rumors about town concerning Kat, she certainly gave no indication of such. The woman had class. She greeted Kat warmly and even complimented her on her unusual dress.

Philip Hone recognized her and actually smiled when she asked him how his journal writing was coming along. The man had not forgotten her advice to journal everything about New York's coming and goings and make sure it all went to the New York Historical Society before he died. Would he journal the details of this gala party on this night of all nights, like he would the actual events of The Great Fire?

They steadily moved down the length of the welcoming line where the Hones, their five grown children and respective spouses, joined with the biggest benefactors of the New York Orphan Society to greet each incoming guest. Big bank drafts would be expected by the end of the evening for the Orphan Building Fund. Rem was well respected, despite his indecent attachment to Kat and, like the other attendees, would be expected to donate generously.

Many of them simply wanted his money and continued business. Snippets of elicited import goods advice and politics were exchanged, which she avoided feeling a strange energy in the air. These were his people, and she wasn't sure how she would fit in or ever be accepted.

Kat had caught a handful of disapproving looks directed her way, but Rem had stepped into her line of sight, blocking them from her view. She was quick to note that he steered her away from certain men as well. He obviously knew their names and what they were about but didn't enlighten her on the subject. Was he protecting her from something or from them?

Arriving guests quickly filled the gaslit room, casting a welcome warmth that dispelled the freezing temperatures blanketing the city outside. Some of the women's gowns took Kat's breath away. It was tantamount to stepping into The Met's vast costume collection, only the clothes here tonight were not vintage but brand new.

Rem never looked so handsome in black satin evening coattails and white silk cravat. His height made him stand out amongst the crowd and she caught the glimpses of unmarried women eyeing him wistfully before turning their attention on her, which was not the least bit wistful.

He's taken, so get over it! she wanted to tell the whole designing lot of them.

Kat had outdone her appearance this evening knowing full well that she would be placed under a microscopic lens by the New York luminaries who were always invited to Hone parties. In many ways, this was her personal coming out gala. Rem and she were making a statement together that they were indeed a couple. When one is as rich as he was, elites often learn to overlook any societal improprieties. New York would always be a business-first world, no matter what the century.

The holiday charity gala was already in full swing as they made their way to the end of the receiving line. Fine imported French champagne was uncorked and began to flow. White-suited servers milled through the crowd carrying silver trays laden with champagne flutes filled with the effervescent bubbly, while others offered up assorted finger-food pastries of canapes garnished with savory meat, caviar, and imported cheese spreads.

More than 200 guests had braved the weather to come out to not only raise money but enjoy a festive occasion with the best party hosts and guests in New York Society. After days of below zero temperatures, it was the perfect excuse to escape the confines of one's home. Philip Hone and his wife Catherine, an extremely attractive woman, never sat still. They worked the lavishly dressed society crowd like political experts, moving amongst the candlelit white linen tables thanking everyone for attending and pocketing envelopes which contained Orphan Asylum donations. Kat saw Rem discreetly place a bank note in Philip Hone's hand, not knowing he had made it in both their names.

Kat felt like an observer out of time, which was what she was. This night would start on a happy high note and end in a way history would long remember. Philip Hone was a wealthy merchant and auctioneer. His warehouses would be destroyed in the fire, financially taking a great toll on his fortune, as would other major dry goods importers here tonight. Before the night was over, the fire would decimate the commercial heart of the city taking out landmark edifices like the New York Mercantile Exchange and the main Post Office—causing over $20 million in damages. It was an unheard of amount, the equivalent of over $625 million in her time.

Wintry weather always led to building fires in New York due to the perils of gas for lighting and coal stoves for heat. Two days earlier, like a harbinger of what was to come, there had been other blazes which had exhausted the city's entire firefighting department of 1,500 men. The water supply was depleted and the Coenties Slip and portions of the East River were now frozen from the abnormal 17 degree below zero Fahrenheit temperatures. It was a cataclysmic disaster in the making, especially with so many wooden structures and warehouses.

The scions of Wall Street, along with the Banker crowd, were all in attendance this evening. As to be expected, so was Melanie Van Eaton. It was hard to put aside what Kat knew was coming and just enjoy herself. Rem must have read her thoughts.

"Come," he said taking her hand and whisking her out to the dance floor where other couples were waltzing a dance that often brought couples so close together it was considered scandalous.

"You're leading," Rem whispered in her ear. "Relax, Kat. You're all nerves tonight," he insisted, pressing her closer.

Kat rolled her eyes. Of course, he would catch her leading and call her on it. She hadn't been aware of trying to wrest control, but Rem was right. She *was* a bundle of nerves. She sighed and let him lead, melding against his tall frame and inhaling the scent of his familiar bay rum aftershave, which always sent her senses reeling. Dancing with Rem was like having vertical sex with him. Her thoughts were suddenly flooded with naughty images, causing her eyes to sparkle with mischief.

"Later," he murmured, rubbing gently against her. "Forget everything. Forget history. Forget the fires you say are coming and just let go and enjoy tonight, my little firebrand."

Easier said than done. Being an optimist at heart, Rem believed that shoring up the area with additional Watchmen would avert such a fire disaster. Yes, he had moved much of his own warehouse goods to another location on her insistence, but she had not told him all the gory little details of how bad this fire would be. She just did not want to sound like a doomsayer as they started their new life together.

Kat relaxed in Rem's arms, until the music suddenly changed to a fast and lively polka.

"It's a new dance from Prague," Rem informed. "I haven't quite got the hang of it yet."

Now polkas Kat knew how to do. She had been to a gazillion Polish weddings over the years. She took back the lead. "Here, I'll show you. It's a half-step."

Rem was a quick learner, which did not surprise her in the least. Dancing with him was not only fun but served to take her mind off what was just over the horizon. Dinner was announced and as they wove their way back to their table, a shout rang out through the crowded ballroom. "Wall Street is on fire! They're trying to save the Merchants' Exchange!"

Shock and panic swept through the room as the news sunk in. Gentlemen who had business interests in the area leapt from their seats. Wall Street meant big money and vast fortunes. Both old and young men ran for their overcoats, making a hasty retreat to the streets hoping to save whatever they could. They left wives and loved ones behind wringing their hands with fear and anxiety.

As history had recorded, it was 10 minutes past the hour of 9:00 p.m. when fire bells sounded the alarm from atop the City Hall cupola. The ringing was heard across the city, as other watch towers took up the call to alert the populace that something widespread and serious was occurring. As chaos ensued, the party spirit evaporated and was quickly replaced by a quiet pall.

Rem gave her a desperate yet knowing look. "I'm sorry, but I've got to go," he apologized. "I know what you're thinking. That you were right, but they're going to need all the help they can get."

Kat was suddenly filled with growing apprehension. "Rem, please don't go! You won't be able to stop it!" she pleaded with him, as mayhem spread throughout the ballroom. But her words of warning landed on deaf ears.

"Maybe not," he said, kissing her on the lips, not once but twice. "But I've got to try. Wait for me here." Then, without another word, he dashed off with the others to save the city.

It was the time of year when buildings and warehouses were packed with precious cargos worth a fortune. The city bell towers continued to ring out the fire warning, prompting all able-bodied man to come running from nearby parts of the city with fire buckets in-hand to fight the blaze. The curious and thrill seekers came as well to witness the unfolding cataclysm.

Across the room, Catherine Hone stood there watching her husband hightail it from the ballroom to join the other men. The couple's lavish party had come to an abrupt and unexpected end. Tables were emptied. Dinners were left uneaten. Champagne glasses were left half-full, while musicians continued to play some classical sounding dirge, reminding Kat of the last strains of music played on the decks of the sinking *Titanic*.

The remaining party attendees—the wealthy matrons and forever husband-seeking women of Manhattan, looked around the room to each other, not knowing what to do. Some sat down to finish their dinners and await word from their menfolk of their family's fate. Others looked to be silently praying or calming their fears with the help of alcohol. No one knew what to expect from the conflagration—except Kat. Tonight, many of society's wealthy would be financially ruined.

Kat had no desire to stand by and attempt to make small talk with the other women. It could take hours for Rem to return. She wanted out of there. Melanie Van Eaton chose that very moment to approach her. Draped over her arm was a dark rich Russian sable stole. Such furs were a rare and expensive commodity whatever the period. The woman was preparing to depart and escape as well.

Melanie flashed her a warm smile. "I fear the men will be gone for some time. Might I extend you the convenience and comfort of my carriage? My driver will make sure we both get home safely."

The invitation was expressed with an almost genuine look of graciousness. Since there weren't any other options available to Kat, she took it despite not liking the woman. She thanked Catherine Hone for her hospitality and expressed regret that her festivities had been marred by such a disaster.

"If Mr. Randall returns looking for me, would you please inform him I have secured a ride home," she asked the matron.

There would only be two fire deaths recorded that night, but how accurate the fatalities would be was always questionable. Forensic science didn't exist during this time. If one didn't die in the fire, one might die of freezing to death in the frigid night air where temperatures continued to dip lower. Ice and snow blanketed the city and some of the roads were dangerous and slippery to navigate.

Melanie gave instructions to the driver atop her carriage, who was bundled in several layers of wool blankets to fight the frigid elements. Hot bricks had been placed on the floorboards inside the carriage to warm one's feet. But even with heavy lap blankets to block out the chill, the air was still icy cold.

They could see wispy tendrils of their breath as they spoke. Kat hunkered down under the lap blanket, desperately hugging her wool-lined crimson cape tighter around her to protect her from the sub-zero temperatures. Thankfully, she had thought to bring along an ermine fur muff to keep her hands warm.

Fortunately, there wasn't much in the way of a cordial conversation between her and Melanie. Another man had joined them in the carriage at the last minute who looked vaguely familiar, but when his name was given as Abbott Lockwood it meant nothing to her. The man had a pocked, bulbous hooked nose that was unpleasant to gaze upon. He also looked quite drunk from too much free-flowing champagne.

The twosome silently stared at her from their seat across from her. It made her skin crawl, feeling downright creepy. When they took a turn away from the Old Row, an ominous chill ran through her that had nothing to do with the wintry weather.

"Just a slight detour, first," Melanie explained matter-of-factly when Kat questioned their direction. They were heading straight towards the fire area, not away from it. Something was afoot between the two. They exchanged knowing looks and Kat realized with rising panic that getting into their carriage had not been the wisest of decisions, despite the circumstances.

It wasn't as if she could just get out and make her way home on her own. She was trapped and at their mercy due to the unbearable weather and quickly spreading fire. They knew it and she knew it. Valiantly, she tried not to show her growing apprehension.

Outside the carriage window she could see the city flames getting closer. The distant nighttime sky was suddenly ablaze in ominous blood-red orange streaks of light. Explosions shook the ground like cannon balls on a battlefield as the fire came in contact with ruptured gas pipes and barrels of oil and turpentine that had been stockpiled in merchant warehouses throughout the area. Gunpowder kegs went off, creating billowing clouds of dense black smoke that choked the frigid air.

Their carriage jerked to an abrupt halt, the horses squealing and sending her flying against the cushions as a crowd of rough-looking men surrounded their vehicle. The Hell's Kitchen and Five Points gangs were out in mass like rats scurrying to a looter's paradise. They came prepared with wheelbarrows and carts to whisk away liquor casks and imported valuables while they still could. They drank openly from uncorked bottles of the finest wines and champagne, to keep them from freezing. Empty bottles now littered the streets with shards of broken glass. The bands of marauding hooligans partied and whooped for joy at their unexpected good fortune. It was an open invitation to massive looting and robbery. Christmas had come early to Manhattan's criminal poor.

Their carriage door was suddenly yanked open and dirty hands reached inside grasping at them with the clear intent of divesting them of any valuables. One man clawed at her gown, ripping it and pulling her off the seat towards him. She screamed and struggled to fend the thief off, only to feel a strong and swift booted foot shoved up against her backside. Seconds later Kat was flung out the open door and left to the mercy of a rowdy drunken crowd waving fiery torches. Rifle shots rang out from above on the driver's perch, sending a bullet whizzing past her face. Its heat grazed her cheek, before striking her attacker's arm and hitting home, enraging him even more.

Behind her, she heard the ominous sound of a carriage door being slammed shut, cutting her off as a deadbolt lock clicked into place. There would be no help coming from her former carriage occupants. With a final shout, the conveyance lurched forward, trampling over hellions in its haste to escape. Melanie Van Eaton and Abbott Lockwood fled the scene knowing full well the frenzied mob would make her their night's sacrificial lamb.

Kat didn't have time to consider if that had been Melanie's plan all along. Hands groped her body searching for a purse, causing pure survival instincts to kick in. These men were more inclined to hunt for riches versus gang rape her in the dead of winter. There was no time for bargaining—only distraction. She yanked off the diamond and pearl choker hidden under her cloak which Rem had gifted her that evening. It would be worth a king's ransom to these desperate ruffians. As intended, it broke open, scattering priceless gems and stones in all directions on the cobbled street. The thieves scurried to retrieve the lucrative bounty, affording her mere seconds to attempt her escape. Kat picked up her skirts and, like a marathon sprinter, ran straight into the heart of the fire.

There was no stopping or looking back as she ran for her life, dodging a field of debris everywhere she looked. Her thin satin slippers were blackened and soaked through but still she kept moving. What she saw shocked her to her very core. Entire buildings were ablaze in a wind-whipped inferno from rooftop to cellar as wealthy merchants scrambled to retrieve goods from stores and warehouses the fire threatened or engulfed.

Kat kept on running, desperately hoping to find Rem, or at least a way out of the danger surrounding her. Dirty ash-filled streets were piled high with mass quantities of all types of inventory—some as wide as 60 feet across and 25 feet high. As quickly as merchants tried to save their precious cargoes, looters were brazenly taking off with whatever they could steal away with. There was no stopping them. The merchants were outnumbered, knocked down and often brutalized as the thieves had their way.

Kat saw precious imported Chinese silks and fine muslins strewn about in the street, scorched and trampled with mud and snowy slush. Porcelain dishes, figurines, and broken furniture were scattered everywhere, abandoned for the more desirable stores of canned food, and packaged gourmet delicacies that would provide a later feast for the roving gangs.

It was immediately evident that attempting to fight the blaze was futile. It spread faster than anyone had time and resources to snuff out. Lofty edifices were being leveled like dominoes falling in line, going up with lightning flashes one after the other. Kat's ear's hurt with the loud booms. The sound of destruction was deafening. Everything was combustible, fueling a fire that had a ravenous appetite for wood and perishables. The heat from the inferno was so hot it melted iron bars on windows, turning them to molten liquid, the likes of which had never been seen before.

Well-dressed and rag-torn gawkers alike lined the street, mesmerized by the shooting flames licking up and across the timbers, and wrapping around anything in sight as wind-swept embers spread from one block to the next. With the relentless wind feeding its ferocity, those who had come to help were paralyzed, unable to slow down or stop the inferno. Wall Street and the surrounding area had become a solid wall of fire with as many as 50 buildings simultaneously going up in a sea of flames. It looked like a biblical Armageddon with no way out.

Streets were blocked and Kat knew not where to run. The city had been left to the mercy of a woefully ill-equipped voluntary fire department who stood by helplessly. There were only 1,500 firefighters available to extinguish such a large conflagration. The men were already exhausted from putting out several other fires in the preceding days. Their efforts were further stymied by the narrow, winding streets that didn't allow them to get their pumps through. Hook and ladders barely reached second floor buildings. Some fighters attempted to pile up tables and barrels in the street in an effort to reach higher floors and burning roofs, but such makeshift means proved useless.

Without a sufficient and plentiful source of water, fighting the fire became almost impossible. Men formed long hose lines down to the East River only to find the riverbanks were frozen solid. Try as they might, they were unable to drill holes in the thick ice to get to the life-saving resource underneath. There were no other water options available.

The day before the fire, the Hudson River had been shut down to barge traffic due to icy conditions and six degree temperatures. The Erie Canal had been closed for the same reason. It was a firefighter's worst nightmare. With nothing more than hand-pumping equipment to extract and disperse water, the firemen had to resort to pouring brandy on their pumps to prevent them from freezing over entirely. In no time, their hoses were frozen through and discarded on the muddy ground, unable to pump.

Kat saw it all, just as history had reported, but history could never tell the full story. She skirted around a mob of angry citizens intent on hanging looters from a stately old elm tree that had yet to catch fire. A thief's body now swayed frozen in the wind—the dead man destined for consumption by the all-encompassing fiery wrath of mother nature. Over 400 suspected looters would be rounded up in the days to follow. The constables could be seen chasing thieves through the rubble as chaos reigned everywhere.

Arsonists had also come out to play and create more havoc. One man was caught attempting to burn a building at Broad and Stone Streets. Swift justice prevailed as vigilantes tackled him and hung him on the spot from a nearby lamp post. Another fire starter was thrown directly into the flames of a burning building and left to perish. No mercy was shown to such perpetrators. Those who possessed pistols were not afraid to mete out justice on the spot as well, quickly taking the law into their own hands to protect precious property.

What Kat was witnessing first-hand was worse than anything imagined or historically recorded. Unbridled fear and panic ran rampant in the lawless streets. She passed dead bodies that would never be counted in the final tally of recorded fatalities. Only two deaths would be officially reported. However, Kat now knew that figure wasn't anywhere near the truth. Men ran screaming from buildings, their clothes and flesh on fire, cursing God for their misfortune while others fainted or suffered heart attacks right in the street, their faces contorted with anguish and death as the flames danced demonically around them. These nameless casualties would forever remain individuals without identities, destined to be thrust into some unmarked mass grave and erased from history—becoming the unreported and forgotten.

Kat took note of all she saw as she desperately searched for Rem. Every step she took was a potential pitfall—a minefield of incendiary objects. She was forced to dodge flying embers that swirled on the wind, sweeping their way through the streets of Lower Manhattan and threatening to make their way across the river towards Brooklyn.

Those on the ground knew not where the fire would finally come to a stop. That is, if it could be stopped. Right now, it looked like the gates of hell had been opened and its complete destruction unleashed on an unprepared metropolis. The fierce winds freakishly kept changing direction. Unchecked it would spread the fire north and take out all of Manhattan past 18th Street. If history was correct, Kat knew this would not happen.

There was no let up. Like a never-ending fireworks display, hazardous fire remnants continued to rain down from dense blood-orange skies. The flammable danger to one's apparel was never ending. Several times Kat had to extinguish patches on her clothes that threatened to ignite and engulf her in the inferno spiraling around her. Her gown was scorched and unrecognizable. The hood on her cape barely protected her hair, but still she kept moving. Nothing else mattered to her except finding Rem.

As a lone woman running through the fiery destruction, Kat went fairly unnoticed in the unraveling melee. It was each man for himself as countless merchants, along with loyal employees, frantically hauled out steel safes and stuffed them with account books, bills of lading, insurance papers, invoices, and anything else of salvageable importance before their buildings were forever consumed. Businesses and countless jobs would be lost this very evening as the city burned unchecked.

Thank God Rem had listened to her and moved the contents of his store houses further north beforehand. She knew the fire would also spare his South Street maritime offices off Maiden Lane. Many sea captains, seeing the conflagration raging, had raced to sailing ships to move them beyond the icy shores hoping to escape flying embers. For some it was a precaution that spared them; for others it was too late.

No matter who was or was not affected by this unfolding tragedy, Rem's business colleagues' misfortunes would have a lasting effect on every shipper, merchant, and banker in the city for some time to come. Tonight's Great Fire would change the course of New York forever. Out of destruction would come great and innovative change for the greatest commercial hub in the world, but no one knew it yet. The nightmare right now was too raw and real to think of anything past the moment. The real nightmare of loss would be felt after the tragedy when merchants realized they were financially wiped out and insurance companies failed to pay.

Kat knew that the fire would burn into the early hours of the next morning, decimating the Merchants' Exchange and crippling the Stock Exchange, forcing trading to be curtailed, and bringing the financial community to its knees. In the end, the blaze would reportedly consume 21 blocks and almost 700 buildings, bankrupting all but one of the city's insurance companies.

Kat was chilled to the bone and every muscle in her body strained in exhausted protest. Her feet and toes were blistered and blue, if not bordering on frozen. The adrenaline surging through her kept her moving forward unable to stop in what now resembled a burnt-out war zone.

History told her they would eventually have to dynamite buildings to stop the fire's destructive path. Someone would have to cross the river to the Brooklyn Navy Yard or Red Hook to bring back gunpowder barrels to the burnt district. This would prove to be the only successful measure with which to stop the apocalypse from completely consuming the rest of the city.

Kat shouted to anyone who would listen to get "dynamite" but realized dynamite had yet to be invented. Her mind locked on the alternative. Black powder and nitroglycerin were the primary explosives then. They would have to call in the U.S. Marines to save the day.

"Go to the Navy Yard! Bring back explosives. Blow up buildings! Stop the fire!" she kept screaming at the top of her lungs to anyone who would listen.

~~*~~

Despite everyone's best efforts to save it, Rem stood back to witness the roof of the Merchants' Exchange cave in, taking with it the great cupola atop the edifice where a Watchman had earlier spotted the first sparks of fire. The building was less than eight-years-old, and its majestic light-filled rotunda was like no other. Guards carrying rifles and bayonets swooped in to protect the ruins of the building from looters, as antiquities abounded within.

He sadly turned away from the destruction, only to experience an even greater shock. A fire-ravaged Kat was running down Wall Street, a frantic look on her face as if the devil himself were after her, screaming like a wild-eyed banshee to whoever she passed, only to be jostled aside by the crowd who must have thought her a madwoman. He saw her stagger and fall to the hard wet ground, where an overweight man viciously kicked her out of his way.

Blind rage seized him. Rem sprang forward, pushing his way through the dense throng of citizens to reach her. Without a moment's hesitation he hit the perpetrator square in the jaw, sending the man staggering backward, before hitting him a second time even harder.

Rem would have continued to pummel the culprit but stopped. He had to get Kat out of there. There was blood on her cheek and her lips were blue. Dazed green eyes stared back at him while she babbled something about going to the Brooklyn Navy Yard. He bent down and scooped her up like a rag doll.

"It's Rem. You're safe now," he shouted to her over the pandemonium, and felt her immediately go limp. "Hold strong my love," he urged, frantically hugging her to him as he dodged his way through the frenzied throng as swiftly as his tired legs could carry him.

Kat didn't remember losing consciousness, or how long she had been out—only that Rem was the one who had rescued her from the maddening crowd. When she regained full senses she found herself laid out on a polished wooden office floor bundled up like a cocoon in heavy woolen blankets. Rem was hunched over her, looking like hell. His smoke-smudged face and burnt evening attire told her he had been on the front lines battling the fire.

His strong, warm hands were massaging circulation back into her numb, icy fingers and toes. It caused an intense burning sensation, making her immediately pull back.

"Stay still," Rem admonished. "Any longer in the elements and you would have gotten frostbite."

The word "frostbite" sent shivers of fear through her. Grotesque visions of blackened, gangrenous toes, along with possible amputation and losing one's mobility flooded her senses.

"Is it bad?" she asked, trying to stuff down panic.

Rem gave her a lopsided grin. "You'll be okay. You're in good hands." He let out a loud exasperated sigh, shaking his head in disbelief. "Kat, what in God's name were you doing out there?!"

Kat closed her eyes remembering all too well. "Melanie thought I needed a little more excitement in my life," she replied flippantly, before changing the subject.

"Where are we?" She asked glancing around taking in the unfamiliar setting.

"We're at my Broad Street accounting offices, away from the fire, but a far cry from home," he replied, before getting back to his unanswered question. "Are you going to tell me what happened?"

Kat averted her eyes. It was hard enough to admit she had been foolish enough to take Melanie up on her ride offer, let alone what followed, but she had desperately wanted to go home.

"C'mon, Kat," he prompted, rubbing her hands.

She finally capitulated. He would find out anyway. "It was awful. I was shot at, kicked out of the carriage by those two villains, Melanie and

Abbot Lockwood, and thrown into the hands of a gang of thieves who stole the necklace you gave me."

Rem's face darkened with a look she had never seen before, the kind reserved for one's worst enemy when you have a loaded AK-47 in your hand, cocked and ready to do battle.

Kat's hand went to the bruised cheek that had dodged an incoming bullet. Rem must have cleaned it as it was no longer bloody, but the graze mark still stung like the devil. Carriage accidents had become a pattern for her. Two near-death misses were more than enough for anyone. Old New York had become a dangerous place. Her modern-day survival skills had not prepared her for the likes of this.

She winced. It hadn't helped being kicked in the side by someone's hard-toed boot. Kat attempted to sit up, craving Rem's protective arms to comfort her. He sensed her need and drew her onto his lap, hugging her close.

"If anything had happened, I wouldn't be able to live without you," he quietly confessed. His words were oddly choked with raw emotion. He cradled her head in the crook of his arm, running his hands through her tresses, his eyes never leaving hers.

"I love you Kat. I hope you realize that I would do anything for you. Anything." He paused, dramatically emphasizing his last word, before going on. "I've never felt this way about anyone until now. What I'm trying to say, and perhaps not doing the best job of, so forgive me, is— marry me. Right now, today. Be my wife and let me make you happy so you never live to regret it."

Rem's proposal and sincere declaration of love and marriage was something she hadn't seen coming. The circumstances surrounding tonight had made them both realize that life was fleeting and that they belonged together. Destiny and fate had brought them to this point and the mere thought of going back to her time was a non sequitur. Her life was here with him, and she knew it.

She saw he was holding his breath, awaiting her answer. "Yes, Rem. I'll marry you," she answered, taking in his sooty face and the immediate sign of relief she saw upon hearing her acceptance. "Are you sure?" she added.

To her astonishment, Rem reached into the inner pocket of his singed dress jacket and extracted a familiar-looking ring. Her eyes grew enormous as she realized it was an exact duplicate of the meteorite ring now worn on his little finger.

"There's two?" she gasped. "But where did you get…?"

"Lady Darcy had two made. I didn't know this until recently. I had planned my proposal to be a Christmas surprise," he confessed, "but after tonight, I can no longer wait. Lady Darcy wrote that 'when the time was right' I would know it. I know it now."

Rem removed his ring and gave it to her, while he held the other one. They would make their own private vows without the ceremonial pomp and circumstances that usually went with such unions. Without a moment's hesitation Kat kissed his ring and slid it back on his finger. "I absolutely love you, too, Remington Randall—you crazy wonderful hunk of a man. I pledge to love you now and forever until the end of time."

Rem placed the duplicate ring, emblazoned with his initial, on her finger as well. Soon she would be a Randall, and they would join their lives together. "I love you Katherine Branigan. Now and forever…" he pledged, "until the end of time."

Then the strangest thing happened. The ether around them became charged with an eerie bluish-yellow light and the earth appeared to shake within its very core. Kat's first thought was that they had finally detonated the explosives to stop the fire from spreading uptown. But the truth was far from it as the world began to spin on its axis.

As realization hit, her last desperate thought was *"Oh Fuck, No!"*

PART 3

Chapter 17

When her vision finally cleared, Kat found herself standing in front of an all too familiar wall of floor-to-ceiling mirrors, staring back at her brightly lit reflection. Clothed in the same soiled yellow and white cotton dress from the new donor's 1835 collection, and wearing the signet "R" ring still on her finger, she had been sucked back in time and space to where she had started—her private office in the Costume Restoration Department of The Metropolitan Museum of Art.

"Fuck, no!" she silently screamed, beseeching the universe to *"take me back!"*

But the fabric of time was not budging. No sooner had she embraced her new life with Rem in his world—finding love and a marriage proposal to a man like no other, then she was kicked back to her time to flounder alone. The timing was incredibly cruel and suspect.

Kat checked the calendar on her desk. It still pointed to April 1st while the clock on the wall displayed the correct time. Yet, the world around her felt surreal. Had she somehow become mesmerized by the mirror and dreamt all that had happened? Or had she been sucked into the mirror and transported back to an earlier time? Either explanation felt far-fetched and utterly preposterous.

Her cell phone was buzzing with text messages from Lexi demanding to know where she was and lamenting how she had been hovering and circling the area ad nauseum for what seemed like forever.

"I've already had to fend off two not-so-nice cops threatening to give me tickets for double parking during rush hour. I can't circle around again! Fifth Avenue is jammed!" And even more texts shouting in large caps: "WHERE THE HELL ARE YOU?! GET YOUR ASS DOWN HERE, PRONTO. WE'RE GOING TO BE LATE!!!!!!"

Lexi was hell to deal with when she was riled up. Kat quickly slapped both cheeks, noting they were as creamy and smooth as ever. No sign of the bullet having grazed her or the ravages of being out for hours in a frigid night and fiery inferno. And more importantly, no evidence of Rem anywhere in sight. He had not come with her, if indeed he was real at all, or was he just a figment of her imagination?

Kat shook the fog from her mind and was confronted by a sudden and profound emptiness that threatened to paralyze her with grief. Rem had professed his love to her for the first time. It was not something to be easily erased from one's mind nor heart. For heaven's sake, Remington Randall had said that he loved her!

She almost sank to the floor to weep, but her mind told her to move and move she did with great reluctance, for she knew not what else to do. Scrambling out of the historic 1835 dress, she carefully laid it back in the long, flat, conservation box and donned her traditional New York tournament garb—skinny pencil leg black pants with a starched, black, long-sleeve cotton blouse. Her brain was still on auto-pilot as she grabbed her tournament bag and ran down the steps of the museum whose doors had already closed for the day.

"Sorry, Lexi," Kat said plopping down into the passenger seat of her friend's dark blue BMW Sedan. She tossed her black-leather cue stick case in the back seat and sat forward. "It's been a strange day, and somehow I managed to get distracted by time." No truer a statement could be made.

"Was it the quake?" Lexi ventured, pulling out into rush hour traffic.

Kat stared ahead. "What quake?"

Lexi glanced over in surprise. "For God's sake, Kat. You didn't feel it? I was stuck in my car at a light when it hit like a rolling wave that knocked out power. Traffic lights stopped working bringing everything to a screeching halt. And you say you didn't feel it?"

Kat shook her head. "No. How long did it last?"

"Not long," Lexi shrugged. "But everyone and their uncle was blaring their horns like a football tailgate party."

Kat remained silent. There *had* been a rumble of the earth and the lights going out just prior to her being transported to 1835. That was a quake? And was it somehow related to her being thrown back to another period of time?

"Hey, snap out of it!" Lexi chastised. "And by the way, you look awful."

Lexi had never been one to mince words. "What the hell have you been doing?! Attending a ceremonial costume burial?"

Kat sighed wearily. "You wouldn't believe me if I told you."

Lexi threw her a sharp glance as she turned onto 79th Street. "What's that supposed to mean? That you're not going to tell me?"

Kat stared out the window at the congestion of honking cars and taxis inching past, seeing in her mind the omnibuses and carriages that once graced these streets. "Later, Lexi," she somberly instructed. "Just drive."

"Well, someone is certainly crabby," Lexi proclaimed. She glanced over at Kat, only to zero in and snicker. "Oh. My. Are you going steady or something?"

What was Lexi talking about? When Kat didn't respond, Lexi pointed to the signet ring on Kat's finger. "Where did you get that weird looking thing? And what does the "R" stand for?"

Trust Lexi to not miss a thing. Kat realized she had not removed the ring from her finger and given it to The Met's Costume Curator, as standard protocol required when a personal effect was found in a costume.

"Oh, this," she commented, shrugging to make light of it. "I found it in a costume and forgot to return it."

The last part was an outright lie. Kat had made up her mind not to return it. She would make sure, come tomorrow morning, that any mention of the ring was forever scrubbed from inventory documents.

She was now certain that something profound had happened to her. Her experience felt real and not like a dream at all. Every detail of her sojourn into 1835 would forever be etched in her memory. She was not crazy, but the world would think so if she tried to explain.

Kat glanced down at the ring on her finger with immense regret. It would have been her wedding ring if time hadn't sabotaged things. It was hers now. A loving memento of lost love.

Getting down to the Lower East Side took forever. They skipped dinner and settled instead for bar snacks at the billiards club, *Out of Pocket,* where the tournament was being held.

When her mixed match set was called, Kat half-heartedly approached the pool table. To muster up any enthusiasm at all, she imagined her geeky-looking, Wall Street trader-type opponent, with his close-cropped beard, slicked-back hair, and narrow-set-eyes, was none other than Remington Randall. She beat him hands down by several points. It was definitely one of her better games. The win would put her in the running for the New York State championships.

"You were on fire tonight!" Lexi declared in amazement. "When in God's name did you suddenly get so rock-star good? Have you been practicing on the side with someone I don't know about?"

Kat smiled inwardly. If Lexi only knew that she had indeed been playing with one of New York's very best 1835 players. During their time together she realized that she had picked up some of Rem's technique moves. That alone was too real to have been just a figment of her imagination.

Lexi, who had not been as lucky tonight, openly pouted on the drive home to Brooklyn. "Why are you holding out on me, Kat? Best friends are supposed to tell each other everything. So, c'mon, talk!"

Yet, she couldn't. All that happened was still too raw to put into words—and too unbelievable. "Another time Lex. I have a splitting headache." It was a lame excuse, but she just wanted to go home and escape this reality.

When Lexi pulled up outside Kat's Brooklyn house, Kat got out and froze in place, staring ahead, completely disoriented. There was a different house on the property adjoining her property—an older statelier mini-mansion which hadn't been there before.

"Wait," she called out to her friend before driving off. She spun around, her eyes wide. "What happened to the other house?"

Lexi frowned. "What other house?"

"That one over there!" Kat pointed. Was Lexi deaf?!

Lexi frowned, her eyes narrowing together with obvious concern. "What are you talking about? That's always been there. Please tell me you're joking. You ARE joking, right?"

Kat shook her head. She was positive that house had NOT been there before!

Lexi looked completely bewildered. "Okay, Kat. Now you're scaring me. Are you okay?"

No, she was not "okay" at all, but she was averse to admitting it for fear of sounding like she had lost her mind. "Forget it," she mumbled, attempting a fake smile. "I guess I'm just tired."

But it was now evident that as a direct result of her actions in 1835, she might have inadvertently changed a thing or two—like that strange house now sitting next to hers which looked as old as her own. Had her relatives, Colleen and Duncan Branigan, sold the other property she had entrusted to them? Could she expect other changes as well?

She inspected her house with a keen eye for change but after an exhausting search could find nothing noteworthy. Saturday dawned like any other day—a day she usually loved to chill out and do whatever she wanted, except today would be quite different.

After a restless, sleepless night, no longer having the warmth of Rem next to her, she was determined to find answers. Kat took the subway into Manhattan, heading straight for The New York Historical Society on Central Park West. As a child she had spent so many years there delving through records with her History Professor father, it had become a second home to her. The exhibits, the films, and the Society's own vintage clothing had inspired her to pursue a career in costume preservation which, ultimately, had set her on a life course which would eventually land her a staff position with The Metropolitan Museum of Art's Costume Division.

Kat had made numerous contacts at the Historical Society. The Met oftentimes collaborated with them, like on The Great Fire of 1835 Exhibit soon to open. Her go-to-person was Elizabeth Abrams, who had a photographic memory much like Kat's and was an authority on Old New

York. She texted her that morning asking for a favor on her day off and offering to take her to lunch.

They met in the Smith Family Skylight Gallery right off the main entrance. It's natural light and arched classical columns had been the venue for many an elegant cocktail reception and dinner and was always Kat's favorite go-to meeting place.

"Liz, I need to know everything about New York in 1835," she announced, getting straight to the point of the meeting.

"That was a definitive year, Kat. We have volumes. How long do you have and what are you looking for?"

Kat sighed. "I'm looking for any information you have on a man named Remington Randall."

Liz was thoughtful. "The name sounds familiar. Is he connected to Randall's and Ward's Island?"

Kat shook her head. "I don't believe so. This Randall was a wealthy shipper and owner of the Eastern Star Line during the early 19th century. I need to find out what happened to him after 1835."

Liz raised an eyebrow. "Is this for The Met's upcoming Gala event?"

Kat hedged. "Yes and no—but it's really important I track him down. I couldn't find anything of substance on him after doing multiple internet searches, so I contacted you. I figured if anyone knew the name, it would be you. He might have even been mentioned in one of Philip Hone's private journals for the night of December 16, 1835. Everyone was there for Philip and Catherine Hone's party when the fire alarms in the bell tower went off."

Liz looked at her peculiarly. "Where did you hear that story? There's no mention in his diaries of hosting a party that night. You must be mistaken."

Kat blinked in confusion. Not all of Hone's diaries had been published, but certainly he would have written about the panic of his guests at his party, and this would have been noted in his account of the fire. On the other hand, Liz ought to know what was in Hone's extensive journals. Had he edited it out of his description of events leading up to The Great Fire? If so, why? Was it because it made the Old New York elite look frivolous to be celebrating on the night of a huge disaster? Or had that timeline changed as well?

Kat knew she was going out on a limb. "I have a few other names from that time I need information on as well." She handed over a concise list, which Liz quickly scanned. Her eyes brightened.

"I recognize this one—*Corinda Brown*. She became a well-known psychic during her time—even amassing sizeable wealth. We did a lecture on 19th century New York fortune-tellers a while back. Brown's name was among them. She was Jamaican, I believe. Some called her a voodoo witch who could read the stars."

That was surprising news that Corinda had become wealthy as a result of her psychic ability. Witch or not, Kat was thinking the woman's predictions could stand room for improvement. Her predictive timing had been way off as to when Kat would return to her time. Unless, of course, Kat had misunderstood what the woman had foretold. This had not occurred to her. Perhaps Corinda had not been referring to the December 6th lunar eclipse to take her home, but the day of the actual fire. She struggled to recall the seer's exact words:

Wait until the winter moon is obscured in the sky and snow blankets the earth. When fire and ice commingle to cleanse the land to start anew, and a new union is forged. If the timing is right, and your heart is pure, the way will be made open to you.

Damn! The Jamaican woman *had* been right. The problem was not Corinda, but her. She had failed to correctly interpret the woman's prophetic words. The very moment her heart was wide open, and Rem had professed his love and she hers for him, the way *had* been made open. The "forged union" occurred when they slipped the mysterious identical rings on each other's finger. That was the exact moment the two realities had conjoined, shifted and she had gone *poof*! The Great Fire of 1835 had been the true catalyst to traversing different timelines.

Kat shook her head, trying to clear her thoughts concerning Corinda Brown. The woman's infamous history would have to wait. "Let's focus on Remington Randall first," Kat suggested. "He lived on Washington Square North's Old Row, No. 8."

Liz took her into the back stacks of the Society's vast and distinguished research library where she moved methodically down aisles containing printed graphic and photo collections, architectural drawings, thousands of newspaper publications, and personal and business records on a wide range of New Yorkers who had shaped the future of the city.

Liz wasted no time pulling down several folders and books from an array of shelved material. One such reference book contained a registry of 19th century New York shipping companies. Another chronicled "Resident Families of Washington Square's Old Row." Liz's arms were full by the time she placed them on a study table and fired up the Society's online database.

Her fingers rapidly clacked over the computer keys, cross-referencing names with legal records, census records, and society registries.

"This is odd," Liz readily remarked. "Randall's name is here in the records but there's no data on date of death. He was born in London on August 1, 1802, but there's no records of either a spouse or children. No depiction of what he looked like either. We can usually find a painting or drawing someone rendered, but there's nothing here for facial recognition. The rich always sat for portraits, but in his case there aren't any. I do have a lengthy list of his holdings and net worth during that time and, of course, his accomplishments, which are sizeable, but not much else. There is a brief mention of him fighting The Great Fire that year, along with other wealthy merchants and shippers, but that's not surprising. They all had a lot to lose and ran to protect their wealth."

Liz continued. "It appears Randall's holdings were not affected by the fire. However, he sold the Eastern Star Line Company in early 1836 for a handsome sum, along with other numerous real estate holdings he owned at the time. It is believed he set sail for parts unknown. Some speculated he went to China to live, being an adventuresome sort. But that's where any information on his life seems to come to a dead end."

Kat's heart sank. Rem had sold everything after she left. He must have been devastated. The thought of him being unreachable and long dead, made her tear up. She held back a sob that threatened to break free. Liz glanced at her curiously.

"Let me run you a copy of this," Liz offered. "I can look further if you'd like. Maybe something else will pop up with a more in-depth cross-reference search. And I'll look into those other names as well and get back to you."

"I owe you Liz," Kat said, thanking her friend with a resigned sigh.

Liz was a sharp one. "It's not the news you wanted to hear, is it?" she remarked. "Was Randall some kind of long-lost relative or family member?"

"Something like that," Kat answered.

She was just about ready to thank her friend and depart when a last minute thought popped into her head. Had her entrance into 1835, and the night she departed, caused a quake like she felt in her office the day of the initial event? She had to ask: "By any chance were there any earthquakes in Manhattan in 1835?"

Liz diligently checked the data. "None of record. But there was one in May of 1836 in Upper Manhattan. A minor one, nothing significant. Does that help?"

"Not really," Kat replied. "It's out of my research time zone but thanks any way."

Disappointment set in and the day fast became a walk down memory lane. Kat took an Uber over to the South Street Seaport, but nothing looked the same. Rem's shipping offices were long gone, replaced by a tourist mecca of seafood restaurants, souvenir memorabilia shops, and all manner of street entertainers. Gone were the cobblestones, the sweaty stevedores unloading precious cargo, and the endless parade of horse-drawn wagons. It felt like a sanitized version of its former self.

Kat glanced out at Pier 17 on the water's edge recalling her very first glimpse of 1835 New York. This was where the ship builders, captains, and craftsmen of Rem's time began building their empire, never imagining it would someday become the gateway into the greatest commercial port in New York and the world.

The man she loved, a titan in his time, had helped make that dream a reality. She wanted to shout it to the world but instead sat down at a café table and ordered a glass of Chardonnay. It was too early in the day to start drinking, but she couldn't have cared less. This day called for a drink. She brought the wine glass to her lips only to hear the lamenting strain of Cher's song: "If I Could Turn Back Time" playing somewhere in the background. Its words were haunting and sad.

There was no way she wanted to return to the Old Row, today or ever. The neighborhood of Washington Square would always be a nostalgic reminder of the memories they had created there together. Even the adjoining street names of Old New York brought back a flood of memories.

There was that time in bed when Rem had left a trail of scorching kisses all over her bare body, carving out a map. He had called her breasts "Pearl Street," and the hands that had first thrown a punch at him "The Battery." When he moved down to her red pubic mound he had lovingly called it "Maiden Lane" when she was really thinking "Beaver Street." She would never find another lover and friend like him again.

Kat stared down at Rem's ring, twisting it on her finger, wishing she was a magician who could "Turn Back Time." She vowed never to take it off. In her heart and soul, she would be forever married to him. Such a thought broke open a dam of emotions. Kat sobbed for what had been, what could have been, and what was now lost to her forever.

Chapter 18

Rem's eyes had not betrayed him. She was gone from his world. The woman he had come to love and had just proposed marriage to had vanished within seconds after he had expressed his deepest feelings for her. Rem sank down on the floor of his shipping office, grasping at the empty blankets which had been wrapped around her, waiting and hoping for her imminent return once providence realized its untimely mistake. When it failed to occur, Rem loudly cursed the hands of fate. When she failed to reappear, he finally dropped his face in his hands and wept in deep despair.

The Great Fire had taken her from him, a cruel casualty of time. Rem had spent his entire adult life taking charge, advising, and telling others what to do and now he was at a loss as to how to move forward himself.

He slept the night in his office leather chair, unable to go home and face the emptiness he knew he would find there. In the early hours of the morning, around 3:00 a.m., he heard and felt the continued explosions rock Manhattan as militia arrived with demolition charges to blow up buildings in the path of the fire that wanted to spread northward throughout the city. Clearing a path had robbed the inferno of fuel and for this he was grateful.

As the first rays of morning light descended upon the devastated city, Rem pulled himself together and rose to his feet to face the damage. Despite the freezing temperatures that persisted, he was not alone in surveying the ruins of Wall Street. The fire had been stopped at Maiden Lane to the north, William Street to the west, and was contained by the

East River where it managed to totally damage several vessels still sitting in slips—none of which were his. His ships had been parked out in the harbor at Kat's prudent advice.

Everything would have to be rebuilt, bigger and better, as Kat had predicted. Damage control would be swift. Out of misfortune vast opportunities would emerge, driving the city into greater city planning and expansion. Of that he was certain. Kat had foretold that her version of New York had arisen from the ashes of this great tragedy, despite the $20 million in property damages that would bankrupt many and displace hundreds of tenement immigrants.

Volunteer firefighters were arriving from as far away as Philadelphia and surrounding states as the fire had been visible in the skies for more than 80 miles away. The excessive heat had melted copper roofs, iron bars, and metals thought to be indestructible.

Transportation came to a complete standstill. With no carriage hires anywhere in sight, not even a single omnibus running the rails, the city stood immobile as a result of the devastation and field of debris.

It was a long and somber trek home, wrapped in Kat's blankets, to keep out the cold. Rem moved forward in the deserted streets like a man lost in a trance. It felt like a walk which would never end, turning into a soul-searching journey.

The winds had blown out the dense smoke from the fires, replacing it with bluer skies and an accompanying sense of clarity he hadn't experienced for some time. He marveled that after a losing something beyond precious, followed by a sleepless night which deprived his physically and emotionally exhausted body of rest, his mind was crystal clear, sharp, and determined to forge a new course forward. Whatever it took, he vowed he would go to the ends of the earth, to the very edge of time itself if necessary, to find her again.

~~*~~

When Rem made it home, he found his Old Row house was still intact as Kat had predicted it would be. The fire hadn't made it north of Maiden Lane, but he found his staff was in a fright thinking he had perished in the fire and that the flames would eventually spread north to consume Washington Square and them as well. There were so many rumors swirling around that no one knew what to believe. Many thought they were in the throes of biblical end times—the prophesized Armageddon. Such fears spread panic far and wide.

Explaining Kat's absence was much trickier. He told his house staff that he had sent her to a safe place outside the city until things settled down, which they accepted. That was as much as he could handle right now in the wake of the truth. The rest he would have to make up as he went along.

They fussed over him—grateful he was alive, unharmed and that they still had employment. The kitchen staff hustled to fire up the kettles, draw him a hot bath and dispose of his scorched, dirty clothing. He sank down into the steamy water, submerging his head, only to feel like he was drowning inside. He still felt connected to her, despite being separated by almost two centuries.

Their bedroom was filled with her personal items, clothes, jewelry, perfume, hairbrushes, and her tantalizing scent. His mind was filled with memories, going over each and every one in minute detail and re-enacting them to assuage his grieving heart. But in the end, it only made his loss more profound.

He needed to find answers, no matter what it took. And he needed to do it now. Perhaps Lady Darcy's letter would provide a solution. Unable to wait, he stepped out of the bath, and searched through her things, only to find Kat's lacy red "panties" sitting atop the pile of others she had fashioned for herself in her lingerie drawer. He couldn't help but smile. The little vixen had confided she had been wearing these devilishly tempting red panties when she had originally entered his world. He held them to his face, inhaling deeply—remembering the first time she had brazenly modeled them for him. It was a memory forever etched in his heart and mind. He held onto them, making them his good luck charm— a lasting memento for all time.

Quickly dressing, Rem hurried downstairs to his study. He brushed past a Chinese lacquered nesting box, causing it to topple over and break open, releasing a stack of parchment papers in a familiar writer's script.

Rem picked up one page and what he read astounded him. Kat had never told him about keeping a journal, but here it was. This was what Higgins had been referring to when he wrote him news of the house:

Sir, she hides herself away in your study for long hours every day and will not come out. Her fingers are ink-stained so I can only conclude that she is writing some long missive.

Rem temporarily forgot about Lady Darcy's last letter as he scooped up the pages of Kat's private journal and arranged them in order. It was enough to fill a book. Sinking down in his leather desk chair, the very place where she must have penned these introspective words, he began to read and sometimes re-read certain passages, giving him a whole new perspective.

Late into the night he analyzed the words Lady Portia Darcy had written to him decades ago pertaining to his future, hoping to find the definitive answer to his deep loss:

My Dearest Rem,

I trust you will know what to do with this when the time is right, and the way has been made open. What I have entrusted you with has the power to change worlds. It came down from the heavens on a portentous eve and, when used wisely, will allow you to find and hold what you most desire. Embrace the old with the new, the future with the past, the entry with the exit. Have no regrets and the markings will serve you well.

Godspeed dear one,
Lady Portia Darcy

Into the wee hours of the morning Rem attempted to put meaning to the woman's instructions, but not everything was clear. What exactly did she mean by "the markings"?

~~*~~

Kat spent the next few weeks like a woman in a walking trance. She functioned and did her job, but inside her heart was breaking. There was little joy to be had in her work at The Met, especially being the busiest time of the year with the upcoming Met Gala to take place in a few days. All she could think about was that Rem was long dead and that he would always be her "Greatest of All Time" friend and lover. Too bad they had been born hundreds of years apart.

Frankly speaking, she couldn't fathom any other man measuring up to Rem. He would be a tough act for any suitor to follow. Depression wanted to claim her, but she valiantly fought it off. The crux of the matter was that she desperately wanted to return to his time—something she knew not how to do. She clung to the belief that there had to be a solution and, if so, she would find it.

In her free moments she devoured everything she could find on the theories of time travel, reading other people's accounts, yet no one had a definitive answer to the specifics of how the time continuum was traversed. Some said time was nonlinear and that the past, present, and future were all happening simultaneously. Others claimed it was easier to travel forward to the future and more difficult to go back in time. Yet somehow she had managed to do it! Everyone had a mixed opinion on the controversial subject, with no solid answer.

The internet was a sea of theoretical physics that she nightly attempted to navigate. Her head was spinning with the concepts of time bending, parallel timelines, warp speed, gravitational fields, simultaneous time, and how using an Einstein-Rosen bridge could open a wormhole portal in space to reconnect time periods. Most of it was beyond her comprehension.

There was mention of some kind of Chronovisor device to effect time travel, then mention of the military's Philadelphia Experiment and Montauk Project. Kat was particularly intrigued by Nicholai Aleksandrovich Kozyrev's Russian Academy of Sciences mirror experiments, where he used long sheets of curled aluminum sheeting to affect enhanced extrasensory perception and time bending. Afterall, hadn't she been looking into her office mirror when the time shift occurred? Had Kozyrev been onto something?

Sanskrit writings in the Mahabharata, a sacred Hindu text from the 3rd century, referenced traveling to the heavens where one returned after having been gone for hundreds of years. There was more of the same inferences in the Hebrew Bible, where the prophet Jeremiah was said to have time travelled. Even Nikola Tesla's experimental work on the subject had been quickly reclassified under "National Security" and not made open to the public. The government had been hiding such truth for ages. Had Kat not experienced it herself she might have also dismissed the whole thing as fantasy thinking or outright conspiracy theory.

But dismiss it she couldn't. A friend of hers was a science engineer at NASA, so she called him. When questioned on the subject, he told her off the record of course, that the government had been working on time travel experiments for decades—all black op secret projects. This didn't help her one bit, and she widely chose not to reveal her own experience to her friend or anyone else lest she be turned into an unwilling lab rat. All she knew was that some wormhole in time and space had opened and effortlessly sucked her back to the past and then again to the present. The "how" and "why" of it was still a mystery.

Kat questioned everything. Was The Metropolitan Museum of Art built on some kind of ancient portal or wormhole in time and space? She knew every gallery in the museum, as well as its extensive art collection, its library, and all its workrooms. Never had she heard anyone relate having had a strange experience with time travel such as hers. If they had, certainly no one was talking. The place was filled with "portal" columns, but aside from a few known reports of ghostly apparitions in the Watson Library's stacks, that was about it. Kat wasted no time asking one of the librarians in the Museum's own library if there had been any other strange experiences over the years. She learned that there had been an exhibit on Spirit Photography in 2005, which dated back to supernatural artists' renderings in the 1860s. Ghostly images sometimes appeared on museum paintings as well.

"Ghost Hunters frequently do tours here," one such librarian informed, as she gave Kat the rundown. "They claim The Met sits on a high electromagnetic field (EMF) which is conducive to paranormal activity. According to them, the ancient artifacts we have on display sometimes have discarnate entities attached to them—especially in the Egyptian galleries. There have been many ghostly sightings over the years. And the museum has some unusual cold spots no one has been able to adequately explain. The public gets a big kick out of it all and it drives attendance, so we don't discourage such nonsense."

Nonsense, indeed! But there was not one incident of someone disappearing or someone reappearing from another time. She was reminded that The Met had an online digital "MetKids Time Machine" to transport you to the past where children could explore inventions or items of art from prior times, but that was the closest thing to time travel the Museum offered.

Having found nothing of true interest to help explain her experience outside the fact that the Museum sat on an EMF hot spot, Kat returned her focus to her work. The Met's upcoming Gala event now filled Kat's every waking moment. Every detail of this year's exhibition highlighting "The Great Fire: A Fashion Phoenix 1835-1840" was in her hands as Assistant Installation Coordinator of the Costume Institute's Exhibition and Special Projects Department. The exhibit would show how fashion trends directly changed as a result of the fire destruction in the years which followed.

Having personally experienced the tragedy of The Great Fire, Kat added details and backdrop renderings that she knew to be true which had not been recorded in history. Even the New York Historical Society's knowledge of the event was lacking in its true drama. Kat had captured the magnitude of the fire in all its spectacular detail, making the set decorations and the costumes one of the best collections the Met Gala would ever display going back to its 1948 inception.

Only Kat would know that some of the outfits which had been mysteriously donated through Kendle & Kendle were clothing items both she and Rem had worn during his time. Running her hands over his expertly tailored waistcoats and shirts filled her with a deep melancholy. These costumes would stand out and serve to really make the exhibit spectacular. They were his last gift to her, along with the ring that had initially brought her to his world. Sadly, the fabulous gown she had worn to the Hone party the night of the fire, the one Rem told her she was beyond stunning in, was not amongst the lot. It, too, had vanished into the ethers, like the threads of history.

It occurred to her that after she disappeared Rem must have found her personal journal and read it in its entirety. Some parts, as she remembered, even now made her blush. She had poured out her feelings and all that had happened in those pages. What had he thought? But then how else would he have known to send his ring and their clothes ahead to her time. The preservation had been meticulously carried out. How had he arranged it all?

Kat would have been totally remiss if she hadn't tracked down the law firm of Kendle & Kendle to get some answers. It had survived the test of time. When she phoned to request an audience with the senior managing partner, she was immediately put through to his office.

"I've been expecting your call," Arthur Kendle informed her.

The plan was to meet the next day. She was instructed to produce a valid New York Driver's license or passport upon arrival, which she did. Immediately, she was ushered into lavish 20th Floor offices on Fifth Avenue overlooking Central Park. The law firm took up five floors, with well over 100 attorneys. It had grown immensely since its early days on Chambers Street where Braden Kendle Senior and Braden Kendle Junior had first started their little law practice.

Arthur Kendle, who appeared to be in his late 60s, with short-cropped gray-hair and impeccably dressed in a custom-tailored Italian suit, presented himself as a kindly grandfatherly figure. To her surprise, the seasoned attorney escorted her into his private office domain like she was the Queen of England.

On his desk was a neat stack of thick files bearing the name R. Randall. Kat's pulse raced erratically. Kendle tapped them unconsciously. "Mr. Randall was the very first significant benefactor of this firm. A most unusual man I am told, who claimed to have foreseen the future."

Kat gulped. Okay, so Rem hadn't told them the full story. "Foreseen the future" indeed. *She* was the future. Arthur Kendle continued. "I have waited for this day to come to solve a secret my ancestors have kept for several generations. I am breaking confidentiality now only because your name is listed as sole beneficiary of this trust."

She sat up straighter in her chair, leaning forward. "What kind of trust are we talking about?"

Arthur Kendle cleared his throat and opened the top file on the stack and carefully removed a slew of legal documents. "I have here a perpetual trust, often referred to as a dynasty or time trust meant to span multiple generations. It was set up in the year 1836 by the founding father of this law firm, Braden Kendle, for his client, Remington Randall, the grantor. The terms and requirements are most unusual, but the bottom line is Mr. Randall named you as sole beneficiary of his assets."

Kat stilled hearing such news. What had Rem gone and done?

"In fact," Kendle continued, "Randall placed a time limit on it, specifying this exact month and year for the trust to be opened, dispersed, and delivered to you—something I find quite astounding."

Kendle paused, perplexed as ever. "My position, as trustee, is to carry out our client's wishes without asking personal questions. However, due to the length of this trust and its most unusual terms, I must tell you that it has mystified generations of Kendle & Kendle attorneys who served as its trustee throughout the years. The question they all asked was: *How could this man know your name if you were not born yet?*"

Kendle looked to her for a definitive answer. Kat merely shrugged her shoulders. "Beats me. I guess he really could see into the future like he claimed."

She attempted to switch gears and steer the conversation in a different direction. "As for the assets you speak of—this was the costume collection delivery, correct?"

Arthur nodded. "Yes. It was preserved according to specific instructions and put in cold storage and, as you know, was to be delivered to the Metropolitan's Costume Institute on April 1st of this year, which we carried out."

Kat nodded. "Thank you for fulfilling these instructions. The Met was incredibly pleased to accept this extremely generous contribution. I'm sorry I wasn't there at the time of delivery to personally thank your firm, but I am now. I assume your obligations for this perpetual trust have now been served."

Arthur Kendle chuckled. "I wish it were that simple, Ms. Branigan, but it's not. There's more."

"More?" Kat repeated.

"Yes. First off, there is a sealed letter and package preserved for you as well. It will be delivered to your home address which we have listed in Brooklyn."

Kat's heart skipped a beat, not realizing she was holding her breath. "When?" was all she could stammer out.

"Later today if that's convenient for you," he replied. "I am not privy to the contents of Mr. Randall's letter, only that it will explain everything. Once you have reviewed this correspondence, please get back in touch with me, and the rest will be carried out."

Kat felt like she had lost the ability to string a coherent sentence together. "The rest?"

At precisely 6:00 p.m. that evening Rem's delivery arrived as expected. Like all the other costumes which he had donated, this one was similarly preserved. Kat opened the large, sealed box to find the shock of all surprises. Inside, carefully wrapped and preserved to weather the ravages of time, was an exact replica of the crimson-red feathered gown she had worn for him the night of The Great Fire. Alongside it, there was a gray jeweler's pouch containing a reworked pearl and diamond choker necklace exactly like the one Rem had gifted her.

Kat stilled, barely able to breathe. Tucked into the gown's beaded bodice was a sealed envelope containing Rem's crested initials. Her hands trembled as she carefully opened it recognizing her name in his familiar bold script. Preserved for time, the paper had not yellowed but looked like he had written it only yesterday.

My Dearest and Beloved Kat, it began.

She dropped it, feeling swept up in a sea of emotion. She found it difficult to breathe as she pictured him bent over his desk writing this simple endearment. She stilled her racing heart and picked it back up, knowing she had to know its contents.

My Dearest and Beloved Kat,

I miss you dearly with each passing day. I thought I would die from heartbreak when you left, but it became even more painful after I found your journal writings. Reading your deepest thoughts about your life and us was both a healing balm and an exercise in emotional torture. I am so sorry that I was not there to hold and comfort you when you needed it most.

I came to the realization that if I did not send the costumes and ring to you on the date and time you had chronicled in your journal, that I might never have had the experience of you in the first place. This would have meant forfeiting the best five months of my life and such a thought was simply unfathomable. Better to have known love, than not at all.

We were destined to meet, like Lady Darcy predicted, and no matter what happens in your future I will always love you. I hope to meet again in the next life if there is one for us.

I had Justine make a copy of the gown you wore on our last night together. You looked like a fiery temptress in it, and I was proud and honored to have you on my arm. It is a picture that will stay with me until my last breath. I had to tell Justine the truth of your origins, or she would not have done so. She sends her love and wishes you well in your other life. Rest assured I have made sure she will have the resources to start her own salon, as I'm sure you would have done.

Please wear this gown and necklace at The Metropolitan Museum's Gala to remember that special night of The Great Fire—the night I asked you to be my wife, and you accepted. Did you know the world turned on its axis for me in that moment?

If you are reading this, then you have already learned of the Randall/Branigan Perpetual Trust I set up for you through Kendle & Kendle. It should be quite sizable by the time you take receivership of it. I want you to live the best life possible with no regrets. Can you do that love—for me?

I wish I could be there with you now, but if I can't please know that I will be there with you in spirit—holding this cherished memory forever and always.

With All My Deepest Love,
Rem

It was the love letter of all love letters. The next day Kat learned that with accrued interest and after all legal and trust fees had been paid, she had a staggering new net worth of almost $33 Billion. And that strange house on the property next to hers in Brooklyn, which she had given to Colleen and Duncan Branigan, was also hers and worth an additional fortune in current real estate values. It was as if she had won the New York Mega Lottery several times over.

What does one do when they have just been handed the goose that lays the golden egg? Kat was too shocked to know or answer.

Chapter 19

No matter how much money she now had, which by both sane and insane standards was more than considerable, Kat couldn't conceive of giving up her job at The Met's Costume Institute for a life of leisure. Without true purpose, she would be bored in no time flat. Her passion for fashion, whether old or new, dictated that she belonged in the trenches of historical preservation.

So, for the time being, Kat set aside making any life decisions regarding her windfall trust until after The Met Gala. There was no time to think anyway. She was in the winding down stages of a major production that required perfection.

The Great Fire: A Fashion Phoenix 1835–1840 Exhibition was almost complete, with only a few minor last minute touches demanding her attention. Extra thick safety glass had been installed recently in the gallery rooms to deter potential vandalism, which was always a major museum concern. From behind the transparent glass, Kat observed staff painstakingly dressing the collection mannequins that were molded and sized to fit each individual costume. Staff worked slowly and with great care so as not to tear the delicate vintage fabrics. It was a laborious time-consuming task.

The fashion transformation from 1835 to 1840 was the focal point of the exhibit. Everything had been planned and arranged so museum viewers could easily see and experience the before and after fashion trends resulting from The Great Fire. Virtual 3-D video displays surrounded the exhibit with animated images brought to life with people wearing such fashions amidst the well-known historic structures of 1835 New York, even the City Hotel. Stepping back and taking in the bigger picture, Kat had to admit the metamorphosis and realism of the displays were quite dramatic.

Kat worked down her mental checklist. Each exhibit's lighting was crucial. Not too much light and not too little was the rule of thumb. Illumination of the costume podiums was carefully orchestrated to display the outfits in their best light without causing fading or color damage.

The Gala exhibition was an act of synchronized perfection by an army of dedicated professionals. Over 800,000 visitors would pass through these gallery rooms during the run of the exhibition, many who were oblivious to the early fire history of the greatest city in the world. This would be both an educational and entertaining experience. It required that every detail be precise and accurate.

With everyone working 24/7 in her Exhibition Installation Department as well as in the Museum's Development Department which did the actual planning for the Gala party, there was no time for sleep. Many of Kat's colleagues worked on the gala dinner portion of the event, which was by-invitation-only with upwards of 800 in attendance.

Always held the first Monday in May, a year's worth of planning was nearing its end. Showtime for the fashion event of the year was only a day away. They were already laying the "red carpet" which was often not red at all, sometimes even white. It covered the front entrance of the Museum on a never-ending staircase where celebrities and fashion icons primped and posed for the paparazzi, sometimes changing outfits several times. Each celebrity gown had to be preapproved and vetted weeks or months beforehand. Dressing to the Exhibition theme was mandatory; surprise apparel just DID NOT HAPPEN at The Met Gala.

Gawkers and fashion wannabes lined each side of the crowded red carpet like they did on Oscar Night. The arrival melee would start at 4:00 p.m., followed by a formal meet-and-greet, then a walk through The Great Fire Exhibition before dinner and entertainment by the top musicians of the times.

Dinner was held in the glass floor-to-ceiling Dendur Gallery where scores of tables, decorated with the finest linen and flower arrangements lit the night. Dining was amongst the ruins of the Roman Egyptian Temple of Dendur, a stunning gallery which was often the setting for many lavish Met dinners.

Brand name designers, business moguls, and celebrity actors and musicians, bought up the tables starting at $350,000 apiece for a table of 10. No one knew who they were sitting next to prior to the event, which was part of the excitement. Seating arrangements were done in the strictest secrecy by The Costume Institute's Coordinator and her trusted staff. Couples or spouses were not allowed to sit next to each other; neither were exes or past boyfriends permitted at the same table. Seating was set beforehand, like celebrities' preapproved outfits. Table switching was not permitted. The event was geared to meeting new people, exchanging ideas, and often interesting pairings were made to light a spark between strangers. It was a mastermind endeavor in the art of social matchmaking.

The Met Gala was a strict affair with a litany of other prescribed rules as well. No cell phones or social media postings were allowed inside, or you would be forever banned—which scared many into compliance. Yet, that didn't stop some rebels from skirting the rules to post bathroom selfies.

The finest gourmet food was served, selected for its sublime taste, texture, and presentation. However, no onions, garlic, or foods containing chives or parsley were allowed in order to avoid greens getting stuck in one's teeth or causing bad breath. Messy appetizers were additionally banned to avoid ruining gowns. Dinners were served French style by formal black-tie waiters wearing white gloves who served food individually onto each guest's plate. Run like a tight ship, everyone had only one hour to eat before plates were whisked away.

Kat never sat down at such events despite now being one of the richest women in the room who could easily afford to buy out the entire Gala. It was better people didn't know about her sudden good fortune. Like Mega Lottery winners, she understood the need for anonymity. For God's sake, she hadn't even told Lexi yet. It was just too complicated.

An hour before the event, once again standing before her office mirror, Kat carefully slipped on the duplicate gown Rem had sent from her night of the real fire. It fit like a glove, hugging her curves. With a discerning eye she viewed her reflection and Justine's meticulous handiwork. The ball gown was a work of fashion art, just as Kat had originally designed it to be. It should be in the exhibition, but she wanted to wear it more than anything. Afterwards, she would donate it to The Met's wonderful collection.

A feeling of déjà vu stole over her as she ran her fingers languidly down the feathered skirts. Once again, she looked like a Phoenix Rising. It immediately opened a floodgate of memories—the Hone party, Melanie's deceit in the carriage, the thugs that attacked her, and then running frantically through the fiery streets desperate to find Rem. Kat's breath caught in her throat. It still felt like only yesterday, not hundreds of year later. She slipped on ruby slippers and a pair of long-sleeve red opera gloves, similar to what she had worn that fateful night.

A sculpted head piece of red ostrich feathers closely hugged her face before draping down to press softly against her cheek, making her Gala outfit almost complete. The finishing touch was the diamond and pearl choker necklace Rem had sent along with the duplicate gown. Her hand trembled as she clasped it around her neck and stepped back to view the overall effect. It was beyond stunning. With a quick touch of crimson lipstick, Kat stepped out to meet the arriving public.

It was her job, along with other Costume Institute staff, to greet celebrities and guests coming into the Exhibition Gallery. Tonight's opening night offered a new twist. Before the exhibition doors opened, Kat stepped up onto a gallery's podium attired in her 1835 ball gown. Behind her a computer-generated rendering of the Merchants' Exchange on fire was dramatically lit with flickering flames that threatened to engulf her. It was art imitating Kat's life.

Like a real-life mannequin, Kat remained perfectly still until the first gasp of surprise was heard when she moved within the flames doing a slow 360-degree turn to display the costume's exquisite work. Her gown might be a knock-off of its historical original, but it was still a vintage gown from 1835.

An endless sea of fiery-attired Gala guests moved steadily through the exhibition to accommodate the sizeable attendance flow. Many, who had attended prior costume gala exhibits, were openly impressed with the added virtual video-rendering of Old New York's conflagration. They stopped, totally mesmerized by the destruction, as so many had done on the real night of the fire.

Staff tried as best they could to keep the line moving, reminding the guests that dinner and entertainment awaited them afterwards in the museum's Temple of Dendur gallery. Everyone knew that was where the real partying began. Yet, there were those that chose to linger. For them, Kat answered questions as if she was a woman from that time, re-telling the evening's harrowing events from a first-hand account. It felt cathartic talking about that night for the first time. Emotion filled her eyes remembering all the horror she had seen and how scared she had been. The guests listened, intrigued, probably thinking she was a seasoned actress working off some pre-written theatrical script. Some of her colleagues looked at her strangely, but Kat no longer cared. Let them think what they might. Her little touch of realism in the exhibit— something never done before—seemed to work.

Then the unexpected occurred. It started with a low rumble followed immediately by a tremor that shook the ground beneath the Museum. Seconds later, the floor became a sea of rolling seismic waves sending people screaming and running for the exits. The power went out, plunging the Exhibition and the entire museum into total darkness. Even emergency back-up generators failed to work.

Not again, Kat thought! Museum statues and treasures swayed precariously on their pedestals while unbreakable glass display cases rattled and were put to the test. The movement of the earth felt like it lasted forever, though it was really less than a minute in duration. But one minute can feel like an eternity in a seismic event. Kat fell to her knees only to feel two strong hands pick her up off the floor as the shaking stopped.

She was about to thank her would-be rescuer but was struck speechless when the lights flickered back on in the now empty gallery and she was looking into familiar blue eyes. Shock took hold and she immediately began hyperventilating, her breath coming in gasps, making her unable to speak. Unchecked tears sprang forth from her eyes.

"C'mon, Kat. Don't you dare pass out on me," Rem grinned, all smiles. "That's no way to greet someone who has traveled hundreds of years through time to get to you." He stroked her cheek, brushing away her tears. "Dare I ask if this means you're happy to see me?"

Happy to see him?! Kat was deliriously, ecstatically beyond happy. Her erratic breathing subsided as she moved her hands slowly over his face, like a blind woman attempting to identify its owner. No, her eyes were not deceiving her. She was not dreaming. It *was* Rem, in the flesh, dressed in the elegant black coattails he had worn at the Hone gala on the night of the fire. He was a glorious vision to behold. Damn. Rem hadn't aged one bit for a man technically hundreds of years old. The realization of that actually made her giggle. She threw both arms around his neck clinging to him fearful he might suddenly disappear.

"How?" she barely breathed. "I thought I would never see you again. I thought…"

Rem pressed her to his chest. "First things first, my love," he said as his lips sought hers, preventing her from talking. She melted against the onslaught of ravenous kisses that elicited soft moans of pleasure. Finally, they came up for air, still clinging to each other.

"You've never looked more ravishing," he murmured against her ear. "I dreamt of this moment for what felt like an eternity."

"Well, you certainly made one hell of an entrance," she laughed. "Damn. You even made the earth shake. How in the world did you do that?"

Rem glanced around the empty gallery noting the displayed costumes he had sent her. "I wanted to see your world, but more than anything I wanted to be with you. One of Lady Darcy's letters provided the key, along with a little help from that Corinda Brown woman."

"Corinda? But how did she…?"

"It cost a small fortune, but I managed," he replied. "But you left me an incredibly detailed roadmap in your journal writings, which I will always be grateful for. I have to say that it was the most enlightening reading experience of my life."

Kat blushed. There were some pretty steamy admissions in her journal. Admissions she would never have made if she knew Rem would be reading such intimate thoughts.

"I also had a little help from something from the future which you left behind," he said patting his side pocket.

"What?" she asked, reaching into his pocket, only to pull out a wisp of lacy red panties. Oh. My. God. "My lucky panties helped?" Now she was more confused than ever.

"Lady Darcy's letter instructed I needed something from the future, while you had something from the past. Corinda helped me locate the portal on the land you said the Museum would be built on in the future. It's a natural shifting opening. I was able to use it on May 1, 1836, after several unsuccessful attempts."

The pieces were clicking into place. "So that quake in 1836 in Upper Manhattan was you?!"

Rem grinned. "I wasn't about to give up, but it *was* all about timing. Of course, the markings were also important..."

"What markings?" she asked.

"Inside my ring. But I'll tell you all the details later," Rem promised. "It's quite a story. However right now I want to see this Met Gala of yours and have the honor of dancing with the most beautiful woman in the world."

How could she say "no" to that?

Chapter 20

The Met Gala was immediately canceled for the first time since the Covid-19 years, but this was the first time it was ever cancelled on the spot, shortly after starting. Women picked up their gowns, showing bare bottoms, sans underwear, as they scattered in all directions emptying museum galleries like rats scurrying to flee a sinking ship. Guests feared additional quakes could cause tall stone columns to topple, trapping them inside or killing them outright. Over 800 celebrities and elites practically trampled each other in their haste to escape to safety. Some got in their waiting curbside limousines and never returned.

Rem and Kat watched the exodus knowing the cause of the quake was over. "You certainly know how to clear a room," Kat remarked as they entered and surveyed the Temple of Dendur Gallery. Tables and chairs were upturned, shattered water glasses were strewn across the polished wooden floor, along with trampled flowers, torn linen napkins, and even a few forgotten women's purses.

That year Kat's Great Fire of 1835 Exhibition would be deemed a "smashing" success: the Met Gala not so for obvious reasons. Yet, despite the debris field in the Gallery, Rem took Kat in his arms and managed to sweep her past the slanted floor-to-ceiling glass windows that spanned the length of the brightly lit room. He waltzed them past the two stone statues of Amenhotep III flanking the shallow wading pool, then right through the columned entrance of the small Egyptian Temple. There he stopped, taking her hand in his and fingering the signet ring she still wore which he had given her that fateful night.

His eyes searched hers. "You're still wearing it?"

"I never took it off," she replied. "It was my only real connection to you."

He nodded, pleased, but took it a step further. "Will you still marry me, Kat, and show me this strange new world of yours?"

Kat raised an eyebrow. "Are you asking because I now have all your money, Mr. Randall?" she teased.

"Not everything," he ventured with a sly smile. "As a businessman, I planned accordingly."

She laughed with sheer joy. She just bet he did.

Epilogue

Kat said "Yes" and "I Do" in a small private ceremony at the South Street Seaport Museum aboard the historic 1885 tall sailing ship the *Wavertree*. Only Lexi and a few close friends had been invited to share in their waterfront nuptials. Rem, being Rem, had reserved the flagship, docked proudly at Pier 16, for the entire day. He would have bought the vessel outright had Kat not reminded him of her penchant for seasickness. But sailing the Wavertree up the East River proved to be a doable feat for her sometimes queasy stomach. Rem loved sailing and she vowed to overcome her affliction for his sake. Ultimately, acupuncture would prove to be the cure-all for her malady.

Rem was beyond ecstatic when the Wavertree's ship captain let him steer and navigate the waters surrounding Manhattan. With the wind blowing through his hair, expertly shouting out orders to the crew on deck, he looked like the shipping prince he was. Perhaps they would purchase something a bit smaller in scope to satisfy his sailing needs. They certainly had the resources.

Everything in her world fascinated him, allowing Kat to see New York City through different eyes. Indoor plumbing, cars, televisions, computers, subways, and an endless list of modern day inventions excited Rem to no end. Despite making the transition to her world, he was still interested in knowing how his time had been portrayed in history. Rem was a stickler for truth and accuracy, something she didn't know about him.

He scoffed at some of the South Street Seaport Museum's historic gallery displays and offered to consult with them on the spot, much like she had concerning the details of The Great Fire. Written history was never totally accurate—that much she had learned firsthand. Thank God for Philip Hone's diaries to add realism to how this great city grew and prospered. All those people she had known in 1835 were now long gone, never getting to witness what would become of their beloved Manhattan, except Rem, of course.

There was so much they had yet to figure out together in their new life. She would never forget his stunned awe at his first glimpse of Manhattan skyscrapers, its never-ending gridlock traffic, the neon lights of Times Square, and even the great cable span of the Brooklyn Bridge and others that connected Manhattan to the surrounding boroughs.

Instead of being overwhelmed, Rem seemed to thrive on the technical and industrial accomplishments of the time. He had become a renaissance man, with this new world serving to inspire him. In no time he was drawing up business plans for how to improve global shipping traffic, new maritime propulsion systems and even robotic remote-controlled ship technology. Who would have thought he would so easily become a man of the future, embracing innovation and finding better solutions?

Kat did not say "I told you so" when he saw firsthand how the 19th century opium trade had ravaged millions of his fellow men with the fentanyl crisis. He was a little leerier about China during her time than he had been in his own time negotiating deals in Canton. So much had changed over the centuries, but Rem was quick to learn the politics of the time.

They still played billiards regularly, betting on everything imaginable, and when they made love it always felt like it was their last day on Earth. They were like twin flames in time that the universe had conspired to bring together under the most unimaginable circumstances, only to become stronger both individually and as a team, bridging two totally different worlds. You just can't get any better than that.

Kat brought her lucky gold locket to her lips. If only her parents were here now to see how incredibly happy she was. The mysterious ring markings were the magic that had made it all possible, but that was a secret only she and Rem would share, thanks to the foresight of Lady Darcy. For them there would be no going back—only forward. They were more than content to stay in the here and now.

The End

About the Author

Kathy J. Forti is a psychologist, software inventor and author of several compelling books. Her highly acclaimed *STACKS Library of Truth* 4-book series is a romantic sci-fi action thriller set in The Library of Congress where ancient interdimensional portals are discovered, and secret societies abound. She is also author of the non-fiction book, *Fractals of God*, which tells of Kathy's near-death experience and journeys into the mystical realm. She currently resides in Hawaii.

Check out the Author's other books on Amazon, Kindle & Audible.